# VOW
## OF THE
# SHADOW
# KING

# VOW

## — OF THE —

# SHADOW KING

・・・・・・・・・・・・・・・・・・・・・・・・・・・・・・・・・・・・・・・・・・・・・・・・

**BRIDE OF THE SHADOW KING: BOOK 2**

・・・・・・・・・・・・・・・・・・・・・・・・・・・・・・・・・・・・・・・・・・・・・・・・

## Sylvia Mercedes

ACE

NEW YORK

ACE
Published by Berkley
An imprint of Penguin Random House LLC
penguinrandomhouse.com

Book design by Jenni Surasky

Library of Congress Cataloging-in-Publication Data

Names: Mercedes, Sylvia, author.
Title: Vow of the Shadow King / Sylvia Mercedes.
Description: First edition. | New York: Ace, 2025. |
Series: Bride of the Shadow King; book 2
Identifiers: LCCN 2024024370 | ISBN 9780593952214 (trade paperback)
Subjects: LCGFT: Fantasy fiction. | Romance fiction. | Novels.
Classification: LCC PS3613.E678 V69 2025 | DDC 813/.6—dc23/eng/20240607
LC record available at https://lccn.loc.gov/2024024370

*Vow of the Shadow King* was originally self-published, in different form, in 2022.

First Ace Edition: January 2025

Printed in the United States of America
1st Printing

*For all those who ever wondered . . .*
*You are worthy.*
*You are loved.*
*You are enough.*

# AUTHOR'S NOTE

# VOW
## OF THE
# SHADOW
## KING

# 1
.....
# *Faraine*

Fingertips brush the curve of my neck and shoulder.

I gasp a short breath, hold it. Let it out in a sigh only to catch it again when that touch, hot as fire, moves to my throat, trails along my collarbone. Warm breath tickles the sensitive skin just behind my ear. Then the edge of teeth, applying only the faintest pressure to my earlobe. Just enough that I feel their sharpness.

*Let me teach you,* a deep voice rumbles in the shadows. *Let me learn you.*

I fall back in a bed of darkness. It envelops me in a sweet, heady perfume. I can see nothing, for all is inky black, so I close my eyes, let my other senses come alive.

He is there.

His body pressed flush against mine.

His fingers twirl the delicate straps on my shoulders.

His hands smooth away the silky folds of my gown.

My throat vibrates with a low moan. I respond to his touch, surrender to his lead as he draws me into this sensuous dance. His lips are full and soft but spark against my skin as his kisses explore down my neck, my collarbone, between my breasts. I run my hands across his broad shoulders, up the back of his head, my fingers tangling in the long, silky strands of his hair.

*Is this what you want?*

*Ilsevel?*

My eyes fly open. Low red light illuminates the darkness just enough that I can see the face hovering above mine. Those strong features sharpened to knifelike edges; his eyes black voids brimming with fury, with hatred.

He bares his teeth. They're sharp like fangs.

Then I'm falling. Falling, tumbling, hot air rushing past me. The heat below intensifies, burns away the scant remains of my garments, burns into my flesh, my bones.

I scream—

—and land flat on my back.

Every muscle in my body is tensed, my lungs constricted. For a moment I believe I've struck stone, shattered into a million tiny pieces. Then my heart gives a painful throb. Life rushes through me, quaking my bones. I draw in a ragged breath. It takes a moment to realize my eyelids are blinking fast, because there's simply no difference between open and closed. All is absolutely black. Did I strike my head when I fell? Am I now blind?

But no. I didn't fall. Not really.

Neither has the flesh melted from my skeleton.

It was just a dream.

A sob chokes in my throat. Rolling onto my side, I grip the edge of the narrow cot on which I lie. My addled mind slowly begins to clear. I know where I am again: in a cave. Dank. Cold. Dark. Far beneath the surface of this world. Imprisoned for treachery against the Shadow King.

A shudder rolls down my spine. This darkness is terrible. It feels like a living thing, an oppressive entity preying on my sanity. My senses are already so highly strung due to my gods-gift. Now, deprived of sight, I have no barrier between me and the tiniest, creeping sensations.

If only I could retreat back into that dream! Because it *was* a dream . . . wasn't it? Part of me wants to believe it was a memory. Those touches. Those kisses. Those thrills of both body and soul. They were mine. For a few, precious moments, they were mine.

Only that's a lie.

Those kisses were all meant for Ilsevel.

My sister.

Beloved.

*Dead.*

Tears course down my cheeks. How long have I been weeping? I don't know. Neither can I guess how long I've been here in this dark place. It simultaneously feels like moments and years since the guards dragged me off that execution scaffold, through a bewildering array of stony corridors, and flung me into this cell. I remember sitting here on this same cot, watching the single shining *lorst* crystal dim and go out. I don't know how long ago that was.

My eyes ache from straining. I close them once more and call to mind the last lingering sight in my memory: Lyria. My half sister. She stood just on the other side of the cell bars as we spoke our goodbyes. Where is she now? Halfway home to Beldroth, carrying her report of recent events to Father?

More likely, she was murdered before she ever reached the

Between Gate, her corpse sent as a warning to King Larongar. Punishment for his treachery. And mine.

Sucking a breath through gritted teeth, I sit upright. A wave of dizziness washes over me, and panic roils in my gut. I swing out my arms, searching for something, anything, to touch, to ground myself. One hand hits the stone wall hard. Pain shoots through my bones, and I cry out. Then I bite my tongue. Tilt my head.

When I touched the wall, something . . . happened.

Fingers trembling, I reach out, press my palm against the thick cold slab of stone. These walls aren't carved but have naturally formed over millennia. I close my eyes and with my other hand grip the crystal pendant hanging from its chain around my neck. At first, it is very still. I squeeze harder until I feel the faint pulse in its center, warming against my skin.

Deep in the wall, moving through the heavy stone, comes an answering *thrum*.

The sudden groan of metal door hinges startles me. I yank my hand away from the wall, heart leaping. Was that a real sound? Or did I imagine it? No, there's light. Real light. A faint gleam, but enough to make me gasp and cover my face with both hands.

A sound of soft footsteps. The brush of heavy fabric on stone. They're so loud in the stillness, they seem to echo in my head. I peer between my fingers. The glow comes from beyond my cell. It catches on the cell door bars, casts long shadow bands across the floor. Those bands move as the light draws nearer, like slashes of darkness ready to slice me in two.

Are the guards returning to drag me back to the scaffold? And this time, will the angered king hold true to his purpose? No last-minute stay of execution. I'll kneel before the block and stare down into a box lined with blue silk. The last sight my eyes will see before my head rolls.

I scramble off the bed, yank my skirts into place around me. Standing upright, I grip my pendant with one hand, my other hand clenched in a fist at my side, determined to show no fear. The light draws near slowly enough that my eyes have time to adjust. What had seemed bright as a blazing star a moment ago resolves into a single *lorst* crystal set in a silver holder held by a trembling hand. A figure stands on the far side of the bars. I think it's a man; he's so heavily cloaked, I cannot be certain. He wears a hood pulled low over his face. There's something eerily familiar about him, some resonance from his soul which strikes my gods-gifted perceptions. It isn't Vor. Of that, at least, I'm certain.

He lifts his crystal high enough that the pale, purplish light illuminates my face. I wince but refuse to shield my eyes. Ragged breaths issue from beneath that hood. Then, with swift, jerking movements, he pulls a key from the deep folds of his cloak, jangles it in the lock, then yanks the door open. The bars screech along the deep floor grooves, sending shudders up my spine. The man steps back and motions sharply with one arm.

I swallow hard. "Where are you taking me?"

The man merely stands there, arm extended.

"Am I to see Vor? The king?"

Still nothing.

I try to get a sense of his feelings. I've found it difficult to read the troldefolk. While not impervious to my gift, they seem to keep their emotions behind layers of stone. At first, it was a relief—the unrelenting pressure of other people's feelings too often overwhelms my senses. Now, however, it's frightening. All I detect is a thin vibration in the air between me and this stranger. When I squeeze my crystal a little harder, I can almost, almost . . .

"*Nurghed ghot!*"

I gasp. That voice, so harsh and cold, chills my blood. But what can I do? I won't wait for him to physically haul me out. Better to move of my own volition, to take what control I can.

Gripping my pendant hard, I duck from the cell and into the passage. Deep shadows obscure my feet, and I stumble a little. The floor is relatively smooth, however, so I find my balance, and we proceed down a corridor, past numerous empty cells, through a door, and into a narrow stairwell. I lift my skirts and climb. Each step feels like a mountain my faltering courage must conquer. At the top of the stair, I emerge into a broad passage with a high, arched ceiling. *Lorst* crystals set in silver sconces offer some illumination, but not much.

The hooded figure—My escort? My captor? My enemy or friend?—steps out of the stairwell behind me and motions for me to turn right. "Where are we going?" I demand again.

He answers only with more of that heavy, ratcheted breathing.

I want to run. I want to hike up my skirts and simply take off, following the *lorst* lights to wherever they might lead. But what then? I cannot escape. I couldn't hope to navigate the Shadow Realm and its subterranean ways. I'd never even make it outside the palace walls. And when they inevitably caught me, they would drag me by my hair, kicking and screaming, back to the scaffold.

If I must die, I will do so with dignity.

I turn right as indicated and march. The stranger falls into place behind me. I shiver at the creeping sensation of his hot breath on the back of my neck. But he hasn't touched me. Not yet at least. We take a turn and step into a new corridor, this one a little smaller and less well lit than the one we've just left. I stumble over my feet, put out a hand to catch myself against the wall.

A vibration flickers beneath my palm. Then another answering vibration, rippling out from the figure at my back. A soul echo that strikes my gods-gift with undeniable potency.

*Evil.*

*Murder.*

I stop. My heart throbs against my breastbone.

"*Drag!*" growls the stranger, his voice once more hauntingly familiar.

He's taking me somewhere to kill me. I don't know why. He could have easily overpowered me in the cell, slit my throat, crushed my skull in his big trolde hands. Perhaps he doesn't want to leave evidence of my death. Perhaps he plans to deliver me to someone else who will do the actual deed.

Either way, he intends for me to die.

I have a split second to decide what to do. I glance at him, his hooded face, his hunched and nervous body. He wants to keep my death a secret. Which means I'm not wholly without power here.

I open my mouth and let out an earth-shattering scream. It echoes up and down the stone passage, and the crystals embedded deep within the walls seem to catch the sound and carry it further. Surely someone must be near, someone will come, someone will—

The man grabs my shoulders and slams me up against the wall. It knocks the breath out of me, and then his hand clamps down over my mouth. "*Morar-juk!*" he snarls as his hood falls back.

A cold wave of horror rushes over me as his features come into view. I recognize him. It's the man who stood by the block on the scaffold. The man who read out my crimes, who pronounced my sentence. I'd felt the cold, cruel pleasure he'd taken in the prospect of my death. His malice struck my gods-gift with force enough to knock me off my feet.

There's no such pleasure in him now. At first, I feel nothing but murder, hard and terrible. But that is only the thin veneer over the truth. Down underneath lurks a deeper, stronger, surging feeling: *despair*.

The man's eyeballs shake in his skull. He presses me hard against the wall, his forearm across my throat. His free hand reaches into his cloak, whisks out a dagger which he angles just under my ear. But he's made a mistake. He's pressed my whole body up against the wall. I flatten my palms to the stone, feel the vibration of all those hidden crystals deep inside. Channeling that vibration, I stare into those spinning eyes of his, and—*take hold*.

The man gasps. Freezes. His head tilts slowly to one side.

I feel all of it. Everything he's feeling. Murder. Hatred. Bloodlust and fear. I feel it and hold it suspended between us, even as his knife pricks my throat; even as the edge of the blade cuts into my flesh.

Slowly, I pry one hand free of the wall, press it against his cheek.

*Calm.*

The vibrations in the stone rush through me, ripple through my bones, my muscles, out my pores.

The man jolts. His eyes widen.

Then he drops like a stone.

With a gasp, I sag, just managing to lock my knees and keep from falling. The wall still hums faintly at my back, and my body reverberates with echoes of pulsing energy. Slowly, the reverberations pass. I blink. My vision clears.

A crumpled body lies at my feet.

I stare at it, momentarily uncertain how it got there. Blood rushes into my head, throbs in my veins. Eventually, understanding dawns: *I did this.* I knocked this man unconscious. Maybe . . . maybe more. Maybe worse.

He looks peaceful. Unnaturally so, considering how twisted his expression had been only moments before. I shake my head, my breath thin and tight between my lips. What have I done? I've used this calming trick before. It's the only aspect of my gods-gift over which I have any control. But never to such a degree.

Warmth trickles down my neck. When I touch it, my fingers come away sticky. I must do something. I can't just stand here, bleeding. The knife lies where it clattered, close to my foot. I wonder if I should pick it up. Not that I'd know what to do with it. I could never bring myself to plunge it into another living being.

My back still pressed against the wall, I sidle several paces to one side, away from the fallen man. Then, with a shivering inhale of breath, I snatch up his fallen *lorst* crystal. Gripping it in both hands, I continue down the passage. My lips try and fail to form a cry for help. But I shouldn't alert anyone to my presence, should I? After all, this man may not have been working alone. Someone else might come running to finish what he started.

Is it possible he was sent by Vor? Surely not. Why would Vor spare me from public execution only to send an assassin creeping into my cell? Of course, he might want me quietly dead without a public scandal. It's not as though my father will care whether I live or die.

I come to a place where the passage branches and stop, uncertain. One wrong move could send me into the arms of another assassin. Is there any choice that will lead to safety? Closing my eyes, I reach out with my senses, hardly knowing what I seek. Perhaps nothing. But perhaps . . . perhaps . . .

Suddenly, there it is: a *pull.*

It's so faint I could easily be imagining it. But just now, it's the only guidance I have.

I turn down the left-hand passage, holding the *lorst* crystal before me. Other passages branch off from this one, but I don't let myself be distracted. I continue, my stride determined, almost as though I know where I'm going.

Light shines up ahead. It's so bright, so pure, I want to convince myself it's daylight. Of course, that's impossible in this world under stone. Still, I hasten toward it, eager, strangely hopeful. A doorway arches before me, wide open. I step into the opening and gaze out on the world before me.

My jaw slowly drops.

It's a garden. At least, that's what my brain tries to tell me. Only this is not like any garden I've ever seen. It's all so much bigger, grander, with sweeping heights and winding depths, sheer cliffs and twisting rock formations. Brilliant pops of color trick my eye into believing I see flowers. On second glance, however, I realize they are gemstones. Hundreds and hundreds of gemstones. Some have been polished into perfect spheres. Others have been left in their natural state, while still more have been carved and cut. Diamonds, rubies, emeralds, and more, so many and so varied, I cannot begin to name them all. They gleam in the *lorst* light shining from the high cavern ceiling above.

I don't know how long I stand there, dazzled. Then I feel the *pull* again, this time stronger than before. It draws my gaze to an outcropping in a higher region of the garden. There, on proud display, stands a ring of tall blue crystals. They look very much like the pendant I wear, but so much larger.

I step through the doorway. I have no plan, no clear purpose in mind. I know only that I must reach those stones.

Many paths wind through this incredible landscape. I take the one that seems most likely to lead me up to that outcropping. It's lined with a hedgerow of raw emeralds and leads beneath a bower of hand-cut red rubies, which hang suspended on nearly invisible threads, like tiny droplets of glittering blood. The path beneath them is suffused in a pink glow.

Vor's voice comes back to me suddenly, the answer he gave when I asked him if there was any light in the Under Realm: *More light than you can imagine. More light, more color, more life. More everything.* At the time, I'd not believed him. Now, I could almost laugh. How very sad and gray and pathetic the winter-gripped gardens of Beldroth must have seemed to his eyes!

A chittering sound draws my attention. I turn sharply, peer through the dripping red rubies to a tall rock formation on the other side. Something leaps into view on top of a large white boulder. I gasp, surprised. At first glance, it looks something like a cat, with a long, lithe body. Tufts of white hair trail from the tips of huge triangular ears. Rather than paws, however, it boasts nimble, claw-tipped hands, more like the pet monkey Sister Magrie kept at the convent. I'd never liked that monkey, with its devilish little face.

This creature, however, is rather sweet looking, save for the fact that it has no eyes. There is nothing but dark patches of fur where eyes should be. No socket. No lid. It reminds me unsettlingly of the hideous cave devil I'd encountered upon my arrival in the Under Realm.

Shuddering, I turn away and hurry up the path. More of the little creatures follow me, however. They scamper around, under, and over the rocks, curious noses sniffing, huge ears twitching. If I get too close, they dart away, but never far.

Just as I'm passing under an arch of greenish-gray stone, one of the creatures drops suddenly to my eye level, suspended by its tail. I leap back, a hand pressed to my mouth to stifle a scream. This creature, however, does not scamper away as the others had. It grips the base of its own tail, twists around so that it can angle itself upright. Its pointed little nose sniffs with interest, its tufted ears cupped toward me.

I hold my breath, uncertain what to do. The path I'm following leads directly under this arch. I don't see any other way to reach the tall crystals, which still subtly call to me.

Chewing my lip, I take a step forward. Maybe the animal will squeak and skitter off as the others have. Instead, it makes a little burbling noise and angles its head to one side. Its fur is so vivid: purple and orange, streaked with blue. I've never before seen such brilliant colors on a living creature. It's beautiful.

Slowly, haltingly, I hold out one hand. The animal elongates its neck, touches the end of its wet little nose against my fingertip. A vibration hums between us. I blink, surprised. The creature seems a bit startled as well and puts back its ears.

Then abruptly it curls up its long tail and scrambles to the top of the arch. In the same instant, the sound of footsteps draws my head whipping to one side. Someone is coming. My heart lodges in my throat. What should I do? I can't run—whoever it is will surely see me and pursue. The last thing I want is to be chased through this strange garden in this strange world.

So, I do the only thing I can. I grip my pendant, steel my spine, and turn to face whoever is coming.

## 2

## *Vor*

Needle-sharp teeth pinch my earlobe.

"*Morar-juk!*" I snarl, and sit upright, pulling my hands away from my face. The mothcat on my shoulder lets out a squeak and leaps to avoid my backhand. Tail flicking, it springs to my knee then launches itself onto my chest and scrambles around behind my neck. All so nimble and quick . . . but not quick enough.

I lash out with one hand, catch it by its long, sinuous tail. Surprised, it squeaks again and squirms in my grip as I hold it at arm's length. It pins back its tufted ears, flashes two rows of tiny teeth.

"What?" I scowl at the little beast. "Do you also think it's high time I pulled myself together and started acting like a king again? Perhaps you'd like a seat on my council. There's a place available right between Lady Parh and Lord Rath, I believe. You'd fit right in."

The mothcat chitters and gyrates in my grasp until I release my grip. It drops, lands on its feet, and immediately clambers onto my knee. There it perches, angling its face up at me. I roll my eyes but, succumbing to its charm, deign to run my fingers under its chin and behind one large ear. Then, leaning back in my seat, I gaze out at the view before me.

The bench on which I sit was placed here by my father as a gift to my mother soon after their marriage. This particular spot was her favorite. She would come to the royal gardens often to sit here and admire the crystal cliff and cascading falls. When I was small, she often brought me with her. We'd sit together and enjoy the droplets of rainbow-shot mist settling on our skin and the voice of the falls singing across the crystal-clear lake before us.

Afterwards—after my mother's departure and my father's remarriage—I did not visit this spot for quite some time. But I liked to envision bringing my own bride here. Someday. I pictured it all in vivid detail—a picnic luncheon the lusterling after our wedding night. A chance to show her one of the most beautiful sights my kingdom has to offer. She would still be uneasy, of course, in this strange world so unlike her own. But when she saw this place, everything would begin to change. I would kneel before her, grip her hands in mine, and promise her that all of this—all this splendor along with my own hand and heart—was hers for the taking.

Such a foolish dream.

A growl reverberates in my throat. Startled, the mothcat leaps from my knee and scampers away before it turns, back arched, and bares its teeth at me. "Forgive me, little friend," I say. "I'm not myself this morning."

When I stretch out my hand, the beast allows me to stroke it from the top of its head down its slinky back to the base of its tail. It kneads its little paws in the air, purring loudly, all fear forgotten. Shaking my head, I lift my gaze back to the waterfall. Delicate white streams tumble between ledges of age-shaped crystals. It's a truly spectacular sight. One of the finest to be had in all my kingdom. It holds no attraction for me this day, however. Though I came seeking peace and clarity, my mind is in as much turmoil as ever.

I must make a decision. About Faraine.

Sul departed yesterday, escorting the princess's companion, Lady Lyria, back to the Between Gate. With him he carries a message for King Larongar—my demand for the Miphates mages to be sent at once to serve at my bidding. I worded the message with care so that it contains no overt threat to Faraine's life. But neither have I promised her ongoing safety.

Not that I expect my demands will do any good. I've witnessed firsthand Larongar's disdain for his eldest daughter. He won't be moved to protect her, not if it works against his interests.

I bow my head, bury my face in my hands. And there she is, in my head. Faraine. I hear the soft crooning of her voice in my ear. Her gentle moans as my palms swept across her trembling flesh. The little gasps of delight which punctuated each kiss I pressed to her skin. How sweet she'd tasted—fresh, delicious. And *mine*.

Then I'd opened my eyes. Seen my lovely, delicate bride for what she truly was. A traitor. False and two-faced.

The mothcat makes a sudden *prrrrrlt* and sits up on its haunches, front feet dangling. It angles its ears toward the gardens, then, with another trill, scampers off among the stones. Heart heavy, I watch until it vanishes from sight. I must go soon as well. Return to the palace. I positioned Hael at the main entrance to the gardens and commanded her to let no one through, but I can't hide out here much longer. Mythanar needs its king.

I release a long, slow breath. Then, straightening my shoulders, I rise, turn from the waterfall, and retrace my steps along the path leading from the lake. The mothcats are strangely agitated today.

They prattle in their singsong voices and sometimes emit harsh squawks and squeaks that send flurries of *olk* dancing into the air. Something must have disturbed them. Hopefully not one of my ministers come to pester me with opinions or press for action. I can't take much more of their—

I round a bend in the path. And stop dead in my tracks.

An apparition stands before me.

It must be an apparition. For it cannot be true. It simply cannot be.

Because Faraine is down in a holding cell. Under guard. Hidden away where she cannot distract me, where she cannot cloud my wits and reason as I search for a solution to the problem she's created.

Which means she cannot be standing in front of me, beneath that arch of pale stone. Suffused in the purple light refracted off a blooming amethyst cluster. Gazing up at me from those strange, bicolored eyes of hers. Eyes which blink slowly, long lashes fanning her cheeks as they fall and rise again.

"*You*," I breathe. My lips curl back from my teeth.

As though moving of its own accord, my body lunges a single step. I don't know what I will do. Catch her by the hair, drag her back to her cell? Press her to my chest so that I may feel her heartbeat against mine? Both needs, both desires, rise in my soul with equal and opposing intensity.

Before I can take a second step, however, she collapses to her hands and knees in the dirt.

Once again, I stop short. When she fell, the wide neckline of her gown slipped down one shoulder, exposing the smooth curve of her skin. Her tumbling golden hair catches the *lorst* light, and I cannot help myself. All the blood drains from my face and rushes straight to my gut, where it roils and burns.

With an effort, I master myself. "Rise, Princess," I command. "Come, get to your feet."

"I would. If I could." A shudder races through her body. The muscles in her neck and shoulders tense as she rolls her head around and gazes up at me. Lines of intense pain frame her eyes. "Believe me, it gives me no pleasure, abasing myself before you."

A streak of red stands out starkly against her pale flesh. It runs in a sluggish stream down her throat, dries across her bosom. I stare, not understanding what it is I see. Then in a terrible rush I remember: *humans bleed red.*

"Faraine!"

The next moment, I'm beside her, kneeling, gathering her in my arms. She resists, her hands pressed against my chest. Her arms shake in her efforts to push me away. But she's weak. With a little moan, her eyes roll back, and her head lolls, affording me a clear view of the crimson gash just under her left ear. I touch trembling fingers against it, stare in horror at the blood seeping through. "Who did this to you?" I growl.

She cannot answer. When I pull her closer and rest her head against my shoulder, she merely moans. Her hair falls in soft waves across my breast, and when I look down, I can see only the curve of her cheek . . . and the much more expansive curve of her bared shoulder and bosom. It would be an alluring sight indeed were it not for that ugly red stain.

"Faraine?" My voice is rough in my own ears. "Faraine, can you hear me?"

"Yes." She shivers. One hand reaches up, clutches the front of my tunic with desperate urgency. "You needn't shout. I'm right here."

That's a lot of impertinence coming from someone whose throat has just been cut. Taking heart, I shift her in my arms so that I can tilt back her chin and get a closer view of the wound. Now that the first flush of panic has settled, I can see that it's no more than a shallow graze. So why is she fainting in my arms?

She moans again and drops her head into the crook of my neck. "Let me go," she breathes. One quivering hand rises, pushes against my chest, but without any force. "You're hurting me."

Hurting her? I force my arms to relax, but the moment I remove my support, she crumples to the ground in a boneless heap. Hastily, I catch her up again, my grip tight despite her agonized groan. Dark God spare me, what am I supposed to do? I can't very well drop her in the path and leave her there.

A frustrated growl deep in my chest, I slip one arm under her knees, force her head back against my shoulder, and rise. She utters a little bleat, gripping the front of my shirt. "No! No, let me go!"

"Don't struggle," I say against her hair.

"I'll struggle if I want to." Her voice is fainter than before. "Please . . . please, don't . . . send me back to . . ."

Her body goes suddenly limp.

My chest tightens as I gaze down at her face. Her mouth is slack, her lips parted, but her expression remains tense. A faint line puckers between her brows. Is she unconscious? I cannot tell. I must do something, must take her somewhere. Lifting my gaze, I search among the rock formations. "Is anyone there?" I shout. "Anyone?"

No answer. Only my own voice echoing among the blooming crystals.

With no other option, I march back along the path, muttering curses with every step. How in the Deeper Dark did Faraine manage to break out of her cell? And then to find her way here, of all places? It doesn't make sense. As though dragged by an irresistible force, my gaze slides back down to the smooth white curve of her shoulder and breast. She's tucked up under my chin now, so small, so delicate. How easily I might crush her in my arms. And yet everything about her is womanly, soft, and warm. The pleasure of simply holding her like this is more than I dare admit.

"Hael!" I wrench my gaze away and bellow across the garden to the south entrance. "Captain Hael! Gods damn it, where are you?"

At last, Hael appears in my line of sight, standing in the entrance arch. My captain of the guard looks uncertain, which is not normal for her. She's usually so poised, but recent events have shaken her to the core. As they should. My own confidence in her is certainly not what it once was.

She takes one look at the bundle in my arms, and her stone-hard expression breaks into utter shock. "What is this?" she cries, and leaps forward, reaching out as though to take my burden from me.

I pivot neatly to avoid her grasp, then continue swiftly around her into the palace. "The prisoner has escaped her cell," I bark over my shoulder. "Someone needs to find out how. *Now.*"

Hael ducks down a side passage to sound a deep-bellied *zinsbog* horn. This brings other members of her guard scurrying to our location. Too soon, I'm surrounded by gawking faces. Which is not ideal. The last thing I need is for rumor to spread that I was seen cradling in my arms the very bride I'd nearly had publicly beheaded mere hours ago.

"Make way," I growl, and they part before me. Hael issues crisp orders for some of them to hasten to the holding cell and speak to the guard on duty; for others to search the nearby passages for possible accomplices. Then she trails after me, blurting the occasional "Where are you taking her?" or "What are you planning?"

I don't have any answers. So I hold my tongue and continue forward. Ignoring the stares of any onlookers I pass, I storm through the palace halls. I don't return to the holding cell. Instead, my feet carry me to the royal wing and the Queen's Apartment. Hael, finally realizing where I'm headed, rushes ahead of me and opens the door.

"Get out of my way," I snarl, and she leaps back. I bear Faraine into the bridal chamber, lay her down on the soft bed. Blood from her throat wound has soaked into the askew neckline of her gown and left a stain on my shirt. I touch the cut again and grimace, then shift my gaze back to her face. So stern, so lined with pain. Gently, I brush a strand of hair back from her forehead. She stirs slightly, turns her face a little toward me. My breath catches.

"Your Majesty?" Hael enters the room, bearing a pitcher, bowl, and cloths. She sets them down on the washstand close by. "Your Majesty, allow me to—"

I push her hand aside, take one of the cloths, and dip it in the water. Carefully, I dab at Faraine's throat. "Send someone for Madame Ar," I say without looking Hael's way. She darts from the chamber. I hear her gruff voice demanding the palace healer be brought to the Queen's Apartment at once. She returns a moment later and starts to say something, but I cut her off: "Out, Captain."

Though I don't look back, I feel the tension in the air as she freezes. Then, tentatively: "Your Majesty—"

I whip my head around, fix her with a level stare. "Did I not make myself clear?"

For a moment, the expression in her face is agonized enough to almost make me regret my words. Then her features harden. She salutes with her big, boulder-like right hand, steps from the room, and pulls the door shut behind her.

So. I am alone with Faraine. With my bride.

I focus on bathing the cut, on wiping away the red stain from her neck. After a moment's pause, I continue to wipe her soft breast as well, careful not to let my fingers so much as brush her skin. The wound itself is blessedly small. Certainly not deep enough to require stitches. If Faraine is lucky, she'll end up with only the faintest scar.

My gaze lingers longer than it should. I can't seem to help myself. The truth is, I'd almost forgotten what she looked like. I'd known her for so short a time. Other than our memorable meeting and our ride together beneath the terrifyingly open sky, I only encountered her a handful of occasions in her father's house. I'd spent more time with her sister, Ilsevel, with whom I'd danced each night.

But somehow, those moments with Faraine had left a greater impact. She spoke with both earnestness and humor. Always a little reserved, which lent her an intriguing air of mystery. And despite her reserve, she was warm. Her soul was so bright, it drew me like an *olk* to a moonfire lantern. I wasn't foolish enough to think I *loved* her. There was something about her, however . . . something which led me to think . . . to wonder . . . to hope . . .

Not that it mattered. She'd made her position clear: if I cared about my people and my kingdom, it was her sister to whom I should be making my proposals. I had honored her insight, set my course, and never once looked back. I bade her farewell and thought I would never see her again. I'd made my peace with the way things were, the way things had to be.

Now I sit on the edge of our marriage bed, gazing down at the unconscious woman before me. Her fair brow, tense with pain. Her straight nose with its round little tip. Her full, soft lips, pressed together in a hard line. Giving in to impulse, I reach out and let my finger trail down the curve of her cheek, round my knuckle along the line of her jaw. A mistake. Her skin is soft as silk. Just that mere touch is enough to strike fire in my soul.

Scarcely aware of what I do, I clench my fist and press it into the pillow beside her face. Slowly, I lean toward her, lower my face to hers until mere inches separate us. Her lips part. Do I imagine it, or does she tilt her chin up, as though in invitation? Her chest rises and falls beneath me even as her breath hitches in her slender throat.

What am I to do with this cavernous need? This ache in my core? I feel like a man parched to the brink of death who lays eyes at last on the cool, clear stream. Surely one touch should be enough to soothe this thirst. One little brush of my lips against hers. Is that too much to ask?

I could take it. Take the relief I desire. She could not stop me. The barest inclination of my head, and we would be joined once more. Only this time, that joining would be so much fuller, so much richer. Because this time, I would know it was Faraine I kissed.

Faraine.

*Faraine.*

Sudden commotion erupts in the outer chamber. "Get out of my way, get out of my way!" a familiar voice barks. "If the king must drag me from my good work, you might as well let me through."

I push back from the bed, stand, retreat by several paces. Gods, what came over me? Maybe I truly am bewitched. Hastily, I run my hands through my hair, composing my face as I turn. The door opens. Madame Ar steps into the room, her healer's bag in one hand. She shoots me a withering look. "Well, Vor? What's so urgent that you'll set a poor old woman scampering clear across the palace at your beck and call?"

I bite back a retort. Ar is certainly old, but one would never know it to look at her. Her stout trolde body bears the age of centuries with ease. She's one of the few people in the palace who dares use my given name, with or without permission.

"I need you to take a look at her," I say, and sweep a hand to indicate the figure on the bed. "Something is wrong. I don't know what."

"Ah!" Ar's eyes light up suddenly. Her face creases in an unexpectedly delighted smile. "I'd forgotten! Your new bride is a human! How fascinating."

"She's not my bride," I growl.

The old healer ignores me, sets her bag aside, and begins a thorough inspection of the princess, muttering to herself as she goes. I stand close by, until finally Ar shoots me a withering stare. "You're hovering," she snaps, and makes a shooing motion with one hand. "It's distracting. Be off with you! I'll let you know when you're welcome back in."

I open my mouth to protest, to remind her that I am king. But it's not as though Ar would pay any attention.

Instead, I step from the room and stand a moment in the outer chamber, oddly disoriented and uncertain. I close my eyes, lean my back against the door. Stepping out of Faraine's presence is like leaving behind both light and air. My chest feels oddly tight and uncomfortable, and I struggle to draw a full breath.

"Your Majesty?"

I look up. Hael stands by the door. The sight of her drawn face is enough to make me pull myself upright. "Well?" I demand.

She salutes smartly, her face severe. "We found Lord Rath."

"Rath?" I repeat, confused. Lord Rath is my minister of tradition, as slimy an eel as was ever dressed in ministerial robes. What he has to do with recent events is beyond me.

Hael shifts on her feet. "He was discovered unconscious not far from the holding cells, clad in a cloak and hood." She pauses then holds up an object. "He had this on him."

It's a knife. A small dagger with a handle carved in the shape of a dragon's head. The edge of the blade boasts a red stain.

I stare at that stain.

Then rage explodes inside my chest. "*Where is he?*" I demand, my voice a barely subdued roar.

"In his chambers, Your Majesty. We thought it best if—"

I don't wait to hear the rest. I push past Hael, out into the passage, and storm from the royal wing. I don't pause until I reach the region of the palace where my ministers live in ostentatious apartments. Though we pass others, I see no faces, hear no voices. My mind has tunneled into a single purpose which leads me straight to Rath's door.

The latch resists when I put my hand to it. With a single vicious turn, I break the lock and slam the door wide. Rath's wife and members of his household are gathered in the front room. Lady Rath screams at the sight of me and faints into someone's arms. I ignore her. I ignore all of them. I pass through their midst without pause and burst into Rath's bedchamber. He lies on the bed, his skin white as polished marble. His eyes are open but unseeing. I'd think he was dead, save for the ratcheting rise and fall of his chest.

Hael appears beside me. She reaches out as though to grab my arm but stops herself. Part of me wishes she would. Part of me suspects I need to be restrained before I do something irrevocably terrible. Red mist films my vision. I blink it back, draw a deep, steadying breath.

Then I march to the bed, stand over my minister. "Why did you do it?" I demand, my voice cold as a cavern. "Why did you try to kill her?"

He stares up at the ceiling. His mouth moves. Opens. Shuts. His eyelids flicker, but don't quite blink.

"Answer me, Rath," I snarl. "Answer me, or by the Deeper Dark, I swear I will—"

"Your Majesty! Please!"

The shout in my ear brings me back to myself. I turn to find Yok, Hael's brother, gripping me by one arm. Hael is on my other side, her strong hands latched onto my shoulder. When I look down, I find I'm squeezing Rath's throat. His eyes goggle and his tongue protrudes between his lips, thick and purple.

With a gasp, I let go. Yok and Hael drag me back. I sag in their holds. Gods above and below, what came over me? One moment, I was standing there, talking to the man, and the next . . . I don't remember.

"Unhand me!" I cry. "At once, you fools!"

"You can't murder him, Your Majesty," Hael says, her hand still firmly locked on my shoulder. "Not even you are above the law."

I turn sharply, catch her eye. "Let go of me, Captain. You've failed me one time too many."

My words strike Hael like blows. She drops her hold on me and backs away. "We must question him, Your Majesty," she says, pulling herself straight. "We must learn what he was attempting. Had he simply wanted to assassinate the princess, he would have sent a proxy."

I nod. My breath is hard and heavy in my lungs. I can't bring myself to look at the stricken lord again for fear another murderous rage will overtake me. I run my hands through my hair, push it back from my face. "You're right. There's something more afoot here. Have him carried to Madame Ar's infirmary as soon as possible. Set a watch around him. Only your best men, Captain. Let no one near. I want him alive, do you understand me? If something happens to him, it will be on your head."

Hael swallows hard, the muscles in her throat constricting. But she offers a crisp salute.

I turn from her, step toward the open door. There I pause and shoot a last look back at the man on the bed. He looks so pathetic, so small. My eyes narrow. "Tell Madame Ar, I want him tested as well."

"Tested for what?" Yok asks quietly.

I pull my lips back, showing my teeth. "*Raog* poison."

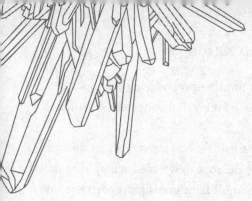

# 3

## Faraine

I fall.

Tumble, career through darkness. Through shadow, through heat, through smoke.

My arms flail uselessly, struggling to grasp something, anything. My fingertips brush stone only for the skin to be ripped away as I continue my endless plummet. A sound like rushing wind roars in my ears, underscored by the keening of a thousand mourners, their voices upraised in endless woe.

There's no escape, no hope, no help.

And down below me . . .

Far beneath the heat and the darkness . . .

Something watches.

Something waits.

Suddenly, a voice breaks through the rushing in my ears. Though I cannot understand the words, something in my heart jolts with recognition. It's like a delicate, shimmering thread has unfurled before me. When I reach out and take hold, that thread solidifies, becomes a stout rope. I wrap myself—my body, my consciousness, I don't even know what—around it and hold on with everything I have.

Now the rushing stops, the mad descent forestalled, for the moment at least. Slowly, slowly, the rope draws me back up through the mist and black obscurity until faint gray light penetrates my eyelids. I'm lying on a soft pillow. My body is perfectly still. No tumbling. No rope either. I lie with my eyelids cracked, and a flickering glow filters through my eyelashes.

Voices murmur on my left. Two voices: one male, one female. One I would recognize anywhere, despite the growling intonation of trolde language. The other I don't know. Elderly, animated, it dominates the exchange, with the other only managing to insert a few blunt words here and there.

Summoning all the strength I possess, I part my eyelids a little further. Two blurry figures stand at my bedside. One is short, for a trolde at least, and a little hunched. The other is the unmistakably broad and powerful form of Vor.

Fear lurches in my heart at the sight of him. Fear and . . . something else. Something stronger. And more dangerous. Something I don't care to acknowledge.

With a last flurry of grunting talk, the smaller of the two figures reaches out and pats Vor on the arm. A strangely maternal gesture, incongruous with the intimidating size of the recipient. Then she seems to be gathering various tools into a bag, which she snaps shut before vanishing from my narrow range of sight. I hear a *clunk*, possibly the door shutting.

My heart rate quickens. I wish I could make myself sink back into unconsciousness. My body aches all over, and my head rings with pain. Meanwhile, the source of that pain—the source of that throbbing, stabbing ache between my eyes—even now draws a chair up to my bedside and takes a seat.

*My husband.*

I tense. I wish I could physically recoil from him. At least his emotions are currently held in check. When we encountered one another in the garden, the wave of his feelings had bludgeoned me as brutally as a blow from his fist. Gone are the days when I felt nothing but peace in his presence. Perhaps it was all a dream.

Is he going to sit there and wait until I wake up? Dear gods, I hope not. Vor is the last person I want to speak to just now after everything that's happened. Dropping my eyelids, I lie in complete darkness once more, my breath shallow, my chest tight. Maybe he will grow bored and leave. I count the seconds and then the minutes passing. He shifts position only once. Either he knows I'm awake and is toying with me, or he really has determined to wait around until I regain consciousness. Hesitantly, I extend my godsgift toward him. So many complicated emotions roil through his spirit. He's calmer now, at least. Mostly.

I frown. There's something there, something underneath the turmoil of fear, mistrust, concern, impatience. Those feelings, all readily recognizable, simmer along the surface of his being. But there's something deeper. Something dark, coiled around his core. Cautiously, I peer through my lashes. Peer at this man who ordered my execution only to stop it at the last possible second. This man I thought I loved.

Suddenly, Vor rubs both hands down his face, pulling at the skin under his eyes. Then he turns, looks straight at me. His expression tightens, his brows drawn together. And I realize that while I've been studying him, I've unconsciously opened both eyes. For a series of long, silent moments, we stare at one another.

"You're awake," he says at last.

I blink once in acknowledgment. Then, gritting my teeth, I push my elbows under me, force my body into an upright position. One sleeve catches and pulls off my shoulder, slides down my upper arm. A wave of heat rolls out from Vor and hits me. I look up sharply, momentarily catching his eye. He turns away at once, stares fixedly at something on the wall across the room. The impression passes. I'm left shivering in its wake.

Hastily, I tug my sleeve back into place. "How long have I been unconscious?" I ask. My voice is rough and dry in my throat.

"An hour." Vor glances at me, looks away. Swallows. Faces me again. "Maybe two." Shifting in his chair, he rests an elbow on one arm. His fingers rub together nervously. "Our *uggrha* healer says it was not loss of blood that caused your fainting spell, but shock. A few more hours of quiet, and you should feel much better."

My hand slips to my neck. There's a sticky puckering right where the assassin's blade grazed my skin. My jaw tightens. "Shock," I repeat softly. "Yes. Of course." I drop my hand back into my lap. "Did they catch him? The man who . . . ?" I can't quite bring myself to finish.

Vor's face darkens. "He is not yet conscious. He's under watch until he can be questioned." Another long, painful silence falls between us. I'm still struggling to think of something suitable to say when Vor turns abruptly to me again. "I owe you an apology."

My eyes flick to meet his. "What?"

He drops his gaze, his forehead puckered. A line deepens between his brows. "I had assumed you would be safe. In the holding cell. I thought security measures down there would be sufficient."

"So . . ." I pause, pull my lips in, and bite down hard. "So, you locked me away in a box-sized cave without light for my *protection*?"

Another flash of feeling rolls out from behind his barriers. If I didn't know any better, I'd think it was shame. "I admit," he says, "I neglected to consider how much worse the darkness would be for you than for one of my own people."

"The darkness? And what about the rest of it? Such as the cold. The lack of privacy. The hard cot for a bed. No blanket, no chamber pot. Not to mention the total ignorance of my coming fate or future. Did you neglect to consider these as well?"

His shame sharpens to a knifelike point. It pricks hard enough to make me wince. But I don't back down. I maintain a level stare, daring him to meet my gaze.

He doesn't. When he finally speaks, his voice is very low. "I did not think beyond simply placing you somewhere secure."

"Secure enough that an assassin could simply walk in, take me from my cell, and march me forth at bladepoint?"

Vor's lip curls. His teeth flash in the low light from the *lorst* crystals hung from the ceiling above. But he answers only, "Lord Rath has always enjoyed certain privileges in the palace."

"Do these privileges extend to the assassination of political prisoners? Is this Lord Rath's role in service to his king?"

"No!" The word is adamant, spoken with another flare of intensity. "I do not keep an assassin on retainer. Even if I did, I could certainly find someone better suited to the task than Rath."

"On that, at least, we can agree." Settling back into the mounded pillows behind me, I rest my head against the stone headboard. "Your Lord Rath was a poor assassin. It's not as though I'm a particularly lethal target."

"Aren't you?" Vor's eyebrow twitches. There's an uneasy gleam in his eye as he considers me. "I'm curious, how did you manage to subdue Rath? There were no marks found on his body."

I don't answer. I merely look at him.

"Was it the same thing you did to Lady Lyria on . . . when . . . ?" His voice trails away.

My nostrils flare slightly. "You mean when she tried to stop your people from cutting off my head? When I had to save her from being torn apart by your guards? Is that what you mean?" Gods above, who knew I possessed such wellsprings of defiance? I've always been the demure, shrinking, people-pleasing, disappointing princess. Perhaps this is what multiple near-death experiences in quick succession will bring out in a person.

Vor's jaw tightens. The muscles in his throat constrict, causing a vein to stand out. "About that—"

"About my near decapitation?"

He draws back from me slightly. "I wasn't myself. I don't want to make excuses, but . . . there were other factors at play. I want you to know that I have no intention of . . . of . . ."

"Of separating my head from my body?"

"Yes. That."

"Such a comfort." I draw myself a little straighter and fold my arms across my stomach. "In that case, what *do* you intend to do with me?"

Another sharp wave of emotion. Not shame this time. This is something hotter, stranger. Something he quickly tamps back down behind his walls, but not before I sense it. My blood warms. Suddenly, I'm uncomfortably aware of where I am. The last time we were in this room together, he was with me in this bed. And there was a lot less space between us. And a lot less clothing.

The heat in my blood pools in my center. My skin is alive, prickling, as though I can feel his breath stirring the hairs on my arm even at this distance. But I won't let it show. I know how to mask my own feelings, and I'm not about to give him any advantage over me.

"I don't know," Vor says at last. His words strike my ears like the inevitable toll of funeral bells.

I knot my fists. "What's to prevent you from changing your mind again? From sending me back to the block?"

"I would never do that to you."

My lip curls. "I find that hard to believe, given recent history."

"Indeed?" His gaze flashes at me from beneath his drawn brows. "And I would not have believed it possible for you to deceive me as you have done. Perhaps it's time we both readjusted our expectations of one another."

I don't answer. Why should I? I simply look at him, my eyes slowly narrowing. Let him realize the foolishness of what he's just said. Of comparing my deceit—a deceit forced on me by outside powers against which I had no sway—to his murderous rage. They are not the same. *We* are not the same.

He holds my gaze for three silent breaths. Then his eyes widen, and the stern line of his brow softens. Another wave of feeling rushes out from him, this time strong enough to drive him to his feet. His chair scoots back several inches across the floor, and he looms above me. So tall, so powerful. So beautiful. "While you are a guest in Mythanar," he says coldly, "you will be under my protection. You can take that for whatever you deem it worth, but I intend it for your peace of mind."

I want to tell him that I'll keep his intentions in mind the next time I'm being dragged up a scaffold. Instead, I lower my eyelids in a slow blink of acknowledgment. When I look up at him again, I say only, "Is that what I am then? Your guest?"

"You are certainly not my *wife*."

Of everything he's said to me, this strikes the hardest. The whole room seems to rock. Nausea whirls in my head, and my stomach pitches. But I won't let it show. I won't. I lift my chin, draw a firm breath. "In the eyes of my people, I am. By the will of the gods and of Gavarian law, I am your wife and therefore deserve all the rights of a wife."

My words have power because they are true. I watch them hit the mark, watch my supposed husband reel. He's unwilling to give an inch, however. Where a moment ago, I sensed shame, now I sense an equally profound indignation verging on anger swelling from behind his protective barriers. "Mythanar recognizes no law that allows one person to take the identity of another," he growls. "Thus, I do not accept you in place of your sister."

My sister.

My Ilsevel.

*Dead.*

My chin crumples. I try to stop it, try to suppress the sob as it rises in my throat. But I can't. Nor can I stop the shuddering gasp, the sudden prickle of tears. Though I blink hard, a tear escapes through my lashes, races down my cheek.

Vor draws a sharp breath. For a terrible moment, I feel his walls cracking. But that's the last thing I want right now, for him to let down his barriers, to reach out to me, to try to comfort me. "Faraine," he begins.

I cut him off. "Go. Please."

He hesitates. Then, with a frustrated exhalation, he lurches into motion, strides for the door. Just as he draws it open and takes a step through, however, I whisper softly, "Wait."

He stops. Looks back.

"Will I be returned to the holding cell?"

He's silent. I cannot bear to look at him. I stare down at my crossed arms, at the bloodstain on the scooped neckline of my gown. Waiting. Tense.

"Until further notice," he says at last, "you will remain in the Queen's Apartment. I will appoint a personal guard for your safety."

"Am I your prisoner then?"

"As I said before, you are my guest."

"And how long will I be your guest?"

"That remains to be seen."

"So, I am a guest who may not come or go as she chooses?"

"Yes."

I nod. "Very well, good king. I think we understand one another."

He waits. Possibly hoping I will say something more, offer a softening word to make the tension between us less horrible. I cannot deny the urge to look up, to meet his eye. To beg him not to go. To fling myself out of this bed and into his arms and discover whether or not I can call back to life some spark of the heat we experienced the last time we were alone in this room together.

But those stolen moments were intended for Ilsevel. Not me. I was the thief in the night, taking from him that which was not mine. Something sacred. Something which I rendered profane.

So, we merely look at one another. And finally, Vor turns away. His long, silvery hair slips over his shoulder, ripples down his back as he marches to the door. One moment, he's silhouetted in the opening. The next, he's gone. The door shuts fast behind him. A low boom echoes against the stone walls.

I sag back against the pillows, suddenly weak and shivery. Fury and fear and shame and sorrow course through me by turns. But at least these feelings are my own and no one else's. My hand slips to my neck again, touching the awful gummy substance used to patch up my wound.

Then, almost unconsciously, I let my fingertips trail down my throat. Slowly, lingering. Following the same paths Vor's fingers had explored on our ill-fated wedding night. First his fingers, then his lips, then his tongue—

*Gods!*

I clutch my crystal pendant so hard it digs into my flesh. Tilting my head back, I close my eyes and seek the resonance inside that will lead my storming mind and body back to a place of calm.

# 4

# Vor

I stand outside her room at war with myself.

When I close my eyes she's there—vividly before me, seated on that bed, her sleeve yanked off one shoulder. That beautiful, creamy shoulder with its pinkish undertones, so unusual here among the pale, blue-toned troldefolk. Even in my imagination, I long to reach out, to touch, to taste, to know—

*Morar-juk!* What is wrong with me?

"Your Majesty?"

I wrench my eyes open, staring blankly before me into the outer chamber of the apartment. Hael stands in the open doorway. She blocks the way as solidly as any barricade. I don't know how long she's been there. "What?" I growl.

She salutes, her face hard and unreadable. "Madame Ar has requested your presence in the infirmary. She wishes to speak to you. Concerning Lord Rath."

I nod. There are only two people in all of Mythanar who have the audacity to summon me across the palace: my stepmother and

Madame Ar. In this case, at least, I'm eager to hear what our *ug-grha* healer has to say.

Stepping briskly to the door, I make as though to pass by Hael. At the last moment, however, I stop and turn to her sharply. She meets my gaze. Stoic as ever. Her skin is grayer than usual, the soft white darkened until it's nearly a match for the ugly gray stone that creeps up her neck and over her jaw. Despite her deformity, she is a handsome woman with proud, dignified features. Hers has always been the face of one of my most trusted friends.

My heart twists painfully. I want to punish her. She's the one who put me in this situation. Twice over, she could have spared me. She was supposed to protect me against a deceit like this—first at the Between Gate, again in the bridal chamber. Twice over, she has failed in her duty—left me exposed, vulnerable. Humiliated.

"Captain," I say coldly.

"Your Majesty." She's calm. But she knows what's coming.

"You are relieved of your post."

Her eyes widen ever so slightly.

"You will no longer be in charge of my personal guard. I have a new role for you instead."

I can almost hear the words she forces back down her throat. The pleas, the apologies, the excuses. They clamor in the silence between us, shine in the dark depths of her pupils.

"From now on, you are solely responsible for the safety of Faraine Cyhorn of Gavaria. So long as the princess remains in our care, her life is in your hands." I take a menacing step closer and drop my voice an octave. "If anything happens to her—anything at all—I will hold you personally responsible."

Her breath quickens. She holds my gaze, but I wonder if her

resolve will break, if the flood of protests will pour forth. At last, however, she offers another salute. "As you wish, Your Majesty."

I don't wait for more. Leaving her in the doorway, I flee the room, flee that whole wing of the palace. But I'm not quick enough to flee the betrayal shadowing my heart. Everywhere I turn I see only traitors and those who failed to protect me from them. I trusted Hael with my life. I would have trusted Faraine just the same. Yet here am I, a proven fool.

And what of my brother? Sul's face springs to mind, craning to look up at me from the ground as I pinned him down, my foot on his neck. *I would never do that to you*, he'd insisted, when I accused him of lacing my drink with poison. *I would take the draught myself first.*

Do I believe him? I did in that moment, but now? I don't know. The truth is, I fell under the influence of *raog* while in a locked room with only Sul and Hael present. Sul was the one who ordered drinks, the one to pour, the one to hand me my cup. He and Hael could be co-conspirators, of course. Working in secret to bring me down . . . for what purpose? To place Sul on my throne? And Hael, how would she benefit? Would she finally gain the love she craves from my handsome half brother? Would he make her his queen?

My footsteps stumble. I lurch to one side, lean hard against the wall, breath ratcheting in my lungs. Dark, terrible doubts burn in my brain. Surely, these cannot be sane thoughts. It must be the poison, still working through my blood. If I go on like this, I will cease to discern reality from suspicion and end up paralyzed with dread.

I close my eyes, draw several long breaths. Then, a growl rumbling in my chest, I push away from the wall and continue at a slower, more sedate pace. Anyone I pass can see nothing but calm resolution in my face. Nevertheless, no one dares address me or make a bid for my attention.

So, I make my way unhindered to the infirmary. Three members of my personal guard stand outside the door, including Yok, Hael's younger brother and the newest member of the cohort. They snap to attention as I pass. Yok opens the door for me. I step through and down the short stair into the catacomb-like space in which our healer works.

Right there on the front three tables are the chopped-up remains of a cave devil. The gruesome head lies on a platter on the foremost table, long black tongue spilling out from its sagging jaw. The sight makes my stomach turn.

Madame Ar is busy at another workstation across the room. She measures something with great care, adds a bit of a dark mixture, swirls, then holds the tall vial up to a globe of moonfire light. Her face is a study.

I clear my throat. "You wished to see me, Ar?"

She whirls on heel. "Vor!" she bursts out, and fairly launches herself at me, shoving her strange brew into my face. "Do you see this? Do you smell it?"

"What is it I'm supposed to be seeing and smelling?" I put up both hands and try to back away, but she pursues, determinedly waving her concoction under my nose.

"It's the same!" she says. "Traces of *raog* in the blood. I found plenty of it in the *woggha* you brought me, particularly in the brain matter"—she nods at the cave devil head on its platter—"which proved my hypothesis. These rabid devils are indeed being poisoned. That's what's driving them mad."

I frown. "I thought cave devils were immune to *raog*, living down deep as they do."

Ar waves a dismissive hand. "Perhaps they are to the gaseous form we're familiar with. This, however, is much more concentrated. They must have ingested it somehow. In the water, perhaps. And see here?" She shakes her brew in front of me. It's black and sludgy with strange particles floating around inside it. "Do you see it?"

Baffled, I shake my head.

"I took a bit of blood from that unconscious lord you turned over to me. When mixed with *vitgut* and *baguolg*, it reacts thusly."

"And?"

"And? *And?* And this proves he too was suffering from ingested *raog*! Albeit on a much lesser scale." She blinks up at me, her eagerness palpable. "Don't you see? Dispersed in gaseous form, *raog* influence is widespread. This was a targeted poisoning. We will have to see when he wakes if it has driven him to total madness or merely temporary insanity."

So. My instincts led me true. While Rath is a ruthless man in his own way, he's never been one to get his hands dirty. He would have to be mad to do something as foolish as break a prisoner from the hold and attempt to murder her. At worst, he would find someone else to do the job for him.

I grimace. Now that I know, I cannot legitimately march back into Rath's chamber and rip his arms from their sockets. Instead, I must wait patiently for him to regain consciousness and try to learn how he came to be poisoned. In so doing, perhaps I will discover the source of my own poisoning.

"Is it possible it was self-induced?" I ask without much hope.

"Possible? Perhaps, but unlikely." Ar shrugs. "It isn't a pleasant poison either to ingest or to endure, not even in small doses. I cannot imagine one would take it willingly."

I nod. Having experienced *raog* myself, I can't deny the truth of her assessment. "But why," I go on, more to myself than to Ar, "did Lord Rath target the princess in his madness? All other reported cases of *raog* poisonings have resulted in savage, unhinged violence followed by suicide. Why would he focus only on Faraine?"

Madame Ar chews the inside of her cheek thoughtfully. "It may be a matter of timing. It may be the dose was administered when she would be the next person he saw, thus imprinting a murderous impulse toward her upon his soul. Or it may be a piece of the victim's hair or skin or blood was mixed in with the poison. I've taken samples from Lord Rath's mouth and will conduct more tests."

I should probably volunteer my own body for testing. It would be easier for Ar to find answers with a broader field from which to take her samples. At the moment, however, I cannot afford to be trapped in this infirmary and experimented on for hours on end. "What are you doing to treat Rath?" I say instead. Though it pains me to think of that wurm receiving any help or healing, I need him alive. For the moment at least.

"A brew of steeped *miraisis* petals," Ar answers dismissively, turning back to her worktable.

"Will this help?"

"It will or it won't. It's been known to soothe some cases of lesser poisonings. Most of the time, folks just die. When they don't, it's difficult to say whether it was due to any real healing properties in the *miraisis* or simply a lesser degree of poisoning. Either way, it can't hurt."

I grimace. "And if I were to ask for a dose, would you give it to me?"

"Why?" Ar turns too-cunning eyes my way, one of them enlarged by the curved-crystal eyepiece she's pressed into her socket.

"Merely a precaution, Madame."

She raises an eyebrow, and the eyepiece falls out to dangle on its chain. But she says only, "Send a page by in an hour. I'll have a dose prepared for you."

I incline my head in thanks. Then I toss a glance back to the doorway leading to the healing ward. The sickbeds are there, one of them presumably containing Lord Rath. Another guard stands in view, keeping watch over Madame Ar's new prisoner-patient.

"Madame," I say, and turn once more to my royal healer. She's already bent over another worktable, fiddling with strange implements. "Have you had a chance yet to run the tests I requested? On those two goblets I had sent your way?"

"On those?" Ar asks, pointing to yet another table. There I see the two *krilge* goblets I'd recovered from the antechamber of my council hall. They're both submerged in clear vats of some thick, gooey substance. Little bubbles rise off them and streak to the surface, where they form a greasy-looking foam. "I'm still performing the initial *gulg* bath," she says. "Give it a few days."

I nod and suppress a heavy sigh. If I'm honest, I'm not sure I want the answers my healer is working to find for me. But if someone in this palace is targeting Faraine with *raog* poison, I need to find out who. Before it's too late.

# 5

## Faraine

The canopy overhead is blue silk embroidered with silver stars. A strange design for a trolde bedchamber.

I remember all too vividly the tension experienced by Vor and his people when they crossed the open plain beneath the night sky on their way to my father's castle. I've not sensed such fear in Vor before or since. Not when I first met him in the heat of battle with wild unicorn riders. Not when he saved me from the vicious cave devils soon after my arrival in this kingdom. In both instances, he was all courage and determination, underscored by a deep and dangerous ferocity. He was only afraid when under the open sky.

Which makes this canopy odd indeed. Perhaps Vor thought it would be easier for my sister to submit to his caresses if she could gaze up at a vista of stars.

I shudder. Dull pain still echoes through my body, aftershocks of the pummeling I took in the garden. Vor's emotions were so strong, and I'd not been prepared. There'd been no chance to put up any mental fortifications. Still, it could be worse. Back home in Beldroth, such a flood of emotion would have left me totally incapacitated for days on end. Here, though I ache in every bone, I can at least form coherent thought. Better still, when I try to move, my limbs obey.

I grip my crystal pendant, reach for the vibration deep in its core. It pulses gently into my palm, flows through my body, easing the aches and pains like a salve. Suddenly, the stone gives a strange shiver. In the same moment, I hear a faint, humming whine, just on the edge of awareness. And with it a *pull*.

I frown, open one eye, peer around the bedchamber. My gaze lands on two chalices, set aside on a table near the opposite wall. My stomach tightens. Vor and I had held those chalices when we toasted our wedding night. I remember the taste of the fae liquor on my tongue, the burn as it slid down my throat. I'd coughed, unused to such strong drink. Vor had called it *qeiese* and said it was a Lunulyrian brew. He'd claimed he'd seen me partake of it in Beldroth. But it was Ilsevel he'd observed. He had no way of knowing the bride before him had never before touched a drop in her life. Yet another in the long list of my deceptions.

A shiver ripples in my gut. I don't like to remember those moments when we were alone at last. Before he kissed me. Before he undressed me. When I still could have told him the truth. He would have been shocked, yes. Horrified, perhaps. But at least then he would have known that I did not wish to deceive him; that I was only here at my father's command. That I would never intentionally do anything to cause him harm. How can he believe me now? I took so much that was not meant for me . . .

I start to roll over, intending to bury my head under the blankets and slip once more into sleep. Instead, the *pull* comes again, an insistent tug. This time, I'm almost certain it's coming from those chalices. But why?

"Fine," I mutter, and drop the pendant. It settles against my breast as I push back the coverlet and swing my legs over the edge of the bed. My feet are bare, and the floor is cold. I hurry from stone to fur rug back to stone again as I cross the room to the table and peer into one of the chalices. A collection of broken crystal shards meets my view.

"Oh." My lips part softly. I remember now the sharp agony stabbing across my senses when Vor hurled these stones against the wall. Afterwards, they'd drawn me to them. I'd knelt, gathered them in my hands, held them as they vibrated with a song of pain. Vor's pain. Shivering like music. They'd shuddered in my hands until one by one they . . . died.

Which is foolish, of course. Stones don't die. They're stone. Yet, I'd felt their pain. And when they finally stilled, I'd placed them in this chalice for safekeeping. I don't know what I intended to do with them. I wasn't thinking clearly. And I certainly don't know what to do with them now.

They're unsettling. Seeing them like this, in the bottom of that cup, is like finding a nest of dead spiders. I grimace and set the chalice back down. The moment I do, however, my pendant gives another sharp, insistent tug. "Fine, fine, fine," I growl again, and stick a finger down into the broken shards, stirring. They're dead and cold, only . . . I pause. Push my fingertip a little deeper. There. Right at the bottom of the pile. I felt something. An answering vibration.

Biting my lower lip, I fish out a small sliver of crystal, no bigger than my thumbnail. The shape is irregular, but beautiful. It doesn't feel dead like the rest of them either. I turn it over, watch the way the *lorst* light glints against its faceted planes. It feels *alive* in some inexplicable way. Like a stem from a pruned rose, tossed aside on the rubbish heap only to bravely put out little white rootlets. Determined to live, to thrive.

Acting on impulse rather than thought, I pluck my pendant from where it rests against my heart and hold it suspended from its chain. Draw the two stones close, the one larger, stronger, the other smaller, more fragile. When I touch them together, there's an undeniable spark. Not visible. Not audible. Not discernable by any ordinary human sense. But strong enough that I jump and nearly drop the tiny stone.

For a moment, I see again the murderous face of the trolde man as he pinned me against the wall. I feel the reverberations at my back, under my palms, how they'd traveled through me, burst into him, dropped him like a sack of potatoes. That these crystals influence my gods-gift in profound ways, I have no doubt. I just wish I understood *how*. There's power here. Far greater power than I've ever believed possible for a gods-gifted mistake like me.

Slowly, I lift my own pendant up to eye level. It's set in delicate silver filigree, intricately wrought. An *urzul* crystal—that's what Vor said it was. I had no idea. Neither do I know how I came by it. When questioned, Lyria had told Captain Hael that it came with the various bridal gifts Vor had sent to Ilsevel, but that wasn't the truth. I've had the necklace in my possession for years, since soon after my gods-gift manifested.

Darkness like a shadow passes over my memory. My magic came upon me unexpectedly like the sudden arrival of my womanly cycle. I was thirteen at the time. I'd always been sensitive to the feelings of others, but nothing like that sudden crush of emotion. It was as though every living soul in Beldroth Castle suddenly cried out in agony, battering my ears, my spirit. I'd crumbled into my-self, too wracked with pain even to articulate what it was I felt.

They'd taken me to my rooms. Closed all the curtains, driven everyone out. Shut the doors. Once a day, my mother would enter, care for my most basic needs, and leave again. Even that was more than I could bear. I would scream at her to leave, to go, to stop hurting me, until she finally retreated and left me alone in the dark again. Thus, I existed. I do not know how long.

Then one day, I woke from dreams of pain to find my fingers wrapped around this very stone. The warmth in its core pulsed through my skin, down to my bones, and deeper still. Down into my very soul. It was the first relief I'd had in days, maybe months. I'd lost all track of time. When my mother visited me later, she found me sitting up in bed. Surprised, she inspected the stone I showed her, her brow puckered and curious.

Later, she managed to pry it from my fingers long enough to have it set in silver and hung from this chain so that I would not risk losing it. My life changed for the better then. I was still sus-ceptible to the soul storms, but I now had means to manage it. And though in my secret-most heart of hearts, I still thought of my gods-gift as a curse, I no longer viewed it as a death sentence.

Funny though . . . I'd never stopped to wonder how I came by this stone. I'd always assumed Mother gave it to me. But how would she have come by an Under Realm crystal? And how could she have guessed how it would affect me?

I angle the crystal now, studying it, as though I can make it give up its secrets to me. There's a mystery here. One I believe I'm meant to solve. Was it more than a happy accident that brought this stone into my possession? Is it possible that powers greater than my fa-ther's machinations drove me into this world? Am I meant to—

The room begins to move.

I gasp and drop the broken crystal. It bounces by my feet, and the table with the chalices rattles and tips over. The rest of the broken crystals scatter, and the two empty vessels roll across the floor. A stream of dust and pebbles falls from the stalactites overhead, raining down on me. I let out a yelp, leap to one side, grasp one of the sturdy bedposts. It shakes in my grip, and the whole bed moves to one side.

Then, as abruptly as it began—everything stills.

I stand frozen, my hands latched around the post, my breath caught in my lungs. What was that? I stare around the room. Everything seems to be all right. Did I imagine it? But no, the table is overturned, the dead crystals scattered. And my shoulders are covered in a thick layer of dust.

A knock at the door. I choke on a cry and whirl in place, heart leaping. "Princess?" a voice calls from the next room. "Princess, are you all right?"

"Yes," I bleat, then shake my head and try again. "Who is it? Who's there?"

"Captain Hael. I've been assigned to your personal guard."

Oh. Yes. I know her. One of Vor's entourage. Not exactly a friend of mine, but in that moment, it's a relief to hear her voice. "Thank you, Captain," I say, though what exactly I'm thanking her for is unclear. I wet my dry lips. "Wh—what was that?"

A long pause. Then, finally: "Nothing. Merely a stirring. No cause for alarm, Princess."

My hands are still wrapped tight around the bedpost. I try to peel them away but cannot quite manage it. "Is it a common occurrence here in Mythanar?"

"It's nothing you need worry about. Do you require assistance?"

I look around the room, at the little piles of dust, at the scattered crystals. I shake my head, then, realizing I need to speak, hastily say, "No. All is well in here."

"Are you certain? Do you need anything at all?"

*Freedom. Escape.*

*Hope.*

"Nothing. Thank you. I'm all right."

Another pause. This one longer than the others. Finally: "Very well, Princess." These words are followed by the sound of retreating footsteps, and I'm left with a strong sense of aloneness once more.

Prying my fingers free of the post, I climb back into bed. It's relatively free of debris, thanks to the canopy. I lie back on the pillows, stare up at those embroidered stars in their blue-silk sky. There are numerous little indentations where fallen pebbles have caught. Someone will need to climb up there and sweep them away at some point.

For now, however, I lie here and wait for my heart rate to calm. Counting the stars and twisting the chain of my necklace round my fingers.

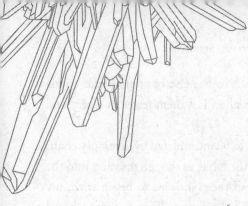

# 6

## Vor

By all that is dark and deep and holy, what *are* you going to do with the human creature?"

I train my gaze on Lady Parh, my minister of war. She doesn't blink or budge but stares right back at me. Violence and vengeance spark in her eyes.

Once again, my ministers have gathered at the crescent council table to press their many and conflicting opinions upon me. Umog Zu and another priestess sit at the far ends of the table, deep in prayer. The low drone of their voices is meant to sustain us throughout our deliberations, but Zu is perhaps not as far sunk into her *va* state as she would like us to believe. Every now and then I catch the glimmer of her eye peering out through a mostly shut lid.

The other ministers take great care not to look at the conspicuously empty seat which should be occupied by my minister of tradition. Only Lord Brug, my blunt minister of agriculture, dared ask after Rath's whereabouts. When I offered no answer, he turned to his fellow ministers, his brow puckered, curious. He was met with nothing but blank stares. No one else has dared take up his question. Good. Let them wonder. Let them fester in worry and speculation. For now.

Parh, however, isn't about to be intimidated by an empty chair. She leans one elbow hard on the table, as though pressing into the throat of her enemy. "You had the right idea to begin with, my king," she urges. "The blade. The box. And all your court gathered to observe. Now what is it they have seen? A fickle monarch, undecided and easily swayed by a mere slip of a girl. A *human*, no less. Is that the image you want to project to your people?"

I sit back in my chair, assuming an easy nonchalance which belies the pulse of my heart. I should not let such disrespect stand, but to reveal any fury or frustration will only further compromise my standing in the eyes of my ministers. I must remain untouchable, unreachable.

So, I let the silence last for just long enough that even Lady Parh's burning gaze begins to falter. Only then do I look from her to Lord Gol, seated on her right, then on to Lady Sha. One by one, I stare down each member of my council. One by one, I silently ask the question: *Was it you who poisoned me? Was it you who poisoned Rath? Is it you who seeks to force my hand?* One by one, I watch their eyelids flicker until finally they drop in silent submission.

Only one person holds my gaze without flinching. Roh. The dowager queen, my stepmother. She has chosen her place on the right curve of the half-circle table, several places down from her former position beside the king's own seat. When my father died, and I ascended to my throne, Roh made every show of deference. She removed herself from the queen's quarters, took a lower place at the table, abdicated all the privileges of her former station as the king's wife. Instead, she turned attention to the practice of her faith in the Deeper Dark.

Yet I know how dearly she wished to see her own son—a full-blooded trolde, not a half-breed like myself—on the throne.

She sits now with her hands folded, her face a perfect mask. For all her serenity, I know how adamant she can be. Roh was opposed to an alliance with humans from the beginning. When Faraine's deception came to light, hers was one of the foremost voices urging me to take swift and brutal action. Still, she is my stepmother. Would she really stoop so low as to poison me?

The silence has gone on long enough. Lady Parh's question still needs to be answered. I blink and turn a measured gaze back to her. "I am still giving the matter some thought," I say at last.

My ministers wait. Breath held, expectant. I seal my lips, rest my head against the back of my seat, drape my arm easily across the table. Offering nothing. Finally, Lady Parh growls. She's just opening her mouth to begin yet another tirade when a sudden burst of applause interrupts. Parh starts in her seat, turns. We all swivel our gazes to the door.

There stands a figure leaning one shoulder insouciantly against the frame. He claps his hands with gusto. "Oh, well done, good king!" he says, nodding approvingly. "That's the way to shut them up! Who can question a thoughtful monarch after all? There's not a fair lord or lady present who couldn't do with an extra thought or two of their own!"

"Sul." I lean back in my seat once more, idly rubbing one finger along my upper lip. "So, you thought to join us at last."

My brother grins, pushes away from the door, and saunters into the room. "Wouldn't dream of missing a party such as this!" He casts a beaming smile round with a particular nod for his mother. Then he swivels his head to one side, eyeing the guard who stands just within the door. "How now, Toz!" he says, giving the big stone-hided man a once-over. "What are you doing, lurking there? Did our stalwart Captain Hael wriggle out of this dull duty in favor of head-bashing a few new recruits?"

Toz pulls himself a little straighter. He's a big man, more troll than trolde, and obliged to wear customized armor. It creaks as he offers a quick salute. "I've been promoted, sir," he answers in his deep, rock-hard voice.

"Promoted?" One eyebrow slides slowly up Sul's brow. "And what of Hael herself? Has she finally decided to take that holiday to Hoknath she keeps going on about?"

"Reassignment, sir."

"Is that so?" Sul's head turns sharply. His pale eyes flash as they catch hold of mine. "Is that so."

I keep my expression a careful blank. "Was Lady Lyria safely given into Prince Theodre's keeping?"

A muscle in Sul's cheek twitches. "Aye."

"And what of my message for Larongar?"

"My man Hurg is to journey with the prince's party to Beldroth, where he will deliver the message in person. He'll return to the Between Gate in seven days' time with Larongar's answer."

"So that's it then?" Lady Parh barks, her big hands clenched. "We wait at the leisure of human kings now?"

I tilt my head, narrowing my eyes at her. "We must allow for the message to travel to and fro. Even I do not control the passage of time."

"And yet time works against you, my king. Time which leaves you bound to a human's whim."

"I am bound to no human." My voice drops an octave, a growl as low as the droning prayers of the priestesses. "The alliance is not sealed. Larongar holds no sway over me."

"It was not Larongar of whom I spoke."

Ice pulses through my veins. I stare at my minister of war even as my hand slowly slips from the table down to my belt and the dagger sheathed there.

Parh leans across the table again, her eyes burning with the intensity of her words. "You must follow through on your original intent, my king. You must free yourself, once and for all. Send the girl's head home in a box. Rid us all of any further dealings with humans."

Ice in my limbs. Ice in my head.

But down in my gut, fire burns. My hand firmly grips the dagger hilt. The council chamber fades from view, lost in shadows that close in tighter and tighter until I can see nothing but Parh and her hideous, leering face. I want to lunge across this table. I want to plunge this blade into her throat. I want to watch her blue blood gush as her eyes widen in shock and her purple tongue protrudes through her teeth. It would be so easy. My knife is halfway drawn already. I could—I should—

"Where is Lord Rath, by the way?"

I blink, give my head a quick shake. Dropping the dagger back into its sheath, I turn to my brother. He's taken his seat beside me, propped one foot up on the table, and laced his hands behind his head. He tips an eyebrow my way.

My throat is tight, dry. I clear it roughly. "Lord Rath is currently recovering in Madame Ar's infirmary."

"Oh? Did the old *guthakug* meet with some accident?"

"He was poisoned."

The air in the room tenses with a collective intake of breath. Every member of my council looks at one another then away again quickly.

I smile, a grim, hard curl of the lips. "And I will soon find out who did it. So, you'd best ready your excuses, my friends." With those words, I look into each of their eyes, one after the other. Brug and Sha barely hold my gaze for the space of five beats. Gol cannot look up from an earnest contemplation of his own hands. Lady Parh tries to be strong, but even her eyes skirt away at last, her brow stern, her jaw hard. Only Roh remains unaffected. My stepmother, who has spoken not a word. Her face is strangely vacant, as though she, like the two priestesses, has sunk into her *va* state. The only sign of life is a single slow blink.

I rise. My ministers push back their seats and stand as well, inclining their heads respectfully. "We shall convene again the lusterling after next," I say, "at which time, we will not discuss the matter of the human princess. Until we receive Larongar's response, that subject is forbidden."

Something in my tone and demeanor must have struck a chord, for each minister holds his or her tongue in check as I step away from the table and stride swiftly from the chamber.

Once out of their sight, I allow my shoulders to bow. My jaw relaxes just enough to exhale a long, slow breath. Members of my guard stand by. I cannot let them see me as anything less than strong, stern, and commanding. Guards are the worst gossips in the kingdom by far, and I don't want them carrying tales. So, I pull my head a little higher and stride down the passage.

"Vor!"

I pause, look back over my shoulder. Sul hastens after me, his expression wry as always. "Well done, my brother. You've got the old stone feet shaking in their boots. I liked that bit about readying their excuses. Very nice indeed. Granted, it'll make my job rather more difficult when it comes time to question them and their households. But *juk*!" He shrugs. "Such is the life of a spymaster."

"You're not a spymaster, Sul."

He pulls a face. "Informal gatherer of delicate information then." Tilting his head, he studies me narrowly. "You look terrible."

"Thanks." I fold my arms. The shadows on the edges of my vision retreat somewhat. I wonder if my brother knows just how close I was to murdering Parh in cold blood right there in front of my entire council. "I'm glad you're back."

"I know." My brother claps me on the shoulder, turns me around, and marches me down the passage with him. "Tell me, brother, when did you last eat? Or sleep? Or"—he sniffs loudly, his lip curling—"bathe?"

I scratch the back of my neck. "Um . . ."

Sul groans. "Too long, dear king, too long! Come. We shall feast. We shall snore. But first, away to the baths with you!" With a quickening step he guides me toward the bathhouse, a series of rooms full of steam, hot springs, masseurs, and crystalline cool bathing pools. I consider protesting but why bother? I've not properly slept in a full turn of lusterling and dimness. Not since ensconcing Faraine in the Queen's Apartment. My own chambers connect to hers via a conjugal door. Somehow, I cannot relax knowing she is so near. Knowing nothing but a single door separates us. That I could simply walk through, and none would know save her and me . . .

So, I've filled the hours with work. Of which there is always plenty. I stopped once to try to catch an hour of sleep in my private chancery, only to be rudely awakened by the stirring. This left my household in a state of mild upheaval. Much of my attention has been taken up with reports of minor damage both within the palace and in the city abroad, not to mention our nearest sister cities. Prior to meeting with my ministers, I spent several hours walking the palace foundations with my chief engineer. Before that, Chancellor Houg carried a report that the sacred statue of Saint Hurk the Rock-Smasher had been damaged by a falling stone. Before that . . . the list goes on.

Yes. A bath sounds good. Wash. Food. Sleep. The cares of the kingdom can wait until then.

"Tell me, brother, what has happened to our friend Hael in the short time since I've been away?" Sul asks before we've taken more than a few steps. His voice is light, but I hear the tension underscoring his words.

"Hael has been reassigned."

"To what?"

"To guarding Princess Faraine during her stay in Mythanar."

My brother considers this for some moments. I know better than to hope he'll let the matter drop, however. "You're punishing her," he says at last.

"See it as you will."

"You shouldn't, Vor." Sul stops, turns to face me. His expression is uncharacteristically serious. "She doesn't deserve it. You know she doesn't."

I fold my arms, set my jaw hard. "Hael had one task to accomplish: make certain I did not carry the wrong bride across the boundaries of the worlds. A task she failed."

Sul mimics my stance, arms crossed, chin tucked. "As I remember, it was you who climbed into bed with the girl without checking first. Hael didn't make you toss off your trousers and—"

"Nothing happened between Princess Faraine and myself."

My brother snorts. "And has nothing continued to happen? Because from what I've heard, the princess is no longer in the holding cell where she belongs."

"No. She is where I can be certain she will be safe. She must remain alive until I can decide what's best to be done with her. Hael is the best person for that job." I tilt my head slightly. "If you have a problem with that, you may as well come out and say it."

Sul's lips curve in a smile that doesn't quite reach his eyes. But he says only, "What I have a problem with is a malodorous monarch. Come! Let's deal with the most pungent matter at hand, shall we?"

Relieved to have the topic dropped, I allow my brother to guide me to the bathhouse door. We step inside into the warmth and steam. Servants appear, help us out of our garments, and we move into the hot spring water. Taking seats on the submerged benches, we rest our heads back against the lip of the pool. Sul holds his tongue for the time being, much to my relief. Sometimes my brother is capable of surprise. Slowly, my muscles begin to relax. I feel both stress and impurities purging from my pores.

"I saw signs of a stirring when I was coming back," Sul says after a time.

I grunt. My eyes are closed. I don't care to discuss city matters just now.

"Any serious damage?"

"No." I sigh, wait a moment, then add, "The palace foundations are strong, and reports from the lower city have all been positive—"

The words have scarcely crossed my lips when I hear it: a high, trilling giggle. I open one eye. The atmosphere in the room is so dense with roiling steam, I can scarcely make out my brother's form across from me in the bath. "Sul?"

"It wasn't me!" he protests.

Movement in the water. I turn, peer into the steam. A soft, warm body presses up against my side. I whip my head around, and stare in shock at the naked woman seated on the pool bench beside me. She's young, lovely, with a delicate, almost demure face, which contrasts starkly with the voluptuousness of her figure. She smiles at me and flutters her eyelashes shyly even as she trails a hand across my chest and down my abdomen.

I grip her wrist hard. She gasps, and I push her back. With a growl, I wave steam from my face, only to see my brother grinning at me from across the pool, flanked by two more naked women. One of them toys with the tips of his pointed ears, while the other giggles and bats at his hand as he tickles her under the chin. "What is this, Sul?" I demand.

"What do you think it is?" Sul eases back into the water, snugging an arm around one of the girls even as the other drops kisses on his cheek, his neck, his shoulder. "You've not eaten. You've not slept, you've not bathed. And according to you, *nothing* has happened between you and your little bride, which leads me to think you've not—"

"And I'm not about to!" I push the girl's hand away again as she tries to catch and cup my cheek. She pouts prettily and sits up on her knees so that the water is no higher than her navel, displaying her large breasts directly in my line of sight. My mouth goes dry. Quickly, I avert my eyes. "Sul, you know perfectly well I don't . . . I don't hold for bathhouse girls or their work."

"And whyever not? They are an industrious lot. Come, Vor, let the poor girl do her job. She'll scrub your neck for you if you like. I swear, you've never been so clean!"

The girl, voiceless but insistent, runs her fingers along the back of my neck and shoulders. I shiver, pulling away, and yet . . . my gaze drags back to her revealed form. Gnawing hunger gapes in my gut, a hunger which has gone unsated since my disastrous wedding night. A hunger which has only grown since I discovered Faraine in the crystal garden. I look at the girl again. This time I let my gaze linger. She is not Faraine. But she is here. And she is soft and warm and so very willing.

She slides closer to me. One long leg drapes in my lap, hooks behind my knee, pulls me toward her. She leans in. I close my eyes, let myself envision Faraine's face. I let myself believe it is Faraine's breath which tickles my ear, warms my neck. Faraine's hand which cups my cheek, turning my face toward hers. Faraine's lips planting against mine, forcing my mouth open, tangling our tongues. Faraine, Faraine, *Faraine* . . .

*"No!"* The roar bursts from my throat. I yank back and push the girl so viciously, she falls off the water bench with a screech and a splash. "Vor!" Sul shouts, sitting upright. The two girls with him both let out screams and scramble from the pool, their naked bodies glistening. I surge up from the water in a stream of foam, snatch up a nearby robe, wrap it around my body. The fabric clings and does nothing to hide my arousal. Enraged, I stagger to the door, ignoring my brother's voice as he shouts after me.

The cold air outside the bathhouse hits like a slap. I gasp and sag against the wall, shuddering, breathing heavily. Pressing my fingers into my eyes, I try to drive sense back into my brain. But I can't. When my eyes are closed, I see only her.

*Her.*

*Faraine.*

Lying on the bed, her gown askew.

Her knee upraised, her skirt falling open to reveal the long, limber form of her bare leg.

Her eyes, gazing up at me. One gold. One blue. Her smile. Slow, seductive. Dangerous.

*She knew.*

She knew what she was doing, gods damn her.

She intended to humiliate me. All along.

She wanted to take me, to break me. To unmake me.

I am king. But she made me her fool.

Another roar strangling in my throat, I push up from the wall. My lips curl back, bare my teeth in an animal snarl. My body feels as though it's on fire, as though my skin will burn away the thin cloth of this garment and leave me naked, burning, a demon of passion incarnate. My shoulders hunched, my head low, I swing my predatory gaze around.

Then I'm in motion. Staggering but gaining speed with each step, until I'm loping along like a predatory beast set upon my quarry's trail. My footsteps carry me through the palace, straight for the royal wing. Straight for the Queen's Apartment.

I'll make her pay for what she did to me.

I'll make her beg forgiveness.

I'll make her beg for mercy.

I'll make her beg for *more*.

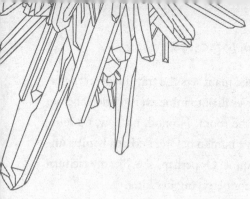

# 7

## Faraine

I'm not sure whose idea it was to finally feed the king's half-starved, unwanted, inconvenient bride. Perhaps Captain Hael thought of it. While I don't flatter myself that she cares for my well-being, she wouldn't want me to outright starve to death. Not on her watch.

However it may be, the door to my room opens unceremoniously, startling me from a semi-doze. Hael stands in the opening and announces in monotone, "Food, Princess." She steps aside to make room for a scuttling little person bearing a tray. The maid—for I take it this must be her role—is an unusual-looking creature. Her skin is rough, gray, and looks to be hard as rock. A condition called *dorgarag*, if I recall the trolde word correctly. Hael suffers from a similar malady, with stone-hard hide covering her right arm, her neck, and creeping up one cheek, while the rest of her skin is alabaster pale and smooth. Vor told me once that more and more trolde children are born with this strange skin, which some consider a sickness and others a holy sign.

"Thank you," I say when the maid sets the tray down on the table beside my bed. Her pale eyes flick to mine ever so briefly before she turns and scuttles from the room. No nod, no bow, no murmur. Perhaps she's never seen a human before. Perhaps I am as unsettling to her eye as she is to mine. Or perhaps she, like my taciturn bodyguard, simply hates me for betraying her king.

Hael stands in the doorway. Her expression is entirely unreadable, her emotions impenetrable even to my prying gods-gift. "Does the princess require anything else?"

I glance at the tray. I don't know what to expect underneath the domed cover—whether I'll find trolde food palatable to my human tastes and digestion. But I merely nod and offer the captain a faint smile. "That will be all. Thank you."

Hael dips her chin once, steps from the room, and shuts the door firmly behind her.

I stare at the platter cover for a long while. I don't remember when last I ate. But while my innards are cavernously empty, I don't have any appetite. Would it be so bad to simply waste away without a fight? After all, I've never been the brave sister, the throw-myself-against-the-odds and claw-my-way-to-victory sister. That was always Ilsevel. And even she never faced odds like this: a husband's rejection, a kingdom's hatred. No home, no allies, no help.

Closing my eyes, I bow my head and summon up a vision of my sisters' faces. Ilsevel, fierce and fiery; Aurae, sweet and kind. I press a hand against my heart, feel the emptiness there. Even when I lived apart from them, I always held my sisters close and dear. To know they are gone from this life . . . to know I'll never see them again . . . never hear Ilsevel's wicked laugh or feel Aurae's gentle hand in mine . . .

A sob chokes in my throat. I press the back of my hand to my mouth. The truth is, I've scarcely had time to process my grief. And grief is such a wild, untamed creature, always returning at the most unexpected times to bite. But I must be strong. My sisters are lost. Killed. And those who killed them, who slaughtered them without mercy? Those monsters still run rampant throughout the kingdom, butchering innocents, setting fire to towns and villages. Pillaging, raping, destroying wherever they go. My kingdom. My people.

Gavaria needs this alliance. It needs these powerful trolde warriors to set Prince Ruvaen and his forces fleeing across the boundaries of the worlds, back to the dark realms where they belong. Gavaria needs King Vor and the might he wields.

Which, for the moment means . . . Gavaria needs me.

My jaw firms. I may not boast Ilsevel's spirit, but I've spent my life fighting against my own body's betrayals. I've not given in yet. I've always found some strength deep down, underneath the pain. Some reason to hold on, to fight, to forge ahead. So I will eat. I will live. And I will prevail.

I lift the platter lid. My eyes widen. I'd expected roasted cave crickets or fungi prepared in outlandish manners. Instead, I feast my gaze on hard-crusted rolls, butter-and-herb fish, sugared fruits, and pastries which, when cut into, reveal succulent roasted game and vegetables. Human dishes. My stomach growls. Suddenly, I'm more ravenous than I ever remember being. Niceties forgotten, I cram as many delicious mouthfuls in as quickly as possible. It's only after I've polished off my third game pie that it suddenly occurs to me: all of these dishes were Ilsevel's favorites.

My too-full stomach knots. Sitting back, I stare at the remains of the meal. Evidence of Vor's consideration. He took the time and care to notice Ilsevel's preferences while courting her in Beldroth and saw to it that the Mythanar larder was supplied appropriately. In the face of such kindness, how long would it have been before my sister truly fell in love with the bridegroom who so terrified her? Or would she soon have discovered the cruel, unrelenting, vindictive side of the Shadow King? The man who would send a woman to the block for daring to offend him.

A shiver races down my spine. Rising, I leave the platter on the table and step to the window. A view of the city lies before me, all white stone, carved and shaped by trolde artisans so that it seems to have sprung naturally into existence. So strange, so pale, so fantastical, ringed by high walls and accessible only by vaulting bridges. All beneath a stone ceiling set with shining crystals, like a hundred thousand subterranean stars.

The light of those crystals is fading now. What was it Vor called night in this world? Dimness, I think. How many days have passed since I came to this shadow realm? I lost track of time while down in the holding cell. And how long will I remain here? In this place between dimness and lusterling, between life and death, between prisoner and queen?

Determined to take some action, to prove in whatever small way I can that I still belong to myself, I leave the window and move to the wardrobe. It's been too long since I changed from the flimsy white bridal negligee into this lavender gown, which has seen rough wear since. It's time I freshened up. My perusal of the wardrobe is daunting, however. Most of the gowns prepared for the Shadow King's bride are so elaborate, I don't think I could dress myself in them if I tried. Eventually, I find a soft blue robe tucked away in the back. Whispering a prayer of thanks, I shed the purple gown and slip into this fresh garment, fastening the belt at my waist. Then I sit before a large obsidian stone disk polished to a perfect mirror-shine. Finding a silver comb and brush on the low table, I set to work putting my hair to rights. I've just begun dividing it into sections for plaiting when my idle gaze falls on the crystal pendant resting against my breast.

It flares—a warm, red light down in its core.

In the same moment, a sickening thud bursts in my stomach. I gasp, drop my hair, the plait unweaving about my shoulders. Clutching my midsection, I struggle to draw breath through my tight throat. A second blow lands, this one hard enough I nearly fall from the stool on which I'm perched. My hand flies out, grips the edge of the table, knocking both brush and comb to the floor. Sweat beads my brow.

I know what this is. I've lived with my gods-gift long enough to recognize the signs. Someone else's terrible emotions explode against my senses. Only . . . I drag in a gasping breath, panic thrilling in my veins as I scan the room. Where is this coming from? My gods-gift never reacts so strongly if the source isn't in near proximity. But I'm alone in the room. A third blow. I bare my teeth and push myself up from the stool. Nearly doubled over, I stagger across the room to the door and lean there heavily.

Low growls sound from the other side. Voices. Speaking troldish. One is Captain Hael, I'm sure of it. Her tone is sharp, like a guard dog's bark. But the answering voice is more forceful by far— a deep, dangerous snarl. Hand trembling, I find the latch, turn it, crack the door just enough to peer out.

It's Vor. Standing in the doorway of the apartment. He wears a wine-colored robe, open across the chest, only loosely belted. His feet are bare, his hair a pale storm about his head. His eyes are those of some crazed beast. I've never seen him like this, wild and dangerous. Not even in the midst of battle did he appear so savage.

Hael has assumed a defensive stance, her shoulders broad as though she's trying to bar his way. Vor snarls at her again, his voice accompanied by a harsh gesture. Hael shakes her head. Vor takes hold of the front of her jerkin, dragging her face close to his own. He stares into her eyes, and she stares back, a silent battle of wills. I can do nothing but watch, my heart in my throat. My body shudders from the violence of emotion assaulting my every sense.

Then Hael bows her head. Vor lets go of her. She staggers back, head still bowed, and steps past him into the passage. There she pauses, looks back across the room to my door. Our gazes meet through the crack. Hael's eyes widen ever so slightly. She shakes her head, opens her mouth—

The door slams. Vor stands in front of it, both hands pressed into the panels, leaning heavily against it. His shoulders heave with the force of his breath. I can see the terrible tension in his hands, in his fingers, all the way down the line of his back. I should retreat. I should shut this door. But I can only stand there, staring.

He turns at last. His hands clench into fists at his sides. Another wave of feeling rolls out from him, strikes me like a blow to the head. I cry out, stagger, grip the door frame for support. Shaking my head, I pull my gaze up, only to find him looking. At me.

His lips pull back, revealing his teeth. "Found you."

I push the door shut with an ear-rattling slam and I cast my gaze wildly about for some lock or bolt, some way to secure it against him. There's nothing. And Vor is already there. He pushes the door open so hard, I'm only just quick enough to keep from being struck. I stagger back, nearly tripping on the hem of my robe. I brace my feet, shake hair out of my eyes as I try to meet his terrifying gaze. I dare not look away.

He stands in the doorway, one arm up and gripping the frame.

His robe sags, revealing the whole broad expanse of his torso. Light from the fading crystals casts deep shadows across the planes and contours of his muscular chest. He's breathtaking, like a statue of living marble. But his face is animalistic, and the heat radiating from his core sears my brain.

This is the man who ordered my execution. The man who wants me dead.

He stalks toward me. One step, two. Another terrible wave rolls out from him. A soul-darkness so dense it's almost visible. It hits me, and I cry out in pain. The sound of my voice seems to startle him. He pauses, giving me a chance to recover, to wrap my arms around my quivering body. "Vor," I breathe raggedly. "Vor, please."

He lunges.

With a desperate cry, I grab the table close at hand and wrench it over. A useless defense. Vor does not stop. He picks the table up, hurls it into the wall, where it smashes into kindling. Then he whirls upon me, chest heaving, teeth bared.

"You humiliated me," he snarls.

I shake my head. "Please, Vor. I didn't mean—"

He springs. I put up my arms in defense, but he's too fast, too strong. One large hand catches my wrist while the other grips me by the shoulder, whirls me around, slams me against the wall. My breath is knocked from my lungs. Instinctively, I try to push him away, but he takes hold of both my wrists, pins them above my head. His eyes burn down at me.

Our faces are so close. The heat of his ragged breath blasts against my lips. My chest swells, struggling to drag in air. I'm painfully aware that the front of my robe has fallen open. His gaze rakes over me, lingering, lascivious. I squirm, desperate to hide myself, and his eyes shoot to mine again, freezing me in place. There's more than hatred in his gaze. There's lust as well, hot and pulsing. Terrifying. I drop my head, squeezing my eyes shut.

"Look at me," he snarls.

My eyelids jerk back up. I'm caught in his stare, like a mouse hypnotized by the serpent.

"Beg," he says. "Beg my forgiveness. For what you have done."

My lips quiver. "Forgive me, Vor," I whimper.

"No."

Then his mouth crushes against mine. It's not a kiss. It's too rough, too violent to be anything like a kiss. A bruising, terrible claiming. I scream into his mouth, twisting, struggling to pull away, to escape. The heat of his lust pours into me, pools in my chest, in my gut, in my loins.

He breaks away at last, stares into my eyes once more. "Beg me to stop," he says.

I shake my head. Part of me wants to plead with him, to implore his mercy. But I cannot find the words. Not anymore. He is so close, so overwhelming. I can scarcely discern where he ends and I begin.

"Beg me, Faraine." He shifts his grip so that he can hold both my wrists with one large, powerful hand, freeing up the other. Slowly, languorously, he trails one finger along the line of my cheek, my jaw, down my throat. There, he encounters the chain of my necklace, which he loops once, twice, around his thumb. With a vicious tug, he breaks it and tosses my crystal pendant to the floor. "No!" I cry, trying to dart after it. He grips my shoulder and pushes me back into the wall. I'm helpless in his grasp.

"I'm waiting," he says. "I might yet hear you. If you weep." He bends in closer, nuzzling my cheek, his breath against my ear. "I like tears, Faraine."

I shake my head fiercely. I won't do it. I won't give him the satisfaction. His lips press against my temple, my jaw, my neck. The hand on my shoulder tightens around a fistful of fabric. With a predatory growl, he yanks it back, exposing more skin. His mouth, hungry and hot, moves down my throat, tasting, ravenous. Teeth scrape against sensitive flesh while his tongue flicks over my wildly racing pulse. I sink further, deeper into the well of his pain, drowning.

He draws back, hisses through his flashing teeth. Slowly, he releases his hold on my robe. His hand slides instead to my waist, fingers working to undo the belt buckle. His knee nudges between my legs, forcing them apart.

"Beg for mercy, Faraine. Your king commands it."

"Vor," I breathe. "You don't want to do this."

"Don't I?"

I'm weeping now. Tears stream down my face. Never would I have believed this man could be so cruel, so base, so violent. How could I have been so wrong? How could I have thought I loved him? Desperately I look up into his face. Gone are the pale, silvery eyes of the man I knew. Instead, I gaze into two black voids.

Suddenly, I am standing outside of my body, poised on the brink of a terrible chasm. I stare over the edge, down into impenetrable darkness from which hot blasts of air belch, burning my skin. I wheel my arms, trying to find my balance, trying to draw back again. But it's too late.

I fall.

Unembodied, helpless, hopeless, I pitch into oblivion. The heat intensifies, until I'm sure it will burn away my very being, leaving nothing but the hollowed-out core of my body behind. I try to scream, try to grasp at the walls, but I can do neither. I can do nothing but fall and burn and fall and burn—

With a painful gasp, my whole body spasms. I blink hard, shocked to find myself embodied once more, still pressed against that wall. Vor's strong hand grips my hip bone underneath the skirt of my robe, his fingers hot against my skin. I jerk my head up, look into his eyes.

Silver eyes.

Wide with shock. With horror.

"Faraine?" he gasps. "Faraine, what . . . what have I . . . ?"

In that moment, the room begins to quake.

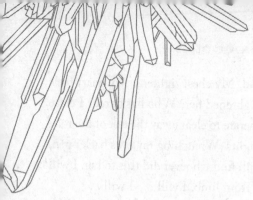

# 8

# *Vor*

Darkness fills my head. Darkness and burning and rage. Pulsing in my veins; pulsing through my bones, my flesh, my spirit.

Soon there will be nothing else.

I am the darkness.

I am the burning.

I am the rage.

I am . . . I am . . .

A sweet note of music bursts in my head, faint but clear. Bright as a silvery morning. I don't know from whence it sings. It dominates my senses, pierces through the storm and fire in my head. So delicate, I feel I could catch it, shatter it in my palm. But when I search, it eludes me. Draws me. Step by step. Suddenly, the darkness parts like clouds of smoke, and I'm staring down into a pale, upturned face.

*Faraine!*

She's afraid. Those strange eyes of hers, so beautiful, so

otherworldly, brim with dread. My chest tightens. My heart feels burned and raw. Who has frightened her? Who has dared? I close my eyes, shake my head, desperate to clear away the last of the roiling dark that clouds my thoughts. Wrenching my eyes back open, I look down at her again. I will find whoever did this to her. I will find him and rend him limb from limb. I will . . . I will . . .

I look down.

Down at my own hand pressed against her bare flesh.

Down at her body. Trembling, exposed to my gaze.

Horror surges through my blood and being, cold as ice. "Faraine?" Her name emerges from my lips in a terrible growl I scarcely recognize as my own voice. "Faraine, what . . . what have I . . . ?"

Overhead, the *lorst* crystals begin to sway. Softly at first, then more and more wildly, casting weird flashes across her face, in the depths of her eyes. The next moment, the whole room quakes, the walls groan. The floor shifts under my feet. Deeper Dark deliver us! Another stirring!

Moving on instinct, I yank Faraine from the wall, pull her flush against my body, and wrap my arms tight around her. Her bare skin presses into my chest, but I scarcely have time to register the sensation before the *lorst* lights begin to fall. They crash to the floor, shattering in jagged shards. Darkness envelops the chamber.

An earsplitting crack overhead. I dive to one side, dragging Faraine with me. Rolling, I place my body on top of hers and brace as stones rattle loose from the ceiling and fall in a stream of dust and debris on top of me. Something huge crashes into the floor where we'd stood an instant before. The whole palace shifts on its foundations, like a living creature writhing in pain.

This is it. This is the end. The end of all things.

I bow over her, pressing my face down, my forehead against

hers. A prayer bursts from the depths of my soul, a silent ragged cry to all the gods both high and low. Let this not be her end! If I must die, so be it. Let my bones be smashed to dust. Only let my body shield her from this fate. Let her live. Let her be spared.

The shaking stops. The room stills once more.

At first, I cannot make either my body or mind believe it. I'm so convinced we must be dead, it takes fifty thundering heartbeats before I can force myself to draw breath. When I do, I inhale dust and cough violently. Only when I finally recover my breath do I realize Faraine is coughing as well.

I draw back. Only a fraction. To be separated from her is unbearable, but I don't want to crush her, not when she's already struggling for air. Darkness surrounds us. No matter how my eyes strain, I can discern nothing of her features. "Are you all right?" I ask, my throat raw. The words emerge as a rough growl.

She coughs again, seems to struggle. Then, finally: "Let go of me."

Her voice stabs through my heart like knives. Cold, sharp. Unyielding.

I shift my weight. Stone and debris tumble from my back. Thank the Deeper Dark for my hard trolde hide. I sit up, peer into the gloom. It's too dark to get a sense of the extent of the destruction. "*Hira!*" I growl, without much hope it will do any good.

To my surprise, a single *lorst* crystal, unshattered and unburied, responds to my command. It's a meager light, but in that pitch black it seems bright as a fallen star. The pale white glow reveals several large pieces of stalactite which lie on either side of us. They would have shattered my spine had they struck. One wall is partially caved in. Dust and stone cover every article of furniture. The whole chamber looks as though it's been unearthed from a landslide.

I look down at Faraine. She gathers her limbs together, trying to pull her garment closed around her body. Her hands shake like two frightened birds, but her jaw is firm, the lines around her eyes tense. She seems both fragile and impenetrable at the same time.

"Are you hurt?" I ask. "Please, I need to know if—"

"I'm fine." She shakes her head sharply, refusing to look at me. I can't blame her. Any concern from me must seem sickening. What kind of monster asks after its prey's well-being after nearly tearing out its throat?

Pulling my limbs under me, I rise, stagger back, and take a look at the wreckage around us. A pile of stone blocks the chamber door. I make my way to it, pull back stones, and tumble them to the side. At last, I've cleared a narrow way and can reach the door latch. It gives. But when I begin to draw the door open, I feel a sudden, terrible pressure of stone on the far side. Hastily, I shut it again. We're trapped. Entombed like ancient warriors.

Slowly I bow my head, press my brow against the door. My breath is tight again. The air seems thicker than ever. I close my eyes. What happened? When I think back over the past few hours, everything is a blur of darkness punctuated by flashes of red heat. Only impressions come back to me like momentary sparks in my mind.

The touch of Faraine's skin under my hand.

The intoxicating thrum of lust in my blood.

The pulse, the drive.

The rage.

I remember some part of me fought, desperate to stop. But it seemed as though that part was locked behind fiery bars while the animal took over. A wild, savage animal that rent my reason into shreds. All I knew was my desire for *her*. To take her. To break her. To make her suffer. To make her mine.

I've felt this madness before. The last time, it had driven me to order her execution. This time, it drove me to savagery. But the impulse stemmed from the same place.

I've been poisoned. Again.

Movement behind me. I look over my shoulder in time to see Faraine stand and yank her robe tight around her body. The delicate fabric is gray with dust, but it clings to her soft frame. Heat flares through my body. Not as intense a flame as it was, but present, dangerous. There's still poison in my blood. I grit my teeth, determined to fight it back. A growl rumbles in my throat.

Faraine starts. Her eyes flash to meet mine. She freezes in place, like a rockdeer poised for flight. Then her hands move, shaking hard as she struggles to tie the belt of her garment. I wish I could offer to help, wish I could do something to ease her fear. My throat clogs with dust when I try to speak her name.

It's Faraine who breaks the silence, at last. "We're trapped here. Aren't we." Her voice is small, hollow. Almost lifeless.

I draw a deep breath. "It appears to be so."

She nods slowly. Gathering her robe close, she steps over debris to the bed. A huge chunk of stalactite fell from the ceiling during the quake, crashed through the canopy, and pierced the mattress. Faraine puts out one hand, touches a fold of tattered canopy, fingering the blue cloth. She rubs away a film of dust to reveal the silvery threads of an embroidered star. This she studies with intense concentration for some long moments. Finally, she looks at me again. Her expression is impossible to read. "Will they come for us, do you think?"

"Of course," I answer quickly. "Hael knows where we are. She will have us dug out in no time." If Hael is alive. If any of them are alive.

I survey the room again. The *lorst* stone has brightened somewhat since I spoke it back to life. By its flickering light, I can see the walls aren't in imminent threat of falling. As the dust settles, the air clears, and I feel a draft of air coming in from somewhere. We shouldn't suffocate at least.

But I know what so often follows the great stirrings. I saw the decimation of Dugorim village just days ago—the spread of poison, the madness. The death. Will Mythanar's fate be the same? Or will tumbled buildings, crushed roads, and buried citizens be the worst of our troubles?

A curse hisses through my teeth. I cannot stay here. I cannot remain trapped in this dark space while my people suffer. How many able bodies are even now fighting to liberate me when they should be applying themselves to the relief of the city? Perhaps this is punishment. Perhaps the gods looked out from their heavens, saw the atrocity I was about to commit, and chose to smite both me and my city for my sin.

My sin which, even now, still simmers hot in my gut.

Faraine moves. Even the slightest shift of her weight is enough to draw my hungry gaze back to her. But she merely folds her arms tight across her breast, as though determined to hold herself together. Her eyes meet mine, hard as stone.

"Are you going to kill me, Vor?"

The abruptness of her question hits me like a blow. I draw my head back, eyes flaring.

She continues, relentlessly: "When you are through with me, I mean."

"Faraine." I shake my head. "Faraine, I—"

"I'd rather know." Her fingers tighten, knuckles standing out white. "Will your thirst for revenge be satisfied by my degradation? Or do you intend to murder me as well?" She refuses to break my gaze. I feel as though she's stabbing me with two knives, one of ice, one of fire.

"I didn't mean to do it." The words fall from my lips like heavy weights.

She jerks her chin up. Her nostrils quiver with a sharp intake of air.

"I . . . Faraine . . ." My shoulders bow as though the rest of the palace has caved in on top of me. She hates me. Of course, she hates me. She should hate me. I hate myself, hate these pathetic excuses crowding on my tongue. What will I do? Plea for pity, for forgiveness? I don't deserve either. Yet, I must say something.

I let out a long breath, force myself to meet her gaze. "I never meant to harm you. Not the execution. Not . . . not this. That person . . . the person who did those things . . . that wasn't me." Her lip curls in an expression of deep disgust. Hastily, I take a step toward her, but she startles back, trips over debris on the ground. "No, please!" I hold out my hands, trying to look as nonthreatening as possible. "Don't run. I will . . . I will sit here."

I ease my body slowly onto a fallen slab of stone, careful to keep the flimsy robe I wear closed. She watches me, her chest rising and falling with the quickness of her breaths. When I make no further move, she finally perches on the remains of the footboard, one hand gripping the front of her garment, the other clenched tight around a fistful of torn canopy fabric.

And so, we sit. In silence. Staring at one another.

It's coming back to me now. Bit by bit. Staggering away from the bathhouse, my body aflame with desire. The embraces of the bathhouse girl, her warm willing flesh pressed against mine, her tongue in my mouth. The heat of lust mingling with the fire in my blood, growing into a furnace of rage.

Hael tried to stop me. I remember that now. She'd seen the madness in my eye and guessed my purpose in coming here. She'd tried to talk me out of it, tried to reason with me. But I'd overpowered her. Gods! Why didn't she fight harder? She should have taken me down, stopped me from ever setting foot in this chamber! Her duty was to protect the princess. She should have honored that duty over all other loyalties, even her loyalty to me.

I would have killed her, of course. In my need to get to Faraine, I would have slaughtered her where she stood.

I rub my hands down my face, groaning softly. The fire is still there, burning in my blood. For the moment, at least, it does not drive me. I am master of myself. I'm not sure what brought me out of the darkness. Something must have shocked me, jolted me back into reason, just as it had at the execution, before the *drur's* ax fell.

I feel Faraine's gaze upon me. When I finally dare glance at her again, she's watching me closely. Once more I feel the pathetic use-lessness of my words before they even leave my mouth. But I speak them nonetheless. "I swear, Faraine. I won't touch you again."

Her head barely moves, a tiny, almost imperceptible shake to one side. The muscles in her forehead tense. "I don't believe you."

"I know. I don't deserve your belief. But I swear it even so. As soon as they dig us out of here, I will send you home to your father. You will leave Mythanar, never think of us again. Put all of this behind you. Forever."

Another tiny shake of her head followed by an interminable si-lence. I bury my face in my hands, unable to bear that look on her face. At long last, however, she speaks again: "You are in pain."

I look up, startled. Are those tears brimming in her eyes, spilling through her lashes onto her cheeks?

"I felt it before," she continues, her voice soft and gentle, her face pale as an angel's in the flickering *lorst* glow. "This pain. This resistance."

My brow puckers. I don't understand what she's saying, and yet . . . strangely, part of me does.

Faraine rises from her seat and picks her way across the room to the window. Her back is very straight, very firm, her shoulders like a wall, blocking me out. The curtains over the window have partially fallen, but she grips them, pulls them to one side.

The whole wall shifts dangerously.

I'm in motion before my mind has a chance to catch up with my body. In three swift bounds, I cross the space between me and her. Even now, with terror surging in my veins, I do not forget the vow I've just spoken. Rather than touch her, I throw myself between her and the stone that breaks and falls from above. It would have brained her. I take it in my shoulder instead. Pain shoots through my body as I'm driven to my knees.

Faraine leaps back, one hand pressed to her chest, the other to her midsection. She stares at me, at the broken stone, at the unstable wall. At last, her gaze fixes on my shoulder. It throbs as though in response to her notice. I grimace, put up a hand to touch the sore place. My palm comes away sticky with blue blood.

"Vor!"

The sound of my name on her lips shoots straight to my core. Before I can speak a word of reassurance, she crouches before me and works to tear a strip off the hem of her robe. "It's fine," I protest when she presses the fabric to the wound. I wince but shake my head firmly. "No, leave it. It's nothing Madame Ar cannot patch up."

Faraine frowns, lifting her cloth and looking at the cut. "It looks deep."

I twist my neck, trying to see. "I've had worse."

She shakes her head, gets to her feet, and hastens to the bed. There she fetches a remnant of torn canopy fabric, shakes out the dust as best she can, before folding it into a square. "Here," she says, returning to press it into my shoulder. "Can you lift your arm?"

I can and do. She winds her strip of fabric around my body to hold the square of blue fabric in place. "It's not an ideal bandage, I know," she mutters, "but we must stop the bleeding. It'll have to do."

Her nearness intoxicates me. The curve of her neck and shoulder, revealed against the neckline of her garment. The softness of her hair, even beneath the film of gray dust. The smell of her, so sweet, so delicate. Like a flower of the human world, bathed in sunshine and starlight by turns. So different from the subterranean blossoms of Mythanar.

She doesn't belong here. But I cannot bear the idea of her going.

Which is why she must go. As soon as possible.

She steps back. The stern line between her brows deepens as she inspects her work. Then her gaze flicks sideways, catching mine. I don't look away. I can't. I wish I could make her see the truth in my eyes, could make her know that I could never intentionally cause her harm. I would sacrifice far more than I should to see her safely free of me and the danger I pose to her.

She tilts her head slightly. "What is that inside of you?"

I blink, surprised. But then, somehow it makes sense that she would know what question to ask. "It's *raog* poison," I answer.

She nods as though she understands, though she's surely never heard the word before.

"Someone administered a dose in my cup while I was in council with my ministers," I continue. "We were discussing what to do with you after . . . after I realized who you were." Grimacing, I roll my throbbing shoulder. A mistake. Pain shoots up my neck, and I hold still once more, head hanging. "At the time, I'd been listening to them urge for your death. When the poison entered my body, it . . . played on the deepest, darkest part of me. That part which wanted to listen to them."

"So, you *did* want to kill me."

"No!" The word bursts out a harsh bark. She starts back, and I hasten to modulate my tone. "No, Faraine. Never. But I felt betrayed. Stripped down. Humiliated before the eyes of my court, my kingdom. And . . . and that part of me . . ." I shake my head, pinching the bridge of my nose. "Gods, I don't know how to describe it! It was like the poison latched onto me. Fed the wickedness in my heart, nurtured it. In my mind, you were no longer yourself. You were something different, something dark and terrible. As the poison strengthened, you transformed into a monster in my mind. A demon. I felt I must be free of you, must kill you to break your hold over me. It was so *real*."

She regards me silently, her eyes traveling over my face. As though she's reading more in me than my feeble, fumbling words can express.

"I've not yet discovered who delivered the poison," I continue, "but I believe this same person poisoned Lord Rath in another attempt to have you killed. And now . . . today . . ."

"You were poisoned a second time," she whispers.

I nod slowly. Hating that I've just made excuses for what I did. Relieved that she allowed me to make them. I swallow hard but force myself to meet her eye. "As soon as we are out of this chamber, I will send you home. You and I need never see one another again."

Faraine sits back on her heels, her arms tight around her body. She swallows hard. Her gaze drops. Her jaw is tight. One of her hands moves to her chest, feeling for something that isn't there. Her necklace, I realize. In a flash, I remember ripping it from her neck, tossing it to the floor. It's here somewhere, buried beneath all this debris.

"Let me look inside you."

"What?" I frown, uncertain I heard her soft voice correctly.

In a single swift movement, she sits up. Before I can react, she takes my face between her hands. I gasp and try to jerk away. "Hold still," she says sharply.

I freeze in her grasp. The exquisite pain of her skin against mine is almost more than I can bear. The darkness inside me roils, seeking to rise up, to send poison shooting through my veins. I must be strong. I must resist the urge to catch hold of her arms, to drag her to me, to crush her in my embrace. My fists curl tight, squeezing so hard I could grind stone to powder.

But Faraine gazes into my eyes. Deeper and deeper.

Something is happening. I don't understand. It's as though she's sent a silver thread of music into my mind, a bright clear note. It hums, a point of light and connection between the two of us. I feel that note taken up, faint but present, pulsing in the air, in the walls, in the broken rock under our feet.

What is she doing? Is this magic? Her gods-gift? It's so strange, so unlike trolde magic in every way. And yet it is inexplicably familiar, though in the moment, I cannot place why.

Suddenly, I gasp. My body goes rigid. I feel as though the top of my head has been opened. A bath of liquid sunlight pours into my mind, flushes through my soul. I see it, feel it, perceive it with every sense so vividly. It's painful and glorious and purifying. All the dark and dirty particles of poison are swept up and sent rushing out through my extremities, out into the atmosphere where they dissipate to nothing.

The vision ends abruptly, like a sudden dousing of light. I drag a painful gasp into my lungs. Despite the dust in the air, it feels like the first clear breath I've drawn in days.

"What was that?" I demand, shaking my head and looking once more at Faraine.

She steps back from me. Her hands drop away from my face. There's a strange, far-off, unfocused look in her eyes. She sways heavily.

"Faraine?" I say. She seems to hear me, seems to tip her head my way.

Then she collapses to the ground at my feet.

# 9

.....

# *Faraine*

I don't faint. I wish I could. It would be easier when the pain hits simply to step out of awareness entirely. To float off into some other plane of consciousness and wait until the pain dissipates, or at least until I'm more ready to face it.

Instead, my body simply . . . folds up. I cannot move. Cannot speak or offer any form of reaction. I can only lie there while pain like waves churned up by a storm crash on the shores of my senses, battering me, pulverizing my bones. I am naked, helpless, defenseless. Unable even to gather myself and flee the onslaught.

Somewhere, through the howling gale-force winds, through the roar of ceaseless thunder, I hear Vor's voice shouting my name over and over again. His panic is palpable. If only I could say something, do something. Give him some sign that I heard so that he would just, please, stop that gods-damned bellowing!

But I can't. And maybe it's for the best. The irritation gives me something to hold on to. My soul—that pale, naked thing lying on the shores of my mind—reaches out and clings to his voice like an anchoring chain as another wave of pain hits, and another, and another. Each crash and roll tries to wrench me back into that eternal sea of torment. I cannot fight, cannot hide. I can do only what I have always done: *endure*.

All storms must cease eventually. And sometimes the greater the storm, the more swiftly it blows itself out. Such is the case here. The wind lessens, the waves retreat. The clouds of my awareness part, allowing me to feel something other than agony once more. I find myself cradled in Vor's strong arms. Apparently, he's forgone his vow never to touch me again in favor of shifting me into a more comfortable position. Which is just as well, for I seem to have landed with one arm twisted awkwardly underneath me. Now, on top of the other sharp pangs still rippling through every muscle and sinew, I've the added unpleasantness of returning blood flow through that arm. Somehow, it feels like an extra spite from the gods.

Vor seems to have gathered blankets and cushions from the ruined bed and mounded them together into a makeshift pallet. He eases me onto it now, resting my head on a pillow. His large hand lingers, cupped around my skull, fingers tangled in my hair. My wide-open eyes stare vacantly at the ceiling. I cannot see him save for a blurry impression of a face, half bathed in *lorst* light. It doesn't matter. I *feel* him. All his tenderness, concern, and anxiety, like a pulsing aura which gives him shape and form to my senses.

And underscoring all those feelings is another, deeper emotion, which sparks from the tips of his fingers as he slowly brushes a strand of hair off my cheek: *longing*. He cannot hide it. Not anymore. I've been inside his head now. All the way down to where that dark *thing* had festered. That poison. That twisted parasite wound tight around his soul, fusing with his emotions. It was like a strangler vine, wrapped around a living tree, creeping along every bough and twig until the tree inside was dead and rotten and only the vine remained. An ugly, twisted parody of the proud original.

When I'd looked at that darkness winding around Vor's spirit, I knew I could do *something*. A layer of calm would give him only temporary relief. What he needed wasn't another layer. What he needed was cleansing. *But is it possible?* I'd wondered. Could I push my calm inside him? Hard enough, deep enough, that it drove the darkness out?

Apparently I could. At great cost to myself.

I wish I could sigh. I wish I could close my eyes. Anything to relieve some of this tension from my rigid body. For the moment, I have no such control. I can only lie in the position in which he has placed me.

I let my gods-gift reach out tentatively to Vor. He's been silent for some time now. Pacing the room, shuffling around, moving stones and broken pieces of furniture. I don't know what he's doing, but it's a relief to have a little distance from him, a chance for my scalded senses to recover. But will they recover? Will I? Or have I pushed my powers too far this time? Is this to be my existence? This trapped awareness within an inert body-prison? A thrill of panic stirs in my gut. Desperately, I try to move something: a toe, a nostril, an eyelash. But the paralysis is complete, and my vision remains cloudy.

Suddenly, Vor reappears beside me. I cannot see him save for a blurry silhouette, but the shape of his feelings is strong. "I found it," he says, kneeling. His voice, a deep, earthy rumble, stirs something warm and liquid in my core. The next moment, he reaches out, hesitates. Then he breaks his vow one more time to take my hand, open it, drop something into my palm, and curl my fingers over it.

My breath catches. My necklace! I'd know it anywhere—its silver filigree setting, the broken chain, the stone itself warm down in its core. For a long moment, I can do nothing but hold it. Then, with a supreme effort of will, I tighten my fist. Just a little. The throb in the stone's heart quickens under my palm. Its resonance works down inside of me, and my body responds. I begin to . . . to *unlock*, somehow. Muscles tense, relax, and every limb goes limp. Finally, I draw a long, long breath. Hold it. Let it out in a measured count to ten.

Vor's awareness shoots to me, his eyes intent. "Faraine?"

I cannot answer. Not yet. By now the unlocking has spread all the way to my toes. When I try to move them, they respond. Next, I flex my calves, my knees. I draw another long breath before attempting a blink. First one eyelid. Then the other. Then together. With each rise and fall of my lashes, the world comes into better focus.

Vor's worried face hovers above me. His eyes are no longer terrible black voids, but bright and silver, ringed by incredibly long lashes. His mouth is full and sensuous, lips parted to release short, tense breaths. Pale hair falls across shoulders so broad, so strong, they might bear the weight of mountains. "Faraine? Can you hear me?"

Part of me doesn't want to answer. I'd much rather close my eyes, turn my head, and sink into proper sleep. Though the paralysis seems to have passed, my body aches from my ordeal.

But I must face him. Now or never.

"Yes. I can hear you." The words emerge raw in my dry throat. I cough. The convulsion sends new sparks of pain bursting through my body. Rolling to one side, I wait for it to pass. Vor's anxiety re-doubles, pressing against my senses. He reaches for me but stops himself. His hand hovers in the air above my shoulder. By the time the spasm has passed, he's already withdrawn from me again.

My eyelids fall again. In that moment, in the darkness of my head, I see the ugly twist of his features looming over me, feel the heat of his breath right before his lips crashed into mine. The black voids of his eyes. His hands scorching my flesh with their fiery touch.

Shuddering, I turn away. "Water," I say, thickly. "Is there water?"

"I'm sorry," Vor answers. "I tried to get through to the wash-room, but the wall is unstable. I found the remains of a meal, but the ewer was smashed."

I nod. Another shiver works its way down my spine. Then, set-ting my jaw, I start to sit up. Vor reacts at once, reaching out but not quite touching me. "Should you be doing that?"

My robe catches under my arm, pulling open across my chest. Hastily, I grab the fabric and draw it closed again, then adjust my legs under me on that pile of dusty blankets. "I'm fine," I growl, even as the room tilts and my head spins. I plant a hand on the ground. My other hand still grips my crystal. I look down at it, al-most to convince myself it's really there. Thank the gods it wasn't smashed to dust beneath the fallen stones.

Vor's eyes are fixed upon me. I open my lashes, peer at him. "Thank you," I whisper.

Pain flashes in his soul, a sharp stab of guilt that makes me wince. He shakes his head, gets to his feet, and crosses the room to the door. It's a relief if I'm honest. His emotions are too strong for me in this weakened state.

"I can hear them working on the other side," he says after a long silence. His back is to me, *lorst* light gleaming on the silvery strands of his hair. "They'll break through to us soon. Hael will drive them hard until they do."

I watch him, studying the set of his shoulders. Shame surrounds him like a cloud. He hates himself. Hates what he did to me. I wrap my arms around my stomach, drawing another careful breath. How am I supposed to feel about this man now that I know about the poison? He had me dragged to the chopping block, bowed over and facing that blue-lined box. He tore off my clothes, put his hands on me. These were such terrible, violent actions.

But were they truly committed by him? I saw that darkness. I felt how it enwrapped him, a separate, living identity. I felt the rage, the lust, the betrayal, the horror, all swirling around a core of pulsing, living *despair*.

I lift my chin, staring hard at his back. When I speak, I make certain my voice is calm and clear. "These tremors."

His spine stiffens. His hands clench into fists.

I continue: "Are they why you need my father's Miphates? Are they the danger you hinted at? Mythanar's great threat?"

He does not answer at first. Finally, he lets out a huge breath, turns, looks at me. "It doesn't matter."

My brow puckers. "Why not?"

"You need not concern yourself with Mythanar anymore. I am sending you home. The moment they break through that door, I will give the order. You may carry word to your father that I have no further need of his Miphates. The alliance is off."

A chill shivers in my gut. No. This cannot be. The alliance *cannot* be off. Not after everything I've been through. My people are still suffering. They need Vor. They need the powerful trolde warriors. And besides . . . I study that cloud of emotion surrounding

Vor, bowing his shoulders, threatening to crush him beneath the weight. He needs this too. He needs the hope this alliance offers. He needs it as badly as I do.

"And what if I do not want to leave?" I say softly.

"What?"

I rise. I'm a little unsteady, my knees buckling, my head swimming. But I brace myself, grip my crystal, and hold the Shadow King's gaze. Then I approach him. One step. And another. He backs away, so I stop. Breathe. Then advance two steps more.

"I'm not ready to give up," I say. "Not yet."

His face is stone. But I feel the heat flaring through him. The confusion. The hope. And again, that painful longing. It's real. It's so real, he can't hide it. Not even when he tries.

"You cannot be serious," he says, his voice tight. "Not after everything . . . not after what I almost . . ."

I swallow hard, dust clogging my throat. "There's still a chance, isn't there?" The words are difficult to speak, but I force them out. "There's still a chance for us?"

Vor looks away. Then, slowly, as though compelled by a force he cannot resist, his gaze meets mine. "If your father agrees to the new terms I've demanded . . . yes. Yes, the marriage could still go forward."

"And what are those terms?"

A muscle in his jaw ticks. "That he will send his Miphates now. At once. Before I lead troops to Gavaria."

I nod. Let a slow breath out through my lips. "If my father agrees, you will take me as your bride?"

"No!" Vor quickly shakes his head, his hard expression breaking. He presses the heel of his hand to his forehead. "Gods, no,

Faraine. I wouldn't ask that of you. I will find some other way for Mythanar."

I know what he's doing. I feel his guilt and shame trying to smother out every other feeling. Hastily, I take another step toward him, half stumble on a bit of rubble, but quickly draw myself straight once more. "What if there is no other way?"

He looks at me, his expression agonized.

"Prince Ruvaen is sure to overrun Gavaria by summer's end," I continue. "If you send me home, I'll only be murdered by the fae, just as my sisters were. Gavaria needs Mythanar even as Mythanar needs Gavaria." I take another step, then another. There's scarcely two paces between us now. I could reach out and touch him if I dared. "Which means . . . maybe you and I need each other too."

The surge of feeling from Vor is so strong, I nearly draw back. It's hot and red, longing and lust so intertwined they cannot be separated from one another. But when I look into his eyes, I don't see the dark voids which had bored so viciously into my gaze. The poison is gone. Only the man remains.

But what manner of man is this? The otherworldly king? The fierce protector? The strong leader? The tender lover? Or the vengeful, dark, dangerous, secret self that underlies all these? Even now, he holds himself back, fighting the urges pulsing in his veins. Determined to honor me. No matter what.

Because that is the truth of his character. The real man. The man of honor.

Summoning my courage, I stretch out a hand. Take hold of his. A spark seems to shoot from his touch, sending ripples of lava across my senses. But it's not painful. In fact, quite the opposite.

"Faraine." My name is rough on his lips.

"What if there is no other way?" I say again softly. "What if we are each other's only hope?"

He looks at me like I truly am his lifeline, his salvation. My heart quivers, thrilling anew at the possibilities inspired by his touch. I'm not sure I will ever again feel the peace I once knew in his presence, but . . . but maybe . . .

I draw a step nearer. The air between us is alive. Lightning leaps back and forth from my body to his.

"I don't want to give up hope," I whisper, lowering my eyes to his lips. "Do you?"

Without a word, he slips his other hand around my waist. His palm is warm through the silky fabric of my robe as he draws me toward him. I tense, but the pressure he applies, though firm, is gentle. The emotions rippling from his soul are so different from what they were under the poison's influence. There's nothing dark here. Terrifying, yes, but a thrilling, heady sort of terror that intoxicates rather than frightens. The warmth in his touch is not the heat of destruction but the fire of life itself.

His hand slides slowly up my back, molding my spine so that I bend toward him. He takes my hand, presses it against his bare chest. I feel his heartbeat throbbing under my palm. "Faraine," he says again, bowing his head toward me. I find my mouth drawn irresistibly toward his, until the space between our lips is scarcely more than a breath, a whimper. Suddenly my body remembers how it felt to lie beneath him, to give myself over to him. To feel him delighting in my curves and contours. To experience his pleasure every time he elicited another low moan from my throat.

Only this time, how different might it be? Because this time, he knows who I am. I stand before him as myself and no other. Unmasked. The shunned princess. My father's embarrassment. My mother's shame. The eldest daughter, but the second choice. And yet . . .

And yet I've always known that with Vor, I was never second. He would have chosen me first had the choice been his all along.

What will he choose now? Hope? Duty? Restraint? Despair? I feel each alternative swirling around us like a storm. All I want is to stand up on my toes, to close that tiny space between us. To make the choice for him. But I cannot. This is a choice that must be made together or not at all.

The tip of his nose brushes against mine. That touch alone is nearly enough to undo me. I have no dread anymore. Only need. My breath is quick and fast, my heart thudding so loud, I'm sure he must hear it. And still he holds himself in check.

"Oh, Faraine, Faraine." His voice is like a prayer. "What if I hurt you? What if I . . . ?"

"I am not afraid, Vor." My eyes close, my body and soul wholly concentrated on the warm sweetness of his breath against my mouth. "*Please.*"

His chin dips. His lips just brush against mine, maddeningly light. Not even a taste. Like a single drop of water on a parched and desperate tongue. I open my mouth to him, but he's already retreated. "Vor—" I begin, urgently.

A great, crashing groan of rock.

Every fragile thing in the air between us shatters. We spring away from one another just as a second groan and crash follows the first. Then a rough troldish voice shouts from the other side of the door: "*Vor! Morar-juk, crorsva-tah, Vor?*"

Vor's eyes flash in the *lorst* light, meeting mine. He looks frightened and then angry and then . . . I don't know. His barriers slam back into place, pushing his emotions beyond the reach of my gods-gift. "My brother," he says shortly. Turning to the broken doorway, he bellows back, "*Grakol-dura, Sul! Mazoga!*"

I retreat further into the room, pulling my robe tight around myself. My body is still warm and alive, but what am I to do with these feelings? I don't know what will happen once the troldefolk break through. Will Vor be true to his word? Will he send me home directly?

The door shudders in its frame. More shouts, more voices. Finally, the door slams open hard. Two figures step through in a cloud of dust. The first of them launches himself at Vor, but the second spares not a glance for her king. Instead, Captain Hael's eyes fix upon me. Very wide. Very tense. Every line of her face is etched deep with shadow.

She strides across the room to me and drops her voice to a low pitch. "Are you hurt, Princess?"

Hastily, I shake my head, then draw my shoulders back and answer out loud, "I'm fine." My bodyguard tosses her gaze between me and Vor, her mouth disbelieving. I catch her forearm, draw her eye back to me. "Truly, I am unhurt. Nothing . . . happened."

Hael's eyes spark in the *lorst* light. She opens her mouth then closes it on whatever questions are piling up on her tongue. Instead, she puts an arm around me and says only, "Come. Let's get you out of here. Find you some proper clothes." I can't very well protest, especially as more and more people are now crowding the chamber, cutting me off from Vor. So I let her guide me toward the door.

"Hael!"

At the sound of her king's voice, Hael's arm tightens around me. My heart leaps to my throat and catches there. Is this the moment? The moment when Vor issues the command for me to be sent home? I force myself to turn around. To meet his eyes. They glow so strangely by the flickering lights of the multicolored *lorst* crystals carried into the room by our rescuers.

He wrenches his gaze away from me, focusing on Hael instead. "Have the princess taken to fresh chambers and made comfortable."

Hael offers a sharp salute. "At once, my king."

Then she pushes me through the door, and Vor is lost to my sight.

# 10

........

# Vor

"See here, Big King? These are the worst of them. And another, here."

My chief engineer, Ghat, scurries along the wall, a *lorst* crystal attached to a band around his thick skull. It casts an aura in the darkness as he leads me through the deepest levels of the palace, among the foundation stones. He pauses at one stone through which deep cracks have formed and puts his whole hand down into one of the fissures. His arm disappears all the way to the elbow.

Pale beady eyes glitter up at me in the crystal light. He looks more excited than terrified, as though he's made a fascinating discovery. Meanwhile, a pit of dread opens in my core.

It's been a long two lusterlings and one eternal dimness since my people dug me out of the queen's chamber. I emerged into chaos. I've been in motion ever since, meeting with members of my household, soothing fears, receiving reports, putting on a kingly air, issuing commands and official statements, making decisions for both major and minor repairs. No time to rest, no time to eat. Scarcely enough time to breathe.

The initial word from the lower city is encouraging. A handful of deaths, the loss of a few ramshackle dwellings on the outskirts, no major damage. One bridge is potentially compromised and has been barricaded, all traffic diverted. Otherwise, the reported destruction appears to be relatively minor and should be cleared up within a few days.

The city itself seems to be in a state of frozen shock. It's preternaturally calm, as though the citizenry as a whole have drawn a collective breath and still hold it. Waiting to see what I will do. Waiting to take their lead from me.

I've had my chancellor put together an official statement and sent runners into the streets proclaiming the message that I am looking into the cause of the disturbance and encouraging everyone to go about their daily business. A statement of calm, order, and reason.

Then Ghat summoned me to the lower palace. Which is why I find myself here, watching as he shows me the various cracks in our foundations. Some are mere hairline fractures. Others, like the one his arm is now sunk into, are more significant.

He turns his broad, stone-skinned face to me, one corner of his wide mouth tilted severely down. "I've been watching this one for some time now," he says. "Last time I was down here, it was scarcely big enough to fit my fat thumb. Now . . ."

He doesn't need to finish. I can see for myself. I run my hand over the wall, gliding my fingers along the edge of the crack. I can't help feeling it wouldn't take more than a good grip and a single hard tug to make this break run straight up through the palace and bring the whole thing crashing down upon my head.

Ghat watches me. His hard eyes blink slowly, one after the other. "It's bad, Big King," he says, in his distinctive low-stone dialect. "I've seen cracks like these in some of the other big buildings in the city. The temple. The old watchtower at lower east bridge. The base of Urzulhar Circle."

"Indeed?" The Urzulhar Circle is one of the oldest, most sacred sites in all the Under Realm. I chuckle mirthlessly. "I assumed the Circle would be protected by the gods."

"'Fraid not, Big King." Ghat shakes his heavy head. "If these stirrings go on, the Circle will be first to fall." He sets a second *lorst* in a holder so that it casts a pool of light over the floor. Taking up a measuring rod, he begins to draw in the thick dust at my feet. In a few quick strokes, he renders a rough but accurate and recognizable map of the city. Ghat may be crude and stone hided, but he is a genius in his own right.

"Here and here," he says, indicating points on the map. "Another here. These are where big breaks will start when time comes. East city will fall first. The rest will crumble soon after. When it goes, it's all gonna go."

I study his drawing. My vision is dull, uncomprehending. I don't want to comprehend. I want to stomp my foot in the center of those sketches, kick them, smear them, obliterate even the memory of them.

"It was always gonna be like this," Ghat says at last, stepping back and surveying his work. "Sometimes I think the plan for the city's fall was built into the city itself. No stopping it."

"How long do we have?"

He shrugs. "If there are no more stirrings, could be another thousand turns of the cycle. More even. But if the stirrings are gonna increase at the rate they've been . . . I wouldn't give us one more cycle."

I don't respond. I can't. My stomach has dropped, my throat closed up. It's all I can do to stand there, staring at that map. Staring at those grooves he's driven through the sketched-out lines of the city I love. "How far will the destruction go?" I ask at last, my voice rough. "Do you mean Mythanar alone?"

"Oh no. When we go, we're all gonna go. The Big End will start here—right here." He points to the Urzulhar Circle. "The city will fall in a few hours at most. Once it starts, it'll spread fast. Before dimness, the whole Under Realm will be broken into . . ." He pauses, his eyes rolling back in his head as he does a quick calculation . . . "I 'spect 'bout four hundred small-bite islands. Maybe seven big ones."

"Will any of the cities be spared?"

"Unlikely. Maybe Valthurg? It's closer to the surface, away from any big cracks. But the others . . . no. They're done for."

"And what are our options?"

Ghat shrugs, the rough stone of his shoulders mounding. "Prayer?"

I harden my jaw. "Evacuation."

At this, however, the chief snorts. "And where do you think we're gonna go, Big King? Aurelis? Noxaur? Troldefolk don't belong anywhere but with other troldefolk."

"Perhaps the human world," I say slowly, hardly liking to admit the thought out loud. I did not enjoy my brief time spent in that world, but it boasts many high mountain ranges beneath which no humans have dared to delve. Perhaps we could find a place of sanctuary in the caverns and deep places.

Ghat, however, laughs outright. "Good luck making troldefolk follow you. Far from *quinsatra* and all that makes life good. No, no." He wipes a hand down his broad flat face and shrugs again. "When I go, I'm gonna be buried under rock and rubble as is my home. It's not so bad an end. For a troll. Some say it's the only good end."

*Troll.* I note the word but do not call it out. Instead, I growl, "You sound like Targ and the Cult of *Arraog*."

Ghat grunts. "Umog Targ is strange but he makes good sense. Why fight what can't be fought, eh?" When I offer no answer, he reaches out, claps me on the shoulder. "Don't worry, Big King. Most folk are never gonna see the city fall."

"Really?"

"'Course not! Most folk are gonna die of poison long before."

On that word of encouragement, I thank my engineer and make good my escape. It's a long climb back up the many steep stairs to the lived-in floors of the palace above. As I go, I could almost swear I feel the stones around me expanding and contracting in a slow, rhythmic pulse, like deeply drawn and exhaled breaths.

Closing my eyes, I rest my hand on the wall and lean in. Trying to sense that Presence. Deep, deep down. That unfathomable consciousness, so utterly unaware of me and all my kind. There's no understanding a mind like that. I have a better chance of connecting with a rockflea mere moments before squashing it under my boot.

Setting my jaw, I pull away from the wall and continue up the stair. As Ghat said, there's no point in fighting what can't be fought. But I'm not done fighting just yet. I have a few more maneuvers to play. Somehow, I must bring the Miphates to the Under Realm. I have heard tales of the staggering feats these human mages have achieved as they use their words to draw magic directly from the Source and manipulate it to their will. If there's any truth to those tales, surely they can use such power to help Mythanar.

But if I'm going to get the Miphates, I must have leverage over Larongar. Which means . . . Faraine. Faraine, whom I promised to send home. Faraine, who has faced death three times now since coming to my realm. Who still insists she wants to stay.

*Faraine.*

*My life or my doom.*

"Are you really going to march right past me like I'm not even here? Or have I blended into the rockwork rather better than usual?"

I stop. Turn my head slowly to the shadowed alcove on my right. There I can just discern my brother, leaning against the wall, all insouciant grace and dangerous grins.

My heart rate quickens. I draw a short breath and remind myself that Sul is not my enemy. Not my proven enemy in any case. He is still, for better or for worse, my brother. "Well?" I say, choosing not to respond to his quips. "Did you find her?"

Sul pushes away from the wall and saunters from the shadows into the light of the lantern hanging from the high ceiling. "Sorry, my brother." He rubs the back of his neck, his expression chagrined. "I've had my people scouring the palace. She seems to have disappeared following the stirring. Her description is exactly like any number of other working girls in the bathhouses. With no other distinctive qualities or marks to inquire after, I cannot get so much as a name."

I regard my brother silently. Sul answers my look with one equally stony before finally shaking his head and growling, "Gods above and below, Vor! Don't give me that disappointed-elder-brother stare of yours. Don't you think I feel *guthakug* enough about the situation as it is? I put you in a vulnerable position. I know that. Never in a million turns of the cycle did I expect that girl to be used as another vessel for poison! If there's any truth to your theory to begin with, that is. You must admit, it does sound rather implausible—"

"Tell me how else it was accomplished, then."

At the sharpness of my tone, Sul takes a half step back. "I don't know." His eyes narrow. "While it may surprise you to learn it, my sources of information aren't infinite. I'm working with the best I have and will get you what answers are within my power to grasp." He snarls then, cursing softly. "I'm just relieved you didn't do something that would have put us all in danger."

Resisting the impulse to grab him by the front of his shirt, I turn abruptly and continue on my way down the passage. I know what my brother is saying; his hints are broad enough. He's not in the least concerned that another dose of *raog* poison nearly drove me to murder Faraine. All he cares about is that the marriage to Gavaria's princess remains unconsummated. Had I gone through with the violent lusts the poison stirred inside of me, I would have bound myself and all of Mythanar to the terms of the written agreement between myself and Larongar. The written word of humans holds power over all the fae. The deed would no sooner be done before I found myself marching into war in the human realm with the best of my warriors. Leaving Mythanar under threat. Without a king.

It was close. Too close.

Sul hastens to catch up, matches his stride to mine. "Brother," he says, and puts out a hand. I stop abruptly and turn another cold stare upon him. He offers a mirthless smile. "Come now, do you still suspect me? Is that what this is about?"

I don't answer.

Cursing again, Sul steps back and throws his arms wide. "What do you want me to do? Would you feel better if you pinned me to the ground again? Shall I lie prone and offer up my neck for your royal foot? Because I'm perfectly happy to humiliate myself as many times as it takes to make you trust me."

His eyes are wide, sparking with the passion of his words. But there's something else, something about the set of his jaw, the tension in his brow. Something I cannot name. I don't like it. I don't like not being able to read my brother as I used to.

The truth is, Sul is the one who handed me that goblet of poison. Sul is the one who arranged for the bathhouse girls. Who else could have poisoned me except for Sul?

"Chancellor Houg has received word from the cities of Ulam and Jolaghar." My voice is abrupt, devoid of emotion. "But not from Hoknath." Sul blinks, momentarily disoriented by the conversational shift. I continue relentlessly, giving him no time to find his footing. "Ulam and Jolaghar both report only minor effects from this most recent stirring. Lord Korh of Hoknath has sent no message."

"It's only been two lusterlings since the quake, Vor." Sul shrugs one shoulder. "Korh may be distracted with his own recovery efforts."

It's true, of course. I know how busy I have been, managing Mythanar's needs these last two lusterlings with scarcely a moment to eat, to close my eyes, to breathe. Hoknath is the nearest city to Mythanar, and if it suffered similar shocks, Lord Korh is likely pushed to his limits. But he should have found time to send a message to his king.

"Chancellor Houg is concerned," I say. Then, with emphasis: "*I* am concerned."

"Send couriers of your own then, if you're so impatient."

"Good idea." I tip my chin, looking at Sul from under my brows. "Take Hurk and Jot with you. Go by riverway and return as swiftly as you may with word."

My brother blinks. Then he angles his head to one side. "So that's it then. You're sending me away. To Hoknath."

"I require news of our sister city's situation. I need someone I can trust to retrieve that information. You are the logical choice."

Sul scoffs. "Be honest, Vor. Is this some precursor to my ultimate banishment? Are you trying it out for size to see how it feels?"

"My only concern is for my kingdom."

"*Morar-juk* it is!"

"And what does that mean? Speak plainly, brother."

"I think I'm speaking plain enough." Sul takes a step closer. Now his face is mere inches from mine. His brow is dark, his eyes spears of accusation. "It's been a long time since Mythanar and the Under Realm was your first concern. Since the moment you snatched that mortal wench off her feet and placed her before you in your saddle. As long as *she* is here, you're not the monarch your people need. And you know it."

His words lance into my head, red-hot and burning. Perhaps all the worse because they are true.

I keep my voice low and hard. "If you set off at once, you may be back by tomorrow dimness. I shall await what news you bring with interest."

Sul draws a long, ragged breath, his nostrils flaring. Then he steps back, runs a hand through his hair, smooths it back from his forehead. "My king," he says, and offers a salute. Only the faint curl of his lip betrays his true state of mind.

The next moment, he turns on heel, marches down the passage, turns the corner, and vanishes from sight. I remain alone. Standing beneath the vaulted ceiling under the cold, revealing light of the *lorst* lantern. Feeling the weight of an entire nation threatening to bow me under it. Never in my life have I felt so alone.

How long can I stand it before I must inevitably break?

# 11

## Faraine

If my calculations are correct, it has now been five days since my near death by execution. Or five lusterlings, as they are called here in the trolde world. How their lusterlings equate to my understanding of a day—whether the cyclical hours of dark and light are comparable—I cannot say.

What I can say is that it feels like forever.

I stand on the balcony outside the window of my new residence. Once we were dug out of the former queen's chambers, Hael placed me in a single room of the same wing, but a floor higher. The furnishings are all distinctly troldish—strange angles carved from solid blocks of stone. It's uncomfortable to my sensibilities, so I spend much of my time on this balcony overlooking the courtyard far below. Occasionally, I see movement—messengers in household livery, guards in bristling armor. The sweep of a long robe, the flutter of an elaborate headdress. All the people of this palace, going about their lives. Now and then, a wave of emotion rises high enough to strike the edges of my gods-gift. Always the same emotion: *fear*.

Sighing, I bend to rest my chin on my forearms. A breeze whispers across my face, wafts strands of hair against my cheeks. Not for the first time, I wonder where that breeze is coming from. My gaze lifts to the high cavern ceiling where the *lorst* crystals gleam. Are there air shafts overhead, leading from the world above?

Another movement in the courtyard below draws my gaze. My heart quickens with momentary hope only to be disappointed. Yet again. It's just another house guard, marching by on his way to or from his post. Not Vor. Never Vor. No matter how many hours I've lingered here at this very rail, I've yet to catch a glimpse of the Shadow King.

At least he hasn't followed through on his vow to send me home. Not yet.

A murmur of voices sounds in the room behind me. I turn, peer back through the wafting curtains which cover the open door at my back. Someone has entered my little chamber. Not Hael, of course. My bodyguard has been as determined as ever to keep her distance from me. I think she feels guilty. Though she's not questioned me in detail as to what happened between Vor and me, she watches me from the tail of her eye whenever she's in the room, averting her gaze the moment I look at her directly. It's always a relief when she leaves, though it does mean a return of my isolation and boredom.

It isn't Hael who enters now, however, but the squat and familiar figure of my chambermaid. She carries a silver platter in her block-shaped hands and doesn't so much as glance my way. She's been as cold and unfriendly to me these last two days as she was at our first meeting. But at least she's alive. Right now, that's all I ask in a potential companion.

Stepping hastily into the doorway, I push back the curtain and fix the trolde maid with a determined smile. "Hullo," I say, my voice falsely cheery.

She looks up. Her eyes narrow beneath the severe ledge of her browbone. It's not at all a friendly look.

I step into the room, moving slowly so as not to seem threatening. "Is that tea?" I ask, indicating the platter. I know perfectly well what it is. Every day at approximately this time, the same girl has entered with the same silver pot, cups, assortment of rolls and biscuits—all very familiar to my palate. She's set them down on that same stone table and scuttled from the room without a word or a nod for me.

She grunts now, turning to do just that. But the last few days have made me desperate. I spring forward several paces, hold out one hand, and bark, "Wait!"

My voice comes out sharper than I intend. But it does the trick. The trolde woman stops. Slowly, her heavy head swivels on her thick neck, and her pale little eyes peer back at me.

"What is your name?" I ask.

She blinks, uncomprehending. But of course, she doesn't know my language. Still, she has stopped. That must count for something.

"My name is Faraine," I say, touching my chest. No point in giving a title—*princess, queen, prisoner*. It's all the same to her. But a name is as good a place as any to start. "Faraine," I repeat, and offer what I hope is an encouraging smile.

She doesn't move. If I hadn't seen signs of life just a moment ago, I could almost swear she was nothing more than a lump of rock. Instinctively, I reach out again with my gods-gift, searching for a sense of her. I hit stone. Just stone. I lean in a little harder, hard enough to get the faintest squirming impression of . . . something . . .

"*Guthakug.*"

Her voice is so abrupt, I jump from my skin. Hastily, I recover myself and blurt, "Is . . . is that your name?"

"*Guthakug.*"

I clear my throat and make an attempt: "*Guth-ah-kug*?" It sounds limp on my tongue, without the proper resonance or rasp. I try again with more aggression. "*Guthakug.*"

The trolde woman shakes her head. The crevices of her lip rise and roll strangely, revealing a flash of diamond-hard teeth. "*Guthakug, kurspari. Udth r'agrrak.*"

She doesn't sound friendly. Then again, nothing spoken in this rock-grinding tongue sounds friendly to my ear. I offer another uncertain smile. The grooves of her brow deepen, rolling down together so that her eyes nearly disappear. With a shake of her heavy head, she turns and stomps through the door. Her feet vibrate the ground in her wake.

"Thank you, *Guthakug*!" I call after her back.

No sooner does the maid vacate the doorway than another figure appears. Captain Hael, staring into the room, her face a mask of confusion. Shock radiates from her, strong enough to break through her barriers and send me stumbling back a pace. "*What* did you say?" my bodyguard demands, fixing her stern eye on me.

"I, um . . ." I give my head a quick shake and draw myself a bit straighter. Hael is a truly intimidating presence, but I must learn to give as good as I get. "I thought perhaps I should begin to learn some names. As I am to be your king's, erm, guest. For the time being."

"Learn names?"

"Yes." I nod at the still-open door through which the maid just disappeared. "Perhaps you don't know her. She's *Guthakug*. I think."

"I think not!" Hael's voice chokes a little. It takes me a moment to realize she's struggling to swallow back laughter. "I *hope* not. Do you know what it is you're saying?"

Warmth floods my cheeks. "Well, no."

"*Guthakug* translates to . . . Well, there is no direct translation. The closest might be *horse leavings*."

"Horse leavings? You mean—oh!" I clap a hand to my mouth, as though I can somehow catch and stuff back the foul word I've just been determinedly trying to pronounce.

Hael, much to my surprise, utters a bleating giggle. She looks almost as shocked at the outburst as I am and swiftly pulls her face under control. She can't take it back, however. Neither can she hide that tiny glimmer of humor rolling out from behind her barriers. It's a crack in her armor. A small one, perhaps, but a crack.

"Well," I say, "I've picked a pretty place to begin my studies of troldish. Tell me, was my accent good at least?"

Hael's eyes snap with another laugh wanting to escape. She shakes her head, however, and says firmly, "It does not matter, Princess. You have no need to refine your accent nor any reason to fraternize with the household staff. I will see to your needs for the duration of your stay, however long it may be."

Something about the way she speaks makes my stomach dip. Has word come from Gavaria yet? From my father? I want to ask, want to barrage Hael with my questions. But something in her expression warns me not to. After all, I already know my father will not give in to Vor's demands. If I don't want to be tossed over the pommel of a morleth saddle and sent ignominiously back to Beldroth, I'm going to need to find a place for myself here in Mythanar.

The first step in that process could be making a friend.

Captain Hael is already backing out through the door, ready to resume her post in the passage. "A moment, Captain," I say, and she pauses. I step across the room and take a seat at the table where the maid set the tea tray. My hands shake, but I manage to lift the pot, swirl, pour myself a cup all without spilling. "Tell me where I went wrong," I say, blinking innocently up at the stern captain. "Was my intonation not guttural enough? *Guthakug*," I try again, this time drawing the sound up from the depths of my gut.

Hael blinks, shocked all over again to hear such a word fall from my lips. She masks her expression, however, and offers only, "What if the princess picked a different word with which to begin her studies?"

"Very well." I take a sip then lower the cup, breathing in the steam as it wafts under my nose. "How about something practical. Like *hungry*."

Hael shoots me a narrow look. She knows what I'm trying to do. And she has no interest in letting a bond form between us. She doesn't like me, might even hate me.

Still, I feel I have a fingerhold at least. I must grasp on tight. "Come now, Captain Hael. You know it will make your life easier if I'm not wholly dependent on you for every little thing. What if I wander off and end up fallen down a hole somewhere? It's as likely as anything in this world of yours. At least if I'm able to cry *Hungry, hungry!* I should be able to draw attention to my predicament."

Hael's jaw tightens. I can almost hear her wishing I *would* go lose myself down a dark hole somewhere. My mouth quirks in a half smile. Somewhere beneath that tough warrior exterior, there must be a kind side to her nature. Otherwise, I can't see why Vor would depend on her so implicitly.

"*Makrok*," she says suddenly.

I blink. It sounded almost like a bark. "I beg your pardon?"

"That's the word. *Hungry*. In troldish. *Makrok*."

I preemptively clear my throat then take a stab at the word.

"No." Hael shakes her head and touches her own throat. "A softer sound. In the back." She opens her mouth wide and makes a soft, rasping noise. I widen my jaw and try to mimic her, and there we sit with our heads thrown back, making inarticulate, throaty growls at each other. If someone walked in on us now, we would appear positively mad.

A little giggle burbles up inside me. It's so unexpected, I hiccup, trying to swallow it back. Hael prickles. Is she irritated? No, for one side of her mouth twists. "We look like a mother coaxing her babe," she says.

"Really?" I rub my poor throat ruefully. "I thought we looked rather like a pair of dogs getting ready to howl at the moon." Hael tips an eyebrow, not understanding the analogy. They don't have a moon in the Shadow Realm, after all. Or dogs, apparently. "Never mind." I wave a hand. "Am I close?"

"Yes, Princess. If you can just pull the sound out from below your chest a bit more."

I draw a long breath and take another stab at it. "*Makrok!*"

"Ah! That was good!"

I shake my head, rubbing my throat again. "I don't think I could ever shout that from the depths of a dark pit. I'd go hoarse long before anyone heard me. Do you have any simpler words I might try? How about a greeting?"

Hael agrees, and the word—*hiri*—proves much easier for my human vocal cords to manage. We progress through a series of simple vocabulary: *me, you, need, eat, drink,* and a particularly choice word that pertains to answering the call of nature. By the end of all this, my voice is raw. As I've already drained the pot of tea, I beg another. Hael goes to the wall and pulls a rope hidden behind a tapestry. It must be connected to a bell somewhere, for not half a minute later, the door opens, and my maid appears.

*Horsescat.* The word pops into my head before I can stop it. I bite back a giggle, and instead whip out one of my other new words for a try: "*Hiri.*" I pause, watching the effect on my subject. She doesn't even blink. I continue: "Would you be so kind as to bring a fresh pot of tea?"

The maid's gaze swivels from me to Hael. "*Kurspar-oom,*" the captain barks. "*Mazoga.*"

The maid inclines her head and begins to retreat, but Hael speaks again sharply, stopping her in her tracks. Another stream of incomprehensible troldish follows. From the maid, I feel a faint flash of fury. It's gone before I can be certain of it, however. When Hael is done, the maid hastens from the room, shutting the door behind her. "What was that about?" I ask.

"I simply reminded her that you are the king's guest. As such, you must be afforded appropriate deference." Hael's eyes gleam. "I told her if I find out she's been using coarse language while on duty again, I will have her replaced and sent to work in the *scorlors.*"

I nod solemnly. But my heart warms a little. Hael defended me. Me! Dare I call this progress? Do I now have an ally in Mythanar?

The maid returns shortly thereafter with a fresh pot of tea which she exchanges for the empty one. Hael maintains a stoic silence, but I attempt a tentative "*Salthu*" in thanks. The maid flashes me a short glance. At a low growl from Hael, she bobs a curtsy before turning for the door. Hael halts her with a word. She looks back, warily. Hael speaks another stream of harsh-sounding troldish. The maid seems to consider. Then she says in response, "*Yrt.*"

Hael waves a dismissive hand. When the door shuts behind the maid, she turns to me. "Her name is Yrt."

I consider this as I lift the warm pot and swirl the brew inside to loosen the leaves. Curling steam escapes the spout and carries an inviting aroma to my nostrils. "I'm starting to detect a pattern to your troldish names," I muse as I pour a dark stream into my cup. "They're all quite short, aren't they?" Hael grunts, a questioning sound. I elaborate: "Vor. Hael. Sul. Yrt. Nothing longer than a single syllable. Am I right?"

"For a trolde, a longer name would be considered"—Hael pauses, choosing her words—"I believe you would call it *pretentious*. They would be seen as trying to mimic the elfkin with their long, elaborate names. No one wants that."

I sip my tea thoughtfully. "I've heard that among the fae each is given two names—a secret name and a name used by the public. Is this true?"

"Only among elfkin," Hael says. "We trolde are not so susceptible to the kind of ensorcellment that would make our own names dangerous to us."

"And do your names bear meaning? Yours, for instance—what does *Hael* mean?"

My new bodyguard eyes me narrowly. She doesn't appreciate my attempts at bonding. If she could, she would end this conversation here and now, but some trolde concept of decorum keeps her in place. "My name," she says at length, "refers to the single drop of water poised at the tip of a stalactite."

I raise my brows in surprise. "That is unexpectedly poetic."

Hael grunts again, but I'm almost certain her pale cheek flushes a soft lavender. Perhaps there's a gentle side to her nature after all. And the trolde language itself, which has seemed like nothing but a series of growls and grinding consonants, may possess more beauty than I first suspected.

What would it be like to remain here in the Shadow Realm? To throw myself into the learning and knowing of these people and their ways? It's a more exciting prospect than I like to admit. Even as I've fumbled through these first few, halting words, I feel a whole new world opening before me. A world much broader and more enticing than anything I could ever have known back home.

A world that was meant for Ilsevel.

A dart of guilt pricks my heart. I set down my teacup, drawing a short breath. But I'm not going to let this feeling drag me down. Not now, not when I'm just starting to find my feet. Ilsevel is dead. I am not.

The silence has lingered too long. I glance up to find Hael's brooding gaze upon me. Suddenly self-conscious, I touch a hand to my chin, my cheek. "Have I spilled something?"

"No." She gives her head a short shake. "It's your turn, Princess."

"My turn?"

"Your name. *Faraine*. What does it mean?"

"Oh!" I laugh a little. "Faraine means *far horizon* in Old Gavarian. I've always thought it rather unsuited to me. I was never one for travel and ultimately destined for life in a convent."

Hael tips one eyebrow slightly. "Perhaps there was portent to your name after all."

My mouth quirks, my laugh not quite faded. I raise the cup in salute. "I'll drink to that." Then, softly, not entirely certain I want to be heard: "What does *Vor* mean?"

The air in the room goes very still. I count my breaths up to ten before daring to peer up at Hael. Once more, her too-keen gaze is fixed on me with lancelike sharpness. Have I made a mistake? But when I reach out with my gods-gift, it's not resentment which emanates from behind her barriers, merely caution.

"*Valiant*," Hael says at last. "It is an ancient troldish name, a name of kings. And yes, if you're wondering," she adds, angling her head to one side. "It is well suited to him."

Heat warms my cheeks. Hastily, I look away, take another gulp of tea. It's a bit too hot. I grimace as I force the mouthful down. "All right," I say, determined to break this tension in the air, "let's have another word." I glance around the room, seeking inspiration. A fireplace dominates one wall, set with a huge stone mantel elaborately carved in the image of a dragon. It catches my eye. "How do you say *dragon* in troldish?"

Something strikes me. Not a powerful blow, but sudden and sharp enough that I jump in my seat. I turn to find Hael's face drawn into a deep, dark scowl. The lines around her mouth are tight, the muscles of her jaw tense and hard. "I cannot speak that word," she says. "Not to you. Not out loud. It is sacred."

"Sacred?" I blink at her, my mouth sagging. "I'm sorry, I was given to understand troldefolk worshipped Lamruil, the God of Darkness."

"Some sacred things are not meant to be *worshipped*."

Her words seem to echo in the space between us. I'm still trying to figure out a response when she bows and moves to the door. "The princess must excuse me," she says. I can feel her pushing her emotions back down with a firm, practiced hand. "I shall resume my post. If you have any need, do not hesitate to ask."

I open my mouth, more questions on the tip of my tongue. But she's out the door already, pulling the door firmly shut behind her. And I'm alone once more. A prisoner in my husband's household.

"Far horizon," I whisper, my eyes shifting to the window and the world beyond. But there are no horizons here. Not in this world under stone.

# 12

## Vor

The whole town was swept away. Only a handful of survivors have made it into the city thus far. We anticipate more will arrive in the next lusterling or two."

Chancellor Houg's voice drones relentlessly in my ear. It's as though the more dire news she must deliver, the more monotone her delivery becomes. Perhaps it's a good thing. After all, the word she bears is hard enough without added emotion.

I rub at my shoulder, trying not to obviously scratch the itchy bandage underneath my shirt. Madame Ar patched me up following the incident in the queen's chambers, and her gluey healing salve is starting to peel away, leaving my skin raw with rash. As king, I cannot be seen to squirm and scratch. I must be the solemn figurehead my people need in this time of uncertainty, even in the privacy of my own office. Stoic. Unmovable. Solid as bedrock.

Still, lusterling follows dimness, and dimness follows lusterling, and reports continue flowing in. One after another they pile up, each small concern adding to the weight of the mountain I must somehow bear upon my back. And who is there to come alongside me, to help me with this burden? Sul is gone. Hael is dismissed from her post. And my wife . . . my bride . . .

"Your Majesty?"

Houg's voice breaks through the mental fog clouding my brain. I drag my head up, meet the three pairs of stern eyes staring down at me from across my desk. Lord Dagh, my household steward, stands on Houg's right, with Umog Zu, the low priestess, on her left. Both look ready to launch at the throat of the other. I ignore them and focus my attention on Houg. "Yes, Chancellor. Do go on."

"The river folk require refuge. They ought to be sent to the Temple of Orgoth, but—"

"But we are already overrun with orphans and refugees from our own city!" Though characteristically a living enigma of calm, Zu positively vibrates with ire in this moment. "My brothers and sisters of the Dark can scarcely enter into the *va*, so distracted are their minds and souls. How can we expect to keep the city healthy and thriving if the prayer vibrations so necessary to the well-being of all Mythanar are so rudely interrupted?"

I am no theologian, but I know enough to comprehend Zu's frustration. The *umogar* take it in turns entering into various states of *va*, which is to say, oneness with the stone of our birth. In this state, they send their life force vibrations down through the many layers of rock to the heart of our world, to soothe that which dwells in the heat and the darkness there. It is said these constant prayers are the only reason the Under Realm still exists.

I don't know if this is true. In fact, I rather doubt it. But I'm not about to voice such blasphemy to my low priestess. I have far too many vivid memories of this woman boxing my ears when I was an impudent young prince. I doubt the crown on my head would stop her from boxing them now.

"Very well, Umog," I say. "Send the river folk up to the palace. Lord Dagh"—I turn slightly to address my steward—"we can house any number of refugees in the East Hall, can we not? There's ample room for some makeshift beds."

Dagh pulls a face, contriving to look even more put-upon than usual. "The East Hall is currently in use by the household staff. If Your Majesty may be pleased to remember, a large section of the staff quarters was severely damaged in the stirring. As restoration efforts have concentrated on other parts of the palace—those occupied by members of your court—the staff have been obliged to manage as best they can."

I frown. "East Hall is huge, Dagh. It's positively massive. Surely there's room for a dozen families or so."

"East Hall *was* huge, Your Majesty. One end is shored up and in need of repairs before it may be safely used."

With a sigh, I bend my head, momentarily unable to maintain the façade of kingly strength. I'm tired, so achingly tired. I've not slept in days. Last dimness, I managed to chase everyone from the room long enough to put my head down on this very table and catch a few uncomfortable but blissful hours of slumber . . . only to be rudely awakened by Houg's pounding fist at the door. "Fine," I say heavily. "Forget the East Hall. What about the guest wing? There are several spare apartments currently not in use. Lady Xag's, for instance."

Speaking my friend's name sends a stab of pain to my gut. It's not been long since Xag met her end. Poisoned. Along with the rest of her town. My engineer's words echo hollowly in the back of my head: *Most folk are never gonna see the city fall. Most folk are gonna die of poison long before.*

Shuddering, I drag my awareness back to the present and Dagh's vehement protest of "They'll get *muck* on the *tapestries*! Their muddy brats will climb the pillars and moldings! These people are positively barbaric. Bargemen! Fishers! Shallow-scrapers!"

"Come, man," my chancellor interrupts, shooting him a disapproving glare. "The palace just survived the largest stirring in the last hundred turns of the cycle. Surely it can survive a few dozen river children. Besides—"

Before Houg can finish, sudden commotion erupts outside the door. Upraised voices, most of them muffled, punctuated by the high, determined voice of young Guardsman Yok: "You cannot go in there, Your Highness!"

There's a deep, rolling growl, followed by a *thunk*. The next moment, the door opens, and a stern, terrible figure stands there. Gray skin, eyes like two white gems. Long white hair hanging across massive shoulders. Naked, save for a thin cloth across his loins, he moves as though clad in the richest royal raiment.

A shiver races down the back of my neck. I do not like this man. Targ, the so-called priest and self-proclaimed servant of the Deeper Dark. A cultist, if you ask me. He commands a loyal following of devotees who hang upon his every word and gesture. One of whom happens to be my stepmother.

Sure enough, no sooner does Targ enter the space than he steps to one side, making way for Queen Roh's entrance. I glimpse Yok behind her, wide-eyed and desperate. "I'm sorry, Your Majesty!" he stammers from under his helmet. "I couldn't— I wasn't certain— I—"

"Peace, Yok." I hold up one hand. The boy means well and is certainly determined to prove himself. But he has much to learn before he'll be of any real use. "Back to your post. Do your best to see that no one else disturbs me, will you?"

Flushed with embarrassment, Yok ducks back outside, pulling the door shut behind him. Roh does not so much as acknowledge him. She stands there, clad in somber black glinting with flecks of broken gemstones. Her white hair, heavily streaked with strands of charcoal, is swept back from her high, proud forehead and falls to her waist in thick waves. She is a beautiful woman. But then, one would expect no less in the wife of a king. Far more impressive than her beauty, however, is her will. It shines in her eye, hard as diamonds, unyielding as the stone of ages.

She casts a cold gaze first at Chancellor Houg, then Lord Dagh. Only to Umog Zu does she offer a faint, polite nod. At last, she fixes me with the full force of her diamond stare. "May we have the room?"

I want to deny her. But I can see she has no intention of backing down, and at present, I haven't the energy for a fight. "Go," I say, waving an easy, dismissive hand. "Lord Dagh," I add, as my steward scuttles from the room. "Find *some* place in this whole vast mausoleum of a palace where we can safely house a handful of rivertown families. Understood?"

Dagh bows himself out, still muttering. Houg and the low priestess follow after. When the door is shut, I turn to Roh, ignoring Targ, who looms silent against the wall. Generally, I find it best for everyone if I pretend he doesn't exist. "Well, Stepmother?" I say pleasantly. "To what do I owe the delight of your company?"

"Where have you sent my son?"

She doesn't beat around the basalt, does she? "To Hoknath," I answer smoothly, and lace my fingers behind my head. "Will that be all? I do have such a lot to see to this lusterling."

"No." Her lip curls. It somehow only makes her more beautiful. "Why are you punishing him?"

"Punishing him? There's a thought. Do you know of a reason why I should punish him?"

Her nostrils quiver. She takes a step closer to my desk. If I didn't know any better, I'd say she was trying to menace me. "Sul has only ever been loyal to you. Even when there were those in your own court who urged him to take a stand against you. Sul could not be swayed. He could not be wooed, reasoned with, cajoled, bribed, or threatened. He is *rock*. He is *jor*. You know this."

"I do."

She presses her fists into the stone tabletop, leaning heavily, cold eyes flashing. "Then why have you sent him from you? Sent him out into gods-know-what dangers, far from your side?"

I draw a slow breath, regarding her through half-closed eyelids. "Why should you care?" I ask at length, and watch the way her cheek twitches, her jaw clenches. "Is it not your wish to see us all succumb to the inevitable Dark in any case? What does it matter if Sul faces a little danger? What does it even matter if he perishes? It makes no difference to you, does it?"

Her lips curl back. Her teeth are very white against the dark purple of her gums. "If that's what you think, you grossly misunderstand the ways of the Deeper Dark."

"Maybe so." I tilt an eyebrow Targ's way. "What then? Are you and your little pocket priest here to endarken me?"

"A mind such as yours cannot understand the hope of *va-jor*," she snaps.

"A mind such as mine?"

"A *human* mind."

It has been many turns of the cycle since I saw my stepmother's face so raw with feeling. Since the death of my father, she's thrown herself into her religious studies so completely, assuming the hard, impassive, emotionless mask of a priestess. In this moment, however, she is unmasked. I see again the woman I once knew—the passionate, even volatile creature my father took as his bride and offered me as replacement for my own lost mother. A woman I knew, from the first moment I set eyes on her, I could never love.

I rise, push back my chair, and face her straight on. I'm taller than she, but not by much. I am part human, after all, whereas Roh is purely troldish, as though she were carved from rock rather than birthed from a mother's womb. But it doesn't matter. "Trolde blood or human," I say, my voice cold and hard as the founding stones of this very palace, "I am Gaur's eldest son. It was I, not my brother, whom the gods determined should rule Mythanar."

"The *gods*?" Roh spits. "Leave the *gods* to the elfkin. We trolde serve only the Dark and That Which Dwells Below. We—"

"Your Majesty! Your Majesty, I'm sorry to interrupt!"

Yok's voice outside the door jars through my senses. I yank my gaze away from Roh's face and scowl across the shadowed antechamber. "Not now, Yok!" I snarl.

"Forgive me, Your Majesty! It's Hurk and Jot. They beg leave to speak with you at once."

My blood runs cold. Roh, her quick gaze studying my face, lets out a little breath. "What's wrong?" she asks.

I don't bother to answer. I don't bother to tell her these are the names of the two guards who accompanied Sul on his journey to Hoknath. "Send them in," I say instead. My knees suddenly weak, I sink back into my chair and assume an easy manner even as my heart gallops painfully in my chest.

"What are you doing?" Roh growls, as the door opens to admit the newcomers. "We're not done, you and I!"

I silence her with a gesture as two figures—one male, one female—stagger into the room. The female holds her companion up, his arm across her shoulders, but they both look the worse for wear. His left leg hangs limp, the bone obviously, painfully broken. His skin is sickly gray, shiny with sweat.

I jump up at once, hasten around from behind my desk. "Jot! Hurk! What has happened? Are you all right?"

Hurk tries to offer me a smile through his pain. "I've been better, Your Majesty. I wanted to deliver this word in person, then I'm off to Madame Ar."

"What news of . . ." I try to speak my brother's name, but it freezes on my tongue and lies there, a cold, hard lump. ". . . of Hoknath?"

Jot shakes her half-shaved head, floppy white curls falling over her left ear. "We never made it that far, Your Majesty. We were taking the riverway, but the cavern was flooded from the stirring. Prince Sul thought we could make it, but then the ceiling began to give. Sul kept our craft from breaking against a boulder, but he ended up in the water. Hurk and I barely made it out alive. We had to shore the craft and crawl back. I was sure the whole thing would come down on top of us long before we made it out."

"And my son?" Roh demands, drawing the two guards' gazes her way. "What became of him?"

"We searched as long as we could." Jot hangs her head dismally. "But then Hurk here . . . he wasn't going to make it, not with his leg like this. I had to get him back, you see? There was no sign of the prince."

Roh turns her head sharply, fixing her stare on me. As though I'd planned this; as though I'd somehow rigged the riverway to murder her son. I feel every accusation she silently hurls at me.

"We'll find him, Roh," I say. My voice carries all the kingly confidence I can muster in that moment. "I will go personally. I will bring him home."

She holds my gaze hard. Her pupils are large black disks, like hollows in her pale face. "If you don't," she whispers, "may you never find your way again in the Dark."

With that, she turns and sweeps from the room. Targ, who stood all this while silent and still as a boulder, reanimates, gathering his powerful limbs and rolling into motion behind her. He never so much as glances my way.

I wait until they are both clear of the room before turning to Jot and Hurk once more. "Jot, are you fit enough to accompany me?"

"I . . . I think so, Your Majesty," she responds, but I hear the dreadful hesitation in her voice. She's not what I need. Not now. Not when Sul's life is on the line.

"No, never mind. Get him to the infirmary," I say, waving them off. "Have Ar look you over as well. Yok!" The boy's face appears in the doorway, his expression drawn, his eyes wide. "Yok, I need you to find your sister and send her to me. At once, do you hear?"

# 13

## Faraine

I press my palm flat against the wall, lean my weight into my arm, and close my eyes. My other hand grips my pendant hard, searching for the warmth in its heart. It responds to my call with a gentle pulse. It almost feels like a greeting.

Taking hold of that pulse, I channel it from my palm into my wrist, my arm, my heart. There it swirls for a moment before continuing down my other arm and into the wall. It's a subtle sensation, a faint whisper of vibration. So faint, I could almost believe I made it up.

But no. Deep down inside the wall something answers. Something *stirs*. This is nothing like when the assassin pinned me to the wall and held his knife to my throat. Then, both his feelings and mine were such a wild storm, the crystals embedded in the wall had seemed to scream out in response. Now my heart is quiet, calm. When I reach for the crystals, they barely whisper in response. But they *do* respond.

I open my eyes, drop my hand, and take a step back. The wall is smooth, slightly curved, and etched with delicate patterns of cave flowers and creatures for which I have no names. Just a wall, though. Just unyielding stone. No one would guess the amount of life vibrating within.

Frowning slightly, I pluck at my pendant, hold it up to the level of my eyes. No matter how I turn the question round in my mind, I cannot come up with an explanation for how this crystal of the Under Realm came into my possession. It's almost as though . . . as though someone *knew* about my gods-gift. Knew how my powers would react to the stones of this world. But that's a wild thought, surely. No one knows or cares about my gift.

With a sigh, I drop the crystal to rest against my breast. All these questions without answers are going to drive me mad. I feel itchy in my own skin, uncomfortable, desperate for a change of scene. I cast a glance around the room. It's far less human in style than the queen's chambers had been. My gaze lingers for a moment on the narrow bed that stands along one wall. It's covered in white furs and thick blankets and is much smaller than the big bed in the bridal chamber. Room enough to sleep only me.

Vor has not come. It's been days now. Or lusterlings, I should say. Too long. Agonizingly too long.

Cursing softly, I begin to pace the room. Unsettled frustration burrows deeper and deeper into my soul, turning to anxiety, even panic. I cannot take much more of this isolation! What would happen if I opened the door and told Hael to summon the Shadow King? Would he come? If he did, what would I say?

I close my eyes. Let my mind still, let the storm of emotion fade. Vor's face appears in my memory, illuminated by a single *lorst* crystal. I hold on to that image, let it pull me deeper. I feel his strong hand warming my lower back, pressing me against his body. The

warmth of his lips hovering over mine, no more than a breath between us. I touch my lower lip with the tip of one finger, trying to
recall the sensation, that brush of connection. That instant—there
and gone again—when he'd dared lower his mouth to mine.

Our first kiss.

Our first *true* kiss.

Not a kiss intended for my sister. Not a vicious attack driven by
poison.

A kiss meant for me. Gentle. Tentative. So full of longing it
had wrung my heart.

Oh, why does he not come?

A sudden burst of voices in the passage outside. I start, my eyes
flaring open, and turn to the door. It remains shut fast, but I can
hear voices clearly on the other side. Hael and another. Male. My
heart leaps then sinks again. That isn't Vor's deep, reverberating
tone. It's higher, softer, sweeter.

Frowning, I step across the room to the chamber door and lean
my ear close. With a gasp, I spring back. A sudden flash of feeling
rippled right through the stone and struck me hard in the chest.
For a moment, I stand with both hands pressed against my heart,
half believing I've been struck. But it was my gods-gift. Responding to some sharp and unexpected pain. Whose?

Gripping my crystal for support, I step forward again, take hold
of the latch, and crack the door open an inch. Hael stands watch
just outside. She's speaking to a boy whom I immediately recognize. *Yok*, I believe his name is. The young escort Vor charged to
watch over me and Lyria when we first arrived in the Under Realm.
His face is animated with frustration, a sharp contrast to Hael's
stoic grimness. They growl at each other in troldish, deep in some
argument and unaware of my scrutiny.

I bite my lip. Perhaps I should retreat, shut the door again. Give them privacy. Before I can decide, however, another wave of feeling bursts from Hael. It's so sharp, I gasp.

Hael turns, sees me. Her eyes widen. "Princess. There's nothing to concern you here. Go back inside."

I push down the pain of her ire. Then, squaring my shoulders, I turn to the boy. He stares at me, mouth gaping. "What has happened?" I ask.

Yok blinks, swallows, and shoots Hael a swift glance. "Vor . . . That is, the king . . . He's, um, he's requested my sister join him. On a special mission. To find Prince Sul."

At the mention of the king's brother, another stab of emotion shoots out from Hael. She stifles it at once, but not fast enough. In that split second, she's revealed the true state of her heart. "What's happened to the prince?" I ask, still addressing myself to Yok.

"He's missing," the boy says. He turns to Hael and speaks in troldish again.

She shakes her head and growls, this time in my own language, "My duty is to the princess." Her words are heavy with resentment. "Tell the king—"

"You tell him!" Yok barks. "I already tried. I told him I would go instead."

"You?" Hael looks the boy up and down, her expression disdainful. "You're not ready. He needs someone he can trust."

"He can trust me," the boy responds sulkily. "But he wants you."

Hael's mouth shuts fast. Then she growls through her teeth. "I cannot leave the princess."

Yok utters a string of troldish. I don't need an interpreter to guess what he's saying. Hastily, I step forward and touch Hael's arm, resting my fingers on the leather bracer strapped to her fore-arm. "It's all right." I offer a small smile when she turns to me. "I'm sure this brave young guardsman will perform his duties admira-bly. I promise not to cause him too much trouble while you're away."

Hael opens her mouth to protest, but I can feel her desperation. Even with a barrier of leather between my fingers and her arm, her emotions are so strong, so tumultuous.

"Go on," I urge gently. "Find the missing prince. And . . . and bring Vor back safely."

Her eyes flash to meet mine. Wary, hopeful, frightened. With an effort, she draws her feelings in check, locking them down fast. Only then does she turn to Yok, a stream of troldish falling from her tongue. It all sounds so harsh, so heavy. I can almost see the boy's shoulders bow under their weight. When she's through, how-ever, she turns to me and says, "Stay safe, Princess. I will return soon." With that, she strides down the passage. When she reaches the turn at the end, she breaks into a run and vanishes from sight.

Thus, I find myself alone with my new young bodyguard. I look at him. He gapes back at me. "What was your name again?" I ask, though I remember well enough.

"Yok," he answers. "Guardsman Yok."

I nod. "You fought bravely to protect Lady Lyria and myself from . . . from . . . what were those creatures called?"

"*Woggha.*" Yok clears his throat. "Cave devils."

Memory of the hideous monsters flashes through my mind. Those eyeless, bone-plated faces. The gray, sagging skin. The huge, stone-piercing claws. The Under Realm is full of beauty, but there are horrors lurking in its shadows. Still . . . I remember what it felt like to connect to that beast. Just for a moment, when I stood gripping a large *urzul* crystal, facing down that leering maw. I'd touched the mind trapped inside the madness. A mind lost to savagery and bloodlust. A mind sunk in despair.

I shiver, the fine hairs on my arms prickling. Pulling my mind back to the present moment, I offer the young man a cool smile. "You have proven your courage and loyalty already, Guardsman Yok. I believe you and I shall get along well."

"It is my honor to serve you, Princess."

"Excellent. So long as we understand one another." With that, I turn on heel and reenter my room, leaving the door open behind me. When Yok reaches out to shut it, I call over my shoulder, "I will inform you when I require privacy."

The boy freezes. But he doesn't protest. After a moment, he simply lets go of the latch, backs away, and assumes position outside my door. This could work out rather well, actually. It will be nice to have a bodyguard who isn't as ferociously intimidating as Captain Hael.

I cross the room and step out onto the balcony. There's a great deal of activity in the courtyard below. I lean over the rail to watch. Morleth prance and pace, lashing their long, barbed tails. Grooms scramble to hold their reins, dodging snapping fangs and cloven hooves. One of the beasts is bigger than the rest. I'm almost certain it's Knar, Vor's own mount.

I chew my bottom lip. My fingers grip the rail. Vor is going. On a mission to find his missing brother. A dangerous mission no doubt. And he hasn't bothered to take his leave of me. Not that I should expect any such courtesy. Why would a king take leave of his prisoner?

Clenching my hands into fists, I turn and march back into the room. Yok has just assumed a comfortable position at the wall when I appear in the open door. He starts at the sight of me. His eyes nearly dart from his skull. "Princess?"

"Take me to the courtyard." I hold myself very straight and tall, summoning all the queenly poise of my heritage. Yok's mouth opens, closes. I watch him try to decide whether or not he should protest. To drive my point home, I add an imperious, "At once."

That does the trick. Yok leaps into action, indicating the way with a wave of his hand. I fall into step beside him, and he guides me down several flights of stairs and through bewildering stone passages. I try not to stare as I go. But it is difficult. I've seen little of the palace so far. It's truly a wondrous, magnificent structure, unlike any I've ever before seen. Ancient and ageless, cold, echoing, and full of shadows. Yet here and there, glowing crystals reveal awe-inspiring rock formations. I spy homely touches as well: woven rugs and tapestries, glimpses of salons and private galleries; of statues and intricate moldings. All of these flash in the tail of my eye as I hurry at my bodyguard's side.

Most impressive of all, however, are the people. The tall, terrible, beautiful trolde men and women, denizens of the household. I take care not to meet their gazes . . . gazes which no doubt observed both my wedding and my near execution with the same interest. They openly stare at me, however, their pale eyes intent. I feel positively dwarfed by their towering stature, humbled by their otherworldly beauty. But I carry myself as tall as I can, determined to move with confidence, to betray no fear.

We come at last to the entrance hall, which I recognize from my first arrival at the palace. It seems so long ago now that I was carried through the city in a curtained litter and deposited here in the center of this floor beneath that huge, domed ceiling. The echoing space is full of activity now—servants assisting warriors into armor, strapping on greaves, pauldrons, and bracers. I spy Captain Hael among them. She's just lifting her helmet to her head when she sees me and Yok under an arch on the edge of the hall. She opens her mouth, prepared to call out.

A voice speaks directly behind me: "What are you doing here?"

Shock like lightning streaks down my spine. Thrilling, almost painful. My knees go weak, but I lock them fast and school my face into a careful mask. Drawing a breath, I turn around to face the speaker. Vor. Tall and towering, a figure of majestic strength, clad in beautiful armor etched in intricate patterns. The pauldrons' edges are sharp as blades, the bracers and greaves set with spikes. He looks like a legend come to life, and the sight is enough to make my head spin and my heart shiver in my breast.

Then I lift my gaze to his face. He's not yet donned his helmet, and I can see him clearly. Though his features are hard and stern as stone, his eyes betray him. They are the eyes of a man half-starved. When they meet my gaze, I feel the surge of his emotion, red and blazing. So many feelings—a cacophony of fear, anger, anxiety. And underneath it all, like the deep beat of a drum, *desire*.

I fight the impulse to reach out to him. Every urge tells me to take his face between my hands, to draw him down to me. But I cannot. Because, though his feelings are strong, they are not clear. I do not know what he truly wants. So I fold my hands neatly before me, and lift my chin a little higher. "You are going away?" I say, my voice low and calm.

He nods. "As you see."

"How long will you be gone?"

"I don't know." His lower jaw works. His teeth flash in the *lorst* light. "Not long, I hope."

"Is it dangerous? Where you are going?"

"I don't know." Another hesitation, then, "Most likely."

My stomach twists. I'm painfully aware of all the eyes watching us, of the sudden silence filling the cavernous hall at my back. "You will be careful." Try though I might, I cannot help the slight quaver in my voice.

His expression tightens. Another wave of emotion radiates from him, another burst of that complicated storm. He fights it back valiantly, however; shuts it down hard behind the walls of his heart. "I will." He glances at Yok then back to me again. "You shouldn't leave your room, Princess."

"I am not a prisoner," I remind him sharply.

He shakes his head. Then, abruptly, he lifts the helmet in his hands and puts it on. The long cheek plates cover his face, and the brim shadows his eyes so that they are no more than two bright sparks. "It's better for all of us if you stay out of sight," he growls.

With those words, he pushes past me, striding into the hall. I turn, and watch him go. My heart aches so badly, I want to grab my chest, desperate to ease the pain. But I dare not betray myself so obviously. So, I simply watch him as he speaks a few low, rumbling words of troldish to his people, then strides into the courtyard. The others follow after him, though Hael pauses in the doorway long enough to shoot a final warning glance at me and Yok.

Then they're gone. Gone to face unknown perils. Leaving me behind in this cold stone world.

A little whimper in my throat, I pick up the hem of my gown, step out from under the archway, and race across the now empty hall, ignoring Yok's yelp of protest. I reach the still-open door and look out into the courtyard, down the broad steps. Morleth stamp and snort, blowing black fumes from their nostrils as grooms struggle to hold them steady for their riders. Vor is there, already astride

Knar. He surveys his people, and I think . . . I hope . . . I wish . . . his gaze flashes ever so briefly up at me in the doorway. But I'm not sure. In fact, I'm almost certain I'm mistaken.

Vor raises a fist over his head. *"Drag-or, ortolarok!"*

His people answer, arms upraised, their rough voices barking: *"Rhozah! Rhozah!"*

Their voices still ringing against the high stone walls, they spur their mounts into motion. Morleth hooves strike sparks from stone as they stream from the courtyard and out into the city beyond. Soon there is nothing left in their wake but a haze of drifting smoke.

# 14

......

# Vor

**D**on't look back. Don't look back.

Everything in my being begs to turn in my saddle, to crane my head, to catch one last glimpse of the slender maiden standing in that doorway. Everything in me urges to yank my morleth's reins, haul the beast about, and gallop back across the courtyard, right up those great stone steps. To leap from my saddle, catch her in my arms, and crush my lips against hers in a cataclysmic kiss.

Gods on high and deep below! How am I to protect myself from this need? I crave her presence like I crave air in my lungs. My hands burn with the desire to run my fingers through her hair, to glide my palms over the soft curves of her body. My lips and tongue starve for a taste of her sweetness. I long to drink her in, every inch of her. To know her and, in the knowing, to claim her. To make her *mine*.

But I cannot. I dare not. For it is not my heart alone which is at stake. It is the fate of all Mythanar. Never can I forget it. I must put up every barrier, every shield. And when those threaten to crumble, I must retreat. Put as much distance between us as I can. It is the only way.

I shake my head, focus on the road ahead. The whole company surges into a gallop, moving swiftly and fluidly down through the city, across the bridge, and on to the tunnels and darkness outside Mythanar. Once we've left the brilliant *lorst* lights behind, the morleth are happier, and their riders have an easier time keeping them under control. I've brought five of my finest with me on this mission, including Hael. Armor clad and helmed, they are ready for action. I can only hope there will be no need, and this mission will prove a simple reconnaissance. That we'll find my misplaced brother, have a quick word with Lord Korh of Hoknath, and be home again by dimness.

Every instinct tells me it won't be that simple.

I turn and catch Hael's eye. She urges her morleth up beside mine. It sticks out its long neck and takes a bite out of Knar's shoulder, ripping away a strip of coarse black fur to reveal the ugly scales beneath. Knar snorts and snaps back, but Hael and I yank their heads and wrestle the beasts into submission. Only then does Hael speak: "What is your plan, my king?"

She's very stiff, formal. Of course, Hael is always professional when on duty, but I cannot help wondering if we've forever lost the easy friendship we once shared, if we'll ever be able to trust one another again. It seems impossible.

"According to Jot, the riverway is blocked," I reply with equal rigidity. "We'll take the old Karthur Channel instead." Karthur used to be a swift, narrow river wending many miles deep through the Under Realm. Following a stirring three generations ago, it dried up, leaving behind a dry channel. It serves well enough as a highway between Mythanar and Hoknath but is rarely used in favor of the swifter river routes.

"It will be dark," Hael says. "Korh does not keep the channel lit."

"We have our own *lorst* stones. And the morleth will like it."

Hael cannot argue this fact. She nods. It feels good to have her back at my side, to know I have her support and strength. Despite everything, she's still the one I trust the most to have my back in a difficult situation. Still, a small part of me wishes I'd left her behind. I would be easier in my mind knowing Faraine was under Hael's watchful eye. But it's high time I gave Yok greater responsibilities. The boy has proven his courage if not his good sense. He's young. Time will season him into a true warrior, like his sister.

Besides, it would be cruel not to bring Hael on this mission. I know what Sul means to her . . . even if, in my personal opinion, she could do much better than that reprobate brother of mine.

After an hour's hard riding, we come to the mouth of the old channel. It's much broader but darker than the road we've been traveling. Hael gives the command, and my companions and I affix *lorst* stones to our helmets. Then I steer Knar's head toward the opening. As we draw near, however, he suddenly rolls his flame-ringed eyes, snorts, and stamps his hooves. I urge him again, and he shakes his whole body so hard, my bones rattle inside my armor. "What is it, boy?" I rub his scaly neck. "Do you smell something?"

He stands at the channel entrance, nostrils flared, ears pricked forward. Every muscle in his body is tensed.

"What's wrong?" Hael asks, driving her own nervous steed up beside mine.

"There's something in there." Tentatively, I sniff the air. Then I hiss through my teeth as a familiar sour stench fills my nostrils. "*Raog!*"

Hael curses. Turning in her saddle, she hastily barks for everyone to don their masks. I've already pulled mine out: a long, ugly beak filled with crushed *miraisis* blossoms. It fits tight over the lower half of my face, covering both mouth and nose.

"We cannot take the morleth in there," Hael says, dismounting. Her voice is muffled behind her own mask. "Morleth are mad enough as it is. Rabid morleth are not a problem I'm prepared to deal with."

I can't argue. Instead, I motion for my people to dismount. Immediately, the morleth slip out of this dimension, vanishing one after another in puffs of sulfur. Soon my five comrades and I stand at the mouth of the channel. The *lorst* stones on our helmets cast weird, long-beaked shadows behind us.

"These masks offer only three hours' worth of protection," Hael says warily.

"Do you want to go back?" I ask.

She does not answer, merely grips the hilt of her sword. I turn to the rest of the brave men and women standing with me. "I cannot predict what lies ahead, either on this road or when we reach Hoknath. If poison has taken the city, we must be prepared for the worst. I will not make any of you continue unless you are prepared to meet whatever lies ahead. If you prefer to return to Mythanar, tell me now."

The four of them exchange looks. They are my bravest and boldest—Toz, Wrag, Grir, and Lur—seasoned warriors with their share of scars. Captain Toz's small eyes spark beneath the stone ledge of his brow. "Let's go find the *guthakug* prince," he growls.

I answer with a grim grin, then step forward. I intend to lead the way, but Hael insists on taking the fore, and I don't argue with her. I've never traveled this winding road on foot before, and I'm unused to such complete darkness. There are no natural *lorst* stones in this stretch of cavern, and none have been set in place to light the way. Our own small lights gleam feebly against the weight of impenetrable black. Trolde though I am, I find it singularly oppressive. It isn't long before I wish I'd chosen a different route.

My light catches on something bright. It flickers in the tail of my eye, drawing my head sharply to the right. I turn. Blink. Shake my head and look again. The light catches on a twinkling necklace of delicate gems, strung around the neck of a woman. A woman whose torso lies at a strange angle among the stones on the side of the road. A woman whose lower half is entirely missing.

My blood turns to ice.

"Look, my king," Hael says, close to my elbow. She points.

I angle my *lorst* light to reveal another corpse. Then another and another. So many corpses. Torn apart. Strewn across the dry riverbed. "*Morar-juk!*" The words escape my lips in a little puff of air as my lungs constrict inside my chest.

"What happened to them?" Lur's voice is high and a little too loud in this terrible black stillness. "What did this?"

None of us can answer. So we continue silently through the horror until we come upon another body, different from the rest. A low, four-legged, blind monster with a bone-plated head and massive, rock-tearing claws.

"*Woggha,*" Hael says. She strides swiftly forward to inspect it and pulls a spear out from the base of its skull. Some brave soul had brought it down. Someone who died soon after, I suspect. No one escaped this tunnel. No one reached the safety of Mythanar.

"One cave devil couldn't have done all of this," Wrag says, turning his head this way and that, his light flashing across the corpses. He's right. *Woggha* are solitary creatures. It's rare to come upon more than one at a time. But this level of carnage could only be the work of many devils.

Where have they all gone? We find four more *woggha* corpses among the other dead. Not enough to account for the scope of this slaughter. I lift my gaze to the high walls surrounding us—all the various nooks and crevices. *Woggha* are like cave crickets: able to slip in anywhere at any time. They can find ways through what looks to the rest of us like solid rock. "Stay on alert," I say. "Weapons out. Be prepared to meet these fiends head-on."

We proceed cautiously, passing more dead bodies as we go. Too many to count with certainty, and only a few of them fighters. Most, from what I can discern in the dim light, were ordinary people. All of whom seemed to be fleeing in one direction: away from Hoknath.

Dread tightens in my gut.

At last, we come to the end of the channel. It opens onto a vast cave, bigger than the cavern of Mythanar. Lake Hoknath, still, dark, and deep, lies some fifty feet below us. Giant glowwurms build webs along the cavern ceiling. They gleam an eerie blue-green, lighting up the space—a very different light source from the crystal light of our home cavern, but beautiful. The glow illuminates the city itself—numerous gigantic stalactites which hang suspended above the lake. The city dwellings are carved directly into the stone with bridges suspended between them. I've journeyed here many times in my life. This city is familiar to me. But it's always been a bustling metropolis of activity and commerce.

Now, all is deathly still.

The water level has risen significantly since the last time I was here. The nearest of the giant stalactites is partway submerged, the lowermost streets and dwellings flooded. Large chunks have broken off one of the other massive formations and fallen into the lake, jutting out like the broken body of a dead giant. Overhead, patches of the glowwurm webbing have gone dark and dead. I see no sign of the great wurms themselves.

"There." Hael points. I look down to the water below us where dozens of small boats have been pulled onto the shore and abandoned. "They must have tried to evacuate," she says. I know she's referring to the dead in the tunnel.

With a grim nod, I scan the cavern wall, the places where riverways emerge, cascading down the rock to fill the lake below. One of those is the channel Sul traveled. I hope when the cave-in happened, the rushing water washed him out on this end, and he managed to keep himself from drowning.

"We'll take the boats," I say. "Search the shoreline. Then we'll venture into the city and see what we can find."

My people fall in line down the narrow stair. We split into three of the smaller crafts. Hael and I take one boat and set off at once for the nearest riverway cascade. Hael's shoulders are tense as she sits in the prow, using a paddle to navigate around large boulders. My eyes are peeled for any sign of my brother, but I can't help casting glances back over my shoulder at the ruinous city. It's so dead. So still. So like Dugorim was when we returned through the Between Gate. But Dugorim was a small mining town on the edge of my kingdom; Hoknath is a mighty center of the Under Realm, an ancient and densely populated city.

"My king."

Startled, I pull my gaze away from the city to meet Hael's wide, pale eyes. "Look down," she says.

Frowning, I cast a quick glance to the water below us. Then I look again, peer under the rippling dark surface. There are lights down there. *Lorst* stones, flickering with the last of their energy, like dying stars. Their glow illuminates a world underwater—a world of the dead. So many dead. Men, women. Children. Too many children, clutched in the arms of their parents. White bodies turned gray in death.

I cannot see far. The light is not strong enough. But I can see enough. "They jumped," I whisper, and look up at the hanging city. All the vitality seems to seep from my body. "Like Dugorim. They jumped to their deaths."

We should go. At once. If the poison is still in the air, our masks will not protect us much longer. We too will go mad, one by one, killing each other before we kill ourselves. We should go, get away from this place. Seal all the riverway entrances to Hoknath and never speak of the city again. We should . . . we must . . .

*"Aruk, hirak!"*

Captain Toz's growling voice yanks me back to the present. I turn to the boat he shares with Lur. Both of them gesticulate wildly to a point in front of my own craft. Frowning, I lean to one side, peer around Hael. A large chunk of broken rock juts from the water off to our left. I look again. There's a figure pulled up on top of that stone, lying there like a broken doll, one arm twisted oddly. It's Sul.

Hael gives an inarticulate cry. Without waiting for word from me, she angles our craft toward that rock and paddles with all her strength. We shoot across the dark water. "Sul!" I cry. My voice echoes hollowly in the dead stillness of the cavern. The figure on the rock does not stir.

Hael is wild in her efforts. She nearly steers our craft into the rock. At the last moment, she sticks out her paddle and pushes away so that our prow does not crash and splinter. "We need to look for a place to—" I start to say. Too late.

Hael leaps from the boat. Catching the side of the boulder, she hauls herself up and clambers to Sul's body. She slips, one foot hitting the water, but adjusts her grip and pulls into a more secure position. Reaching out, she presses her fingers to my brother's neck. "He's alive!" she calls, twisting to look back at me.

"Yes," a thin but silky voice responds, "but not for long if you keep shouting like that. You'll bring the rest of the cavern crashing down on our heads."

"*Morar-juk,*" I breathe, more like a prayer than a curse. That was unmistakably Sul. Alive, and well enough to muster his habitual sarcasm. I angle the boat around, craning for a better look.

Sul rolls his head. White hair trails over his sickly gray face. He blinks up at Hael. "My gods!" he says, the words thick on his tongue. "I never realized just how beautiful you are, Captain. You're such a formidable specimen, it's easy to overlook. But really, you're like a warrior angel come up from the deep heavens to avenge us poor souls above."

Hael shoots me a look over her shoulder. "He's delirious."

Sul grunts. "Very likely. I was just dreaming I was being kissed by an angel. Would you care to kiss me? Purely as a matter of study, of course. I'd like to see if it's the same."

"Shut up, Sul." My captain's trembling hands move over his body, searching for injuries. She looks at me again. "His arm is broken."

"Happened in the cave-in." Sul grimaces. "I thought for sure I was going to be pulverized to dust and then drowned for good measure. But the river shot me out into the lake and washed me up onto this stone. I suppose the Deeper Dark still has some purpose for me. Or maybe the other gods didn't want me hanging about heaven, seducing the angels. Either way—"

A hand bursts out of the water. Before I have time to bark a warning, it latches onto Hael's ankle. She gasps a vicious "*Juk!*"

Then she's yanked off her perch on the stone and dragged under the dark surface.

"Hael!" Sul cries, pushing himself painfully upright. "Vor, she can't—"

I don't wait to hear the rest. I'm already yanking off my helmet and breastplate and diving in after her.

# 15

## Faraine

I stand on my balcony at dimness, lean against the rail, and watch the crystals in the high cavern ceiling go out, one after another. Still, Vor does not return.

I try to pray. I've spent most of this day trying to pray, in fact. I used to be quite good at it. It's a skill one almost can't help acquiring while living among the sisters at Nornala Convent. There, in the high mountain air, so close to the stars, it feels as though prayers have but a short journey to make before reaching the goddess's waiting ears.

Down here, under stone? What god can possibly hear me other than Lamruil, the god of darkness? And him I don't know. I would be afraid to direct any prayers his way.

Eventually, the cavern is plunged into the Under Realm's version of night. It's not as dark as one would expect a subterranean world to be. The city streets below are bright with lanterns, and my own room boasts several *lorst* crystals in silver sconces, and white moonfire flickers on the hearth. I miss the orange warmth of fires back home, but it's bright enough.

Still, I cannot bring myself to go back inside and sit before that fire. I remain where I am, gazing out over the palace wall, down into the city. Hoping. Wishing. *Willing.*

I'd managed to drag a little more information out of Yok concerning the king's mission. He'd told me no word had come from Hoknath City since the quake, and Vor, concerned, had sent his brother and two other messengers to investigate. The two messengers had returned with news of a cavern collapse, while Sul was lost in the river.

Vor is close to his brother. I felt the love between them during their brief stay in Beldroth. My heart aches for Vor, for the fear he must be experiencing. I wish I could do something. Anything. I hate feeling so helpless.

My fingers toy listlessly with my crystal on its chain. I should give up this futile watch, should retire to my bed, try to sleep. Not that it matters. Lusterling will come eventually, and I will face more lonely hours, more helpless solitude. Meanwhile, Vor is out there somewhere in this dark realm, risking his life. Oh, why could the gods not have gifted me with a true power? Something I might use to help this man I've come to . . . to . . . Who I've dared to . . .

Heat flares against my chest. I catch my breath, frown, and look down. My crystal lies in its accustomed place above my heart. My gown is a trolde creation with rather less bodice than I'm used to. No fabric between my flesh and the stone, therefore no protection from a second and equally unexpected flare of heat. Hastily, I grab the chain, pull the pendant away from my skin. It swings in the air, blue and clear. But in its heart, something red flickers. Like a spark.

I tilt my head and lift my other hand to touch the stone with a tentative fingertip. It doesn't burn. It's cool and smooth as ever. Even that flicker of red is gone. Now, however, I feel that same strange sensation I've felt twice before—a *pull*. My brow creases. For a moment I stand uncertain, undecided.

The next I'm in motion. I leave the balcony behind, cross the room to the door. I'd shut myself in when coming back from the courtyard, refusing to admit even Yrt when she brought my supper. Hael would have insisted, but Yok yielded to my demands for solitude and sent Yrt on her way.

The boy is out there now. I can feel him and all his pent-up, nervous energy. He may be trolde, but he's young, and has not yet learned to keep his emotions in check like his elder sister. I hesitate, considering what I'm about to do. The necklace flares again with that strange spark of red light, the pull so strong, I stagger two paces and nearly fall against the door. What is this? What is drawing me so inexplicably, so inexorably?

A little growl in my throat, I grab the door latch, wrench the door open. Yok leans against the wall just outside. At my appearance, he pulls himself together, fumbling with his lance. "Princess!" he gasps, and halfway salutes before thinking better of it. "Do you need anything? Shall I call the maid back with your meal?"

I look at him, my mouth open, my heart thudding. Then: "Out."

"Pardon?"

"Out. I'm going out."

He blinks three times before managing to ask, "Why?"

"Is it your place to question me, Guardsman Yok?"

His pale trolde skin flushes lavender. I sense a prickling of shame. Good. I can use shame.

"I intend to take a walk," I continue. "I am tired of these same walls. I need new sights and a chance to stretch my legs." I look up, hold the boy's gaze hard. Daring him to contradict me. Daring him to shove me back into the room and bar my way. He wants to protest. I feel his resistance. But I won't back down.

At last, Yok swallows hard. The muscles of his throat constrict. Then he nods.

"Good." I step out into the hall. It suddenly seems very large, and I very small. I'm like a rabbit loosed from the snare, too frightened to make a dash for freedom.

Then my crystal warms again, almost too hot to handle. The flare recedes quickly, leaving behind only that unmistakable *pull*. My mouth set, I step into motion. Yok utters a little grunt and hastens behind me, armor creaking. I don't bother looking back. He'll stick close to my heels, no doubt, my determined young protector.

Closing my eyes, I concentrate on the inner vibration of the crystal. Now and then, I peer through my lashes just to make certain I'm not about to run into anything or anyone. The crystal leads me true, however. The more I lean into its guidance, the better progress I make. The dimness hour is late, and we encounter only a few tall, imposing trolde figures as we go. One of them barks out a series of harsh words at the sight of me, but I ignore both him and Yok's response. I simply march on, following my invisible guide.

It leads me at last to a large octagonal chamber. Water runs down each of the high, sheer walls, catches in trenches set into the floor, and runs off in channels away from the room. I step into the echoing space. Condensation beads on my skin. "What is this place?" I ask, spinning slowly to take it in. There are patterns on the walls, beneath the running water. From some angles, they look totally random, abstract. But as I shift my view, images begin to appear—visions of kings and monsters, of dragons and palaces. All caught in ancient stone beneath the ageless flow of water and time.

"This is the upper chapel," Yok says, his voice low, hushed. Reverent. He hunches his shoulders nervously. "We shouldn't be here, Princess."

I don't want to intrude where I'm not welcome. Biting my lip, I take a step back, prepared to retreat. But then, I hear something. A drone, deep and low beneath the sound of falling water. A sound heard not with the ears, but with the bones. Another pulse emanates from my crystal. I turn sharply to see a cleft in one of the walls, a narrow crack around which water flows. Crystals sprout around the edges of the opening, creating an impression of a sideways, toothy leer. Beyond, all is pitch black.

My heart rate quickens. Even as I stare into that darkness, my necklace flares again. The pull intensifies. "Where does that lead?" I ask, pointing.

Yok looks where I've indicated, his brow puckered. "That way leads to the *grakanak-gaakt*. The Altar to the Dark."

A shiver travels up my spine. "A holy place?" I ask.

Yok nods. By the way his soul shivers and ripples, I can tell he's frightened. Of what, exactly? I cross to the gash in the wall, ignoring his whispered protests, and peer into the shadows. It's no use; I cannot see anything. But from here, that deep, bone-grinding vibration is stronger than before. A hum, a drone. Musical and yet unmelodic. As deep and dark as the compressed stone of the world's foundations. My crystal flares again. The pull is so strong now, it's all I can do not to lurch into that opening, fall into that darkness.

Yok appears at my elbow. He puts out a hand to bar my way. "You can't go down there, Princess."

"Why not?" I cast him a quick look. "Are humans not permitted to worship Lamruil?"

"*Morar tor Grakanak.*"

"Pardon?"

"That is the true name of our god. The one you call Lamruil. *Morar tor Grakanak.*"

I clear my throat then give it a try. It's such a harsh, growling sound, my vocal cords cannot manage it. I sound as though I'm coughing up phlegm.

Yok shakes his head, his expression desperate. "Please, Princess."

"If I cannot visit his house, how can I learn of your god?"

"Why do you need to learn of the Deeper Dark? You have your own gods."

"True. My god is Nornala, Goddess of Unity. I've dedicated my life to her service." I tip my head, raise an eyebrow, and hold Yok's gaze. "It is in service to my goddess that I must learn the ways of my husband and his people."

This startles Yok. Another burst of confusion ripples out from him. I can feel him trying to shape a protest, trying to find the words to insist that I am *not* the Shadow King's bride. But he's not sure, and my confidence has put him off-balance.

"You'll find it too dark down there," he tries finally, desperately.

"I'm not afraid of the dark." That's a lie. I am afraid. Because the darkness in this world is so much darker than anything I experienced in my own. Here, the darkness lurks, always just on the edges of vision, ready to overtake and overcome, with no hope of a future sunrise to drive it back into submission. In this world, light is the unnatural state of being. In this world, light is the perversion. In this world, darkness must and will one day reign supreme.

But the pull of my crystal is strong, intensifying along with my need to understand, to know the source. What other choice do I have? Give up this little quest, return to my rooms, and fall back into senseless, endless, hellish waiting?

No. If the dark must devour me, so be it. Better to die in search of answers.

This time, when I approach the crack, Yok makes no effort to restrain me. He mutters in angry troldish, but I ignore him. Holding my crystal out before me, I slide first one foot, then the other. My toes find a sharp edge. A tread. It's a stairway. Leading down, down, *down* . . .

It takes every ounce of courage I possess to continue.

One hand touching the rough and uneven wall for support, I begin my descent. One step. Two steps. My crystal flares. Three steps, four. My crystal flares again, brighter. More sustained now. Only it's not a glow that illuminates or reveals. I'm not even certain I'm actually *seeing* anything, not with my eyes. This light is visible only to my gods-gift. As far as I can tell, Yok cannot discern it at all but follows blindly behind me.

Nevertheless, my confidence grows. Soon, I'm surrounded in red aura. When I close my eyes, it's brighter still, and though perhaps I'm only imagining it, I believe I can *feel* the shape of the stones around me, clearer than sight.

Down below, the grinding, growling drone intensifies. Are those words I'm hearing? Harsh, troldish words. A sort of chant. A prayer? The lower I descend, the more I'm certain of it. It's eerie and more than a little terrifying.

I reach the bottom of the stairwell. A sudden sense of space opens before me. I cannot see, not with my eyes. But the red glow of my crystal ripples out, revealing to my gods-gift a cavernous hall. I feel it, hear it, smell it, breathe it. It's as clear in my head as any image. Boulders of all different shapes and sizes line up in twelve perfect rows in front of me. Or rather, on second inspection, not boulders. *People.* Troldefolk. Both big and small. Bent over in attitudes of abject prayer, faces pressed into the ground, arms outstretched before them. They wear no clothing, but every inch of their skin seems to be covered in a thin layer of dust. Or is it . . . stone?

The worshippers all point the same direction, facing the far end of the hall. There stands a cluster of crystals. Seven in total, the tallest just over four feet, jutting at strange angles. Their polished planes gleam, pulsing like my own pendant with a spark of inner life which radiates from their cores. That pulse washes over the people in wave after rippling wave. My stone responds to the pulse. I feel other responses as well—in the walls surrounding me, in the jagged ceiling overhead, in the floor beneath my feet.

For a moment, I'm so awestruck, I do not notice the two figures standing beside the crystals. One of them is much taller than the other, a massive being with shoulders like a mountain. His long white hair gleams in the strange unlight of the crystals. Though his skin is covered in hard rockhide, he is somehow still beautiful. Chiseled and powerful, like a demigod of stone.

Beside him is another figure. A woman. Smaller than the priest, but no less imposing. Like him she is naked—what use is modesty in such utter darkness? No one can see her, not even me save by the strange nonseeing perception of my gods-gift. But she is undeniably beautiful. Statuesque and shapely and strong. Like the man, her hair falls free down her back, shining like a waterfall. She kneels before the cluster of seven crystals and holds her left hand above them, dripping a steady stream of blood. Blood which, at first, I think she holds cupped in her palm.

Then I realize: her hand is sliced open. The blood is fresh, flowing from her veins.

Even as I watch, the man steps to her other side, takes hold of her right hand, and holds it out above the crystals as well. She does not flinch as he opens her fingers, takes a black stone knife, and draws its blade across her flesh. Blood bubbles up, spills over, dripping in a fresh stream onto the crystals, which flare and pulse with every drop that falls.

My own hand aches as my grip on my pendant tightens. I shouldn't be seeing this. This ceremony, this rite . . . it's not meant to be seen. It's meant to be performed in the dark. But I cannot tear my gods-gifted gaze away from the woman. She sways in time to the priest's deep, chanting voice; in time to her own dripping blood. The crystals blaze brighter and brighter, hotter and hotter. My little stone heats so much, my hand quivers with pain.

Something is happening. The pulse intensifies, beating through my outer layers of awareness, down into my blood and bones. Something wraps around my heart—like a layer of magma, engulfing and then swiftly cooling into hard stone. My chest is suddenly heavy, weighted down. I press a hand against it, nails digging into my skin, as though I can reach through and tear that stone away.

Suddenly, the woman opens her eyes.

She cannot see me. It's too dark.

But somehow, impossibly . . . she looks directly at me.

I gasp and open my eyes. I'd not realized they were closed. I'd not realized how deeply I'd sunk into my gods-gifted perceptions. Now, abruptly, I'm plunged into darkness so all-consuming, my whole being spasms with terror. I stagger back, choking on a cry that comes out a whimper. Even that is swallowed up in the priest's reverberating drone.

Strong hands grip me under the elbows. "Princess?" Yok's voice, low in my ear.

I turn to him, clutch at his arms in my terror. "Get me out of here!" I hiss. I don't know if my bodyguard can hear me. I'm whimpering, pathetic. But he takes hold of my shoulders and guides me back to the stair. I cannot perceive the steps anymore and fall over my own feet. With a grunt, Yok picks me up, tosses me over his shoulder. I can do nothing but cling to his mail shirt, squeezing my eyes tightly shut.

At last, we emerge at the top of the stair into the *lorst* light. Only then does Yok set me on my feet, propping me up with both hands. "Princess? Are you all right?"

I cannot answer. Pushing away from him, I lean against the wall, desperate to catch my breath. Deep inside the stone, I feel the resonance of the crystals, still pulsing. Reaching out with my godsgift, I try to grab hold of their resonance, to steady myself, to purge away some of this pain. Instead, the stone wrapped around my heart tightens.

"I knew it." Yok runs a nervous hand through his hair so that it sticks up all over his head. "Humans aren't meant for this kind of worship. They're not meant for the Deeper Dark."

I tilt my gaze up at him. My vision swims, blurs. "Did you see?"

"See?" The boy frowns. "Princess, one doesn't *see* in the Dark."

I blink stupidly. My head throbs. I cannot for the life of me think of some other way to phrase my question, to ask if he perceived and understood the strange ritual of blood I'd stumbled upon. When I open my mouth, the only words that will emerge are "Get me back. To my room. Now, Yok. Please."

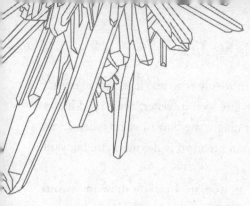

# 16
.......
*Vor*

Darkness and cold shock my senses.

I open my eyes and at first see nothing but white bubbles bursting before my vision. Movement draws my attention. I turn toward it and spy the *lorst* stone affixed to Hael's helmet flashing wildly. Several feet underwater, Hael grips the side of the boulder. Only the tremendous strength in her arms keeps her from being dragged down into the lake depths.

A stone hand latches hold of her leg. When Hael turns her head, angling her *lorst* downward, I see to whom that hand belongs. It's a woman. Slender. Older. Mostly bald save for a few white hairs floating about her face. Fine lines wrinkle her cheeks, surround her eyes and mouth, but those lines are etched in skin as hard as stone. Though her mouth is open wide, no air bubbles escape. She's not breathing. Neither is she drowning. She stares up from the abyss, and her eyes are the only thing about her not stone. They are bright with madness.

I don't have time to think. Hael won't last long, not with her armor weighing her down. I move my arms and legs, propel myself forward. Most trolde do not fare well in water; their solid bones tend to sink. But my mother taught me how to swim when I was young, and I've enough human blood to make me more buoyant than my fellow troldefolk.

I reach Hael and the stone woman. I cannot draw my sword underwater, so I simply grab the woman's arm. She shifts her mad gaze from Hael to me. Darkness swirls in the depths of her pale eyes. I recognize that darkness—the *raog* poison which has stolen her sanity. I know the pain of it, the agony she suffers. I would offer my sympathy were she not actively trying to murder my friend.

I take hold of her forearm with both hands. It's slender, almost delicate, but solid stone all the way through. Summoning all my strength, I bend, twist, and finally . . . *break*. The limb snaps in half, hand and wrist still attached to Hael's leg. The rest of the woman's body sinks down beyond the glow of the *lorst* light. I catch one final glimpse of her mad eyes flashing up at me just before she disappears.

Then I kick as hard as I can for the surface. Hael still holds tight to the rock. She's not pulling herself up. Is she too weak from her struggle? Does she not have air left in her lungs? She's going to lose her hold, sink as fast as the stone woman if I don't act fast.

My lungs burn with a desperate need for air. I ignore them, push myself closer to Hael, using her *lorst* light to guide my hands as I seek the straps of her breastplate. I must pull it off, lighten her load. I must—

Something grabs me by the back of my shirt.

The next moment, I'm yanked to the surface of the lake, gasping in a painfully glorious lungful of air. "There, Big King!" Toz's voice growls in my ear. "I've got you." My great trolde captain flings me onto the rock beside him. I lie where I land, only just able to gasp, "Hael!"

I needn't have worried. Toz leans into the water, grips Hael under her shoulders, and hauls her up next, dropping her beside me. I roll to make room.

"Have a care, brother!" Sul yelps when I nearly knock him into the lake. He grabs me with his good hand, and I grip him by the shoulder.

"I'm glad you're alive, Sul." The words rush foolishly from my lips even as I struggle for another gasp of air.

"I'm glad I'm alive too, Vor. If nothing else, just to witness that feat of kingly prowess you just performed. Gods above! Did you really snap the woman's arm in two? You're a mighty beast, brother mine."

The relief in my heart is so real, so raw. I squeeze his shoulder again, and he manages a ghastly grin before turning from me. His brow puckers. His smile disappears into a grimace. Cradling his broken arm against his stomach, he inches across the rock. "Hael?" He leans over my captain's body, pushes wet strands of hair out of her face. "Take a breath, will you? Come on, I need to hear you—"

Her body convulses. A sudden gush of water fountains from her lungs, splashing Sul in the face. He curses but doesn't draw back. Instead, using his one good arm, he rolls her onto her side, patting her back until she's finished heaving. When she's through, he helps her sit upright. Not once does he stop touching her, his good hand moving from her shoulder to her arm to her back.

Interesting. Very interesting.

Shaking water from my eyes, I turn from them and peer over the edge of the rock. Lur is close, still in the craft she shared with Toz, and holding my empty boat by a line. Grir and Wrag are on their way to us, paddling hard. I raise a hand to let them know we're all right. They nod but don't slow their progress.

"What happened, Big King?" Toz asks, looming over the three of us. His big frame dominates the space. "What was down there?"

I shudder. "I . . . I think it was someone who . . ." The words don't want to come. I force them out. "I think it was someone who had attempted *va-jor*."

"*Va-jor*?" Toz scratches the back of his big hard head. "What the hells is *va-jor*?"

Hael, however, sits up straighter, turning sharply to meet my gaze. "Do you mean to say . . . ?" A shudder ripples from the top of her head all the way down her spine. She wraps her arms around her middle. "Do you mean the dead down there aren't really dead?"

"Oh, they're dead all right," Sul says darkly. "I got an eyeful when I was washed out of the riverway. It's like Dugorim all over again."

I know Sul and Hael remember as vividly as I the aftermath of horror we'd seen in that town on the edge of my kingdom. But this is different. This is something more, something worse. *Raog* poison turns the mind to violence and self-destruction. The woman in the lake was certainly poisoned. But she was also encased in stone. Stone which kept her alive, or semi-alive, even underwater. Long after she should have died and been freed from her madness.

"My king," Hael says suddenly, her voice ragged. I turn to her. She motions with one hand. I touch the lower half of my face only to realize that, in my haste to remove my helmet before diving into the lake, I had also dislodged my mask. I'm breathing the unfiltered air of Hoknath even now.

"It's all right," Sul says, catching my eye. "The poison has already dissipated. Otherwise, I'd be rabid as a *woggha* myself by now."

I study my brother's face, searching for signs of the *raog*. While his eyes are a bit hollow and sunken with pain, he doesn't look poisoned. His gaze is sharp and clear as ever.

"We need to get you back," Hael says. Her own mask is knocked askew and can't be doing her much good anymore. She pushes it back into place and, after a momentary struggle, manages to get to her feet. "We need to get you both to Madame Ar as quickly as possible."

"I won't argue with that," my brother says.

I rise, brace my feet, and turn toward the hanging city. There's something out there, something . . . I can't quite describe it. Like a pulse. Deep down in my gut. A vibration, low, guttural. As though the city itself utters an agonized moan.

I narrow my eyes, searching out the lowest point of the nearest stalactite. That is the site of the Low Temple of Zoughat. I've worshipped there when visiting Hoknath on royal progress. It's half-submerged in the lake now due to flooding, but I'm certain—absolutely certain, though with no reason I can articulate—that I will find the answers I seek there. The pulse emanates from that point.

"You go," I say, without looking at the others. "Hael, take Sul, Grir, Wrag, and Lur. Toz, you're with me."

"What are you intending, my king?" Hael demands.

I set my jaw. "We do not yet know the full extent of the damage in Hoknath. We must venture into the city, find out what we can."

"You and Toz? Alone? In that *raog*-filled ruin? Quite probably crawling with cave devils?" Sul snorts. He's managed to get to his feet and sways heavily, holding his broken arm against his chest. "That sounds like a winning strategy to me. Wish I'd thought of it myself."

"I'm not leaving you, Vor," Hael growls. "Where you go, I go."

I catch my captain's eye. Her loyalty truly is unmatched in all the Under Realm. How could I have doubted her? How could I have pushed her away all this time? I wish I could say something to her now; let her know that I've forgiven her failures—that indeed, there was nothing to forgive all along. Now is not the time, however.

"Fine," I say brusquely instead. "Hael, you're with me. The rest of you, get the prince back to Mythanar as fast as you can."

Sul studies me closely. When I finally turn and meet his gaze, his face is oddly contemplative. "That pulse . . ." He lets the words trail away a moment before finally finishing with "You hear it too, don't you?"

I nod.

"It's been singing in the stones and the water since I got here. I heard it best while I was unconscious. I felt it trying to . . . to pull me in."

"Do you know what it is?"

He shakes his head. "But I have a guess."

My chest tightens. "Does it mean someone is alive? The priestesses, perhaps."

"I don't think so. At least, not in the way you mean."

Captain Toz protests my plan of action almost as vehemently as Hael. In the end, I agree to take him and Hael with me, leaving the rest to watch over Sul. They will wait for us at the channel entrance, under orders to head for home if we don't return within the hour. They're not to come looking for us. They're to hasten to Mythanar and assemble a search party.

"Of course, sure, absolutely," Sul says in tones that imply the opposite. When I growl at him to heed me, he raises his one good hand, protesting, "When do I ever not?"

Hael takes her place at the prow of our craft while Toz sits in the stern, his big arms powering each stroke of the paddle. I sit in the center, wishing I'd insisted on taking the other paddle. Instead, I can do nothing but serve as ballast, trying not to let my gaze be drawn back again and again to the images of death under the water. I can't help it. There are so many of them, lost to the ultimate despair of *raog*. Broken and drowned in dark, glassy reflection beneath their once-magnificent city. What had it been like for these people? To survive the initial stirring only to smell the poison filling the air? To hear the savage cries of their neighbors erupting in the streets just before the madness overtook their own minds and bodies? What would desperation drive them to do under such circumstances?

What would I do, had it been Mythanar and not Hoknath?

The deep moan of the city continues to sound on the edge of my awareness. The nearer we draw, the louder it grows. It ripples on the water, pulses out from the temple. I want to turn back. Something tells me I'm being drawn inexorably into a dark knowledge I will wish I'd never learned. But I cannot turn my back on Hoknath now. These people—both the dead and the undead in the water below—deserve to have their story known, however dark that story may be.

The lowest point of the temple is entirely submerged by floodwaters. Hael guides our craft to a balcony as though it were a pier. We secure our craft and climb over the rail. The door is open, and all is black as pitch inside. Like all temples devoted to the Deeper Dark, there are no windows, no lanterns, no braziers, no light sources of any kind. To walk in the House of the Dark is to walk in Darkness. But we have our *lorst* stones. Though it feels sacrilegious to wear them into the temple, we are not here to worship. We step inside. The droning is more distinct than before, vibrating in the floor under our feet. Sometimes the pulse is so strong, it causes us to stumble and catch ourselves against the wall.

"What is this?" Toz wonders out loud. "It sounds like the *umog vulug*, the prayersong at the turn of *grak-va*."

"This isn't *grak-va*," Hael says, her voice low. "This is deeper dark than *grak-va*."

"What dark is deeper than *grak-va*?"

Neither Hael nor I answer. Hael leads the way, her footsteps slower than before but determined. We come to a crack in the wall. All three of us feel the intensity of the pulse issuing from within. This is it then. Beyond is the source. It's strong and strangely . . . attractive.

I move to enter, but Hael holds up her hand. "Me first, my king," she says. She's not asking permission. With a sigh and a short nod, I step back. She ducks through, taking her *lorst* with her. It's much darker without her light. Toz and I exchange uneasy glances. Then, drawing a breath, I bow my head and slip through the crack after her.

I emerge into a hall. I cannot see much, only that which the little sphere of light surrounding Hael illuminates. Otherwise, the darkness is impenetrable. I feel the largeness of the space, the high ceiling. My breath seems to echo as I hasten to Hael's side. The drone is louder here. Deeper.

"There." Hael points. I turn with her and just discern a flash of red. It's there a moment then gone again. Another pulse comes, another flash. This time I see it: crystals. Seven, arranged in a circle. *Urzul* stones unless I'm much mistaken. And what is that in the center of the circle? That broken, awful shape . . .

The blood freezes in my veins.

"*Morar-juk!*" Toz's voice growls as he steps in close behind us. "This must be the holiest place I've ever been."

It's certainly the darkest. But I cannot say it feels holy. "Stay close," I growl, and take a step forward. My hand and foot both collide with stone. I stop, drawing a short breath. Then, slowly, I angle my head to better direct my *lorst* light and see what it is I've struck.

It's a man. A trolde man, seated cross-legged. Wide shoulders, heavily bowed. Head sunk to his breast. Only a few strands of white hair still cling to his bare scalp. He's covered from head to toe in stone.

I stop short. It's not as though I didn't expect this. But expectation is not the same as seeing. I tilt my light to get a better sense of the man, of his features. The stone is too thick. It's obscured all definition, leaving only a vague impression of who he used to be. I've seen men in *grak-va* before, at the lowest point of the holy cycle, when the faithful enter into deep meditation, becoming one with the stone of our birth. But this is something more. This is the holy state of which Umog Targ preaches, the oneness to which my stepmother aspires.

This is the true state of stone—the *va-jor*.

"*Morar tor Grakanak!*" Hael breathes beside me. I turn to her, see her gaze. She's rapt with wonder. "It's a miracle," she says. "A miracle of the Dark."

My stomach clenches. She's wrong. It's no miracle; it's perversion. But I'm not about to enter into theological debate with her. A growl rumbling in my throat, I continue, making for the crystals on the far side of the chamber. Every few steps, I find another trolde just like the first one—deeply encased in stone.

How had they done this? I've heard Targ preach upon occasion but always dismissed him as a ranting madman. I'd never believed it possible to achieve true *va-jor*. But as I turn my head, my *lorst* light flickers across dozens upon dozens of indistinct figures. There may be a hundred worshippers here, or more. Did they gather to perform the ceremony when the poison first began to spread? Had they deemed this end better than violence?

I pick my way through the crowd. With every step I take, the crystals send out another pulse, rippling under my feet, through my bones, straight to my beating heart. Though their strength is fading, they still have enough power to draw me toward them, closer and closer. At last, I'm near enough to see that which lies in the center of the circle.

A body.

A woman.

She is not stone. Her skin is still soft, pliable. She did not enter into *va-jor* in her final moments. She died here. Bleeding out. Bleeding from numerous wounds.

They bound her. By the pulsing red light of the crystals, I see signs of her struggle, the abrasions at her wrists and ankles. She fought hard against whoever did this to her. But she fought in vain.

Gods above and below! She wasn't very old. And beautiful. So beautiful. But of course, she was. Who would offer less than the most beautiful as a sacrifice to a god? Because that's what she is. A sacrifice. Her body opened and bled dry. Her heart and other vital organs displayed on the crystals around her. Though she's been dead for some time now, her face is still twisted in horror.

"What in the Deeper Dark is this?" Toz whispers at my shoulder.

Hael, on my other side, answers, "To enter *va-jor* requires sacrifice. But . . ." She turns to me, her eyes stricken.

"What, Hael?" I ask. I can barely speak around the bile in my throat. "What do you know?"

"It is the teaching of the Children of *Arraog*," she whispers. "To enter *va-jor* requires a blood sacrifice. A *willing* blood sacrifice."

The three of us survey the tortured remains within that circle. There is no chance this woman offered herself willingly.

I turn in place slowly, trying to see out into the dark hall, to get some sense of the scope of this space, of the number of worshippers gathered here. I think of the stone woman in the lake. She had not joined these people in their dark ceremony. It's as though the pulse of *va* radiated beyond this chamber to catch others in its dark energy.

"The ceremony of *va-jor* is sacred," Hael says, her voice tremulous. "It is meant to be salvation. For all."

"This is not salvation." I turn harshly upon her, my lips drawn back in a snarl. "This is profane. Those people out there, out in the water? They're trapped. Still mad. Still suffering from *raog*, without even the relief of death."

"If the sacrifice were performed correctly—"

I don't wait to hear what else she will say. Turning from the desecrated body, I make my way back through the living statues. The only survivors of Hoknath's ruin.

I feel as though I can see the ultimate fate of Mythanar unfolding before my mind's eye.

# 17

## Faraine

There's a stone wrapped around my heart.

I lie on my narrow bed, atop the piled furs. Above me, the ceiling is jagged with stalactites. There's no canopy, no embroidered silver stars. Just me and that heavy, serrated stone, cast in gloomy extremes of shadow and highlight by the moonfire on my hearth. It's all too easy to imagine those sharp, toothlike protrusions breaking, falling. Skewering me through the eye. Yet, I go on lying here. Over and over again, I imagine hairline cracks forming, followed by a growl as the stone begins to give. The little wobble right before the fall. And me. Immobile, unable to lift a hand to protect myself. Unable to roll away. Trapped beneath my inevitable doom.

My right hand grips my pendant, squeezing harder and harder. It doesn't matter. Ever since escaping that dark chapel, I've not been able to feel its resonance. It's been hours now since I staggered into this room, shut the door in Yok's face, and leaned heavily against the wall. I'd struggled then to find the life of the crystals buried deep inside. Only silence answered.

I flatten my hand against my breast. My heart feels so heavy! So impossibly heavy, as though it will break right through me, fall out between my shattered shoulder blades, and hit the floor below with a thud. Summoning all my strength, I manage to roll onto my side and sit up. Both hands grip the edge of the bed even as sweat trickles down my forehead, my neck, between my breasts. I'm shivering, but my skin feels as though it's on fire.

It's the crystals. They did this to me. Those *urzul* stones down in the chapel. Blood-fed and pulsing with dark intensity. Their pulse petrified my heart. I don't understand how. I don't have to understand. I simply know.

*Oh, gods!* I would give anything for relief! My hand fumbles for my pendant again, raising it to the level of my eyes. I search intently for some spark of life inside. It's too small. Too weak. I need . . .

I need a larger crystal.

A whimper on my lips, I push up from the bed, sway, catch my balance. Shuddering, I cross the room, barefoot. I wear nothing but a sleeveless white shift that only reaches my knees. The skin of my exposed limbs prickles with cold, but I don't stop to grab a dressing gown. I need to get out of here. Now.

I grab the latch, turn it, throw open my door. Light from a near *lorst* sconce falls on Yok's face. The poor boy starts from his doze and blinks stupidly. "Princess!" he gasps. His gaze runs down my body then back up to my face. A flush stains his cheeks. "Princess, is . . . is something wrong?"

I cross my arms, hands knotting tight. "I wish to go to the gardens."

Yok's brow wrinkles. "Now?"

I nod.

"Princess, you cannot go out again. Not this dimness."

"The room is stifling. I need to walk."

The boy shakes his head, his soft features hardening. "I'm sorry, but you must stay in your room. At least until lusterling. It's . . . I believe it's what the king would want."

"What does it matter what the king wants?" My voice sounds almost too harsh to belong to me. I can't help it. The stone around my heart is grinding, agonizing. If I don't find help soon, I don't know what will happen. "You were sent to serve me, not him."

Yok shakes his head. "I always serve the king, in whatever way I can." He tips his chin. "The king bade me keep you safe, so that's what I will do. I . . . I shouldn't have let you venture into the *grakanak-gaakt*. I'm not going to make that mistake again."

I study him silently. Try as I might, I cannot get a sense of him, not with my gods-gift locked down. But I don't need my gift to see the resolute loyalty in his face. Were I not so desperate, I'd admire the boy. As it is . . .

With a little smile and gentle sigh, I lean out of the room, keeping one hand pressed to the wall inside the door. "You're a good soul, Guardsman Yok," I say, reaching out and taking him by the hand. He tries to pull back, but I firm my grip. "I am lucky to be in your care."

With that, I send *calm* into him. Yok's eyes widen. He opens his mouth, begins to speak, to shout. Before more than a strangled sound can emerge, he topples to the ground, unconscious at my feet.

I stare down at him, panting softly. The boy deserved better than this. By now the pain in my chest is so great I can scarcely think of anything else. But I can't leave an unconscious guard's body lying outside my door either.

I grasp his ankles and drag. He's heavier than he looks. It takes everything I have to get him into the bedroom. Any moment, I expect someone to turn the corner at the end of the passage and catch me in the act. No one comes, however, and I manage to get him inside. Then I draw the door shut and slip silently away down the passage.

I must find that garden. I must find that circle of tall crystals. I must find relief. If it's the last thing I do.

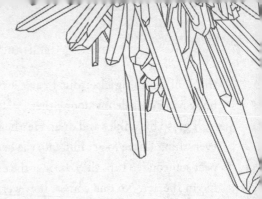

# 18
·······
## Vor

We are a solemn, silent party as we ride our morleth back up through the city late that dimness.

Toz did his best to communicate what we'd found in the temple. Hael held her tongue, and I could not bear to speak of it. Not yet. Toz's report was enough. No one spoke unless necessary for the whole journey home. Even Sul was uncharacteristically silent. He rode on the bow of Hael's saddle, wrapped tight in her arms, his head thrown back against her shoulder, his eyes closed. He looks very gray and grim by the time we reach the palace.

I dismount Knar, allowing the beast to slip away to his own dimension, and hasten to help Sul down. As soon as her feet are on the ground, Hael reaches for him, her manner almost possessive. "Take him to the infirmary at once," I tell her.

"Yes, my king. I've got him," Hael says, and turns for the steps. She pauses, however, and looks back at me. "What about you? Madame Ar should check you over, make certain you haven't inhaled any *raog*."

I shudder. But I know I don't have *raog* in my system. Not this time at least. "Don't worry, Hael. I'll be along shortly. I have something I must see to first."

Hael gives me a shrewd look. I don't like it and turn away hastily to speak a word to Toz and the others. I urge them all to report at once to Ar, then hasten up the front steps and into the palace before anyone can question me. My face must be grim indeed. The household folk I meet as I stride through the winding corridors avert their eyes or bow their heads. I spare none of them a word or a look. My steps carry me swiftly to the west wing of the palace. I know exactly where I'm going.

Fury burns in my breast. It's been growing by the hour, ever since I looked upon that dead girl in the circle of crystals. The devastation of Hoknath was bad enough, but that particular horror? That one will remain with me all the days of my life.

I come to a certain door, brace myself before it, and pound three times with my fist. The sound echoes hollowly against the stones, underscored by my own hard breathing. Perhaps I should think better of this, should wait to have this encounter when I'm in a calmer state of mind. But I cannot wait. Not a moment more.

The door opens. A wide-eyed child peers up at me. Her mouth opens in a little circle of terror. "Where is your mistress?" I demand.

The child swallows hard. "The queen has given orders that she's not to be dis—"

I push through with a growl. Roh's set of rooms are humble indeed, scarcely what one would expect from a dowager queen. Indeed, if one didn't know any better, it would be easy to believe this was the cell of a priestess. All is dark, with only a single *lorst* crystal to illuminate the whole of the space. By its light, I see my stepmother seated before a stone washbasin. She's cleaning her hands. Slowly, methodically.

She looks up at me. Her eyes flash in the crystal glow. "So, Vor. You're back."

I stare at her hands. At the two great cuts slicing across both her palms. Even as I watch, even as she lifts them from the water, blood wells again. She picks up a cloth, grips it tight. A blue stain seeps through the white.

"What have you done?" I demand.

She tilts her head at me. "What have *you* done? Have you found my son?"

"He is home. Safe."

Roh lets out a little breath, then lifts one bleeding hand to make a holy sign. "Praise be to the Deeper Dark. And the people of Hoknath? What word of them?"

I stare at her. In that eerie pale glow, I see the sacrificed woman again. Her desecrated body. Her blood spilled to feed the *urzul* stones. "I think you know," I growl. "I think you know what happened in Hoknath. Did Targ have anything to do with it?"

Roh purses her lips and turns to her basin once more. She takes the cloth, dabs gently at her wounds, and only a faint tightness around her eyes reveals her pain. "You'll have to be more specific, Vor. I cannot read your mind and prefer not to speak in riddles."

"The ceremony. The *va-jor.*" I stride a little closer, my hands trembling with the urge to grab her by the shoulders, to force her to look at me. "They were stone, Roh. Solid stone. From the inside out."

"Really?" she looks up sharply. "What of the others? The people of Hoknath? Were they saved as well?"

"No. They damned well were not saved."

"Ah!" Her expression dims and her shoulders slump. She turns her attention back to her bleeding hands. "I feared as much. They could not find a willing sacrifice. The magic will not reach far if the sacrifice is unwilling. There's only so much even the most faithful can do under such circumstances."

I stare at her. This woman who was my father's wife. The mother of my brother. A proud, dignified queen of her people. How could she have come so thoroughly into the clutches of a madman like Targ?

My steps quick, I cross the room, catch her by the wrists, and turn her hands palm up, displaying the wounds. Ugly slashes in the delicate flesh, blue blood drying almost black. "Tell me the truth, Stepmother," I say. "This is Targ's doing, isn't it. He made you do this."

"Don't be foolish, boy." Roh wrenches her hands free of my grasp and swiftly grabs the towel once more. "No one makes me do anything."

"What is he trying to do? Turn you into his sacrifice? So he can put the *va-jor* on us all, willing or unwilling?"

Her lip curls. "All true troldefolk are willing to return to the stone. It is our natural state."

With a single swipe of my arm, I knock the washbasin to the floor. It breaks in two, water spattering. The heavy pieces of crockery skid away to different parts of the room. "Vor!" Roh cries. For the first time, I hear a note of fear in her voice.

I lean over, forcing my face into hers, forcing her eyes to meet mine. "Hear me, Roh, and hear me well," I say, my words low and hard. "If I catch you or Targ practicing dark magic in Mythanar, I will execute him and banish you without a second thought."

Roh's eyes flash, her pupils like two pits in the center of

white-fire irises. "Is this how it is to be now, Vor? Your little human bride has become your spy. An unexpected turn of events, I must say."

"What?" I draw back from her as though struck. "What are you talking about?"

"Oh, don't pretend with me." A mirthless smile curls the corner of her mouth. "She's been sneaking around the palace ever since you let her out of the holding cell."

I stand up straight, retreat two paces.

"Everyone knows it," Roh continues. "She's quite unmanageable, so they say. Poking her dainty little nose into places it doesn't belong. You'd be wise to lock her up properly, dear boy. This indulgence of a prisoner does not reflect well on you."

Maybe I inhaled more *raog* poison than I thought. Because suddenly, I find myself nearly overwhelmed with the urge to grab her head and dash it against the stone table's edge. My hands slowly curl into fists.

"She found her way to the Dark Altar." Roh looks up at me, her expression vicious. "I don't know if by accident or design. But she was there. She witnessed a *grak-va* ceremony underway. But the *urzul* stones responded to her strangely. It was like . . ." Her voice trails off, and her gaze slides away from me, seems to stare into some far-off place. "It was like something I've seen only once before. But never so strong." Her eyes snap back to mine. "I think your human may be gods-gifted. Perhaps the god who gifted her was *Morar tor Grakanak* . . . and the gift was intended for Mythanar."

My blood runs cold. For a moment, I feel as though I too have been bound in deep stone, incapable of thought, movement, speech. When words finally come, they fall from my lips like molten magma. "If you so much as look at Faraine again, I will end you."

"Is that so?" Roh smiles slowly. "Well, if that's how you feel, dear boy, I do hope you can get over it soon. No passion of yours, no matter how hot, can withstand the will of the gods."

I wrench away. It's all I can do not to murder her then and there. Her laugh trails after me as I march from her chamber. "The end is coming, Vor! It's coming for us all! You must decide if you will die as a human or live as a trolde. The choice is yours!"

Even when I reach the hall and slam the door behind me, her words echo in my ears. I make it down one passage, take the turn, then lean heavily against a wall. My breathing is labored, my body covered in sweat.

Faraine. *Faraine.* I don't understand. What does Roh want with her? Does she intend to use her as a sacrifice? There's no chance Faraine would willingly die for the sake of a trolde cult devoted to a trolde god. But there was something hungry in my stepmother's gaze. No, not hungry—*ravenous.*

I shudder. Images of the murdered girl in Hoknath flash through my mind's eye. I'm afraid. More afraid than I've ever been in all my life. No battle or bloodshed ever moved me like this. My world, my very existence, suddenly seems so fragile.

I need to see Faraine. Just for a moment. I need to see her and know that she is alive, that she is whole and well and *here.* I will not touch her. I dare not. But a mere glimpse would be enough, a single word from her lips pure heaven.

My body is in motion before my mind has come to a decision. My feet carry me swiftly to the royal wing of the palace where I take the stairs three treads at a time. All the exhaustion of the last several days melts away in this need, this compulsion. I reach the floor to her room. There's no guard in the hall outside her door. Strange. Where is Yok? Is he inside her chamber? Or . . . or maybe . . . ?

I hasten to the door and knock five times, a quick percussion. No one answers. "Faraine?" I call. "Princess, are you there?"

Still nothing.

Panic churns in my gut. I reach out, try the latch. It gives. Why is it not bolted? If Yok isn't out here standing watch, she should at least be safe behind a bolted door! Someone's head will roll for this. I push the door open.

It stops partway. Stuck against a body.

My heart stops.

In a surge of terror, I push the door further, step into the room, and fall on my knees beside the prone figure. It's not Faraine. It's a tall, ungainly form in guardsman uniform.

"Yok!" I cry, and roll him onto his back. Terror surges in my veins. Did someone break in, overpower this boy, and kidnap Faraine? Another assassin, bent on her destruction? Or was it Targ and his cultists? Are they—could they—?

I see again that sacrificed woman. A scream threatens to tear my throat in two.

"Yok!" I roar, and yank the boy upright, shaking him by the shoulders. "Wake up, man! I need you!"

Yok groans. His brow puckers. With tremendous effort, he manages to raise one eyelid. "My—my king?"

My fingers dig into the boy's shoulders, leaving dents in his chainmail. "Where is she?" I growl. "Who took her? Tell me, Yok! Tell me what you know!"

He shakes his head. "No one took her," he groans. "I swear."

"What?" Something icy shoots through my heart. In that moment, I can't tell if it's relief or another surge of terror. "What do you mean? What happened?"

"She wanted to go for a walk." The boy forces the words out

painfully, one after another. "But . . . but I thought she should stay. She'd been out once already, and she didn't seem well, so . . . so I insisted. But then she took my hand and . . . and . . ." He looks blearily around the room, his gaze unfocused. "How did I end up in here?"

I drop my hold on him, little caring when he falls back on his elbows. "Where did she go?" I demand. "Did she tell you?"

"She said something about the gardens—"

I don't wait to hear the rest. I'm already bolting from the room as fast as I can.

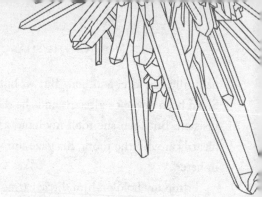

# 19

## Faraine

I find my way to the gardens by luck alone.

Every now and then I stop, hold my pendant, and seek inside for the pulse, the *pull*, which I've felt before. There's nothing. My perceptions are blocked. And my heart aches with each feeble attempt to beat against the encasing stone.

Cursing bitterly, I drop my pendant, let it bounce against my breastbone, as I hurry on through the twisting passages. There doesn't seem to be another living soul anywhere near. The denizens of the palace must have retired at dimness. That, or I've somehow been plucked from my former existence and dropped into an empty world, abandoned to my solitude. Either way, I wander lonely as a ghost through these cavernous halls.

I take turns at random. Perhaps some inner instinct guides me, for after nearly an hour I descend a short stair, step under a tall stone arch, and, to my surprise, find myself gazing out upon the palace gardens. Even in dimness, it's a startling sight. The gemstones are alive with their own inner glow, not as bright as *lorst*, but enough to offer a gentle aura. Blues and violets, a few patches of gold and scarlet. Strange lichens climb the larger boulders, creating luminous abstract patterns that dazzle the eye. Mushrooms nearly half my height bob gently, though there is no breeze. Their gills ripple, and their speckled caps reflect the low light around them. Here and there, tiny flying creatures—*olk*, Vor called them— flit across my vision, trailing glittering dust in their wake. The air hums with the soft music of their wings.

It's wondrous. More beautiful than I remembered. For a moment, I can only stand there, awestruck. Then my heart gives another painful throb. The pressure in my chest is mounting. If I cannot find relief soon, it will burst, shatter my heart, and leave me an empty husk on the ground.

I lift my gaze to the higher regions of the garden, to that outcropping I spied the last time I was here. There stand the tall blue crystals, big as trees, pale and lustrous. My breath quickens with sudden hope. Setting my teeth, I plunge into the garden, take the first path I come to, and stagger on as fast as I can. The ground is rough. Tiny gravel stones tear into my bare feet. I hardly notice. It's like it's happening to someone else, someone wholly disconnected from me. I have my goal in sight and can think of nothing else but to reach it as swiftly as possible.

The path branches. I growl in frustration but choose the way that seems most likely to lead up to the outcropping. It winds off into a grotto, however, and I'm obliged to retrace my steps. I search out another path, slowly making my way deeper and deeper, higher and higher.

The creatures of the garden are alert to my presence. The little *olk* flutter closer, tiny beaks snapping, six feathery wings fluttering. One flies past my face, trailing dust that makes me sneeze. The little catlike beasts appear as well, eyeless faces lining the openings of their cave dens, ears pricked, noses snuffling.

I come to another split in the path. Both branches seem to point back toward the palace. I curse softly. My goal lies beyond, up a steep incline, with no visible trail leading up to it. There's nothing but rough stone and sharp gems between that tall circle of crystals and me. I drag a long breath into my lungs.

Then I leap forward, clamber up and over an onyx boulder. My foot slips as I'm descending the other side. I fall hard to the uneven ground below, and pain shoots through my wrists and one knee. Hissing, I pick myself up. My knee is a mess of lacerations, and my palms have fared little better.

*Prrrrlt?*

I start, turn my head sharply. One of the little cat creatures is perched on the stone behind me. Its eyeless face is level with mine, tilting first this way then that. It burbles softly. By the glow of the nearest crystals, the orange streaks in its colorful coat gleam like ribbons of fire.

I blink. The creature twitches its ears. For a moment, all my urgency filters away. There's just me and this animal. Studying one another. Slowly, I stretch out a hand. The creature responds, elongating its neck so that its dainty nose can just sniff my fingertips. As though deciding it approves, it rubs its cheek against my finger and allows me to stroke the top of its head. Its fur is almost shockingly soft and silky. Amazed, I tickle under its chin. A loud thrum of a purr erupts from its throat. The vibration ripples up my arm, strikes my chest, bouncing off the stone around my heart. It's unexpectedly soothing. For one lovely moment, I can breathe.

Then, for no discernable reason, the creature chitters abruptly and scampers away into the rocks. I watch its long, bushy tail flick out of sight. The stone in my chest feels heavier than ever. So heavy, I wonder if I'll even be able to get to my feet.

Somehow, I manage to gather my limbs beneath me, push upright, and continue my climb. I'm close now. So close. Close enough that I can start to feel the hum of the tall stones even without the aid of my gods-gift. Soon I'll be among them. Soon I'll be able to take that hum into my body, into my soul. My pace quickens as I climb. I stumble often and am obliged to use my hands to pull myself up the steeper portions of the rise. Dirty, exhausted, I stagger on. My feet leave drops of blood behind me with each step, but I don't stop, can't stop. Not until I pull myself to the top of the outcropping and stand at the base of the stones.

They are . . . enormous. Much bigger than I'd realized when looking at them from afar—at least four times a trolde man's height. It would take three of me standing in a circle, fingertip to fingertip, to span the girth of the smallest of them. Seven main stones stand in a near-perfect ring, with other, smaller, but still impressively sized crystals in between. They're uncut, unpolished, and perfect. Their blue is as clear as a summer sky with hearts of dusky purple and deep indigo. But more impressive than the look of the stones is their voices. Their low pulsing tones, so profound they pierce through the stone in my chest to stir my heart. My own little crystal vibrates in response, buzzing like an insect.

They can help me. I know they can.

I step in among the stones. In the very center, there's a smooth place, obviously polished by hand, approximately six feet in diameter and flat as a table. After traversing that rough terrain, the relief of stepping on such a smooth surface is tremendous. I stand in that center, close my eyes, extend my arms. The vibrations around me intensify, fill my senses, work down into my bones. It hurts. Like plunging burning hands into ice-cold water. A blissful pain.

It's not enough, though. The stone in my chest vibrates, but it does not crack, does not break. My heart remains trapped.

I fall to my knees. Right there, in the center, with the great crystals towering above me. I press my palms into the flat surface. The vibrations flow through me. A song, an anthem. A hymn of life and death and all the complexities in between, dancing through my veins, through my soul. I close my eyes, feel how it ripples out from me, out across the garden, across the city, across the whole of this vast cavern. The resonance connects each and every living creature, every stone, every gem. On and on, the heartbeat of song, reverberating from one being to the next, forever.

"Please." My lips form the soundless plea. "Please, help me."

I bow, press my forehead to the stone. The pulse increases, quaking my skull. Still, it's not enough. The stone around my heart is too hard, too strong. I've got to get closer. I've got to . . .

Not stopping to question what I do, I strip off my linen shift, toss it carelessly to one side. Naked, I press my body flat into the ground and let the resonance enter me. Overcome me. It pounds against my imprisoned heart. The stone cracks. I gasp, shudder, but only press myself harder, harder. Now I feel it, the hard outer crust chipping away, one flake after another. Inside, my trapped heart roils, churns.

Then suddenly—it erupts.

All that feeling. All that pain. And not just my own. Everything that had been contained. This is the pain of those trolde men and women in the chapel: their fear, their terror, their desperation.

Their despair. I understand now what I saw in that dark chapel. How the blood-fed crystals drew the worshippers' emotions from their bodies. Trapped them, held them. Left them cold and hard. But that feeling must go somewhere, and those crystals were not strong enough to contain it all. So it had sought a new place of shelter and found it . . . in me.

Now it rolls out of me. Pulse after pulse, as the stone around my heart disintegrates. I'd not realized how that stone protected me, shielded me from these emotions that don't belong to me. If I'd known, perhaps I wouldn't have been so desperate to free myself. Perhaps I would have embraced the stone, given thanks for its weight.

Too late now. I can do nothing but lie here. Exposed. Shuddering. As the music of the crystals flows through me. It will kill me. I'm sure of it. My physical form is simply not strong enough for this.

*Faraine!*

Some part of my consciousness, deep down under the pain, pricks with awareness. I know that voice. I know it but cannot place it. Is it . . . ?

*Faraine! Faraine!*

Echoing. Faraway.

Across the worlds.

And then . . .

Right here, close to my ear: "Faraine!"

*Vor!* He's here, beside me. I would recognize the shape of his soul anywhere, in any plane of existence. His hands are on me. That touch is enough to jar my awareness back to my body, and I'm relieved to find that, though every bone in my skeleton aches, the pain is not what it was. It has moved out from me, poured into the tall crystals, and my heart beats freely in my breast once more.

"Faraine, can you hear me? Speak to me!"

I pinch my brows tight. I want to open my eyes but can't seem to remember how. Neither can I utter a word. When I try, nothing but a pathetic moan emerges from my lips.

"You're alive!" Vor's voice breathes against my ear, his lips pressed close to my temple. He's caught me up in his arms, holds me tight against him, rocking me slowly back and forth. "Praise be to all the gods, above and below!" he rasps.

He keeps talking, murmuring in troldish. Prayers, I think, by the rhythmic cadence. I don't try to decipher the words, for suddenly I realize that I'm leaning against his naked torso. My right hand is pressed flush against a hard, muscular chest. Frowning, I manage to pull my head back, pry my eyes open, and take a look. First at him. Shirtless. Magnificent. Then down at my own body. Loosely wrapped in a trolde man's shirt.

*Oh, gods.*

"Vor," I gasp. My whole body flushes with embarrassment. "Vor, I—"

A bolt of lightning seems to shoot through him. He pulls back, stares down at me, his pale eyes shining in the light of the crystals. "Faraine? Yes, what is it? I'm here. Tell me what you need."

"I . . . I . . ." I swallow. My throat is dry, and my voice seems very loud, ringing inside my skull. "Where is my gown?"

His eyes flash. I get the distinct impression he's refusing to let his gaze drop. "I'm not sure," he admits. "I found you here. Like this." His arms shake, but he tightens his grip on me. "Who did this to you, Faraine? Who brought you here? Was it Targ?"

"What? No." I shake my head then look blearily around. Ah!

There it is. My shift, tossed aside and caught in some of the lower crystals. I work one arm free of Vor's grasp and point. "There. Please, may I have it?"

Vor turns where I indicate. Then he looks down at me, brow puckered with concern. "Can you sit on your own?"

"I think so." I'm still quivering, but the pain is manageable.

Vor sets me down reluctantly, his arms disinclined to let go. I'm painfully aware of my own naked flesh pressed against the smooth stone. His shirt is large at least and covers most of me. Vor hastily fetches my shift and hands it over, keeping his eyes averted. When I have the garment in hand, he turns his back to give me privacy while I dress myself.

I hesitate. I shouldn't, of course. Not when he's being so gentlemanly. But I cannot help letting my gaze linger on his muscular shoulders, his tapered waist. My stomach fills with heat that spreads to other parts of my body, warming my cheeks last of all.

I tear my gaze away, slip Vor's shirt off, and pull my shift over my head. My fingers tremble as I do up the front ties. It's not a lot of covering—my arms are bare, as are my legs below the knee. But it's better than nothing. Better than how he found me.

"I . . . um. Here." When Vor turns, I awkwardly hold out his shirt.

He takes it but doesn't put it on right away. Instead, he stares at it, as though I've just handed him something strange and he cannot puzzle it out. Finally, he lifts his gaze to mine. "There was blood," he says. "All the way up here. I thought . . ."

Fear radiates from his words. It's so sharp, I nearly take a step back. "Oh, that!" I say hastily. "I did not stop to put on appropriate shoes. The ground, you know. It's very rough." I point to my bare, bloody feet and grimace ruefully.

Vor shakes his head. A muscle in his jaw ticks. "What are you doing out here, Faraine?" he says at last. "I thought you'd been taken. Another assassin maybe. Then Yok . . . he said you wanted to go to the gardens. I raced here as fast as I could, and when I saw the trail of blood . . ."

There's something dark in his eye. Something he dares not articulate. "It's hard to explain," I say lamely.

"Hard to explain why you would incapacitate your bodyguard to go for a stroll? Barefoot? Naked? In my gardens?"

A flush roars up my neck. I bite my lip, uncertain where to begin. Finally, I say the only thing I can think of in that moment: "My feet hurt."

He is silent. A long, terrible count of ten breaths.

Then suddenly, he steps forward. Before I have a chance to comprehend what is happening, he scoops me off my feet. A cry bubbles in my throat as I wrap my arms around his neck. "What are you doing?"

"I know a place where you can bathe your feet. It's not far from here." With those words, he steps out from among the tall crystals and begins to pick his way down the rise. I feel a momentary dart of pain, reluctant to leave the crystals behind, but that feeling is quickly subsumed in the undeniable pleasure of being cradled against Vor's chest. He's so strong, moves with such easy, effortless grace. The sheer power of him is enough to make my head spin and my newly released heart pound in my throat.

I should resist. I should fight this, demand he put me down. I shouldn't let myself feel what I'm feeling. If I were wise, I would plant my hands against his chest, push as hard as I can, force him to release me.

But I am not wise. Besides, do I really want to crawl back through this stone garden on my bloodied hands and knees?

With a sigh, I give in and rest my head against his shoulder. I don't ask where we are going or how long it will take to get there. All I want is to live in this moment. To listen to the pulse of his heart, to feel the rhythm of his breath, and let it sink into my soul like the living song of the crystals.

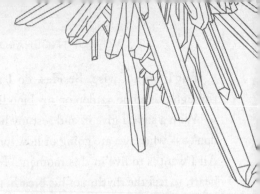

# 20

## Vor

She's so light. It's like carrying a dream.

The relief flooding through me is almost more than I can bear. I must summon all my strength simply to keep my knees from buckling and my body from sinking to the ground, trembling as I cradle her against me. She's alive! Warm, alive, here in my arms. Her soft breath stirs against my skin, her graceful arms drape round my neck, and her hair, soft and sweet as spun silk, brushes my jaw.

When I saw her lying in the center of the circle . . . naked, still, her limbs spread wide . . . Oh, gods above and below! For a terrible, endless moment, I'd thought she was dead. Sacrificed. Like that poor woman in Hoknath.

Then she'd moaned. The sound shot fire through my veins. I'd leapt forward, her name bursting from my lips. In a trice, I'd ripped the shirt from my back and wrapped her body in it even as I drew her into my arms.

Now, I pick my way carefully down the incline, away from the

Urzulhar Circle, taking care not to jostle her. She feels ephemeral in my grasp. As though one wrong move on my part, and she'll slip away, vanish from my life and existence. I long to crush her closer, to prevent her from escaping, but equally fear harming her, breaking her.

I should never have let myself come to this. I should never have allowed my heart to open itself up to this terrible vulnerability. If I'd been wise, I would have sent her home with Lady Lyria. How could I have let her remain in Mythanar? Avoiding her was no use. Avoidance only made my heart long for her more. The simple knowledge that she was *here*, within the walls of my home, breathing the same air I breathed, was exquisite torture.

My teeth grind so hard, it sounds like a growl. I dare not speak, not even to demand what in the nine hells she was doing, lying there among the sacred stones! If I open my mouth, it won't be any of the questions burning on my tongue that pour forth. No, it will be confessions. Declarations. Words I have no business articulating.

So I clamp my jaw tight, refuse to utter a sound. She's peaceful at least. Still and silent as I bear her down to the lower levels of the garden. The last time I carried her like this, she was in pain, resisting me up until the moment she lost consciousness completely. Now, she tucks her head under my chin and simply holds on to me. Like she trusts me. Like I can help her, comfort her. It's the most beautiful sensation I've ever experienced.

I know what I should do. I should carry her to her room, set her on her feet, back away, lock the door, and set a double watch in place. Instead, it's as though my feet have a will of their own. They carry me and her unhesitatingly to a certain path, winding between blossoming amethyst clusters and formations of gleaming anthracite.

Soon, a distant murmur of water fills the air. That murmur grows to a dull roar.

Then I emerge through the stones onto the shore of the lake facing the crystal falls.

Faraine lifts her head from my shoulder. She gasps. "What is this place?"

The delight in her voice strikes me straight to the heart. "This is *Hirith Borbatha*," I answer, my mouth close to her ear. "Lake of a Thousand Lights."

Even at dimness, the falls are spectacular. The living gemstones give off a gentle glow that shimmers through the running water. Cascades dance in many white streams, cutting through rock to fall in a joyous splash of foam. Down under the surface of the lake, small *lorst* crystals gleam softly, illuminating the pale, darting fish and the submerged plant life, a brilliant display of color and life and movement.

Faraine is speechless. I carry her to the edge of the lake and set her down on a moss-covered boulder. Only when she drops her wounded feet into the water does she let out a little bleat of surprise. "It's so warm!"

"Hot spring," I say, and step into the shallows. Before I can stop and think twice about what I'm doing, I kneel before her. Water seeps into my trousers, but I don't care. I strip away the shirt I've tied around my waist then lift one of her feet in my hands. At my touch, she starts and makes as though to draw back. I flash her a swift look. "Please. Let me help you."

She freezes. Then, slowly, she lowers her foot once more. I begin to use the sleeve of my shirt to carefully wipe away the blood and bits of dirt and gravel. Slowly, gently, methodically. Trying not to notice just how lovely her foot is. That high arch, those small toes, and round, crescent moon nails. Dainty, perfectly formed. Like the rest of her.

A little shiver runs down her spine, strong enough that I feel it. I glance up to find her gaze fixed hard upon my face. Realization strikes me like a blow: she's beautiful. Sitting there, disheveled, hair pointing every which way, dirt smearing one cheek. I remember once wondering if I could learn to find her attractive. Now, I almost want to laugh out loud at my own foolishness. I should have known even then, looking at her for the first time, that all my definitions of beauty were suddenly changed. Since that moment, no woman has compared to her in my mind. If I force myself, I can objectively see and list her flaws. Her mouth is too wide, her jaw too square, her nose too prominent. And of course, those bicolored eyes of hers are undeniably unsettling.

Yet how can these features be anything less than perfect? Every small detail is a vital part of the whole that is *her*. That is Faraine.

I've stopped breathing. Hastily, I lower my eyes, clear my throat, force air into my lungs. Placing her foot back in the water, I take the other in hand and begin to clean that one as well. Only when my task is complete, when I've risen from the water, draped my soaked shirt on a nearby rock, and taken a seat on the boulder beside her, do I attempt to speak. "How do you feel now, Princess?"

Her posture is rigid, perched on the edge of the rock, her hands on either side of her. Her fingers are tense against the mossy stone, her shoulders stiff. Mist-dampened strands of hair stick to her forehead and cheeks. "A little foolish," she admits after a moment, then sneaks a glance at me. "I . . . I don't know how to . . ." Her words drift away, lost in the roar of the falls and churning foam.

I should press her with questions. There are so many things I need to know. Why did she come to the garden? Why did I find her naked among the crystals, shuddering, obviously in pain? Why had she knocked out her bodyguard in order to venture here? She could not know the importance of the Urzulhar Circle, for it holds no significance for her or her kind. None of this makes any sense.

But in that moment, I cannot find any words. Not with the shape of her shoulder so close to mine. The air is warm and alive in the mere inches that separate our skin. I remember too well what it was like to touch her. To hold her. To mold her to my body. Then I had not realized it was *her*, however. Now that I know, how much more intense would the pleasure be?

My lips part. Her name is there on my tongue: "Faraine."

"Yes, Vor?"

"Faraine, I—"

Needle-sharp pricks pierce my skin. I let out a yelp as a moth-cat springs from my shoulder into Faraine's lap. She screams, startled. Her feet splash out of the water as she scrambles up on her stone seat. With a little screech, the mothcat leaps to the boulder nearby on which my shirt is draped, arches its back, and hisses at both of us.

Faraine poises in frozen shock. Her bare legs bend under her, her skirt slipped back to reveal rather more knee and thigh than is altogether modest. The view does something to my blood, something which the sight of her lying naked in the stone circle had not inspired. Then, all my concern had been for her well-being. Now . . .

I hastily avert my gaze. *"Morar-juk,"* I mutter, turning instead to inspect my own shoulder. "The little beast got me." Five tiny scratches mark my skin, seeping thin lines of blue. I rub at them ruefully, but at least this wound won't require Madame Ar's ministrations. From the tail of my eye, I watch Faraine settle her feet back in the water and pull her skirt down over her knees again. "Are you all right?" I ask without quite looking at her.

"I'm not hurt." She's still a little breathless. "It surprised me, that's all. What . . . what is it exactly?"

"They're called *varbu*." Smiling ruefully, I extend a hand to the mothcat. The fur on its spine stands upright, but it deigns to sniff my fingertip. Then, with a little trill and a hop, it springs onto my forearm. A long, sinuous tail wraps around my wrist for balance. "My mother always called them *mothcats*."

"Your mother?"

"Yes. She had a special fondness for the creatures, which is why there are so many of them here. They're considered something of a pest, but she was so delighted by them, my father had several breeding pairs brought in and turned loose in the palace gardens. Now there's a veritable swarm about the place, all fat and spoiled and good for nothing."

The mothcat walks up my arm to my still-smarting shoulder. There it nuzzles my jaw and begins to purr noisily. It continues sauntering behind my head, then makes its way down my other arm, drawing level with Faraine's gaze. It sticks out its eyeless face, snuffling.

Her lips curve gently. She strokes the top of its head with one finger. Its purrs redouble as it stretches out both front feet until she extends her arm for it to climb onto. In short order, it's settled on her shoulder, its forefeet on top of her head. Its long tail twitches under her nose.

Faraine laughs. Such a bright sound, like a crystal struck by a silver bar and made to sing. "I'd nearly forgotten," she says. "Your mother was human, wasn't she?"

"Yes." I clear my thickened throat. "She liked to come here. To this very spot. It was her favorite place. She would sit here by the waters for hours, surrounded by her mothcats. She claimed their purrs were soothing to a troubled soul."

Faraine is silent for a moment. The beast crawls down from her shoulders into her arms. She juggles its unruly limbs, trying to keep from being scratched, and only when it finally settles does she say softly, "Was your mother's soul much troubled?"

A muscle in my jaw tightens. "Yes." I have to force out the word. My gaze drops to my fist, knotted on my knee. "When I was young, I did not understand. Looking back, however, I think she did not thrive in the Under Realm, away from the sun and stars of her own world."

Faraine nods even as she contemplates the brilliant falls, the myriad lights and colors. I dare to sneak another glance her way. A slight crease indents her brow, and her lips pucker slightly. After a few silent moments, she lets out a small sigh. "I did not believe a world under stone could be so beautiful. Now that I've seen it . . . seen this place . . . my own world seems rather colorless by comparison."

My heart warms. The mothcat has flipped over in her arms and now lies belly-up, fat and comfortable. Its forepaws lazily knead the air. I find myself suddenly jealous of the little beast, to be held so gently in her lovely arms, pressed close to her breast.

I tear my gaze away, looking once more at the falls. "My best memories of her are here. This was where she could be happy. Father had a stone bench built for her so that she could spend more time here comfortably. I think he hoped he could find a way to draw her out, to give her a place in this world. To make her content. But most of the time . . ."

"Yes?" Faraine gently urges.

I draw a long breath and let it out slowly. "Most of the time, she kept to her rooms. The doors shut, the curtains drawn. I think . . . I think she was in pain."

Faraine is silent. I feel her waiting for me to continue. Suddenly, it's easier to go on than to stop. The words slip out, one after another, as though they've been waiting for a sympathetic ear in which to find shelter all these years.

"She disappeared. When I was still quite young. No one knows for certain what happened. My father sent many brave warriors searching, and he himself ventured to the Surface World. When he returned, however, he called off the search and never spoke of it again. Some speculated that she was kidnapped by his enemies, held hostage, murdered. Others claimed she ran away with some secret lover. Most simply believe she escaped through the Between Gate and found her way back to her own world. All I knew was that my mother had gone. And she'd not taken me with her."

The rumble of the waterfall is not loud enough to drown out the mothcat's snores. Both sounds fill the silence that follows as my voice fades away. I fix my gaze on the foam lapping around my bare feet. Perhaps I should have held my tongue. What good can be had from speaking of such things?

Suddenly, Faraine shifts her grip on the mothcat, freeing up one arm. She reaches out. Takes my hand. Her fingers are so small, so slender, yet there's such unexpected strength in her grip. "You love her," she says. "So much."

I frown, turn away. "I gave up loving her a long time ago."

"You needn't pretend, Vor. I already know."

A shiver ripples down my spine. Slowly, I let my eyes be drawn back to hers. So intense and yet so understanding. So knowing.

"What is your gods-gift, Faraine?" I ask abruptly. I wasn't intending to speak the question out loud. But it's been in my mind since the night I met her, out under that dreadful expanse of star-filled sky. Her sisters were both gods-gifted. Her brother too. Beauty, song, dance . . . the kinds of miraculous blessings one hears about in old tales. But Faraine's gift is unlike those of her siblings. Yok's unconscious body on the floor in her room is proof enough of that.

Faraine blinks. Her mouth works slightly. She's debating how much to say, and all I can do is wait. Finally, she gives her head a determined shake and lifts her chin. "I feel the feelings of others. Deep inside me. Like a pulse. A reverberation. I feel them so strongly, it hurts sometimes." She pauses before adding, "Most of the time." Her eyes flit away from mine, dropping to study the mothcat in her lap. "The crystals of this world—the *urzul*, as you call them—they seem to channel my gift. To temper and direct it. That's why I came out here tonight. That's why I sought the large stones. I was in pain. Ordinarily, *this* is enough to moderate my symptoms." She touches the crystal pendant on its chain around her neck. "But it didn't help this time. Not after . . ."

"Not after what you witnessed in the chapel?"

She shoots me a startled glance. "You heard about that?"

"I did."

"Who told you? Yok?"

"My stepmother. Roh."

Her face seems to shutter. She turns from me again, the muscles around her eyes tightening. "I didn't *see* anything. It was too dark. But the resonance of the crystals was strong, like nothing I've ever before experienced. It was *like* seeing, only without sight. Your stepmother was there," she adds meaningfully.

"And what was she doing exactly?"

Slowly, reluctantly, Faraine tells me. Her words are heavy and low as she describes the ceremony she'd stumbled upon. The faithful deeply sunk into stone. The knife in the hands of the gray-skinned priest. The pulse of crystals. The blood.

When she comes to the end of her tale, she shudders. "Was that an ordinary ceremony? Is this how your people worship your god?"

I shake my head. My teeth grind hard. "It is not. Bloodletting was long ago banished from the worship of *Morar tor Grakanak*. It is dark magic, forbidden in Mythanar."

Faraine considers my words. At last, she asks, "What will you do?"

Ah! That is the question, isn't it? I drag a hand through my hair, pushing it off my forehead. "There is little I can do. I cannot act on mere speculation. Without witnesses to present to my ministers, I have nothing but empty accusations to hold against either my step-mother or her damned priest."

"But there were many in the chapel. Surely some of them could testify?"

"And risk punishment for collusion? You'll be hard-pressed to find one willing."

Faraine nods solemnly. Then she says, "I could testify."

"No!" The word bursts harsh from my lips. Hastily, I modulate my voice and continue, "You are human. And a guest in Mythanar. Your word would mean nothing to the council." I bow over, sink my head into my hands. My fingers dig into my scalp. "I fear it will take greater sins committed before I can take decisive action."

In my mind's eye, I see that poor woman once more. Slaughtered. Her body desecrated. The whole scene is there, so vivid, so gory, so wrong. A sense of inevitability fills my gut with roiling bile. There was nothing I could do to stop that death. But now, I fear, there is no way to prevent another just like it. Or worse.

"What was that?"

I frown and lift my head enough to shoot Faraine a questioning glance. "What was what?"

"That darkness." Her face is paler than it was a moment before. "It rippled out from you."

"You . . . felt that?"

"It would be difficult not to."

I sit upright, drop my hands away from my face. "This gods-gift of yours is a tricky *guthakug*, isn't it?"

She tips her head to one side, another slow smile pulling her lips. "It has its uses." Her face grows solemn once more. "Tell me."

I want to hold back. I don't want to burden her with any of this. But she holds my gaze so intently, so purposefully. Soon I find myself talking. The words simply pour out, a slow trickle at first. Then, as the stones of resistance fall away, a greater rush. Before I know it, the dam has burst, and I'm telling her everything. Of the dead bodies in the lake under Hoknath. Of the temple chamber. The blood-fed stones. The sacrifice. Everything. She listens, leaning toward me. Every now and then I see her wince and wonder if I'm hurting her, if her gods-gift is reacting to the sheer magnitude of horror pulsing from my soul. But every time I pause, she leans in again and urges me in that low voice of hers, "Go on."

I do. And even as I speak, I cannot help thinking how strong she is. How determined, how brave. To take on this pain, like a series of blows, without once turning aside. The blood slowly drains from her face. Her eyes darken, set in shadowed hollows. But the mothcat nestled in her lap goes on purring, and she strokes it gently with one hand. Her other hand grips her crystal pendant so hard, her knuckles stand out like blades.

At last, I bend over, shoulders hunched, elbows resting on my knees, and stare into the water at my feet. Silence lingers, full of the dark things I've just spoken. "Did I hurt you?" I ask at last. "Did I say too much?"

"No," she answers simply, though her breath is tight. "It's not unbearable." She's silent again for a little while before finally asking, "What is *grak-va*, exactly?"

"It's difficult to explain to someone not trolde." I roll my lips musingly. "It is a holy state of mind in which a trolde will allow the life force in his soul to sink into perfect stillness. There he may know unity with the All Dark and be at peace."

She nods. "And *va-jor*? How is it different?"

"According to some theologians, *va-jor* is a deeper state than *grak-va*. It is the state in which oneness with stone is said to be made complete: body, mind, and soul."

"And the dark magic worked in Hoknath was an attempt to spread *va-jor* throughout the city. To spare the people from poison."

I nod. "But it failed. Because the sacrifice was unwilling."

"You think Umog Targ is trying to prepare your stepmother to become the willing sacrifice for Mythanar? So that he may spread this *va-jor* across your people?"

At this, I shake my head. "I don't know. The sacrificed one will not enter into *va-jor*. They will simply die a gruesome death. But Roh's greatest aim is to become one with the stone. I cannot imagine her voluntarily foregoing her chance of achieving this desire."

"But you do believe she is helping Targ prepare for the ceremony. Either on a willing or an unwilling victim."

I don't answer. But it doesn't matter, because she is gods-gifted, and she reads me with ease.

"You think . . ." She hesitates before continuing. "You think they intend to use me. For this sacrifice."

Hearing the words spoken out loud plunges icy daggers straight to my heart. My lips curl back in a snarl. "It doesn't matter! As soon as the message arrives from your father, I'm sending you home."

"What?"

The sharpness of the word bursting from her lips startles me. "I've not forgotten my promise," I say earnestly. "I must receive your father's official answer before I can declare the alliance over. At that point, my ministers can no longer argue against my decision to return you to your world. Which I will do. Immediately." Unable to bear her expression, I turn away, once more staring out at the falls. "I expect the message to arrive tomorrow. The day after at the latest."

A long silence hovers between us. But I feel her anger. My own body tenses as though for battle.

"So that's it then," she says at length.

"It must be so."

"And what of your feelings, Vor?"

I frown. "My . . . my feelings?"

She whirls on me, dislodging the mothcat. It lets out an angry yip before leaping from her lap to the shore, where it begins irritably to groom its tail. Faraine ignores it. She reaches out, catches hold of my hand in both of hers. I see her wince. Does physical touch intensify the strength of her gift? I try to pull back, but she tightens her grip. "Yes," she says, her voice almost a growl. "Your feelings. For me."

All the breath seems to have been blasted from my lungs. "You . . . you know how I . . . ?"

She lets out an exasperated huff. "It doesn't exactly take a gods-gift, Vor."

I stare at her. Frozen.

Then I wrench away, stand up, and splash back to the shore. There I pace, back and forth, my stride quick and agitated. "It doesn't matter," I say at last. "It simply doesn't matter what I feel."

"That's not—"

"You're in danger! All the time." I clench my fists, rounding on her. She sits perched on that stone. So vulnerable. So lovely. So everything I crave. But this craving is an enemy I must face and fight and conquer. "Every moment you stay here in Mythanar is another moment of peril. If not from the cultists then from my own ministers. From the spies within my court. Why, even I have tried to kill you. Twice now!"

"I don't care," she whispers, her expression fierce.

"I do!" The words bark from my throat. "Which means I cannot let you stay here. I cannot let you face death again and again. I cannot risk it."

"And what of my feelings? What of my choice?" Before I can answer, she slips from the stone, stands in the water. Slowly, she comes toward me. Spray from the waterfall has dampened the thin fabric of her shift. It clings to her body, like she's a bride once more, climbing from the sacred waters of the marriage pool. The sight makes me feel hollow and hot inside. And she knows it. She feels it. She can sense my intense arousal.

With an effort of will, I drag my gaze up to hers. She is close now, close enough to reach out, to take my hand. Which she does. Her fingers squeeze mine, while her eyes peer right into my soul.

"You once told me you considered women the equal of men," she says. "Do you remember? Neither one superior to the other. Is this no longer what you believe? Do you intend to strip me of my rights? Of the equality of my voice? Will you deprive me of a choice that is mine to make?"

My head feels heavy as a boulder as I slowly shake it. "The choice is neither mine nor yours, Faraine. The gods themselves have united against us." With that, I wrench my hand from her hold and back away. Firmly, I raise the walls in my mind, around my heart—stone barriers which even her gods-gift must struggle to pierce. It pains me to do so, but I must.

"I will escort you back to your chambers, Princess," I say in a voice as cold as *virmaer* steel. "There I beg you to remain until the message from Beldroth arrives. It is for your own good."

*And mine.*

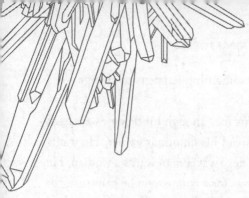

## 21

## Faraine

Vor offers to carry me back to my rooms. I can't very well refuse. Though soothed by the warm lake water and Vor's gentle ministrations, my feet are still quite battered. I'm not sure
I can make it back on my own.

So, I submit to the indignity of being lugged about in his strong
arms. Though, if I'm honest, that's not so terrible a trial. At first, I
hold my body very tense, braced for pain. Long years have taught
me that any amount of physical touch will inevitably end badly for
me. It's difficult to let such habits of wariness go. But Vor's feelings
are carefully locked down once more, and my gods-gift is not un-
duly activated. Instead, I'm extremely aware of the sensation of his
hands gripping my body. His strong arms bear my weight as though
I'm little more than a doll. My skin warms right through the damp
fabric of my shift. My cheeks are flushed, my breath tight and
uneven.

This isn't a good idea.

Or maybe . . . maybe it is? After all, by tomorrow, I'll be on my way back to Beldroth unless something happens to change Vor's mind.

My teeth clench. Vor wants me. Though his defenses are back in place, I know I didn't misread his emotions earlier. He wants me—and not just in the hot, fiery way a man wants a woman. He wants more than that. He longs for a companion he can trust, for someone on whom he can depend through all the tumultuous storms of this life. When he looks at me, he knows I could be that very companion. I could be the one to give his heart safe harbor. Why then does he still resist so vehemently?

I study the hard line of his jaw, the shadows of his throat and clavicle. His tale of Hoknath and the horrors he witnessed there chilled me to the bone. But I'd been able to bear it, far better than I've ever managed to bear such unchecked emotion in the past. Perhaps Vor was holding himself back. Perhaps he wasn't telling me all. He spoke of poison and the damage caused by the quake, but there is more going on here than he's willing to say. A darkness threatening all the Under Realm.

I press my lips into a thin line. If his kingdom is in such imminent danger, doesn't that make the alliance more important than ever? He shouldn't be giving up so easily. My father's mages are Vor's best bet for saving his people. He should strive with everything he has to make this alliance work.

We are silent as Vor crosses the garden. I scarcely notice the beauty of the winding paths, the rock formations and crystals, caught up in my own thoughts as I am. When at length he reaches the palace and steps into the shadowed halls, his stride does not slow. "You can put me down now," I say quickly.

He pauses. His muscles tense. Is he going to protest? To refuse? A shiver of reluctance ripples through his barriers. But when I shift in his grasp, he sets me on my feet, withdraws his arms, and backs up two paces. I wince, pain shooting up my legs, but quickly mask it in a determined grimace. I will not be carried about like a child. I can certainly manage to walk on the polished stone floors and soft rugs of the palace interior. Lifting my chin, I face the Shadow King. Now that we are inside, away from the glowing crystal light of the garden, he is suddenly an ominous, enigmatic figure. Only one pale *lorst* stone set in a wall sconce gleams in the depths of his eyes.

"I can find my own way back," I say bravely.

His eyes narrow. "It's not safe, Princess. You do not know whom you might meet on your way. It's best if I escort you."

I hold his gaze for a long moment. Then nod. He turns, sweeps an arm, and we walk together down the cavernous hall. He matches his long stride to my short one. In truth, I'm glad to have him near. I'm not at all certain of the way and don't recognize anything until we come to the stairwell leading up to my floor. This I recognize well enough based on the distinctive carving of a long, sinuous dragon etched into the wall.

My pace slows. I grip the stair rail hard, willing each painful footstep after the other. Nothing but my empty chamber waits at the end of this climb. My luxurious prison cell. But . . . does it have to be a prison? Or might I put it to better use?

My stomach knots. I cast a sideways glance at Vor, whose gaze is firmly fixed away from me. I can scarcely see him in the shadowed stairwell, but that doesn't matter. I remember every feature of his beautiful face, every line of his magnificent body. I feel his warmth like the draw of the celestial spheres, pulling me to him.

I know what I want. But that doesn't mean I'm not afraid.

We exit the stairwell, emerging into the empty passage outside my chamber. Vor utters a low growling troldish word. "What's wrong?" I ask.

"That boy." Vor grunts and shakes his head. "He's not here."

"Maybe he's in the room?" I suggest.

Vor swiftly crosses to the door, tries the handle. It opens at his touch, and he pushes it wide, puts his head inside to quickly scan the space. "Not here."

"Maybe . . ." I swallow, my throat thickening. Then: "Will you inspect the chamber for me?"

He draws back to give me a look. Does he know what I'm doing? Surely, he does. Surely, he can read my intention plainly in my face. But I offer only an innocent expression, all wide-eyed and blinking. His cheek tightens. Then, without a word, he steps into the room and begins a slow, methodical search, underneath and behind even the smallest bits of furniture—though what assassin he thinks might hide beneath my footstool, I cannot imagine—inside the tall wardrobe, the hearth, up the chimney.

I step into the room after him. Slowly, I shut the door behind me, taking care it should not *thunk* and draw his attention. My heart pounds. Heat pools in my gut, thrills in little bursts through my breast. Unaware of my turmoil, Vor steps onto my balcony to finish his inspection, parting the long curtains and vanishing through them. For a moment, I'm alone. Alone to think through what I'm about to do. Can I go through with this? Have I the courage? The will? Gods help me, I should have listened more closely to Fyndra! My father's mistress had given me many pointed tips on the art of seduction. I'd been so distraught at the time, I'd not registered any of it. But maybe it will come naturally? If I only have the courage to begin . . .

Vor spends more time on the balcony than necessary. I can't

help suspecting he's taken the opportunity to steady his own breaths, firm his own resolve before returning to face me. He reappears at last, pushes back the curtains, steps through, pulls the window shut fast behind him. Then he turns. Faces me. His expression is hard as stone, but his eyes are bright. Very bright and very pale by the low glimmer of moonfire on my hearth.

"There's no one here," he says.

Am I mistaken, or did his gaze flick ever so briefly to my narrow bed? If so, he looks away again almost at once and refuses to let his eyes drift that way again. Instead, he crosses the room in a few quick strides. His shirt was still too wet to wear when we left the gardens, so it's tied around his waist, leaving his torso bare. Firelight catches and plays with the contours of his powerful warrior's body. He looks unreal, like some mythic and magical being.

My mouth goes dry. I lean back against the closed door. "Do you . . . do you think the young guardsman will return soon?"

Vor stops a few paces from me. His jaw is tight, his brow hard. "He may have gone to the infirmary. But he should have thought to send a replacement. I'll have a word with that boy."

"Don't be too angry with him." I put out one hand, lightly touch Vor's arm. A thrill streaks through my fingers just at that barest contact. It's terrifying. You'd think being carried in his arms would make me somewhat immune, but here in this room, in this low lighting, with that bed close by, everything feels so much more . . . *alive*.

Vor feels it too. His careful barriers quake with the sudden surge of feeling in his soul. He stares down at me, at war with himself. "That boy was meant to protect you," he says, his voice rough and low.

I tip my chin up, exposing my long neck, the low cut of my

neckline, the tight heave of my breast as my lungs struggle to draw breath. "Maybe I don't need protecting."

Vor's gaze flashes downward before dragging back up to my eyes. "Nonsense. You're in danger every moment you remain in this realm. Of course, you need protecting."

"Maybe I can protect myself."

"Can you?"

He draws a step nearer, looming and powerful and shadowed and dreadful. My heart rams in my throat, and my gods-gift roils with powerful bursts of emotion. I don't know which of these feelings belong to me and which to him. It's all one. All need. All desire.

I don't mean to do it. Not exactly. But I reach out. Slowly, slowly, I place my palms flat against his chest, hard as stone, but warm and alive. "Yes," I whisper, and flick my gaze up to meet his. "But maybe I don't want to."

His eyes glitter with dark fire.

Suddenly, he takes two lunging steps. I don't pull my hands from his chest but let him push me up against the door. His fists plant on either side of my face, his arms framing me in a cage of strength. He stares down at me, his breath hard and hot on my face. Then he draws one hand down to rest a finger under my chin. His touch is featherlight, gentle, a sharp contrast to the look in his eye. His thumb trails across my mouth just before his fingers glide lightly down my throat to my shoulder, igniting my skin with bright sparks. He brushes his palm along my arm and finally lets it come to rest on my hip. His eyes are ready to devour me with their heat.

I stare at his full lips, so very near. "Kiss me, Vor," I plead.

His teeth flash in the moonfire glow. "You know I can't."

"Why not?"

"If I kiss you again, I won't be able to stop."

"Then don't stop."

With agonizing slowness, he lowers his mouth to mine. But doesn't touch. He angles his face, breathing me in, tantalizing me with the warmth of his lips so near and yet torturously withheld. I feel like a woman starved, ravenous and desperate. One of my hands slips from his chest to the back of his neck and glides up into his hair. I try to pull his face down to mine, to close that space between us. But he turns away. Conflict coils through his soul, equal parts red craving and cold, black resistance.

Time is running out. I can feel the seconds slipping away. Too soon, too soon, we will be parted forever. I need this moment. I need him. *Now.*

"Vor—" I begin.

Then his mouth is on mine. Crushing me with the intensity of everything he's feeling, fierce and hot as the core of the world. I melt into him, ready to burn up in that first kiss, to give myself over to the inferno. He tastes like fire and darkness and smoke, a heady combination that rushes across my senses. My fingers knot in his hair as his tongue slips between my teeth. He flattens me against the door, pins me under the great wall of his chest. The hand at my hip skates down my curves, then grips fabric, and pulls. He hikes my hem up higher and higher, until his fingers are underneath my shift, gliding up my hip bone, my rib cage. I whimper as his thumb traces the lower curve of my breast. So gentle. Too gentle.

I take his lower lip between my teeth and bite. Just enough to shock him, to make him draw back and stare down into my eyes. His eyes blaze, his swollen lips parted, panting. Slowly, they curve in a smile.

A growl rumbling in his throat, he lifts his fist from where it's pressed against the door, wraps his large hand around the back of my head, and drags me into another kiss, harder and hotter than before. Beneath my shift, his scorching fingers slip around to my back, slide down lower and lower still, until he holds me cupped in his palm. He pulls me to him, flush against his body. All my softness melts against his stone-hard flesh.

"What have you done to me?" His voice is a low snarl against my mouth, my cheek, my ear, my neck. "What have you done, Faraine? Deeper Dark damn me for a fool!"

Desire warps my answer into a breathy, wordless gasp. My hands slip through his hair, down his neck, his back. My fingernails dig into his skin. I must have more of him. I must have all of him. I must—

A terrible pounding rattles the door behind me, right where I'm leaning. I swallow a cry as Vor jerks his mouth away from where he'd been kissing sparks of fire against my throat. His hand rips out from under my shift just as Hael's brusque voice barks, "Princess! Are you in there?" The latch turns, hits the small of my back. "*Morar-juk*, you haven't even dropped the bolt! Do you never think of your own safety?"

The next moment, the door begins to open, pushing me along with it. Vor is already halfway across the room, leaving me to stagger and catch my balance as Hael bursts into the room. "Princess!" my bodyguard exclaims. "Thank the gods above and below, you're here. Where did you go? My fool of a brother found me and told me you'd given him the slip, and the king . . . the king . . ."

Her voice trails away even as her eyes take in my disheveled state. My body, clad in nothing but a damp, clinging shift. My hair, mussed and tousled. My face a roaring fire of blush. From there, she turns to the king, standing at the fire, leaning heavily against the dragon-carved mantel. Naked to the waist. His back like a wall.

Hael's gaze snaps back to me. "*Juk!*" she gasps, her eyes widening. Then she veritably leaps for the doorway, muttering something in troldish.

"*Gurat!*" Vor barks, his tone imperative.

"*Juk,*" Hael mutters again, but stops in her tracks. She pulls herself to attention and faces her king. Vor takes a step back, draws his shoulders straight, and gives his head a single shake. Only then does he turn around. His face is a mask, utterly unreadable. He speaks a string of troldish, all very cold and clipped. Hael answers in kind. She doesn't look at me. Or her king. Her eyes are fixed intently on the far wall.

Vor crosses the room in a few quick strides. I try to catch his eye, but he won't look at me. He makes straight for the door without another word and disappears into the hall. Leaving me. My heart still racing, my blood still burning, aware of every place on my body where his hands and lips had touched. Is this it then? Is this the last I will see of him? Will he keep me here, imprisoned in this room, until that cursed messenger arrives from Beldroth? Have I lost my chance?

"No, no, no," I growl, and leap into motion. Ignoring Hael's cry of "Princess, wait!" I dart from the room. "Vor!" I call.

He's down at the end of the passage. One second more and I would have missed him entirely. For a moment, I fear he'll keep going and never look back.

But he stops.

Pulls back his shoulders.

Then, slowly, turns.

I wrap my arms around myself as I hasten down the hall toward him. I'd not felt cold until this moment, but now I can hardly keep from shivering. I wish I dared reach out and touch him. From the way he's poised, I fear any sudden movement will send him fleeing again. I stop a good ten paces from him and lift my chin. The *lorst* light from the nearest sconce gleams on one side of his face, sparks in the depths of his eyes. "You said you expect the message from my father." I keep my voice firm, level. "Either tomorrow or the next day. Is that true?"

"Indeed. It should take no longer, Princess," he replies stiffly.

"And then we must say goodbye? Forever?"

He hesitates. Then nods. Once.

I can see the little bruise on his lip where I'd bitten him. I can still feel the fire on my skin where he'd touched me, gripped me. And yet he stands there, like he's carved from stone, all his feelings locked down fast. It takes every ounce of courage I possess to speak again: "In that case, I would beg a boon of you, great king."

His brow tightens. "A boon?"

"Yes. If tomorrow is to be my last day in Mythanar, I prefer not to spend it alone in my room. I've seen so little of your city. I'd like an opportunity to see more before I am gone. So that I may at least have tales to tell around the winter fires of my own world in years to come."

He stares down at me. "Captain Hael—" he begins.

"I should like you to show me."

He stops. I hold his gaze hard, all my hope and longing in my eyes. I don't know if he can see it in this dim light, don't know if he can be moved to heed me. "Princess," he begins.

I press on before he can finish. "We shall be out in public. In the city."

His jaw works. His resolve wavers.

"Please," I press gently. "When I return to my father, he will send me back to the convent. I don't expect I shall ever leave it again. My life will be . . . very small. Narrow and confined. Give me this one boon. Give me this one last chance to truly see something of the worlds beyond my limited scope. Show it to me as you see it, as you love it."

Vor's head bows. He breathes a long sigh before lifting his brows and peering at me once more. "And this is your last request of me, Princess?"

"It is. If you grant it, I shall never ask another."

He holds his tongue a moment. I'm caught in terrible suspense. Then, finally: "Very well. I shall meet you at lusterling and take you for a short excursion into the city. A *short* excursion, mind. Then you shall be returned to Hael's keeping, there to remain until the time of your departure is at hand. Understood?"

My heart soars, but I take care to keep my tone level when I respond. "Completely."

He nods. His lips part, and I think he'll say something more. In the end, however, he simply inclines his head and touches one hand to his bare chest. "I bid you *grakol-mir*, Princess."

I swallow. My fingers tighten around my upper arms. "Good night, great king."

Without another word, he turns and hastens away, vanishing around the bend. And I stand where he leaves me until I hear the door to the stairwell shut.

## 22

### Vor

"There you are, brother mine! I'd started to think you'd forgotten all about me."

I grab a nearby stool and drag it to the bedside. Sul lies there, looking nearly as white as the bedclothes, his face illuminated only by the hanging *lorst* in the center of the domed ceiling. The crystal's radiance has been dimmed, and the healing ward of Ar's infirmary is suffused in restful low light.

Most of the beds are empty, I note, turning slightly to look around the room. There's only one other bed, closer to the door, that currently holds an occupant. I choose not to look too closely at him just now, however.

Instead, I turn my attention to Madame Ar. She stands on the other side of Sul's bed, having just dosed him with a tincture to make him sleep. Currently, she stands with a brass horn pressed to his chest, listening closely. Her face contorts with concentration.

"How is he, Madame?" I ask.

"He's fine, thanks for asking," Sul answers irritably. "He's also right here. And he doesn't like being talked over. He has a tongue of his own, you know, and can answer queries after his own health."

Ar steps back and uses her horn to bop Sul lightly on the top of his head. "Enough fussing. You'll make yourself sick," she tuts before turning to me. "Well, it's as I thought. Only weak traces of detectible *raog* in his system. Couldn't help breathing in a little, I'd guess, but not enough to do any lasting damage. I suspect he'll be a bit limp these next three lusterlings or so."

"Limp?" Sul pricks an eyebrow. "You don't mean—?"

"I mean you'd best not get out of bed for fear of taking a tumble, that's what I mean. As to the other?" She casts a significant glance down his body. "Let me assure you, you won't be getting a chance to find out anytime soon."

"Just my luck," Sul mutters. He closes his eyes and nestles a little deeper into his pillow. "I swear, sometimes I think the gods must hate me. It's my pretty face, you know. They resent it."

"Indeed?" I give my brother a once-over. He's bruised, battered, and his arm is broken in three places and resting in a sling. Compared to the citizens of Hoknath, however, he's gotten off easy. "I should say at least one god holds you quite dear to his heart."

"Or *her* heart," Sul agrees, smiling serenely. "Much more likely, I should think."

I shake my head and turn to Ar again. "How soon until he's on his feet?"

"No more than a few days. Trolde bones mend faster than trolde minds, I always say. His mind I cannot vouch for, but then, no one ever could."

"Truer words were never spoken," Sul acknowledges with a yawn. Then he shifts on his pillow, casting his sleepy gaze over me. "You're looking a bit worse for wear yourself, Vor. Have you rested

since our return? I'm sure Madame here could whip up a nasty concoction that will quite do away with your fatigue."

Half smiling, I dismiss Ar with a nod. She shuffles away, always happy to leave her patients to fend for themselves in favor of
other, more interesting experiments in her workshop. I settle more
comfortably in my stool, tip it on two legs, and lean my back against
the wall. "I've had no rest," I admit. My voice sounds heavy in my
own ears. "I am king, remember? I haven't a spare moment to my
name."

"And yet here you are!" Sul smirks. "Perhaps I am favored by
the gods after all." Then, despite the sedative, his gaze sharpens.
"Tell me, have you truly been too busy even to visit the bathhouse
and wash some of the travel grime away?"

The thought of the bathhouse casts a shadow across my heart.
I shake away a shudder. I won't dwell on the possibility of my brother's treachery. Not now. Not when I've only just got him back. "You
saw the carnage in Karthur Channel," I say instead. "We need to
discover where the rest of the devils crawled off to before they attack some defenseless river town."

Sul nods slowly, his eyelids heavy with coming sleep. "Yes, that
does sound important. You must certainly attend to it. At once.
Right after you've finished *grundling* the human princess, of course."

Ice shoots through my veins. A low growl rumbles in my throat.
"You're a bastard, Sul."

He smiles silkily back. "Am I? That'll be news to Mother, I'm
sure." Rolling onto his side, he props up on his good elbow. Strands
of pale hair fall across his face. He shakes them out of his eyes.
"Come, Vor. You know what a gossip Lur is. She and Wrag had
quite a nice little chat while we were waiting for the rest of you to
return from your adventure in the temple. They each had an inter-

esting perspective to share on your farewell with your little wife. They're taking bets on whether or not you'll keep her. Lur is for it—she was always a romantic underneath that gruff exterior. Wrag thinks the human's too small for you; says you'll want a bigger wench to satisfy your mighty—"

I let the legs of my stool drop to the floor. Rising, I stand over Sul in his bed. "You should have put a stop to such talk."

"How could I? I was much too fevered and frail." Sul leans back on his pillow and pulls a suffering-invalid expression. "Otherwise, you can bet I would have reminded them both that our king would never forget himself so foolishly. He would never commit to an alliance that would risk the lives of his own warriors without certainty of aid in return. He is far too noble, too good, too wise."

I turn on heel, put my back to him.

"Or would I have been wrong to say as much?" Sul's voice sinks, turns into something dark and slithery. "Is it possible my brother— my great king, our noble ruler, Mythanar's valorous protector—has forgotten his duty?"

"I have not forgotten."

"I'm not so certain."

My fists clench. I let out a slow breath. This time, I cannot blame *raog* poisoning for the sudden, violent urges coursing in my veins. With an effort, I master my feelings before looking back at him over my shoulder. "I am aware of my duty, brother. Are you still aware of yours?"

His eyes are heavy, unfocused. The sedative Ar gave him swiftly takes effect. "I serve the throne of Mythanar," he murmurs, his words slurred. "At whatever cost." With that, his eyelids drop. His head tips to one side, and his face goes slack. I cannot tell if he is feigning sleep in order to escape the conversation, or if he truly did just drift away. In either case, I cannot very well grab his shoulders and shake him awake again. I might rebreak his arm.

Besides, was anything he just said untrue?

Cursing under my breath, I stalk across the room, past rows of empty beds. I pause at the bed nearest the door. There Lord Rath lies. He looks more like a corpse than an invalid. His skin is sunken and gray, his eye sockets deep hollows. Hatred stirs in my heart. Gods, how I loathe even to look at the man! When I think what he nearly did to Faraine . . . But then, what right have I to judge? Under the *raog's* influence, I did worse. Twice over.

"Madame Ar!"

I'm obliged to call half a dozen times before the healer finally pokes her head back into the healing ward. "What?" she demands.

I swing a hand to indicate her patient. "How is he? Has he woken again?"

"Eh, once or twice." Ar regards Rath disinterestedly. "I keep him sedated most of the time. When he comes to, he's frantic, out of his mind. And self-destructive. Seems determined to put his miserable life to an end. Part of me wants to let him, but eh." She shrugs. "*Morar tor Grakanak* determines the length of our days, or so my *mar* always taught me. Best not to question the will of the Dark."

I regard Rath's wasted face. Would I too have sunk into such a condition eventually had the poison remained in my system? A frown puckers my brow. Why had I not thought of it before? Faraine somehow used her gods-gift to drive the poison out of me. Could she not do the same for Rath? But it had caused her such pain. How could I ask her to endure that again? Especially not for a man who nearly murdered her.

Besides . . . I glance over my shoulder at the sleeping form of my brother, so peaceful under the single *lorst* light. My heart twists painfully. When Rath wakes, he may be able to give testimony as to who poisoned him. Then will I have answers. Answers I'm not certain I want.

I step from the healing ward back into Ar's workroom. The *uggrha* healer bustles about a table full of organic matter I prefer not to study too closely. Instead, I scan the cluttered room. On a table near the far wall stand two goblets which catch my eye.

"Madame?"

Ar pops her head up from her work, glaring at me through two gleaming crystal lenses. "What now?"

"Did you finish the tests you were running on these?" I nod meaningfully at the goblets.

Her eyes swivel, the movement exaggerated hugely by her lenses. "Ah! Yes, I nearly forgot." She sniffles then snorts. "Trace amounts of ingestible *raog* powder were found in each goblet. One more than the other, but definitely both." She slips the lenses down her nose, peering at me over the wire frames. "Did anyone drink from those goblets, do you know?"

Ignoring the question, I cross the room and pick up first one goblet then the other, turning them slowly. Sul poured and served *krilge* to me that fateful day. Moments later, I fell under the poison's influence. Did he drink too? I cannot recall. Perhaps he abstained, knowing the poison was there. Or perhaps he was entirely innocent. There's always a chance.

"Thank you, Madame," I say in lieu of an answer. "I will leave you to your business."

She gives me a narrow look. Then, with a shrug, she resumes her work, and I climb the steps from the infirmary and step into the cooler air of the outer passage. Two solemn guards stand watch.

They are meant to keep an eye on Rath until he can be questioned. I'd prefer they remained in the healing ward itself, but Ar long ago chased them out, threatening them with all manner of nasty home-brewed contagions. They salute me as I pass.

I nod. All the while, my stomach churns with bile. Gods, I hate suspecting Sul like this! But I must. At least until Faraine is safely out of Mythanar. Which won't be long now.

One more day. One more lusterling.

Suddenly, I feel heavy. Like a stone has lodged itself in my chest. Leaning against the nearest wall, I rest my head against my fore-arm, close my eyes. And see her. Standing there, with her back against her chamber door. Gazing up at me from those strange eyes of hers. Eyes so deep, so endless, whole worlds might live and die within their dark pupils.

I'd lost control tonight. Utterly. Completely. Were it not for Hael, I would not have held back. She wanted me . . . and Dark alone knows how badly I wanted her! After everything I saw to-day. After believing for those few, terrible moments that she was lost to me. Knowing that she must ultimately go from my world, never to return. All these combined into a desperate urge to claim whatever sweet instant of bliss she and I might share together be-fore our chance is gone.

I must not see her again. Only a fool would put himself right back into a danger he so narrowly escaped. Sure, I'd promised her this little excursion, but it would be easy enough to get out of it. A message sent by page claiming that some important business has come up, that I must forego the pleasure of her company. Hael can act as her city guide instead. Better yet, I ought to forbid the tour altogether. Keep her locked away safe and fast.

But I cannot do that. Not to her.

Her face flashes before my mind's eye. Intense, determined. She's so delicate, so frail, yet her spirit is strong. She's like the captive songbirds I'd seen at Beldroth, fluttering at the bars of their gilded cages. Though I myself have such a horror of the sky, I'd felt their need for freedom, and had fought the urge to break their cages open and turn them loose.

I wish I could break all the cage bars for Faraine. Let her fly free. Let her soar as high into that terrifying sky as her spirit will carry her. Away from all the darkness which haunts both my kingdom and hers. Instead, I must send her from one cage to another.

If circumstances were different . . . But what is the point of wishing for what can never be? Both Faraine and I must face the fates ordained for us by the gods. We cannot save each other. We cannot even save ourselves.

"Big King!"

I pull back from the wall, hastily order my face into stern, stoic lines. Only then do I turn to meet the approach of Captain Toz. He lumbers down the passage, taking up most of the space with his bulk. A slighter figure hurries in his footsteps, armor clanking noisily with each step. Yok. I pointedly turn my gaze away from the boy, focusing my attention solely on his captain. "Yes?"

Toz presses his fists to his chest in a respectful salute. "I've been searching high and low for you, Big King. Word has come in from beyond the walls. Signs of *woggha* in the ruins of Zulmthu Town. Folks was scrounging among the ruins, looking for what's left, and said they was chased out by the beasts."

My chest tightens. Memories of the carnage in Karthur Channel flood my brain. "How many did they report?"

"Couldn't say for certain. One of 'em claimed a dozen, another said there was only two or three. Enough to cause trouble."

226    SYLVIA MERCEDES

"True enough," I agree. "We cannot have wild *woggha* roaming so near trolde habitation. Where one or two have gathered, others may be close by."

"Want I should take some o' the guard to investigate?"

I shake my head. "You must be exhausted, Captain. You need to rest."

"I'm fit enough, Big King." Toz shrugs his massive shoulders. "I'll bring a handful of ready fighters with me, see what's to be seen. If we find a nest of devils, we'll take care of them in short order."

I don't like it. There were fighters among the slain in the channel. They were just as dead as all the rest. "I'm going with you."

Toz puts up a hand, his heavy brow lowering. "No need, Big King. You stay. Go about your kingly duties. Let us do our jobs."

"I would feel more at ease knowing—"

"I'll go with him!"

I turn my gaze sharply to Yok. The boy looks shocked at his own impudence, but he puts on a brave face and continues. "Your pardon, my king! But please, let me go. Let me prove myself to you. I know I . . . I know I let you down. But I can do better. I can do more."

Eagerness shines in the lad's foolish face, all underscored by grim determination. I heave a long sigh. Can I really be too angry at the boy? He hadn't known Faraine was gods-gifted, after all. Nothing could have prepared him for what her touch could do. And he'd done his best to keep her in her rooms, a more difficult task than any of us could have anticipated.

I eye the boy up and down. I've known him his whole life. How many times had Hael strapped her infant brother to her back, carting him around with her as she, Sul, and I went on our childhood adventures? Later, he'd trailed after us on fat legs and tiny feet, demanding to be included. He's now a gangly lad, nearly full-grown. Inexperienced, sure, but there's only one known remedy for that.

"Very well," I growl. Yok salutes smartly, his eyes shining, and I hasten to add, "But both of you, be wary. Cave devils are notoriously crafty beasts. If you find more than a dozen in the nest, come back for reinforcements before you engage. Do you understand?"

Both Toz and Yok give me their solemn oaths. Then they're off, tromping back down the passage, eager to get to their hunt. I'm left watching them go. Wishing I was about to mount my morleth and ride out with them.

Instead, I have my own trial to face. A trial of temptation I fear I may not have the strength to withstand.

# 23

## Faraine

I lie in my narrow bed and watch as the *lorst* lights beyond my window slowly come back to life. The trolde night is over. Morning has come. Possibly my last morning in this world.

Brow knotted, I sit upright, push back my bedclothes with a determined shove, and swing my legs over the edge of the bed. There I sit, gripping the mattress hard. Drawing long, steadying breaths.

Then, slowly, I touch my lips. As though even now I might catch Vor's mouth and force it to connect with mine. I feel him there, so close and yet so impossibly far.

I know why he resists me. I know I'm not the best choice for him. Ilsevel would have given him the leverage he needs over my father. Without her, the alliance is not strong. But that doesn't make it worthless, does it? Perhaps our marriage won't bring the political advantage he sought, but surely we could make things right.

Turning my head slowly to the window once more, I watch the *lorst* light play on the delicate lace curtains. Mythanar awaits. Out there, beyond. This is it: my last chance. My final opportunity to convince Vor that we belong with each other, regardless of kingdoms and politics, regardless of perils and fates. We, the two of us, must choose to make a life together, no matter what dire threats loom in whatever uncertain future.

But if I fail to convince him . . . if he continues to blind himself to the truth that is so plain to me . . .

A little growl in my throat, I push out of bed and stalk across my room to the water basin. There I wash with care, trying to ignore the flutters dancing in my stomach. When I'm through, I turn to the wardrobe, sort through the gowns which were salvaged from the queen's chambers. All these gowns were made for Ilsevel, all in the bold, vivid colors she favored. I shove that thought down as hard as I can. Today, at least, I must not think of my sister. Today, I must be focused.

In the very back of the wardrobe is a gown of dusty pink. Not a color suited to Ilsevel's olive complexion. I pull it out, hold it up for inspection. The color is right, but the style? It's very strange. A simple gown with thin straps over the shoulders and draping, off-shoulder sleeves. The bodice is split in a deep V that exposes far more than I am used to displaying. The skirts at least are ample and layered, and the whole thing is secured by a dainty little belt. It's so much simpler than the gowns I'm used to, with all of their structured undergarments, their stays, their petticoats. Those required assistance both dressing and undressing. This, however, I should be able to slip on easily.

*It will slip off easier still.*

My cheeks heat. Closing my eyes, I fall back into memory of last night. Of my back pressed against the door, of Vor's face hovering just over mine. His breath hot and fast against my skin. I feel his finger on my chin, feel his hand traveling lower, slipping under my shift, smoothing over my body. Such ravenous hunger he'd awakened in me, only to leave me empty, desperate.

Today will be different.

Today must be different.

With a shake of my head, I set about dressing in the lovely gown, securing the belt, arranging the sleeves. Thankfully, I find a pair of soft shoes with sturdy soles to protect my still-sore feet. At least they're not as damaged as I'd expected them to be this morning. I've heard rumor that the air of Eledria speeds recovery. Maybe it's true.

Once dressed, I set to work on my hair, brushing and brushing until it gleams. Then, turning to the polished black stone mirror, I take a step only to catch my breath. The skirt, though layered and voluminous, boasts two long slits right up the front. When I walk, they part, exposing rather a lot of leg. I hastily grab a handful of fabric and pull it back into place, staring at my startled reflection in the stone. Then, slowly, I release a tight breath and relax my hand. Let the skirt fall back, revealing my leg once more. After all, it's no more than most of the trolde women expose on a daily basis. Perhaps Vor won't think anything of it. Or perhaps . . . I bite back a nervous little smile as heat creeps up my neck once more.

Voices rumble outside my door. I turn on heel, layers of skirt fluttering around my feet and knees. Is it Vor? Or has he sent some messenger to cancel our outing? I swallow the lump in my throat, pull my shoulders back, and hasten to the door. The voices are low, speaking in troldish. I cannot discern one word from the next, but I can discern the tension in the atmosphere, the conflict of two souls. One soul is Hael—bright and sparking with frustration and fear. The other is Vor. I'm sure of it.

I step back several paces, grip my skirts with both hands. He's not backing out. Surely he's not. He wouldn't come all the way here, to my very door, just to deliver disappointing news in person. He wouldn't.

I'm still trying to work up the courage to open the door myself when a knock sounds. "Princess?" Hael's voice calls from the other side. "Are you dressed?"

"Yes." I roll my eyes to the ceiling, send up a swift, silent prayer to my goddess. Then, reaching out to the latch, I pull the door open. Hael stands before me, imposing in her armor, but I can scarcely take her in. My eyes are drawn irresistibly over her shoulder. To Vor.

He is like a dream come to life. His sleeveless tunic is made of silky maroon-hued fabric, belted at the waist, and elegantly embroidered at the collar and cuffs in the now-familiar pattern of the knotted dragon that I see everywhere in this world. It's loosely laced, open across the clavicle and upper chest, revealing strong, muscular definition to my admiring gaze. A metal brassard grips his upper arm, emphasizing the powerful swell of his bicep. A thin silver band across his forehead holds his white hair back from his high, smooth brow.

For a moment, I cannot think. I'm no longer aware of Hael standing between us. It's just me and him. Alone in all this world. His eyes flick from my face, travel down my body, taking in the pink gown. He doesn't linger. Doesn't stare or ogle. And yet, in that momentary glimpse, a sudden surge of desire escapes from behind his careful barriers, heating my gods-gifted perceptions.

His gaze returns to mine, locks hard. And I smile. I know where his mind just went. And he knows that I know.

Perhaps the smile was a bad idea, however, for he firmly takes those feelings and shoves them back. His face a mask, he offers me a short bow. "Good lusterling, Princess."

I nod. "And to you, my king."

"You look . . ." He stops. Blinks. Stands there with his mouth still open and his gaze firmly refusing to travel over my body once more. All the while Hael watches, disapproval simmering.

I duck my chin, spread my hands over the folds of skirt at my hips. "I wasn't certain how to dress for our outing. I hope this will be appropriate for whatever you have planned." I peek at him from under my lashes in time to see the dark centers of his eyes dilate.

He adjusts his stance, grips his hands behind his back. "So long as you are comfortable."

*Comfortable* is probably not the first word I would use to describe this gown. "I am. Thank you."

"I thought perhaps you should like to see the great Temple of Orgoth. It is one of the oldest established sites in Mythanar and considered a place of interest. People travel from across the Under Realm to worship there."

"Sounds fascinating."

"After that perhaps a sojourn into Market Rise for a chance to see trolde culture. Then I thought we might end at the Overlook. It offers a view of the city as a whole and is well worth seeing."

He's nervous. It emerges through his barriers in little bursts. But his nerves give me courage. This time together means more to him than he wants to admit. "I'm ready for anything," I say.

His eyes flash to mine again. Gods, is this how it's to be between us from now on? Will every word, every look, every gesture be layered with double meaning which neither of us dares admit?

Hael coughs, dragging our unwilling attention back to her. "My king," she says, touching a hand to the center of her breastplate, "I feel I must join you."

*No!*

"No!" Vor's response is as sharp as my own silent protest. He recovers himself and continues in a milder tone, "That will not be necessary, Captain. Thank you."

The skin around her eyes tightens. "It is my duty to guard the princess."

"A duty which I will assume for the next few hours." Vor blinks coolly at her. "Come now, you've not rested since our return from Hoknath. Take a few hours for yourself. Bathe. Eat. Sleep if you can. I shall have the princess back in her chambers by mid-lusterling." Hael eyes him from under her stern brow. When she opens her mouth to speak further protest, however, Vor cuts her off by neatly sidestepping her and offering me his arm. "If you are quite ready?"

"Yes." The word bursts from my lips in a little gasp. I rest my fingertips on his bare forearm and cast a last glance back at my scowling bodyguard just before Vor leads me down the passage. Hael still looks as though someone has given her a sour brew to swallow.

"Has something happened to distress Captain Hael?" I ask in a low voice as we enter the stairwell. My heart is beating fast. Now that I am alone with Vor, those moments between us last night keep playing across my mental vision. Standing caged between his strong arms. His eyes hovering just above mine, his breath hot against my lips. My hands pressed against his bare, heaving chest; his thumb skating along the curve of my breast. I shake my head, force my focus back to the present.

Vor casts me a sidelong glance. "Did you . . . *sense* our altercation?"

"Yes," I admit. "I'm sorry, I don't mean to spy. I rarely control what my gift detects."

Vor chuckles softly. The sound sends a whole flock of butterflies swarming in my stomach. "To answer your question, yes. Hael and I are currently in disagreement. Over a number of things."

"Such as taking me into the city this morning?"

He chuckles. "Yes. Probably. Hael has not overtly protested, but I doubt she cares for this particular scheme."

"I'm sorry to cause trouble." I smile softly. "What else has the good captain bristling?"

Vor is silent for a moment. Have I pried into private matters? I consider taking the question back, but then he heaves a sigh. "It's Yok."

"Yok? Her brother, the young guardsman?"

"Yes. I've sent him on what may prove a dangerous mission. Hael doesn't think he's ready. So far, he's struggled as a member of my guard. He was wounded by Licornyn Riders on our journey to Beldroth and sent home. Then he nearly allowed you and Lady Lyria to be eaten by cave devils while under his care."

"That was hardly the poor boy's fault! Lyria can be . . . persuasive. And as for last night, truly, I am sorry if my actions have compromised your opinion of him. He seems a loyal and steadfast soul. I know he desires to please you."

Vor grunts. We've reached the bottom of the stairwell, and he holds the door open for me to step through into a large hall with a vaulted ceiling. Thick pile carpet of green and blue depicting fantastical images of heroes, crystals, and, of course, dragons, extends down the center floor like a long river. Vor offers his arm again and leads me onto that carpet, proceeding right down the center under elaborate chandeliers of *lorst* crystals.

"I don't doubt Yok's true heart," he says, picking up our conversation. "That's why I've allowed the boy to go on this mission. But it is difficult. It's always difficult, sending young ones out, knowing these early missions will either be the making or the breaking of them."

His worry is palpable despite every effort to keep it suppressed. Part of me wants to take this opportunity, with my fingers resting lightly on his forearm, to send *calm* into his soul. But he will feel it and know that I've just used my powers on him. I don't want that. I don't want him to think I am in any way manipulating his emotions. Whatever happens between us today, it must be entirely by choice. No tricks. No magic. Just the two of us.

We've scarcely progressed ten paces down the hall before a door opens on our right. Five troldefolk emerge: first an imposing helmed guard, then three ladies with demure headdresses. Last of all is a much taller, broader woman in a magnificent headdress that seems to be decorated with stone-sharpened blades. She is white as bone and boasts a jaw so hard and square, it looks as though it could take a blow from a spiked mace without flinching.

The woman stops, her arms folded deep inside the sleeves of a heavily embroidered red robe. Her eyes narrow when she sees us, her gaze fixing hard on me. A flare of pure fury hits my gods-gift before it's locked down behind her hard trolde walls.

"*Grakol-dura, Shura Parh*," Vor says. I recognize the greeting from my lessons with Hael. He goes on to say something that sounds like a question.

The woman continues to stare at me, her pale eyes like twin daggers. It takes all my courage not to duck my head and look away.

Finally, her lip curls back. She turns to Vor, speaks a series of short, sharp words I do not understand. Vor smiles. He pulls his arm away from me. For a moment, I'm bereft. Though I still stand beside him, I feel alone and exposed.

Then Vor's hand comes to rest on the small of my back. Gently, he pulls me toward him. Warmth floods my senses. Suddenly, it doesn't matter how anyone else looks at me, doesn't matter that I am the only one of my kind in this whole hostile world. Vor is with me, his strength beside me, his power evident in even the smallest of gestures. In that one touch, he sends a bolt of courage straight to my heart. I cannot repress the smile that bursts across my lips.

The woman draws back, her eyes flashing. She snarls another short word before turning in a whirl of robes and stalking down the passage. Her maids and guard trail behind her, casting wary glances back at me as they retreat. "Who was that?" I ask.

"My minister of war," Vor responds.

Something in his tone makes me shiver, despite the warm touch of his palm. "She doesn't care for me much, does she?"

Vor lifts an eyebrow. "Did your gods-gift tell you that?"

I snort. "In this instance, a gods-gift was entirely superfluous, I assure you."

His smile is quick, there and gone again, like a flash of sunlight through thick, rolling clouds. "When alliance talks began between Mythanar and Gavaria, my council was evenly split as to whether or not we should pursue it. Lady Parh was on the opposing side."

A great deal of unspoken meaning lingers behind his words. He's trying to keep his feelings at bay. It doesn't matter, for Lady Parh herself made her position clear. I have no doubt she was among those crying out for my head following my disastrous wedding night.

I swallow and look down at my feet. Vor was probably right—I would be safer in my rooms. Hiding until the time is right for my return home. But no. I firm my jaw, lift my gaze to Vor's once more. I won't be cowed. "Well, I'm sure your minister would not deny me the pleasure of a single day's sightseeing in your beautiful city." I smile quietly and take Vor's arm once more. "Shall we continue?"

We meet others in the palace corridors as we make our way. When I made my request last night, I'd not stopped to think what being seen with me in public might do to Vor's reputation. But he moves with confidence, nodding and murmuring troldish greetings to everyone we pass, then inclining his head to murmur their names in my ear. "That was Umog Hur," he tells me, "a priestess, well connected by blood and definitely one to watch out for," and, "That was Lady Yahg, grandame of the Urbul Family, a notorious tyrant." These and others, all of whom give us a wide berth and shoot curious stares my way. I keep my head up, my face serene, even as I maintain a firm grip on my crystal pendant.

We come at last to the large front entrance. Vor leads me out to the courtyard, where, to my surprise, two morleth wait, held by young grooms. One of them is Vor's mount, big and spined and terrifying. The other, a little smaller and daintier than her counterpart, stomps one cloven hoof, sending sparks shooting across the cobbles.

I stop short. Vor looks down at me, his mouth tipped in a half smile. "You remember Knar, I trust?"

He leaves me at the base of the steps to stride across to the morleth. He pats its scaled neck. The monster snaps at him, sharp teeth just grazing his skin. Vor smacks his muzzle like it's all in play, and the beast rolls its balefire eyes.

I can't move. All my courage seems to have melted away at the sight of that second morleth and its saddle. When Vor turns to me,

I'm standing where he left me, gripping my crystal and trying to remember how to breathe.

"Don't be frightened," he says, his brow pinched with concern. "Here, come. Let me introduce you." Before I can protest, he takes my hand and leads me right up to the smaller monster. "This is Mur," he says, and strokes its broad, flat cheek, taking care to avoid the barbed spines protruding around the eye socket. "Here, let her sniff you. I swear, she's gentle as a mothcat."

"Really?" I grimace. "So, she's inclined to spring out of nowhere and dig her claws into any exposed flesh?" But I extend my hand and don't yank it back again when the morleth stretches out her long nose to sniff. She snorts and jerks her head. Smoke coils from her flared nostrils. I retreat two paces only to find Vor's hand once more firmly planted in support at my back. "I think I've upset her."

"Not at all." Vor chuckles again, sending another swarm of butterflies careening up through my heart. "Mur is just greedy. She thought you were offering one of these." He fishes a chunk of what looks like charcoal out of his trouser pocket and hands it to me. "Go on," he says. "Hold it out. Keep your palm very flat so Mur doesn't accidentally nibble one of your fingers."

With those teeth, she'd probably take my finger right off. Determined not to wince and close my eyes, I do as I'm told, offering the treat to the beast. Much to my relief, Mur uses her long, nimble lips to swipe the black lump from my palm and chomps with noisy satisfaction.

"There." Vor steps away from me. My back feels cold where his hand had been, and I can't help a dart of resentment when he strokes the beast's nose. "You'll be the best of friends before you know it."

I eye the monster and her black, scaly, spined, vaguely horse-shaped body. "She's . . . magnificent," I manage to say.

"I can assist you into the saddle."

"What?" I turn to Vor, search for some sign of teasing in his face. "You mean for me to ride into the city?"

"You do ride, don't you?"

"Yes, but . . . but *horses*."

"Mur is much like a horse, I assure you. She's been gentled from a young age, and I picked her out specially for . . ."

*For Ilsevel.* He stops himself from saying my sister's name, from bringing her into this space between us. It doesn't matter. She's there all the same. The truth is, Ilsevel would be far better suited to this particular adventure. She loved a challenge almost as much as she loved riding. She would have been delighted with this gift of a monster steed.

"I am not much of a horsewoman," I admit, dropping my gaze.

"Ah." Vor is silent a moment, suddenly uncertain. "It's too far to walk where we are going. I had thought perhaps you would prefer a saddle over a litter."

He's not wrong. I vividly remember my arrival in Mythanar, being carried through the streets in that awful, lurching, curtained contraption. Not an experience I care to repeat. But the idea of mounting that morleth is terrifying.

"I would prefer to ride, yes," I say, and look him boldly in the eye. "But with you. As we've done before."

Vor goes very still. "That might . . ." He stops, turns away, rubbing a hand along the back of his neck. "That might send the wrong message."

"A morleth carrying me away in a cloud of smoke and screams is likely to cause more trouble than the sight of the two of us riding together."

A smile quirks his mouth. He's considering it. I hold my breath.

I want this time together so badly. To be close to him. To rest against his chest, to feel his arms around me. If this is to be our last few hours together, I'd much rather not spend them clinging to a saddle for dear life.

Abruptly, Vor turns and barks orders in troldish to a groom. "What's happening?" I ask.

He looks down at me, eyes shining. "I'm having Knar's saddle replaced with one more comfortable for double riding."

My heart soars so high, it nearly escapes my chest. Soon enough, the fresh saddle is brought, this one with a top pommel for me to grip with my knees, allowing me to perch side-saddle in front of Vor. Once it's heaved onto Knar's broad back, Vor lifts me up in his arms. I laugh a little breathlessly as he settles me in place.

A sudden surge of feeling from him shocks me, however. I look down to discover that my slitted skirt has opened all the way to the thigh. Hastily, I pull folds of soft pink fabric over my exposed leg. When I glance at Vor again, he's not looking at me, but seems intent upon checking the saddle girth. I smile a small, secret smile. The next few hours are going to be . . . interesting.

Vor mounts, wraps his arms around me, and takes the reins. A feeling of rightness settles over me. I'd almost forgotten what it felt like, riding like this, nestled in front of him. I lean back against his chest and let a sigh escape my lips.

"Are you ready, Princess?" Vor asks, his lips close to my ear.

I close my eyes. "Yes."

He urges his beast into motion, and we set off on our last adventure together.

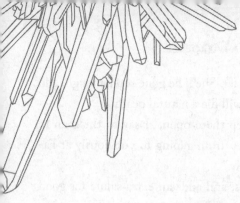

# 24
........
## Vor

Deeper Dark devour me, what have I done?

Everything about this is a mistake. The shape of her in my arms, the warmth of her back pressed against my chest. I'm acutely aware of her round softness perched between my legs, and that awareness is not helped by the way her skirts flutter and part at every other plodding step of the morleth.

At this rate, I will be undone before we have even cleared the palace grounds.

My throat thickens. I face forward, refuse to let my gaze drift down. Not too often, at least. It doesn't make much difference. Not with the sweet smell of her hair just under my nose and the soft music of her voice every so often gracing my ears. I could grow to crave such delights. Which is dangerous. These are not delights meant for me. But I'm in no mood to be cautious.

We approach the gate. I hail the men on watch. They stare at Faraine, openly curious to see her with me. They're terrible gossips, the palace guard. No doubt rumors will fly before the hour is through. It doesn't really matter. She'll be gone soon enough, and any rumors stirred up today will die a natural death.

"Open the gates and keep them open," I say to the man in charge, who struggles to keep from gaping too obviously at Faraine. "We shall return shortly."

"Yes, my king," he replies, and adds an extra salute for good measure. He barks a command, and the portal is opened. Knar tugs at his reins and tries to snap the blade of the guardsman's lance off. The guard lets out a yelp and yanks his weapon back out of reach.

Faraine giggles softly. My blood warms. That sound . . . it's enough to break any remaining vestiges of resolve I have left. But I must take care. With her gods-gift, who knows how much she can perceive of my feelings?

Hastily, I nudge Knar into motion. The morleth stomps under the arch, and we emerge at the top of a steep road leading precipitously down to the lower city. Faraine gasps. Her hands on the pommel tighten. "Are you all right?" I ask.

"Yes! I just . . . When I came this way before, I was in a litter with the curtain drawn. I did not realize how very steep this road is."

"Are you afraid of heights?"

"No! Merely *aware*, as it were."

"You're quite safe, I assure you. Knar is steady. Though he does not like being out under the *lorst* lights, he will behave himself." I tighten my arm around her. "I won't let you fall."

"I know," she responds, and settles the back of her head against my shoulder once more. When I look down, I can see the whole lovely line of her throat to her collarbone, down to the bare skin between her breasts revealed by her gown's plunging neckline. *Gods help me.*

I spur Knar forward. Morleth prefer walking on shadows to solid ground, but he's sluggish at this time of the lusterling and plods along on the paving stones. "This road is called the *aruk-dra*," I say, determined to make the lightest, most impersonal conversation I can manage. "It is the primary highway through the city and leads directly to the very center, where the Temple of Orgoth stands. There, the road branches into six, all of which lead to the chasm bridges."

Faraine nods. Her fingers are still tight on the pommel, but her body relaxes as she accustoms to the morleth's steady gait. "Who was Org?" she asks after a silent moment.

"Pardon?"

"You said the Temple of Orgoth. I'm curious who the temple was named after."

It's a good question. A glow of pleasure warms my chest at her interest in my people and their history. I proceed to tell her about Queen Org, the first ruler of the Under Realm, who united the warring tribes of the troldefolk. It's a long tale, but an exciting one, and Faraine listens with great attention, asking pertinent questions here and there. I tell her how Org discovered the Urzulhar Stones and recognized them as sacred—seven great crystals, representing each of the seven gods. She established her seat of power there. But she never forgot that the true trolde god was *Morar tor Grakanak*. So, to him she dedicated the temple at the heart of the city.

"It is the oldest temple in all the Under Realm," I say to conclude my story, "and Mythanar is the oldest city. And the greatest."

"How many cities are there throughout the Under Realm?"

"Forty-eight of comparable size to Mythanar. That's not including the smaller towns and villages along the riverways, of course."

Faraine shakes her head slowly. "I had no idea your kingdom was so great! Gavaria certainly doesn't boast half that many cities."

"Gavaria is a human kingdom," I respond with a smile. "The

Under Realm, you must remember, is vastly older. Older perhaps than your entire world."

I point out examples of interesting architecture along the road we travel. Something tells me our troldish buildings must all look the same to her human eyes, but she asks intelligent questions and seems determined to learn. When the road begins to level out, she sits up a bit straighter in the saddle. That I don't care for. I fight the urge to pull her back against my chest so that I may feel her and breathe her.

We reach the temple at last. I'm obliged to point it out to her, for it is nothing but a great stone mound without discernable feature. Various entrances dot the surface of the dome seemingly at random, leading into the catacomb interior.

"There are no lights permitted inside," I explain. "Light too easily disturbs worship of the Deeper Dark. And see there?" I swing my arm to indicate the many smaller domed structures surrounding the temple. "Those are residences of the priestesses, who sometimes need reprieve from the more intense darkness."

Faraine looks on in silence for a moment before tilting her head to one side. "Those do not look like priestesses to me."

I follow her line of sight to where a trolde family sits in front of a domed stone domicile. A squat, maternal figure, her skin hard with *dorgarag*, stirs something in a pot over a fire. Several small children, some stone-hided, some smooth and pale, wrestle in the dirt around her. One of them climbs to the top of the dome, beats his chest, and hollers until his mother finally stops stirring long enough to bark at him to come down.

"No, indeed," I say. "Many of the temple dwellings are occupied by refugees at this time."

"Because of the stirrings?"

"Yes."

She considers this for a moment. "Will they ever be able to safely return to their homes?"

I had hoped so. Once. I had hoped I'd be summoning Miphates to our aid, putting an end to our trouble, and all the displaced people of my kingdom would venture back along the riverways to rebuild the ruined towns, villages, and cities. Even Dugorim. Even Hoknath. But that dream has faded. It is all but dead. "We shall see," I say. But I know she feels the truth in my heart. The resignation. The despair.

Not wanting to dwell on such thoughts, I urge Knar on to a remote corner of the temple grounds. There I point out a certain formation of solid black obsidian. "That is Saint Hurk, the Rock-Smasher," I explain, and launch into another tale of legends. Faraine listens, and when I am through, she asks to be let down from the saddle so that she may inspect the statue more closely. I lower her carefully, and she circles old Hurk, studying the way the craftsman of ancient days captured his likeness via old trolde carving techniques.

As for me? I have the singular pleasure of watching her. Of memorizing the way she moves, the sway of her hips, the glint of *lorst* light in her hair. The way those blessed skirts of hers part to reveal flashes of her lovely legs.

*She would have been happy here. As queen.*

*She would not have ended up like my mother.*

As though she heard my thoughts, Faraine turns and looks directly at me. Catches me staring. Heat warms my neck, and I turn away quickly, pretending to be interested in another set of domed priestess dwellings some distance beyond her. I haven't fooled her, though. Not in the least.

Gods on high! Does she realize what she does to me simply by *existing*?

Having finished her inspection of Hurk's statue, Faraine steps lightly back to me and Knar. Just as she draws near, a loud gurgling sound erupts. Faraine gasps, flushes, and claps a hand to her stomach. "What's the matter?" I ask, concerned.

"Oh!" She ducks her chin and gives her head a little shake. "I simply haven't eaten yet today." Her teeth worry at her full lower lip as she glances up at me. When she lets it go, it's suddenly pinker and plumper than before. I'm possessed with the terrible urge to reach out, to run my thumb across its softness.

Wrenching my thoughts back in line, I lift my gaze to hers, firm and steady. "I know a place where we can find food. If you don't mind trolde fare, that is."

She smiles. "I've not yet had opportunity to try it! I'm certainly game."

I help her back to her place on the front of my saddle. We leave the temple grounds behind and pursue the road that leads to Market Rise. This is a tall cliff face dotted with numerous shallow caves. A wide road zigzags all the way to the top. Market sellers display their wares at the cave mouths, the entrances decorated with gems, subterranean flowers, and banners of bright fabric to draw attention their way. It's one of the more colorful, lively districts of all Mythanar—one I don't visit often enough.

I draw Knar to a halt at the base of the cliff. The morleth is unhappy enough with all the light around us; riding him up that winding road would be foolish. We dismount, and I allow the beast to vanish back into his own dark dimension. By now, we've attracted many eyes. All the sellers and market-goers at the base of the cliff have stopped their haggling to stare. Every one of them recognizes us—their king and his human bride.

I meet none of their curious gazes but incline my head to Faraine. "Will you be all right? With your gods-gift, I mean. Will the crowds be too much for you?"

She casts me an appreciative look. "I can manage well enough, thank you. Often with a crowd this large, the swell of emotion is too complex to penetrate my gift. And I have this to steady me." She holds up her little pendant.

I nod, trusting her to know her own limits. "Shall we then?"

"Please." She rests her fingers on my arm, and we set off, climbing the path. The crowd parts for us, still ogling, fascinated by Faraine. Most of them have never seen a human before and find her very strange. At first, I fear their scrutiny will discomfort her, but she carries herself with queenly grace and dignity, a gentle half smile on her lips and a kind nod for any trolde whose gaze she happens to meet. All the while, she holds tight to her pendant.

"The food sellers are farther up," I say as we reach the first level of shops. "We needn't linger if you wish to continue."

But Faraine, despite her hunger, is in no hurry. The sellers here are all stone collectors who have ventured into deeper, more remote reaches of the Under Realm to bring home rare gems and rocks used for various purposes. Some are much sought after by furniture makers, others for tools and weapons. There's a *lorst* crystal seller with some very poor quality stones that would scarcely serve as a child's night-light, but Faraine stops and looks them over with interest. "In the right setting, one of these would make for the most stunning necklace," she says, picking up a particular stone.

I chuckle. "Trolde women would never use *lorst* for jewelry. They're far too common."

"Really?" Faraine sets the stone back down with care. "I suppose you're right—I haven't seen any of your ladies wearing them. Human women would pay for just one of these in diamonds!"

"I don't doubt it. I've seen the quality of diamonds in your world, however. They're worth little more than these. Come! Let's find you some living gems."

Faraine nods politely to the *lorst* seller before allowing me to lead her on to a further stall where sits an ancient trolde woman with a bounty of black-streaked hair pulled severely back from her square face. I've purchased many a stone from her in the past.

"Good lusterling to you, Tril," I call out in troldish as we draw near.

The old trolde's eyes light up at the sight of me. "Big King!" she begins in her strong low-stone accent. She stops, however, as her gaze fixes on Faraine. With a grunt and a groan, she climbs ponderously from her chair, presses her fists to her chest, and bows. "And the new queen!"

I flinch. My gaze flicks to Faraine. At least she doesn't understand what the old gem seller is saying. I should correct Tril, of course. In the moment, however, it is easier to let the mistake slide, so, I say simply, "Faraine, allow me to introduce Tril. She may not look it, but she is quite the adventurer. She mines her gems fresh from the Diamond Fields of Zahgigoth beyond the Fiery Fjords. Although"—I lower my voice, though Tril herself does not understand the language I speak—"I believe it is her grandson who performs the more daring exploits these days."

"It sounds most impressive to me." Faraine flashes her lovely smile at the old trolde woman. "*Hiri*, Tril," she says.

Tril blinks hugely. Then she tosses her head back with laughter, flashing her sharp teeth. "Quite the friendly one, eh, Big King?"

Faraine glances sidelong up at me. "Was it my accent? Do I sound foolish?"

"Not at all," I assure her. "You've used an informal mode of greeting, ordinarily reserved for family and close friends. *Grakol-dura* is the proper form of address."

"I see." Faraine nods, her cheek tightening. "I have much to learn, it seems."

To my shame, I don't correct her. I simply cannot bear to remind her that she has no reason to study the intricacies of troldish language because she will have no use for them in the future. Just now, it's nice to indulge in this little game of make-believe—to pretend she is, in truth, my new blushing bride, and I, her proud bridegroom. That this is only the first of many ventures into Mythanar which we will make together as I teach her the ways of my people and my world.

Tril is more than ready to display her wares. Living diamonds of the brightest, clearest quality, like stars fallen from the Upper World. Also emeralds, rubies, sapphires of various hues. Opals the size of my fist with hearts so fiery, one expects young dragonettes to burst from their centers. Some of these, she has taken time to fashion into jewelry—nothing intricate or delicate like the necklace Faraine wears. This is rough-and-ready trolde jewelry, displaying the uncut stones at their wildest.

Faraine selects one particular tiara of clear sapphires, admiring the way the stones catch the light of Tril's *lorst* lantern. "Try it on, try it on!" Tril urges.

Faraine shoots me a baffled look. When I translate, she hastily puts the tiara back down. "I shouldn't."

"Try it on, I say!" Tril repeats before picking up the tiara herself and setting it on Faraine's head. Faraine tenses, eyes widening. Then, with a delighted laugh, she steps back and looks at herself in the polished mirror-stone Tril holds up for her. She tilts her head, trying out different angles and expressions.

"What do you think, Vor?" she says, turning abruptly and fixing me with a brilliant smile. "Does it suit me?"

And there. She's done it again. Caught me staring. When I'd not realized I was doing so.

I draw a short breath through my teeth. Hastily clearing my throat, I force a smile. "Yes." The word is rough as a growl in my throat. "Yes, it suits you well."

We stand there for the space of ten heartbeats. Silent. Gazing at one another. While the whole of Market Rise and its noisy denizens, the shouting sellers, the irritable customers, the grinding stone wheels of carts, all of it fades away to nothing. There's just the two of us. Sharing a moment so bright, so perfect.

I know something then with absolute certainty. Perhaps the only certainty in my whole sorry, uncertain life. I know this image of her—clad in that pink, trolde-style gown, wearing that crown of uncut gems, her hair tumbled about her face and shoulders, her eyes uplifted to mine—will stay with me to the end. When the world comes all undone, when the cracks spread and the caverns fall, her face, just as it is right now, will be the last vision my mind's eye sees.

"Half price today!" Tril breaks the moment with a smack of her palm against the stone tabletop across which her gems are spread. "Half price for the Big King. A present for his new bride."

I wrench myself back to reality and turn on the old gem seller with a wry grin. "How much would half price cost me exactly?"

She names an outrageous sum, provoking a burst of laughter from my lips. "What is it?" Faraine asks, carefully removing the tiara from her head. She tries to offer it back to the woman.

"No, no, no!" Tril waves her square hands. "For the queen! For the new queen! And only half price!"

"She's trying to make a sale," I answer. "A very generous sale . . . in her favor."

Faraine's brow puckers. "Will you inform her, please, that I have no trolde currency in any case?"

I should, of course. I should make our apologies, offer Faraine my arm, and lead her in a hasty escape. Instead, I fish a handful of polished *ginugs* from my pouch—not as many as Tril's demanded, but more than the tiara is worth. She makes a great show of inspecting each coin. She always does, as though it's not an insult to her king to doubt the quality of his purse. I roll my eyes, fold my arms, and wait for her eventual grunt of acceptance. She sweeps the *ginugs* into one palm and motions for Faraine to take the tiara.

"What is happening now?" Faraine asks, raising her eyebrow at me.

"The tiara is yours," I say. "Tril and I have come to an agreement."

"What?" Faraine stares down at the arrangement of sapphires set in silver. She puts a hand to her mouth, as though she's just said something embarrassing. "Oh, Vor! I did not mean for you to—"

"I know." I pick up the tiara and, before she can utter a word of protest, set it on her head. "As I said, it suits you well."

The look she gives me from beneath those shining gems makes my heart light up like a *lorst* stone. It's all I can do not to cup her cheeks in my palms and plant a kiss on her lips there and then. Instead, I step back quickly and clasp my hands at the small of my back. "Shall we continue?"

We leave Tril to gloat over her ill-gotten earnings and progress to the next level of the market. By this time, the whispers are flying. I hear the word *bride* coupled with *queen* more often than I like. I certainly haven't helped matters by purchasing that tiara. But I cannot bring myself to regret it.

We come to the food sellers. I watch Faraine's eyes goggle as she takes in the many offerings, all so strange to her palate. There are cakes sweetened with *jiru* nectar and shaped like little domes—*mog* cakes, we call them, in honor of the priestesses and their domed dwellings. There are flatbreads made of *grus* flour, a variety of edible lichen—very earthy and a bit dense, but satisfying. The scent of fried mushrooms catches her attention, but I guide her to a vendor selling sizzling *ugha* fish seasoned with rock salt.

"*Ugha* live far from all light," I tell her, as she recoils from the ugly, eyeless fish, cooked whole on little skewers. "Divers use line cables to plunge up to thirty feet into blind depths to set their traps." I select a plump one from over the coals, holding the skewer's handle out to Faraine.

She makes a face but gamely accepts my offering, turning it slowly as though to find a less repulsive angle. "Am I supposed to eat it whole?"

"Not yet." I pluck a jar of bright purple salt from the seller's display and sprinkle it over the *ugha* until it glistens. "Now, be brave! Bite the head off first."

She casts me a dubious look. Have I pushed her too far? By now, however, her stomach has started growling almost constantly. She screws up her face, pops the fish head in her mouth, and bites. Chews. Slowly opens her eyes again. "That's actually . . ." She hesitates, considers. Then: "Good?"

"Is that a question?"

"It might be?"

"Would you like a second bite to verify?"

She makes a wordless whimper. But she does take a second bite. Then a third. In the end, she finishes the whole thing and eats another. From there we move on to a mushroom vendor who points out certain varieties safe for human consumption. After that, Faraine staunchly refuses to try seared cave cricket legs, so we end our makeshift meal with some *grus* bread served with a minced grottoberry relish. This she finds much to her liking and eats a sizable portion.

"You must have found the food at Beldroth quite bland," she remarks, licking her fingers delicately before wiping them on the little cloth provided.

"Strange, to be sure," I acknowledge. "But I quite enjoyed the experience. I travel so little beyond Mythanar and appreciate the chance to encounter other worlds and ways of living."

Hunger sated, we proceed now at a leisurely pace through the textiles market. Faraine admires garments of pure *hugagug* silk, delighted by their iridescent colors. Another vendor offers skeins of the spun *hugagug* thread, which Faraine inspects with great interest. I'm just trying to decide if I dare buy her another gift when a sudden trill of music ripples through the air. Faraine's head pops up. "What is that? Where is it coming from?"

"It's the *gujek*—traveling minstrels." I tilt an ear and pinpoint the direction from which it comes. "I believe they're right above us. Shall we go see?"

Faraine agrees, her eyes shining and eager. We climb to the final level of Market Rise, high at the top of the cliff. There, on a broad flat platform, the *gujek* minstrels have gathered with their great frames strung with dangling crystals. Each crystal gives a pure, sweet tone—some high, some low. The minstrels beat them in swift, complicated patterns, generating a shimmering song, like the rushing cascade of ice water. Other players on *zinsbog* horns create a bright countermeasure, and a single drummer beats a rumbling growl on his skin drums.

Wonderstruck, Faraine watches the performance. And I watch her. I can't help myself. All the beauties of Mythanar pale by comparison to the joy of watching her face. The subtleties of expression, every slight shift of her brow, her cheek, her jaw, her lips. It's like watching a living, breathing work of art. I could sit and make a study of her all day.

I find myself wondering what her face would look like in . . . *release*?

"Oh! Look!" she exclaims suddenly, and turns to me. "Who is she?"

Reluctantly, I tear my gaze away from her to look where she points. A trolde woman in traditional garb has taken her place before the minstrels. She wears a massive headdress of balancing black stone weights. A single wrong tilt will send the whole thing toppling, but the woman holds herself so perfectly straight and tall, the muscles of her neck bulging with strength, that the weights scarcely tremble. The rest of her clothing is simple—a loincloth, a sheer wrap across her bosom, and a belt of small animal skulls.

"She is a *morn* dancer," I say, bending to speak in Faraine's ear so that she can hear me above the sudden blare of the *zinsbog*. "It's a very old art form. Watch!"

The woman begins her dance, a performance of balance and strength, so unlike the dances back in Gavaria. Faraine is enthralled. She cannot tear her gaze away as the steps become ever more complex. The *morn* dancer stomps hard enough to shake the ground under our feet, raises and smashes rocks together, crumbling them to dust. In the end, she utters a deep, guttural roar that rises to the cavern ceiling above, all without disturbing the balance of her weights.

When the dance is complete and the music resolves, Faraine applauds after human fashion, clapping her hands together and shouting, "Well done! Magnificent!" The folk gathered to observe the dance smile curiously at her antics. A few of them try to copy her behavior. After all, if she is their new queen, any outlandish customs she brings will soon be all the rage with the younger set.

The *morn* dancer exits, and the minstrels begin another song, this one lighter and faster. Suddenly, one of the men in the crowd shouts out, "A dance! Big King, a dance! A dance with your new bride!" Before I can react, the cry is taken up. Soon the voices of the spectators nearly drown out the song itself.

Startled by this outburst, Faraine leans closer to me. "Is something wrong?"

"No." My face heats. I hope she's not reading my feelings just now. "They want me to dance with you."

Her eyes flash to meet mine, alight and alive. "Is that so? And . . . do you think the people should have what they ask?"

It's suddenly difficult to swallow. "Considering the tensions in the city these days, it wouldn't be terrible for them to see their king at ease, dancing." *Enjoying himself immensely.*

"Would you say it might uplift their spirits?"

"It might."

Her smile is bright as a *lorst* stone suddenly ignited. "Well then, shall we?"

I laugh and shake my head. "You don't know any trolde dances, remember?"

She shrugs, her lips quirked prettily. "I know how to stand still, how to clap to a beat, and how to be spun on demand. Will that not do?"

Another laugh rumbles up my throat. Suddenly, I don't care anymore what a dangerous idea this is. This whole morning has been foolish from the beginning. I might as well embrace it.

Taking her hand, I lead her to the clear space vacated by the *morn* dancer. The people cheer, and the minstrels shift effortlessly from their light, sparkling melody into something . . . different. A low, sensual song with a driving beat. The first few strains are enough to suggest dimly lit rooms, wafting curtains, discarded garments on the floor.

I catch Faraine's eye. Hold it. She feels it too, that thrum of lust and longing. It ripples through the air, surrounds us in an atmosphere of unrelenting sound. She draws herself very straight, very tall, all the laughter suddenly gone from her eyes. Instead, I see only . . . *challenge.*

Following the beat, letting my body move as it wills, I approach her. Strong. Powerful. My feet carry me close to her, so close that our skin warms but never quite meets. She does as she said she would—she stands firm. Swaying a little in time to the beat. Turning slowly to follow me, to hold that eye contact like a fiery cord binding our souls, even as the dance carries me away from her again. This is an ancient dance, and yet it is all new.

Suddenly I am singing, though I had not meant to:

*"Jor ru jorrak.*
*Ur ru urrak.*
*Dor ru dorrak.*
*Hav ru havrak."*

*Stone of my stone.*
*Blood of my blood.*
*Flesh of my flesh.*
*Heart of my heart.*

The words are simply there on my tongue. They must be spoken; they must be sung. And soon, those who watch us take up the chant, singing it in rumbling voices, deeper even than the reverberations of the skin drums.

*"Jor ru jorrak.*
*Ur ru urrak.*
*Dor ru dorrak."*

Faraine's face, flushed and brilliant, shines before me like the last light of life itself. The dance draws me back to her. I move around her, passing my hands in the air over her breasts, her shoulders, her throat, down her back. Never touching, only manipulating the energy between us. She sways with me, bending and responding to every gesture. Only when the music swells to its crescendo do I finally grip her waist and swing her off her feet. Round and round we twirl, and she holds my shoulders, her gaze never once leaving mine.

The music ends. The people roar their approval, stomping their feet and smashing stones together. Cries of "The king and his bride! Behold, the king and his bride!" echo across Market Rise.

I scarcely hear them. I stand as though frozen in a sliver of suspended eternity. My arms are wrapped around her waist, holding her face level with mine as her feet dangle above the ground. Faraine stares into my eyes. Knowing me, knowing my heart. Knowing that truth which, until this moment, I've struggled so hard to deny.

I am falling irrevocably in love. With my wife.

# 25

## Faraine

I wish I could stay here. Right here, in this singular point of time, suspended in the air. Held in his strong arms.

My hands rest on his shoulders as I gaze deeply into his eyes. Mere inches separate our parted and panting lips. Were it not for the crowd gaping at us, I would grab his face and drag him to me right now. Then, in that touch, in that burning point of connection, I would know for certain. I would know that he isn't going to send me back. I would know that I will stay here and be his wife. His queen.

A pulse of excitement emanates from the crowd. I feel it, but faintly, like the distant murmur of wind. The rest of my awareness is taken up with Vor. His feelings. His love? Perhaps. Or something very close to it.

Slowly, slowly, he lowers me back to the ground. My slippers touch stone, but I do not remove my hands from his shoulders, nor do I break that eye contact which we have held since the beginning of our dance. If I look away, I fear something between us will snap. Something I must find some way to secure, soon.

Vor's eyes shine above me, eclipsing all other lights in that vast, light-filled cavern. They're like two moons, drawing me with their gravity, brightening my very existence.

Suddenly, his expression darkens. He blinks, and his brow constricts. To my pain, he lifts his gaze and stares over my head. Only now, with our connection broken, do I sense the disturbance in the atmosphere. A deep throb of drums rumbles like thunder, reverberates under my feet.

"*Morar-juk*," Vor curses. "What are *they* doing here?"

The crowd is restless, shifting. I twist in Vor's arms to look where every head is turned. I feel before I see what has drawn their attention, however. Like a blow to my gods-gift—a battering weight of *void*.

This is wrong. Impossible and wrong. I shouldn't be able to stand here, in the midst of this crowd of living beings, and experience such an absence. Absence of feeling. Absence of life. An emptiness, a nothingness. My head spins, and my stomach churns.

Suddenly, the crowd parts, and a strange procession comes into view. Trolde men and women both, twenty at least, perhaps more. At their forefront march two tall women, both of them naked save for loincloths and the long white hair covering their bosoms. Behind them come six drummers in rigid formation, also naked, their only covering the animal-hide drums hung from their necks and suspended before their groins. Their hands beat the drum skins in perfect synchronization, raising a thunderous din of *doom, doom, doom*.

Behind these, six massive, stone-hide troldes carry a litter on their backs. Unlike the curtained contraption in which I rode through Mythanar on my arrival, this is a broad, open platform. It is trimmed in black cloth, so that it gives the impression of a wafting shadow.

Targ sits in its center.

The priest sits perfectly still. His bare stone skin looks grayer than ever, without the faintest trace of life. Strands of white hair drift from his head, but he's lost more of it since last I saw him. His skull is craggy like a boulder. It would be all too easy to believe this is not the man himself but instead an incredibly lifelike statue carved in his honor.

The moment I lay eyes on him, I know the source of that void.

Muttering and grumbling, the crowd pulls back, makes room for the procession. Some drop to their knees, abject and submissive. Others scoff, and one brave soul heaves a clod of mud straight at Targ's face. It splats against his forehead, dribbles down his cheek. The priest offers no reaction. Marching in time to the beat of the drums, this strange parade continues straight on, straight toward Vor and me. Each footstep is somehow inexorable, as though ordained by the gods themselves in ages past.

The minstrels behind us gather their instruments and scatter, unwilling to be caught in the path of these terrible worshippers. But Vor does not move. He stands with his shoulders straight, his chest wide. With one arm, he draws me behind him. That I don't like. I don't want to cower at his back. I want to stand beside him. But when I resist, his arm tenses. I go still. Perhaps it's better not to fight. Not yet, at least.

The two women, white as alabaster, their faces beautiful beyond description, stop a few paces in front of Vor. Neither of them look at him. Their gazes are vacant. Behind them, the drummers beat out a last, synchronized *doom*, and the litter-bearers lower their burden to the ground.

Silence holds the air captive. My knees tremble so hard, I have to stop myself from grabbing hold of Vor for support. I don't know what is happening, but I can see the unease in the crowd all around us, all their whispering and pointing and shifting of feet. I cannot sense their feelings, however. That pulsing void emanating from Targ is much too oppressive.

Suddenly, the priest's eyes open.

He doesn't make a sound. Doesn't move save for that quick flick of eyelids. Yet every one of the observers gasps out loud. Someone screams. Vor's spine stiffens in front of me, while I choke back a terrified cry of my own.

Targ stares straight at Vor. Their eyes meet. The air between them charges. The void rolls out from inside the priest, a dark force emanating from his soul. I feel it, almost *see* it, with that strange, unseeing clarity I'd experienced in the dark chapel. It swells as it nears, until it's a huge shadow, ready to overwhelm us, to swallow us up in its inescapable *nothing*.

Vor stands firm. When I look at him, my gods-gift sees the shining strength of his spirit rise to meet that darkness. Light and shadow clash in that space between the king and the priest. No one else sees it. No one else feels it. But suddenly, that churning storm of battling wills is more real than anything else.

I watch in mingled horror and awe as sometimes the darkness of Targ's void seems to dominate, only to be fought back by the light that is Vor's indomitable soul. But the dark is stronger. It has the weight of inevitability behind it—a hard, cold certainty of ultimate triumph. Yet Vor does not back down. He braces himself, his vision clear and firm. He will not go quietly into that dark. He will hold on until the last spark of life—the last spark of hope—is extinguished. But . . . but . . .

But he cannot do this alone.

Part of me wants to stay in hiding. That storm of souls is greater than anything I've experienced since my arrival in this realm. To step out of Vor's shelter and face it feels foolish. But when I look up at Vor's face, I see the strain in his eyes, the first lines of defeat beginning to etch themselves into his cheeks. I know what I must do.

I reach out. Take his hand.

It's a simple gesture. The simplest.

But in that touch of our palms, I offer the only thing I can, the only power I've ever been able to wield from this gift of mine: *calm*. It flows between our skin, up his arm, straight to his heart. I hear his sudden intake of breath, watch his eyes flare.

Then, to my surprise, his mouth curves in a smile.

The effect is instantaneous. The roiling void which had so nearly subsumed his light gives way. The energy of Vor's soul intensifies until it is so bright to my gods-gifted senses, I almost turn to hide my face in his shoulder.

As abruptly as it began, the battle is over. Targ remains seated on his litter, having never once moved save for the raising of his eyelids. Vor stands at my side, grips my hand, his stance strong, his face set. The storm of spirits dissipates like clouds. Though they are unaware of what truly just happened, the crowd lets out a collective sigh of relief.

Moved by some unseen force of will, the two pale women speak at once: "*Morar tor Grakanak! Morar tor Jor!*" The litter-bearers bend and heave their burden back onto their shoulders. Targ's eyes glitter one last time before he shuts them. The criers and drummers turn on heel, and the litter is ponderously brought around. Then the whole procession marches slowly back in the direction it came from, the crowd parting and closing behind it. Soon, even the deep voices of the drums are drowned in the regular noise of the city.

Only when they're truly gone does Vor finally turn to me. "Are you all right?"

I can see in his eyes that he knows his silent staring contest with the priest had a far more profound effect on me than on others present. I nod and offer a weak smile. The truth is, I feel strangely numb. That encounter has shaken me more than I like to admit. "What was that about?" I ask softly.

"One never knows with Targ." Vor shakes his head and rubs a hand down his face. Then his brow puckers. "I should take you back. You look tired. It's been a long lusterling already, and if you're to travel soon . . ."

My eyes widen. I cannot believe what I'm hearing. Travel? Soon? Is he truly still planning to send me back to Gavaria? My head spins. All the blissful certainty I'd experienced while dancing in his arms shatters.

I shake my head, drop my gaze to focus on his collarbone. "I don't want to go home." The words slip out. Soft but clear.

Vor stills. He seems to hold his breath, waiting for me to continue. But what more can I say? There is nothing else. Just that one, simple fact. I don't want to go. I don't want to be parted from him. Not now. Not ever.

"I've already kept you out longer than I should," he says after what feels like an age. "Hael will be starting to worry."

With those words, all the barriers between our hearts slam back into place. I'm too weak, too numb, too powerless to fight them. I want to scream with frustration. Instead, I simply nod.

Vor summons his morleth from its dark dimension. Soon, I find myself holding on to the saddle pommel once more, Vor's arms wrapped around me. Rather than ride by the main road, Vor urges his beast into flight. It glides out from the top of Market Rise, its strange feet walking easily on air. This is the first time I've ridden like this, but the wonder of it all is lost on me. My heart lodges painfully in my throat, choking back a sob. Tears slip down my cheeks as we soar across this city I've only just begun to know. Over the little domed houses of the priestesses where the refugee children scamper and play. Over the highways and byways of the intricate trolde lives going on below.

Vor waves to the gate guards as we glide over the wall. I expect him to bring Knar down in the courtyard. Instead, he guides the beast up to a window many stories up. Seen from this angle, I don't recognize it as my bedchamber window until Knar lands, setting his massive cloven feet with surprising delicacy on the balcony rail.

I blink, surprised. Why has Vor brought me this way back to my room? To avoid being seen? Is it possible he doesn't want anyone to know he is with me here? Is it possible he might intend to . . . to . . . ?

My stomach flutters. A sudden strong rush of *last chance* quickens in my blood. I pull in my bottom lip and bite.

Vor slips from the saddle, landing a little hard. He catches his balance then turns and holds up his hands to me. With Knar perched on the edge of the rail, the distance between us is greater than before. I look down into Vor's eyes.

Then I reach out, wrap my arms around his neck. He pulls me from the saddle. My head whirls, and I tighten my hold. Just a little. Just enough that he doesn't immediately put me down. He stands there, holding me. Very like how we ended our dance, with my arms around his shoulders, his hands at my waist, my feet dangling. Only this time there's no one watching. This time, there's no reason for him not to kiss me if he wishes to.

But he doesn't.

Before I can utter a word, he sets me down and withdraws his hands. I back up, cheeks hot, straightening my skirts and pushing stray hair from my face. My throat is tight, but I force out the first words that spring to my tongue. "I . . . I quite enjoyed my tour of your city, Vor."

"Yes." He looks off over my shoulder, avoiding my eyes. "I will . . . never forget our time together. Brief though it was."

My stomach drops. This is his goodbye. This moment, right here on my balcony. He intends this to be our last. Perhaps we will glimpse one another again, but never in private. He might even avoid me entirely before he sends me back to my own world.

His gaze flicks to mine. His lips part, and I hear him draw a little breath. I'm not ready for whatever he's about to say. I can't bear it.

So, I blurt out the only thing I can think of: "Would you like to come inside? For . . . for a drink?"

He blinks. His brow puckers, one eyebrow quirked.

"You must be parched," I ramble on hastily. "I know I am. I believe there is some refreshment inside. The maid, she often brings something in the mornings. I . . . I can see. If you like?" I'm not certain it's possible to sound more foolish. I have nothing to serve him. And I think he knows it. Which means he can easily guess at my ulterior motives.

Before he has a chance to protest, I whirl in a flutter of pink skirts and hasten to the window. My hands shake as I push it open, and butterflies careen wildly in my chest as I part the curtains and step through into the room. Part of me fears Vor will take the opportunity to mount his morleth and depart without a word while my back is turned. But he is a gentleman; surely he wouldn't do anything so rude.

I hasten to the center of the room, cast about for something, anything I might offer him. There's nothing but a silver ewer of water and two small cups on the table near the door. I hasten over to it, every sense in my body aware when Vor steps through the open window. His presence seems to fill the space behind me. My hands simply won't stop trembling. It takes all my concentration to lift the ewer and pour a trickle of water into each cup. Then, closing my eyes, I breathe a silent prayer before I turn to face him.

He stands in the middle of the room. How strangely awkward and uneasy he looks, especially for such a powerful, graceful man. He meets my eye only for an instant before looking away. "Here," I say, a little too brightly, and step forward with the cup. "It's not very cold, I'm afraid."

"I don't mind." He accepts my offering and stares down into it. As though it's a scrying pool and he seeks to discern the future. "What should we drink to?" he asks at last.

This moment reminds me rather too vividly of our wedding night. Does he remember too? I shiver, turn the cup around in my hands. "How about to new experiences?"

His mouth tips in a small smile that sends warmth spreading right down to my toes. "I'll drink to that." He touches the lip of his cup against mine before downing the contents. I take a more tentative sip, moistening my lips. Then we stand there. Mute. Vor stares into his empty cup, but I know he's as aware of me as I am of him. Aware of me, of this private space. Of the narrow bed up against the wall.

"I should go." Vor turns, sets the cup down on the nearest available surface. He's already taken two strides for the window before I have a chance to react.

With a little gulping cry, I lunge after him, take hold of his arm.

"No, please! Stay." Do I sound desperate? I can't help it. I am desperate. Desperate that this will be the last time I see him, that once he walks back out onto that balcony, I will never again share his atmosphere. "I . . . Hael isn't back yet," I add lamely. "I would appreciate the company."

His gaze fixes on my fingers, gripping his bare forearm. Slowly, he lifts his eyes to mine, then glances to the window, like it's his escape. Hastily, I let go and step back, move to one of the chairs pulled up near the hearth. I take a seat, like the proper gracious hostess my mother raised me to be, and sweep a hand to indicate the other chair. After a short, awkward stillness, Vor complies. He perches stiffly on the edge of his chair.

Great gods spare me, what am I supposed to do now? I know what I want, but . . . but I can't very well launch myself across this space between us and kiss him. Can I? No, surely not.

"I enjoyed my outing today," I say lamely after the silence has lasted far too long.

"Yes. You said that." Vor's lip twitches as he studies the back of his own hand.

"Oh. Of course."

We're silent again. I'm almost certain I hear Hael's returning footsteps on the stairwell, marching down the passage to this room. I don't have much time. I can't afford to hesitate. And yet I sit frozen, afraid to act.

Finally, Vor clears his throat. "I hope you will think well of me, Faraine." Still, he does not look at me. His gaze is fixed on the dragon carved into the mantelpiece. "Your time here in Mythanar was full of peril and darkness. I know I contributed a great deal to both. But I hope your memories of me will dwell on whatever good I managed to show you rather than the bad. When you're gone."

"When I'm gone?" I echo softly. All the air seems to leave my lungs.

"Yes." He says it again more firmly: "Yes."

Suddenly, I'm not afraid anymore. Or rather, something other than fear rises to the surface of my heart, swallowing up all other feelings. I gaze across at Vor as realization rises, firms. Becomes conviction. For too long, I've let other people decide my fate. For too long, I've let them push and prod, manipulate and mold me into something I don't even recognize, until I myself am lost.

No more. I know what I must do.

Without a word, I rise. Vor's head comes up sharply, but I don't look back. My fists clenched, my jaw set, I step away from the chairs, cross the bedchamber, my skirts rustling in my wake. I reach out to the door latch, make certain it's fastened. And drop the bolt. Then carefully, delicately, I remove the tiara from my head. It sparkles as I set it on the table beside the water ewer.

Only now do I turn. Look at Vor.

"I don't want us to be disturbed," I say. "Not this time."

His barriers fall. One after another, they simply melt away, and a storm of feeling rises inside him. He wants me. He wants me more than he can bear. It's burning him up from the inside, an exquisite torture.

Slowly, I cross the room to him. Any moment, he might spring up and flee. But he doesn't. Soon I stand before his chair, almost between his knees. For once, I look down at him. Down at that broad brow, knotted and tense. Down at those full lips, the warmth of which I know so well. He drops his gaze once more, stares down at my feet. But that won't do. Not at all.

I lift one hand. Hold it beside his cheek, let it hover there, less than an inch from his skin. He breathes out, closes his eyes.

Then he leans into my touch. That mere contact sends my gods-gift singing, dancing. I catch my breath, unable to help the smile that bursts across my face. He looks up, abject longing in his eyes. Whatever doubts I may have harbored vanish.

I bring my other hand up, cup his face gently as I lower my lips to his. My kiss is light at first, a gentle pressure. Testing the waters, eager to discover how my senses will react to his. It's all warmth, all sweetness, all delight. I press more firmly, nudging his lips open, urging him to receive me, to take everything I have to offer.

Vor surges to his feet. "No!" he cries. "No, no, no, we cannot do this." Turning from me, he storms once more for the windows.

"Vor, stop!" I've never in my life used a tone so commanding. It works. He halts mid-step and stands as though rooted. "Tell me why not," I demand. Lifting the edge of my skirts, I hasten to him. My gaze fixes on his tense spine, between his shoulder blades. "Give me one good reason why you won't turn around and kiss me right now."

"Because I'm sending you home!" The words break from his throat, low, agonized. "Today. Or tomorrow or the next day. It doesn't matter because you are going. Sooner, not later."

"But not *now*." I take another step closer. "This is our time. This is our moment. If we don't take it, it may never come again."

His hands are fisted at his sides. His whole soul shakes. Ordinarily, such a storm of feeling would be enough to drive me back. Not this time. I reach out but cannot quite bring myself to touch him. My hand hovers over his shoulder.

"I don't care about the risks, Vor. I'm ready. I'm ready to risk it all because any risk is worth it to be with you. If this moment is all we ever have, I'm willing to accept whatever pain may come." I blink hard, try to force back the tears sparking in my eyes. "I won't live my life aching for what I never had the courage to take."

"You feel that way now." He shakes his head, breathing heavily. "What about later? You will feel I have used you. Taken from you that which was not mine."

"No." The word whispers from my trembling lips. "I will know only that I gave what I wished to give, and in that knowledge, I will be glad. Glad that for once I had a choice. And I made it. For my sake, for yours, and no one else's."

"*Morar-juk!*" He lifts his head, rakes his hands through his hair. "Gods give me strength!"

Am I losing him? After all this, will he still resist me? "Vor, please—"

He pivots on heel, grasps me by my upper arms, and pulls me to him. His lips find mine in a kiss that makes my mind, soul, and body explode in a light-storm of sensation. It ripples through me, melts my insides, until I am weak-kneed and leaning into him for support. Were it not for his grip on me, I would fall at his feet.

Then my hands are around his neck, and his are in my hair. He angles my face so that he can kiss me more deeply, and I open my mouth to him. Our tongues meet, tangle. That intimate touch makes all the colors of my heart dance.

He cups my cheeks, pulls me back just a little, stares down at me in absolute wonder. "What have you done to me?" He kisses me again, gently. A sweet touch, like a promise, a prayer. "I would hazard it all. My realm, my crown, my kingdom. Even my honor. All for you. Only for you."

His hands slide from my cheeks down to my neck, my shoulders, my arms. When he pulls me against him this time, I cannot ignore the hardness of his body revealing the full intensity of his need for me. It's enough to make my breath catch. I roll my head back, and his kisses move from my mouth to my jaw, my neck, down to my collarbone. He molds me against him, and I bend backwards, dizzy with desire. My blood turns to liquid lava, pulsing hot through every limb.

A little growl in my throat, I grab hold of his tunic, wrench it free of his belt so that I can slip my hand underneath to press against the small of his back. He gasps. As though that mere touch is enough to undo him. I explore further, sliding my palms around to his abdomen, up his chest. Then I yank the garment. Obeying my unspoken command, he rips it over his head and tosses it to one side.

Now he stands before me, chest heaving. I step back to sweep my lingering gaze over his body. But looking isn't enough. I cannot resist reaching out, touching the hard muscles of his chest. His skin is such a strange, otherworldly color to my human gaze. I should probably find him unsettling. But I don't. He's so beautiful it almost hurts.

He closes his eyes, groans softly. Then he takes hold of me suddenly, turns me around, pulls me against his chest. Once more I feel his hardness, and it both thrills and intimidates me. For now, I lean my head back against his shoulder and glory in the sensation of his fingers tracing my throat, slipping under the sleeve of my gown. He pulls the sleeve down and presses scorching kisses against the curve of my neck.

A shivering moan escapes my lips. I reach up, rest my hand lightly on top of his for a moment. Then I take hold. With gentle determination, I guide him down under my bodice until he cups my breast.

Turning sharply, I look him straight in the eye.

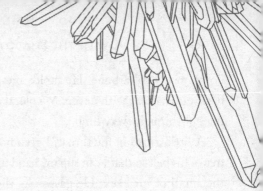

# 26

# Vor

She's like a miracle. So perfectly formed, her warm softness against my palm; her strange, bicolored eyes piercing mine.

She wants this. She wants me.

Despite all I've done. Despite how I've made her suffer. She wants me.

Thoughts of duty, crown, kingdom, and chaos can no longer fit inside my head. There's no room for anything but her. For all I want to give her, all I want her to know and experience. She is a miracle. *My* miracle. And I won't waste whatever time we have.

I caress her gently, my thumb playing across her nipple. Her eyes widen and her lips part in a little gasp. Leaning back against me once more, her body quivers in response to my touch. I bend my head, kiss her beautiful white shoulder even as my fingers continue their delicate play. She shivers and moves, her hips pressed against me. Is she unaware of how the pressure of her round curves drives me wild? Perhaps. The ways of love and lust are new to her. But she will soon learn. We will learn together.

She utters a protesting whimper when I draw my hand away from her breast. The sound is so sweetly petulant, it brings a smile to my lips. Taking hold of her hips, I turn her to face me. She gazes up from beneath her lashes, her eyes slightly unfocused. She looks intoxicated. Drunk on my touch.

I back her up a step. Like a dancer, she moves at my silent bidding. One step, then another, then another, until I've guided her across the floor and we come to the bed. There I sit her down in front of me. Her head is level with my abdomen. Her breath pants against my navel. My body surges with longing for the things I want from her. But no. This moment is not about my needs. Not now. Maybe not ever. I don't know how much time we have left together. What I do know is that I want whatever time we have to belong to her.

I kneel before her, my eyes only a little lower than hers. Smiling, she drapes her arms around my neck, pulls me to her. Her lips claim mine in another kiss. Slow, lingering. A kiss that tells the world to stand back and wait for us.

When I finally pull back, she leans in after me, catching my lower lip between her teeth. Her bite is sharp and sweet. I smile and kiss the corner of her mouth, her jaw, her neck. How her pulse races, like a fluttering bird! I twirl her delicate sleeve with one finger, pull it out of the way. Her bodice slips to expose her breast, and my kisses wander farther still, all the way down to that pink nipple.

Faraine gasps. Arches her back. Presses her hands into the mattress and pushes herself into me. My body surges with power and triumph at her responses. I want to taste and tease her, to devour every inch of her. I pull her other sleeve as well until the whole bodice falls around her waist. Nuzzling close, I first kiss the skin between her breasts before moving to take the other nipple in my lips. Meanwhile, my hands find that slit in her skirt. Fingers dancing and light, I discover her calves, her knees, the soft swell of her outer thighs, the fascinating slope of her hip bones.

"Oh, Vor!" she gasps, and suddenly grasps my head. I look up only for her to crush her lips against mine. She slides her grip to my shoulders, tugging, pulling. She doesn't have the strength to move me, but I obey her urging. Rising from my knees, I lay her back onto her little bed, climb on top of her. I'm so much larger than she, I must take care not to overpower her. But she's not afraid. She runs her hands over my body, as though she cannot get enough of me. Her bare breast presses against my chest, her heart beating in time with mine.

My tongue enters her mouth again. She groans in response, the sound a song of pure delight. She bends her knee. I feel the hot inside of her thigh pressed against the side of my abdomen. It's too much temptation to bear.

I slip my hand under her skirts. My searching fingers find the sensitive nerves of her secret core.

She sucks in a breath, pops up onto her elbows. Her mouth is open, her eyes wide; her lips swollen, parted, and panting.

I hold her gaze. Stroke her again.

"Wh-what are you doing?" she breathes.

"Do you like it?"

"I . . ." She bites her lip. Nods. I stroke, and her body quivers in response. Her eyelashes flutter, and her eyes go unfocused.

"You are so beautiful," I murmur, drawing my lips close to hers. "Like an exquisite little bird of the Upper World, trapped here below. I want to make you sing. I want to make you soar."

I stroke her again, my fingers attune to her least response. Her hips move. Her head lolls back, exposing that lovely white throat once more. I kiss her, lick her, rest my teeth gently above the rabid flutter of her pulse. My hand finds the little sash still holding her gown in place. With a twist, I snap it in two and let the whole flimsy garment fall away. She sits up in the ruins of pink fabric, completely bare, and crosses one arm over her chest with virginal timidity, but no fear. Flushing, her eyes lift to meet mine.

That look is pure devastation.

I kiss her lips again. Full and deep. Then I pull her hand away from her chest, pin it behind her back so that I may kiss the rest of her, worshipping every inch of her exquisite form. With each passing moment, I feel her give herself over in absolute vulnerability. To me! To the man who nearly killed her. To the man who let his pride and pain punish her far too long when she never deserved it. If this is not forgiveness, I do not know what is.

How can I possibly let her know what I feel? How honored I am to be offered the gift of her trust? I want to give to her. I want to throw the world at her feet. I want to bring her joy and comfort and delight, to be the one she turns to for every need, for the fulfillment of each secret longing.

I have to show her.

And I will. *Now.*

When I lay her back down on the bed, her golden hair pools around her face. She breathes out through those parted pink lips, gazing up at me without blinking as I kiss her again and again. Then she rests her hands on top of mine as I run my palms over her body. My mouth continues traveling down, between her breasts to her navel. My tongue flicks, both light and languorous.

As though suddenly shy, she presses her legs together and twists to one side. I glide my palm over her hip, admiring the smoothness of her skin, the womanly shape of her body. Then I slip my fingers between her legs, easing them apart.

Her eyes fasten hard on mine, bright with sudden anxiety. I can see the thoughts racing across her brain. She's been taught enough to know the basics of how men and women join. Of the pain she will endure. She looks down at the front of my trousers, still laced up, but unable to hide the evidence of my mounting need. She bites her lip. "You . . . you will be gentle with me, Vor?"

"Oh, Faraine." I bend down and kiss her stomach again. "Faraine, Faraine. I will be more than gentle."

## 27

# Faraine

Vor shifts on the bed. It's so narrow, I fear there won't be room for him, for what he is about to do. But he moves with leonine grace, easing himself down, lowering his head to press his lips against my abdomen.

Then he ventures lower still. And lower. Now his mouth is hot against the soft skin of my inner thighs. Each kiss is a brand, searing me with pleasure. I burn at his touch and long only to be consumed in this flame.

Then he's not kissing me. Instead, his tongue is moving. Licking. First against my legs, and then . . .

My breath catches in my throat. Reaching out, I touch the top of his head with one hand. I try to speak, but my words melt away in a little squeak of surprise. He looks up at me, along the length of my hot, quivering body. His lips hover just over my core.

"Do you trust me?" he asks, grinning roguishly, his lips full, his teeth flashing.

I'm panting too hard to speak. Do I trust him? I don't know.

His brow puckers, and the smile vanishes. "Do you want me to stop?"

"No!" I shake my head so hard, strands of hair fall across my eyes. I push them back hastily. My chest rises and falls, unable to draw a full breath. "Oh, gods, no. No." *Please, don't stop.*

His smile returns, devasting and beautiful enough to stop my heart. "I'm going to make you soar, Faraine," he murmurs.

Then he lowers his mouth. Kisses me.

Licks me.

One stroke, and I gasp.

Another, and I bleat his name: "Vor!"

A third, and I fall back on my pillow.

I am his. Wholly and completely. I've given up whatever control I thought I had, placed myself in his hands, in his keeping.

And now, he makes me new.

Again and again, he strokes me, creating a rhythm just for us. I whimper. My fingers grip the blankets, my knuckles white and tense. My hips move in time to his tempo, back and forth, chasing something I don't understand but feel flitting there, on the edge of my awareness. So close. A bird beating its wings against the bars.

Part of me is afraid. Afraid to give in. Afraid of the release I long for. Afraid to let my walls down, to let my soul fly free.

It's safe in the cage. It's safe in hiding.

But there's no hiding. Not anymore. I am here, bare, vulnerable. And his.

I can try to hold on to the last fraying threads of control, or I can . . . *let go.*

I cry out. My back arches and my body spasms as something bursts inside of me. Something that soars and spins dizzyingly high to the heavens, beyond this world of stone. I quake, unable to breathe, as waves of pleasure pulse through me. A deep, guttural moan erupts from my throat as I twist, turn, writhe, all while his hands hold my hips firmly in place.

He doesn't stop. Not even when I grip the top of his head once more. And just when I think the ecstasy has passed, just when I think I'm about to come back down to earth again, another powerful updraft sends me soaring higher than before.

"Vor! Oh, Vor!" I cry.

I feel his lips curve against me in a smile.

## 28

## Faraine

I lie in a golden haze, Vor's name still hovering on my lips. Even now, long after cresting the last heights, I feel like I'm floating on a cloud far above this world under stone. Never have I felt so alive, so complete. As though some missing part of me has finally been found, reclaimed, and restored.

Vor. Vor is the missing part. My soul knew it from the moment I first heard his voice in my ear. It was as though I recognized him from some existence beyond time and space where we have always been inextricably linked. I am his just as he is mine.

He kisses my stomach, then plants another kiss between my breasts before settling beside me on the narrow bed. We scarcely fit together, but I angle my body to create more room and gaze up into his face. Into that smile of his, which seems as though it could go on forever. He gently smooths hair off my sweat-beaded forehead then cups my cheek. I want to speak, want to say something. But my emotions are all a tangled blur which has nothing to do with my gods-gift.

"I . . . I didn't know . . ." is all I can manage at last.

Fyndra had explained in detail the pain and degradation await-
ing me on my wedding night. She'd spoken of men's animalistic
desires, of instincts and rough satisfaction. She'd spoken as well of
the secret power a woman may wield over her oppressor if she learns
to lever his desires against him.

Nothing she'd said had any place in this experience. This was
no dance of instinct and pain, but one of tenderness. A dance of
passion, awakening my body and my soul to possibilities I'd never
dreamed. Possibilities that could only be made reality in a space of
absolute trust.

I've always had to be so guarded. It's the only way I've survived
against the storms that assail my senses every hour of every day. I'd
never known it was possible to let my defenses down so completely,
to give myself over to someone else like this. Who knew surrender
could be so exquisite?

"I gathered," Vor says, and smiles. His fingers trail down my
neck to my collarbone, finally coming to rest over my heart. "I'm
delighted to be the one to introduce you to that particular pleasure."

I flush and drop my gaze, suddenly shy. "Oh, don't do that!" he
says.

"Don't do what?"

"Don't look away. I want to look into those strange, beautiful
eyes of yours."

I raise my gaze to his. There are no barriers between us. His
heart is open to me now, and in that openness, his soul shines with
such beauty. I could drown in his gaze and die happy.

My hands slip up, wrap around the back of his head. I pull him
to me, press his lips to mine. He answers my desire, opens his
mouth to receive my eager tongue. His hand slides down to press

against my back, then lower still, pulling me against him. I'd thought I was spent a moment before. Now I find I'm hungrier than ever. Absolutely ravenous for him.

I wrap my leg around him, hook him behind the knee, draw him close. His hand grips my thigh, and I feel the swell of him pressed up against me. I know what it means. In this, at least, Fyndra's instruction doesn't fail me. Hand trembling, I slip my fingers down to the front of his trousers, fumbling with the laces.

Vor moans and draws back. His long hair falls in his face. "Faraine." His voice is husky, rough. "We can't."

Like the slam of a dropping portcullis, his barriers fall between us. It's so sudden, I'm left reeling. Sparks explode inside my head. I stare up at him, shocked and uncertain. He's still here, physically. I feel his warm blood, feel the tight swell of his need. But his soul retreats from me. That bond, that closeness, which mere moments ago I'd thought could never be broken is . . . gone.

I start to shiver. Not with cold, but with a terrible soul-freeze. Maybe I did not hear him correctly. Maybe my gods-gift is overwrought and needs to settle once more. Gritting my teeth, I reach down to touch him again. He gasps, closes his eyes.

Then, grimacing, he shakes his head and slips off the bed. "No!" he growls. He turns away from me, chest heaving, and hastily refastens the front of his trousers.

I sit up in the bed. The shivering is worse now. A dull throb begins to beat in my temples. "Vor," I breathe, his name no longer the ecstatic song on my lips. "Vor, please. Come back to me."

He shoots me a look over his shoulder. His expression is alarming. "I told you, Faraine. We cannot do this. Not now. Maybe not ever."

"But . . . we are married. Truly married." I blink at him, struggling to comprehend this coldness, this wall of ice. "Are we not?"

"Not by the laws of my people. Not until the marriage is consummated."

A knot tightens in my gut. With one hand, I grip the tumbled blanket, pull it up and over my bare body. "So that was . . . We are not . . ." I don't know how to form the words, how to shape the question I'm trying to ask.

His brow is hard and forbidding. "Consummation, according to the law, involves one specific act. An act we have not committed."

I cannot think straight. I watch him cross the room to pick up his discarded shirt, shake it out. The throb in my temples increases with each breath I drag into my lungs. *Do you trust me?* he'd asked. And I had. In that moment, I'd chosen to trust him. Completely. Through the surging emotions and sensations, all so new and delicious and terrifying. I'd trusted him, cast myself wholly into his hands.

"You won't give this to me?" I whisper. "You won't give me this one thing I need?"

His eyes flash to meet mine. I'm struck again by a blast of ice. He yanks his shirt back into place. "I cannot." His voice is hard, almost angry. He tempers his tone, however, when he adds, "You must understand that."

I don't understand. I don't understand at all. Is he still intending to send me home? After this? After what we had together? Did I mistake his intentions so completely? I thought we were choosing together to risk it all, to be with each other. I thought . . . I thought . . .

"What is your plan then, Vor?" The words slip bitterly from my tongue before I realize I intend to speak them. "Will you use me like some harlot? Take your pleasure from my body then send me on my way?"

That breaks through the ice. A hot flare bursts from his soul. It's painful, but in that pain, I feel again some of the true emotion seething behind his restraint. The passion, the pain. "How can you say that?" he grits through his teeth. "I took nothing from you! I gave and would give again and would go on giving. I would never use you, Faraine! I am not that man."

I shake my head, reeling as each word strikes my senses like a blow. "But you won't give me yourself."

"No. And you know perfectly well why not." I cannot see him anymore. The dark sparks have closed in on my vision. But I feel his footsteps pace across the room as he retreats still more from me. "You know exactly how I am bound if I . . . if we . . . if the agreement I made with your father is fulfilled."

So. This is it. He won't share his body with me. Which means he won't share his crown. I will never be his queen, never bear his children. The pleasure I just experienced with him was intense, but it wasn't whole.

Gods, what a fool I've been! Just a moment ago, I gloried in the freedom of lying beside him, so exposed and yet so safe. Now all those feelings of safety have fled. I am truly naked. Possibly for the first time in my life.

"I do know." I pull the blanket closer to my body. "I know very well all the lives at stake. Not just your people. Mine as well. The man who murdered my sisters still ravages my land. Even now, he's killing, looting, burning, destroying. My father hasn't the means to stop him. He's thrown everything he has at Ruvaen for the last five years. It's not enough." I swallow, lift my chin. "Gavaria *needs* this alliance."

I cannot see him through the pain. I cannot feel him through the wall. But finally, his voice reaches me: "I should have known."

"What?"

"For all your sweetness, for all your delicate modesty, you are your father's daughter after all."

A blast of anger—my own this time—shoots straight from my heart, driving back the fog, the dark. I see him standing there, his shirt still disheveled, his lips still swollen with my kisses. I see the pain in his face, but also the coldness. Like he's wrapped his own heart in stone.

Rising from the bed, I drag the blankets with me, let them pool around my feet like royal robes. "Speak plainly, Vor," I demand. "Say what you mean or say nothing at all."

He turns away, puts his shoulder to me.

"My father is a two-faced viper," I persist, hurling the words at him. "Is this your opinion of me as well? I suppose I shouldn't blame you. But since that night—since our wedding night—I have spoken nothing but truth to you. My people need this alliance. I do as well. I do not wish to remain a shadow princess, either in your court or my father's. I do not wish to beg for kisses or favors, to never be truly free, truly safe."

"So, you would seduce me to ensure your own safety."

"Seduce you? Is that what you call what has happened between us?"

"What would you call it?"

He can't look at me. Won't look at me. I stand there, staring at those impervious shoulders, too dumbstruck, too horrified to speak. The truth is, I did lure him into bed. I did push for consummation and not purely from desire. The desire was there, of course. But more as well. I need him, need his body, need the consummation of our marriage. It's the only way I can secure my place in this world.

When I don't speak, Vor growls softly, "I thought as much," and turns for the balcony.

"Do you blame me?" I lunge a step after him, trying to get between him and his exit. "Would you do less in my position?"

His head turns sharply, his eyes like two knives cutting straight into me. "I would never stand in your position. I would never do what you have done."

"No." I meet his gaze, refusing to be cowed. "Because you had the good fortune to be born a man. I did not. I am forced to make the best of a situation over which I have no control, and to try to manage it with my honor still intact."

"Honor?" His lips draw back in a snarl. "Would you call this little game you've played honorable?"

"I have confessed my sin. Of the rest? I am not ashamed. I want this alliance, and I want . . . I want . . ."

He tips his head, stares at me from beneath the harsh ledge of his brow. "Go on, Faraine. Speak the truth."

But I cannot say it. Not now. Not with his angry accusations still ringing in my ears. I can only shake my head. Though a moment before I'd impeded his escape, my only wish now is for him to go, to give me some relief from the pain of his presence. I back away, folding my arms and the soft blanket tight around me. And I hold my tongue.

Vor draws a ragged breath. "Today was a mistake. But it will soon be rectified. I will have Hael make ready for your return journey. We won't wait for the message to arrive. You will leave Mythanar before dimness." With those words, he turns, strides for the window.

*Wait.* The word is there, on my lips. I try to speak it, try to give it strength and sound. But I cannot. It is no more than an agonized breath which Vor cannot hear.

He pushes through the wafting curtains, mounts his morleth, and urges it into flight. I cannot watch him go. I can only stand there, my gaze fixed on the floor as his soul withdraws from me. The pain of his tumultuous emotions fades the greater distance he puts between us.

But when the pain is gone, there is only emptiness. And that is worse by far.

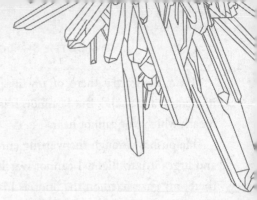

# 29

·······

## Vor

K nar's hooves hit the ground hard, jarring every bone in my body. He tosses his head and takes a vicious snap at me as I slide from the saddle. I smack his muzzle. "Begone!" I snarl.

With a shiver of his black coat, the beast folds himself up into his dark dimension, leaving me alone. I stand a moment, staring blankly at the world around me. Upon leaving Faraine's chamber, I couldn't bear to go anywhere I might risk encountering another soul. So, I'd guided my morleth to the palace gardens. These paths through the living crystal groves have always been a place of solace for me in the past. But now . . .

Now I see Faraine. Everywhere I look. The chittering mothcats leaping from stone to stone only make me think of the mothcat purring belly-up in her lap as we sat together by the lake. The gleaming of the living amethyst reminds me of the way her skin shone under its light when I first encountered her here. The very path on which I walk, I walked last night while carrying her in my arms. She is everywhere, in everything, every thought, every breath.

Because I let her into my heart. And it's the worst mistake I've ever made.

I stagger like a drunken fool, my feet finding their own way to the falls and the mist-shrouded lake. There I continue on, splashing into the shallows and further until I stand waist-deep in the steaming waters. Beads of moisture accumulate across my skin. It's too hot, but I don't care. I want it to scald me; to cleanse my body, mind, and soul.

"*Juk!*" I growl through gnashed teeth. "Gods damn me to the deepest hells!"

I should have known better. I *did* know better. Everyone warned me. But they didn't have to. I've known all along how dangerous her mere presence is to my self-control. Like dancing on the edge of a knife. Fool that I am, I'd danced anyway.

I turn slowly. Ripples flow out from me across the misty lake. Another ghostly image of Faraine appears before my eyes, perched on the boulder where I'd sat her last dimness. Where I'd knelt before her, washing her feet. She knew. She knew what I felt for her. And she used that knowledge against me. She and her cursed gods-gift.

I surge forward, grab that boulder. A grunt, a strain, and I heave the whole thing over my head. With a roar, I hurtle it across the lake. It crashes into the crystal wall, shatters, the pieces falling like a small avalanche into the mist and foam.

Chest heaving, I bow my head. Rage roils in my head. But if I'm honest . . . I'm not angry at Faraine. Not truly. No, this rage is for me alone. For my own stupidity and selfishness. How can I blame Faraine? It's not her fault. She couldn't understand. She isn't fae; she isn't of this world. How could she possibly comprehend the power of written magic over my kind? She cannot grasp how I will be bound by the words of the marriage if it is fulfilled.

Suddenly heavy, I sag to my knees, there on the edge of the lake. My own futility and weakness threaten to crush me under their weight. I'd thought I could give Faraine everything she wanted. But when the moment came, I could not give her what she needed. I could not give her me. Not completely. Because I do not belong to myself. I am Mythanar's king. I belong to my people, my city, my realm. I belong to the warriors I lead and all the denizens of this world I have sworn to protect.

In the heat of passion, I'd half believed I could deny the fates, become what she needed as both husband and lover. But to give her what she desired would only bind me forever to Larongar. To consummate our marriage would mean serving her father in his wars. I would be forced to lead trolde warriors, good men and women both, to die on foreign soil.

I drop my head to my chest, close my eyes. Exhale a long breath. In the darkness of my mind, I see Faraine again. Her naked body. Her slim legs, her soft breasts. The lovely curve of her waist and hips. Her long, elegant neck.

Most of all, I see her face. Gazing up at me in such wonder and delight. Her lips parted in the shock of unexpected ecstasy. So full of trust. So full of shining promise.

What a fool I was! To lash out at her like that, to accuse her of seduction and deceit, when all along, the fault was mine. I never should have let myself be alone with her, never should have given in to the temptation of her touch, her taste, her spirit. It was too easy to forget everything else. To be just a man and a woman. A husband and a wife.

Sitting back on my heels, I raise my head, gaze up at the cavern ceiling high above. If Nornala can see me through all these layers of stone, I pray the goddess of unity will show me some way forward. Some path I might walk that will lead me back to Faraine. But I fear no such path exists. We are destined to be drawn ever away from one another.

"*My king!*"

Stiffening, I turn, look back through the gardens. Water pours off me as I rise and wade swiftly back to the shore. I'm just stepping from the shallows when Hael rounds a corner and skids to a stop. Her eyes widen in shock at the sight of me, dripping wet on the edge of the lake. "Your Majesty!" She pulls herself together and offers a hasty salute. "Someone said your morleth was seen flying this way."

"What is it, Hael?" I demand, my voice low and calm despite my quickened pulse.

"It's Yok."

"Yok?" I stare hard at her, noting all the cracks breaking across her stoic face. "What's happened?"

"No one knows." Her words tumble out in a terrible rush. "He was with Captain Toz, hunting cave devils in Zulmthu. They found a trail, and it took them deep down, below Mythanar. There was a cave-in . . . the ground gave way . . ." Hael stops a moment, as though the next words are too painful to speak out loud. She forces them out: "Yok, Toz, and four others . . . they fell. Deep."

"And no one bothered to go after them?"

She shakes her head. "Only Lur came back. She said it was too dangerous on her own. There was a nest of *woggha*."

"How many?"

"A hundred. More. She couldn't say for certain."

My blood runs cold. A hundred cave devils? In one place? Even a single devil is a dangerous beast, capable of decimating half a town. The damage a hundred of them in swarm might do is . . . is . . .

An image of the ripped-apart bodies in the Karthur Channel flashes vividly across my mind's eye. "We must destroy them," I say. "We must find Yok and the others. And then we must put an end to those beasts."

"Yes, my king." Hael salutes. "I'll muster the guard at once, and then we will—"

"No!" The word snaps from my lips. "You cannot come with me, Hael. Not this time. Your duty is to guard Faraine."

"But you need me for this!"

I do. There is no one I would rather have with me when facing a whole nest of rabid *woggha* than my brave captain and friend. But if something were to happen . . . If that swarm were to get into Mythanar . . . No. I cannot bear to think of Faraine facing even one of those monsters without Hael at her side.

"You have your orders, Captain," I say firmly. "Summon the guard. Then report to the princess's chambers and see that she remains safe. Have I made myself clear?"

Hael's eyes are bright with desperate fire. But she lifts her chin, sets her jaw, and answers only: "Perfectly clear, my king."

# 30

# Faraine

The door latch rattles.

A frisson races through my body. I lie on the tumbled mess of my narrow bed, every muscle tense, my heart in my throat. My hands grip the blanket I've partially pulled over my naked flesh. The latch rattles again. Stops. I stare at it. But the bolt is dropped. My privacy is still protected, for the moment at least. I let a shivering breath ease out through my lips.

After a pause of several seconds, Hael's voice emerges from the far side of the door: "Princess? It's me. Are you in there?"

I don't want to answer. I can't trust my own voice. I feel raw and ragged, like my insides have been carved out and emptied.

"The king sent me," Hael continues. My heart lurches to my throat. The king? Vor? Did he leave my presence and go immediately in search of his captain of the guard? Has he ordered her to haul me back to my own world, willing or otherwise? Are those last, anger-fueled moments with him truly to be the end of our story?

Hael holds her tongue for some moments. She is loyal to both her king and her own sense of duty, however, so eventually, she rattles the latch again, harder this time. "Please answer me, Princess. I need to know you're all right, or . . . or I'll have to break the door in."

I squeeze my eyes tightly shut. I can't very well ignore a warning like that, can I? "Yes," I manage. Then, clearing my dry, thick throat, I try again. "Yes, Hael. I'm all right." By some miracle, I sound almost normal. Scarcely a quaver or hesitation. But then, I've learned to hide my feelings well over the years. "I'm just a little tired. That is all."

Hael is silent again. It's an uncomfortably knowing sort of silence. "Very well," she rumbles at last. "I am at your service should you need me."

I nod, unable to offer a verbal response. My heart falls back to my breast where it belongs and starts to learn how to beat once more. So. I'm not about to be dragged from the room by my hair. Not yet anyway.

Sitting up slowly, I swipe a hand across my tearstained face and look dully around the room. How empty it feels. Devoid of Vor's presence, which had filled my senses so completely such a short time ago. How could everything have gone so wrong so fast? How could we have misunderstood one another so completely?

"*Juk,*" I whisper. I'm not entirely certain what the word means, but I've heard it uttered often enough, accompanied by strong emotions. Just now, it's the only word in my possession capable of expressing my true feelings. "*Juk!*" I growl again, my hands forming fists.

Here I am. Once again. Trapped in this cursed room. Waiting. Waiting for Vor to make decisions about *my* life. So much for taking control! So much for asserting my will! Growling wordlessly, I tilt my head back, stare up at the stalactites overhead. Gods on high, why did I let myself hope like that? Why did I open myself up, place my trust in his hands? What was the use? I once believed in the divine purposes of the gods, in the ultimate goodness of Nornala, my goddess. I'd even dared to believe there was a plan in place for me. A plan to transform my pain and suffering into purpose. That I'd been divinely guided into this world to become Vor's substitute bride.

For a handful of glorious moments—as my body burst with passion and my soul soared to the very heavens—it had all seemed so real, so possible, so true.

Rough trolde voices erupt suddenly outside my window. I'm up so high, they seem far away, but the stone walls of the palace catch and echo the sound all the way to my open window. Soon the shouts are punctuated by the now-familiar bray of morleth.

My skin prickles. Though I'm too far away for my ears to detect words or my gods-gift to pick out any strong feelings, uneasy instinct coils in my gut. Gathering the blanket close around me, I slip from the bed, pad across the room. With one hand, I part the curtains and step out onto the balcony. The *lorst* crystals of the high cavern ceiling are already beginning to dim. The shadows in the courtyard below are long and deep. From those shadows, brave trolde grooms drag angry morleth out of their reality and into this one. A lot of morleth, all stamping cloven hooves and snorting sparks and sulfurous smoke.

The flash of armor draws my attention away from the beasts to the armed men and women congregated on the palace steps. Far more than last time—twenty, maybe thirty in total. My heart quickens, rams against my breastbone. What is happening? Something must be terribly wrong for this many of the household guard to be mustered. Has there been another tremor? Some new disaster?

Vor appears. Suddenly, like the moon emerging from behind storm clouds. The sight of him shocks me all over again, his beauty and majesty both awesome and terrifying. He carries a helmet under one arm, while his other hand clasps the shoulder of a broad guardswoman with whom he exchanges earnest words. My heart catches painfully. Even at this distance, a mere glimpse of his face is enough to set my blood rushing.

"*Vor.*" His name breathes through my lips, a voiceless whisper. Is he going to mount his monster and ride off to face unknown danger without another word between us? If only I dared call out to him! But he wouldn't hear me from this distance. Even if he could, what would I say? Too much anger stands between us, like a wall of daggers.

I lean against the rail. The blanket slips from my shoulders, and my hair tumbles free across my bare skin. I drink in the sight of him, knowing too well it may be my last. Terrible foreboding grips my heart.

Or perhaps it isn't foreboding . . . perhaps it's my gods-gift, discerning the rising swell of feelings from the men and women below. The proud trolde warriors cannot suppress the fear that simmers in their veins. They are setting out to face a terrible foe. Some of them will not return.

Vor dons his helmet, mounts Knar. He turns the beast around, surveying his men and women. Then with a cry and an upraised fist, he leads the way to the palace gates. A surge of dark beasts flows into formation behind him. I try one last desperate time to call out his name. My throat closes tight, trapping my voice.

It doesn't matter. At the gate, in the last possible moment, Vor turns in his saddle. Looks over his shoulder. I cannot see his face from this distance, hidden beneath his spiked helmet. But somehow, I feel the moment when his eyes lift to meet mine, when our gazes connect and lock.

My heart leaps, suddenly alive with nameless feelings so strong they steal my breath away. "Vor," I whisper one last time. "Don't go. Don't leave."

Then he faces forward in his saddle and rides on. Beyond my sight. Gone.

# 31

# Vor

I almost wonder if I imagined that glimpse of her, high up on her balcony. The way she leaned over the rail with her pale white shoulders bare and her golden hair tumbled across her bosom. It's too much like a dream, too much like the deepest longings of my heart to be real.

I turn away, face the road ahead of me. I cannot let my thoughts dwell on Faraine right now. I cannot wish I'd marched up to her room to speak with her before venturing out. There is no time. Not for Yok, nor for Toz and the others. Besides, what could I say? I can make her neither promises nor apologies. To apologize for the time we've had together would be like apologizing to an angel for receiving a blessing bestowed. I can never regret what she gave so willingly . . . only what I could not give in return.

But we are not destined for one another. Fate or the gods or both have conspired against us. The price has now come due on those beautiful moments we so joyfully took—a price neither of us is prepared to pay.

Better to focus on the mission at hand. I will find Yok. I will make certain he's all right and safely returned to his family. I sent the boy on this mission. If something happens to him, I will never forgive myself.

"*Drag-hrukta!*" I cry, and spur Knar forward. My beast leaps from the cobbled road and the other morleth surge into flight behind him. Together we soar above the city, pass over rooftops and roads, over the domed temple and the hovels, over Market Rise, and all the familiar sites that make up Mythanar as I know it. I find myself looking for Sul and Hael on either side of me. But my brother remains in Madame Ar's infirmary, and my captain stands outside Faraine's bedchamber door. I am bereft without them. As though both my right and left arms have been hewn from my body, and I'm left maimed and alone to face whatever dangers await.

We fly over the high city gates, out to the chasm bridges that connect the city to the cavern walls. I turn in my saddle. "Lead the way!" I call to Lur, who rides on my right.

She looks gray and strained following her ordeal. Worried for Toz and the others, no doubt, and guilty for returning without them. Bravely, she turns her morleth's head downward. We follow her, plunge into the chasm below the city, down under the bridges. Down, down, and deeper still, until the rising fury of the fiery river makes our armor heat and sweat break out across our skin.

I'm just starting to think we cannot safely venture lower, when Lur pulls on her morleth's head and guides it into level flight. Down here in the dark, far from the cavern lights and the glow of the city, the morleth are much happier, fluid and graceful, like inky black smears, only just holding on to their physical form. Lur gives a whistle and points to a crack in the stone wall.

I narrow my gaze. She cannot be serious! Is this the opening to the lair she reported? Did Toz and the others pursue the *woggha* trail all the way down here, under the foundations of the city itself? Somehow, until this moment, I'd not believed it truly possible.

Our morleth fly in a holding pattern, circling on the hot updrafts of air from the river below. That cavern entrance is much too small for a morleth. We'll have to leave our mounts behind. I signal four of my riders to follow me, including Lur. Then, guiding Knar as close to the wall as I dare, I gauge the distance and spring from the saddle. For a terrible, weightless instant, I hang in the air above that death-plunge. Then I hit the wall, grapple, catch hold of the ledge. In a few quick, heaving breaths, I haul myself into place and stand in the opening of the cave.

The darkness is deep. And hot. Even with the *lorst* crystal on my helm ignited, I feel as though the shadows will crush me. Nevertheless, I step into the cave, making room for Lur and the other three to join me. "Where next?" I ask once they've caught their breaths and stand in the darkness with me, eyes bright in the crystal glow.

"Straight ahead," Lur says. "The tunnel curves and takes a steep plunge in about twenty feet, but it does not branch." She hesitates a moment before adding, "I should lead the way, my king."

But I shake my head. If there are indeed a hundred *woggha* waiting for us at the end of this dark path, I won't send anyone ahead of me to act as my living shield. "Stay close. Stay wary," I say. Then, drawing my sword, I set out down the narrow path. It's difficult not to imagine the too-close walls are closing in. But despite my human blood, I am trolde at heart. I will not give in to such weakness. The dark under stone is where I belong.

I angle my head to let the *lorst* light illuminate my path, choosing my footsteps with care. While I'm no expert, I suspect this cave is a relatively new formation caused by one of the recent stirrings. A perfect hiding place for any number of *woggha*.

The *lorst* gleams on a wall ahead of me, revealing a smear of blue. Blood.

I stop. Lur steps close behind me. "We're getting close," she whispers.

"Do you recognize this way?" I ask.

She shakes her head, her face uncertain beneath her helmet's brim. "I don't remember these landmarks, but . . . that blood . . . One of the beasts grabbed Hud and dragged him off. That's when Toz and Yok went after him, and the ground gave way under their feet."

I nod. Glancing back, I look into the wide eyes of the others, crowded in the narrow space behind me. I give a signal for silence. If there are indeed cave devils near, the least sound could disturb them, draw their attention. We progress again, more cautious than ever, our footsteps nearly soundless as we inch our way along.

Suddenly, my light gleams on an edge of stone at my feet. Beyond is nothing but pitch-black emptiness. We seem to have found the pit. I lift my head, try to see beyond the black. My circle of light can just reach the far side where the path picks up again. Sheer walls rise on either hand, and below . . . Well, below might as well be a mouth straight to the deepest of the nine hells.

Lur inches up behind me, her voice a faint hiss in my ear. "That's where they fell," she said. "Toz. Yok. And the others."

I nod. Then, cautiously, I creep up to the edge of the break, put my head over, and shine my *lorst* light down inside. At a single tap of my finger, it brightens, extending its light over a wider radius.

I drag in a sharp breath.

I was right. This is the mouth to hell. And all along the walls of the pit are hell's devils, clinging to the stone. Their eyeless faces are tucked under their hairless arms. They dangle, suspended by their great hooked claws. There's more than a hundred. A lot more. Two hundred, three hundred . . . I cannot see them all. I never imagined the solitary *woggha* capable of congregating like this. And not so far up. They are Deep Dwellers, belonging in the low country, down among the fiery rivers. Yet here they are.

I swing my head silently, trying to take in everything that I see. A flash of silver, and I turn sharply for a second look. Armor. A backplate. It's one of my men, nearly fifty feet below. Could he have survived such a fall? Perhaps not. But I must discover for certain.

I turn, catch Lur's eye. She shakes her head, unable to speak for fear. "Wait here," I mouth to her. Her eyes widen, and I know she would protest if she dared. Thank the gods I didn't bring Hael with me. She would never allow me to attempt what I'm about to do.

I swing out over the edge of the drop, taking care not to disturb any of the sleeping devils. At least when *woggha* sleep, they sleep soundly. Little enough can disturb them. Using the spines protruding from my forearm braces to help me cling to the wall, I begin my descent. It's tricky business, navigating around the inert cave devils. I move with care, make as little sound and disturbance as possible. One of my men starts to come after me, but I shake my head, and he stops. I won't have them adding to the risk.

Looking down to check my next foothold, my light flashes across something. I stop short. A face, a trolde face. My blood jolts with recognition. Hud. A brave fellow who has served in my guard for some years.

His head, neck, shoulders, and part of his torso are all held in the upper arms of a sleeping *woggha*. Where the rest of him is, I do not know.

I swallow back bile in my throat. Then I climb down beside the sleeping devil, draw the knife from my belt, and plunge it into the base of its skull. A little shiver goes through its body. It drops, carrying Hud's remains with it as it falls. None of the other devils stir.

Heart throbbing, I continue. I'm close to the fallen man now, close enough to realize that he lies not on the floor of this pit as I originally thought, but on a ledge. The pit itself goes on much deeper. Down lower, the *woggha* are more densely gathered. Gods spare us! My initial calculations were far too conservative. There are more devils here than I ever imagined dwelt in the whole of the Under Realm. Something must have driven them up from their habitat to seek shelter in the upper regions. Something . . . I don't have to guess what.

I test my weight on the ledge before letting go of the wall and hastening to the side of my fallen guard. He lies belly-down and seems to be stretching one arm into the darkness below. I kneel, catch him by the shoulders. With a heave, I roll him over in my arms.

It's Yok. Thank all the gods above and below!

With an effort, I swallow back his name. Instead, I search his body for signs of trauma. His leg is broken, bent at a terrible angle. Much of his armor is savaged, great chunks ripped away. He bleeds from numerous gashes. But he's alive. By some miracle, he's alive.

Gently, I pat his cheeks. Yok stirs. His young, boyish brow puckers, and his teeth flash in a grimace of pain. Slowly, he opens his eyes, his gaze unfocused and strange. Then he sees me. I clap a hand over his mouth as he sucks in a sharp breath. Shaking my head, I flick my gaze around us to indicate the sleeping devils. Yok's eyes widen. He nods his understanding.

Carefully, I ease the boy into a seated position. Yok winces, but swallows back all whimpers of pain. Then he turns suddenly, points down into the dark below us. When I don't immediately respond, he grips my hand hard, urging me to look. I lean over the edge, cautiously angling my *lorst* light.

Toz lies another twenty feet lower. He's dead. His armor is stripped away. Cave devil claws have penetrated his tough stone hide, ripped his torso wide open, spilled his guts. He looks gnawed. Mutilated. I'm thankful I cannot see his face from this angle.

I draw back. Sickness roils in my gut. Toz was my friend. As was Hud.

What happened to them must not happen to the people in the city above.

I firm my jaw. I won't let it happen.

Leaning over Yok, I place my lips close to his ear. "Let's get you out of here. Then we'll deal with these *guthakug* devils."

Yok nods. Silent tears course down his face. I cannot blame him. A lesser man than he would have perished of sheer fright by now. I motion for the boy to stand, but he cannot manage it, not on his leg. He grabs my shoulder, draws me to him, and gasps into my ear, "Leave me, my king. I'll only slow you down."

As if I would even consider such a plan. "Get on my back," I answer. "Put those scrawny arms of yours to use and hold on fast, do you hear?" Yok shakes his head, but I add a growling *"Now."*

Yok shudders, nods. He's gray as stone under the *lorst* light, but I'm relieved to feel strength in him yet when he grips my shoulders. I don't know if it will be enough. But I won't leave him. Hael would never forgive me if I did.

I begin to climb. At first, I'm not certain I can manage it—not up a sheer rock face, navigating between sleeping devils, with Yok's dead weight on my back. From deep inside, I summon the strength of my ancestors, the ancient trolde kings, to aid me. Slowly, slowly we make our way up. Now and then, as we pass too near a devil, the scent of Yok's blood seems to rouse them. One or two stir slightly. I see curled lips, flashing fangs. If one awakens, that will be it. Its savage snarls will soon alert the others, and there will be nothing I can do but pray we are devoured swiftly.

But our god of darkness must see us in our plight, for somehow, we reach the top of the pit. The relief when Lur's strong hands grip Yok's arm and take his weight from my back is so much, I nearly lose my hold. But Jork, a stalwart warrior, catches me by the hand and hauls me up beside him. "You're a gods-damned lunatic, Big King," he whispers almost reverently.

I grin back. Then I glance into the pit once more. We've not brought enough warriors to dispatch that lot. Not by a long shot. I give the signal to fall back. We need to regroup, come back with a real plan. Perhaps my chief engineer can rig an explosive, and we'll find a way to safely bury them. A tricky business considering this lair lies directly under the city, but if anyone can manage it, it's Ghat.

I take Yok back from Lur and nod for her to precede me back up the passage. She doesn't like it, but none of them dare protest. Yok and I follow after her, dragging a little behind the others, while Jork guards our rear. When we're far enough away from the pit, I whisper, "What happened?"

"I'm not sure." Yok breathes out through pain-gritted teeth. "We were pursuing one *woggha*, and Hud was up ahead. Suddenly he screamed. There was . . . blood . . ."

His voice trails off. At first, I think perhaps he's fainted. Then

I feel it—a tremor under my feet. I stare down. Small stones and pebbles begin to vibrate and move. The walls on either side of us shiver, dust and debris crumbling over our heads.

"Brace!" I cry to the others.

They don't need my warning. They flatten themselves against the stone, holding hard. Someone cries out, struck by a falling rock. One man loses his balance and tumbles into Lur. I manage to press Yok against the wall, shielding him with my body. With every flash of *lorst* light, I believe the walls are caving in, crushing us.

It doesn't last long. Not a large stirring, possibly not even strong enough to be felt in the city above. Lur struggles to get to her feet, but neither she nor any of the others seem to be harmed. "Is everyone all right?" I call.

One by one they answer, ending with Jork, a few paces behind me. "Alive and in one piece, Big King!" he growls. "Only hope that we—"

He breaks off as a terrible shriek echoes up the passage behind us.

We freeze, stare at one another.

Another shriek follows the first.

Then another.

And another.

I turn my head slowly back down the path. My *lorst* crystal, still beaming bright, casts a wide swath of light through the dense shadows.

I see it. The first of the writhing forms. Charging up the narrow way behind us.

A single word bursts from my throat: "*Run!*"

# 32

## Faraine

A tremor rumbles under my feet.

I sit idly in one of the chairs before my hearth, staring into the dancing moonfire flames. It is dark outside my window. I don't know how long I've been like this, still as stone. My head rests heavily in one hand, my eyes glazed and dull.

But then the room starts to vibrate. The stones in the walls growl, and my stomach drops. I sit bolt upright, grip the arms of my seat. For a moment, my mind flashes back to the last time this happened. Only then, I was sheltered in Vor's embrace, shielded from the worst of the falling stones.

There is no such shelter now.

By the time I've fully grasped what's happening, however, the tremor is almost over. Then it stops completely without having disturbed so much as a stick of furniture in the room. Though my hands are still white-knuckled to the chair arms and my gaze shoots this way and that, I detect no sign of damage. I almost wonder if I imagined the disturbance.

Then Hael pounds at the door, her voice a bark: "Princess? Princess, are you all right?"

So, I didn't imagine it. Hael has been standing silent watch for hours. I've felt small pulses of uneasy emotion from her through the wall between us, but nothing more. Now, her emotions are spiking.

"Yes, Hael," I answer, if nothing else to get her to stop that pounding. "I'm fine."

My bodyguard is silent for a moment. Then, "Please, Princess. Unlock the door. It doesn't seem right, you barricaded in there. What if you needed me, and I could not reach you swiftly enough?"

Breathing out a long sigh, I close my eyes. What sort of danger does she expect to assault me in an upper-level room with only one entrance? Still, I cannot put her off forever. Slowly, stiffly, I stand. In the hours since Vor's departure, I've put on the simplest gown I could find in the wardrobe. It's dark and a bit heavy, the fabric richly beaded, with long trailing sleeves and a deep V across my chest. It doesn't suit me at all, but at least it's some covering.

Holding the skirt out of my way, I cross to the door and lift the bolt. Without a word, I turn away and move to the window, where I stand with my back to the door when it opens. I feel Hael's gaze fixed upon me from behind. Anxiety radiates off of her like heat-waves. "You are well, Princess?" she asks.

"Yes, Hael," I respond without looking around. "I am well."

She doesn't go. She remains there, trying to come up with questions. I wonder if she suspects what happened between her king and me during this morning's interlude. It doesn't matter; I've no interest in discussing such private matters with her. Let her stew in her own curiosity.

Schooling my face into cool, disinterested lines, I finally spin on heel and face my bodyguard straight on. "Is there something you require, Captain?"

She presses her lips into a thin line. Then, with a quick shake of her head: "Nothing, Princess. As long as you are all right. The stirring did not disturb you?"

"Do I appear disturbed?"

"No. Certainly not." She begins to back away. One hand reaches for the door.

"Wait."

Hael stops. Her brow puckers as she catches my eye.

"Where has the king gone?" I ask. When she hesitates, I take a step closer, the black gown dragging behind me. "I saw the morleth riders muster from my balcony. They were heavily armed."

Hael's gaze skirts away from mine. A stronger pulse of anxiety throbs from her heart, enough to make me wince. "There's been . . . trouble," she admits.

"What sort of trouble?"

"I . . . I'm not certain I should . . ." She takes a step back, as though she wants to retreat. Then she drops her head and lets out a heavy huff of breath. "It's my brother. He may be in danger."

My brow tightens. "Yok?"

Hael nods.

"What kind of danger?"

Hael opens her mouth to answer. Before she can utter a word, however, a scream rips across my awareness. It's faint. Distant. So distant, it doesn't quite feel real. But the pain of it, the sharpness, is enough to make me start and turn. Frozen, I strain my ears. When the second scream comes, distant as a waking dream, I realize I didn't *hear* it. It was my gods-gift which reacted.

"Princess?" Hael steps back into the room. "What's the matter?"

I hold up a hand for silence. Turning to the window once more, I push through the curtains and onto the balcony, out under the dimming *lorst* light. Mythanar still glows bright with the many light sources used by its denizens, the streets alive and busy and full of life as ever. The *stirring*—as Vor calls the tremors—wasn't strong enough to cause much disturbance. So what is this I feel? I rest my hands on the rail, lean out into open space. Did I imagine it? Are my senses still so distraught from earlier events, they play tricks on me?

Ah! There it is again. Faint, echoing. But real.

Screaming.

Terror.

My eyes widen.

A terrible black swell seems to rise from the lower city, close to the wall. My gods-gift recoils, but I cannot turn away. It's a wave of darkness, of emotion—so massive, so unlike anything I've ever before seen. Higher and higher it sweeps, rippling across the city, swallowing up street after street.

"Gods!" I whisper. I can do nothing but stand there. Watching. As the black, roiling horror grows greater, until it towers over all Mythanar. It comes to a crest.

I scream, put up both hands in feeble defense just before it crashes down on top of me.

Somewhere far away, I hear Hael crying out, "Princess!" But I'm already crumpled in a heap, shrieking as my senses are overwhelmed in darkness.

# 33

# Vor

**L**ight gleams from the cave mouth ahead of us.

We race for it. Our *lorst* crystals flash, casting our shadows like wild phantoms on the narrow walls. Most of the others are ahead of me, stumbling and staggering on the uneven ground. I am slow, burdened by Yok's weight on my shoulder.

"Leave me!" he cries when he can find breath. "I'm too heavy! Leave me behind!"

I don't bother to answer. There's no chance in the nine hells I'm leaving this boy to that swarm. Instead, I put my head down, angle my *lorst* to illuminate my feet, and simply run, run, *run*.

We hurtle up the path. I lift my gaze just in time to see the first of the men reach the cave entrance. There's nothing there but that tiny ledge—nowhere for him to go. He stops, arms pinwheeling. The man behind him can't slow down fast enough and hits him in the back. Only by sheer luck do they both manage to grab hold of stone and keep themselves from plummeting.

"Climb!" I bellow. My voice is nearly drowned in the rising

cacophony of *woggha* shrieks and squeals. They each come to the same conclusion simultaneously. Swinging out onto the wall, they begin to scale it as fast as they can. It's hopeless, of course. No trolde could ever outclimb a *woggha*. But it may give the riders in the holding pattern outside a chance to see us and come to our aid.

Lur reaches the cave opening ahead of me. She spins, leaps, catches the wall, and hauls herself up swift as a spider. I'm only a few paces behind now, still holding tight to Yok. Jork lumbers behind us. Suddenly, I hear him scream.

I turn. I shouldn't. I'm so close to the opening, but I turn anyway, and look back to see Jork grappling with a cave devil. Green foam falls on his skin as its slavering jaws clamp open and shut mere inches from his face. He grips it by the throat, holds it off, even as its claws tear into his armor. Ice freezes my spine. Every instinct tells me to go back, to help him. But Yok . . . if I leave the boy . . .

Jork twists his head around. A terrible gash gushes blue across his forehead and into one eye. "*Go!*" he roars. "*Get out of here!*"

I pivot on heel and race on. The shrieks of the *woggha* are deafening as they bottleneck in the narrow passage behind Jork and the fiend he battles. They'll overwhelm him soon. Rip him to pieces like they did poor Hud and Toz.

But I will get this boy out of here safely. If it's the last thing I do.

We reach the opening. Up above, I see our fellow riders bringing our morleth down to us. Even as I watch, Lur springs from the wall, catches her beast's saddle, and pulls herself onto it. The others haven't spied me yet, and I cannot see Knar. Did the fool beast take the opportunity to disappear back into his own dimension? Just my luck!

"Hold on, Yok," I say, and swing the boy back around onto my shoulders as I had when I carried him from the pit. The next moment, we're climbing. I use the spikes in my bracers to assist me in my ascent, and Yok clings to me with all the strength he has left. I feel him weakening. I don't know that he can make it.

"My king!"

It's Lur. She's angled her beast down close to us. She extends a hand to Yok. "Catch it, boy!"

I hold still long enough for the lad to adjust his grip on me and reach out with one hand. His fingers just brush against Lur's.

A cave devil launches itself out from the cavern mouth. It leaps straight for her morleth, savage and snarling and utterly mad. Her beast rears back in the air, and Lur curses as she nearly loses her seat. The *woggha* falls, shrieking. Others are coming, streaming out from the cave mouth. Many of them fall too, while the rest flow up the side of the cliff as easily as though running on level ground. There's no way I can outpace them.

"They're coming!" Yok cries.

"I'd noticed," I growl through my teeth. Up above, one of the other men on the wall makes a leap for his morleth as it swoops by. He misses, falls, and the beast plunges after him. I can only hope it will catch him but cannot turn to see. I climb, climb, as fast as I can. *Woggha* stream up the cliff on either side of me. One of them catches at my leg, claws hooking into the armor. It tugs, and I nearly lose my grip.

Abruptly, it lets go, utters a hideous scream, and falls. I turn to see Lur flash by on her morleth, sword stained with devil's blood. The other riders are doing their best to keep the beasts off me. But where is Knar?

Another *woggha* draws level with us on my right. It turns its hideous, eyeless head, as though suddenly aware of us. Its mouth opens. Its long tongue lashes hungrily as it alters course straight for us. I let go of the wall with one hand and punch it straight in the flat part of its bone-plated skull. The blow seems to shock it, but only for a moment. It roars and lunges again, claws lashing at my face.

I feel Yok's arms tense. His breath catches in my ear.

I know what he's about to do. Before I can react. Before I can move to stop him. I know.

The boy springs from my back, catches hold of the *woggha* around its neck. There he dangles, broken leg useless, hands struggling for purchase. He adjusts his hold, squeezing hard. His one good leg kicks wildly against the wall.

"*No!*" I lift one hand, try to swing myself toward them. My other hand slips. I'm forced to grab the wall. "No, Yok! *Stop!*"

Yok wrenches hard and adjusts his grip, locking his arms around the beast's throat. It shakes its head, its whole body writhing. Yok doesn't let go. With his one good leg, he presses into the wall. I see him grit his teeth. His eyes flash to meet mine for just a moment.

"Yok!" His name rips from my chest in a furious roar. I reach out, my hand grasping, desperate. Too late, too late.

He pushes off from the wall. Wrenches the devil's claws free of the stone.

They fall. Tumble. Still grappling together. Plummeting through shadows and down to the fiery river far below.

# 34

## Faraine

"Princess? Faraine, can you hear me?"

Hael's voice echoes distantly, beyond the hideous *throb-throb-throb* in my temples. My whole being shudders with pain. I cannot see. The darkness is too great, too overwhelming.

All around me, I hear screams. Hundreds of voices crying out in terror, each voice battering my senses like an individual blow. I'll soon be bludgeoned to death and all without my body bearing a single bruise.

I fumble blindly, grasping for my pendant. My hand finds it and squeezes hard. Its vibration is just enough to clear a small, narrow path of awareness through the dark, through the throb. Enough to realize I still lie on the ground with Hael crouched over me, her rough voice barking, her fear adding to the rest of the assault. Another javelin thrust straight to my brain.

But if I'm on the ground, then . . . maybe . . .

I put out my other hand, press it palm-flat against the floor. And there. I feel it. Deep down in the stone. The answering vibration of other crystals—small, but alive and responsive. I draw the vibration into me. Slowly, slowly, they drive back the pulsing power and pain of all that emotion, giving me a small space in which to stand, to exist.

I open my eyes. Hael is there, her face alarmingly close to mine. Her eyes blaze with concern. "Princess?"

I groan, grimace. We're on the balcony still. How long have I been unconscious? It feels like hours, but it may have been mere moments. Even with the song of the crystals in my head, I can still hear those screams. So many screams—vicious, animal, shredding at the edges of my sanity. "What's happening?" I ask. The words shudder as they fall from my lips.

"I don't know." Hael supports my shoulders, and I pull myself into a seated position. "You fainted. I thought you were—" She stops as a scream rends the air, this one audible to her ears. Whirling in her crouch, she springs to her feet, stares out over the balcony.

Another scream. And another.

They're coming from the city, beyond the palace walls.

"Something's wrong," Hael says. Her hands grip the rail so tightly, I wouldn't be surprised if the stone cracked. "Something's happened."

Shouts rise from below, sounds of pounding feet and activity. Then Hael draws back a step, her eyes widening. "*Morar-juk!*" she snarls. "*Woggha!*"

The word sounds familiar, but in that moment, I cannot place it. My head pounds too hard as darkness threatens to close in my vision. I shut my eyes, press into the stone floor under me, search for the answering stir of crystals. Whatever traces of *urzul* are here in my balcony, it's not enough. I cannot clear this pain.

My eyes flash open. "Hael."

She turns, stares down at me. Her fear jolts through my senses, and I wince, drawing back slightly. But I need her strength. Now. "Hael, take me to the gardens."

"What?" She shakes her head, brow puckering. "What are you talking about? The gardens? You can't mean—"

I rise. It's an agony, and doing so means removing my hand from the stone. I kick the slippers from my feet so that I may ground myself through my soles instead. It's enough to help me hold my balance as I face down the tall trolde captain. "At once, Captain," I say.

She wants to protest. She wants to lock me up in this chamber, trap me inside like the prisoner we both know I am. How could I stop her? She has the brute force. I have nothing. No power, no authority. Nothing.

But I throw the full force of my spirit into direct combat with hers. It takes everything I have, gripping my pendant, bracing my feet. Hers is not a will to be trifled with.

In the end, however, she dips her eyes. "Very well," she murmurs, and steps around me, leading the way from the balcony back into the room. She's nearly to the door when she stops, looks back. "Are you coming?"

I swallow hard. The humiliation is almost more than I can bear, but I keep my head high and my voice even. "You will have to carry me."

She blinks. Swallows. Then, without a word, she crosses back to where I stand and scoops me up in her strong arms. She's not gentle like Vor. She carries me like a sack of potatoes, slung over her shoulder. But she moves with easy grace, strides to the open door and out into the passage beyond. By now, screams erupt from inside the palace. Some of them are audible, but the rest crash inside my head alone. I press my fist to my forehead. Without the grounding touch of stone under my feet, I'm nearly overwhelmed by my curse of a gift.

Hael steps from the stairwell into the arched hall. The moment she does so, more screams burst nearby. She turns toward the sound, catches her breath. "What's happening?" I manage to ask. "What do you see?"

"Nothing yet," she replies. Her jaw is tight, her teeth grinding. With a little growl, she hastens the opposite direction. "The palace is vulnerable. So many of the house guard went with the king," she mutters, more to herself than to me.

"Is the palace under attack?"

Rather than answer, Hael lifts her head and barks something in troldish. A cluster of women rush by, clutching their skirts, their mouths open in terrified screams. Hael shouts after them, demanding answers, but her voice cuts off in a ragged cry.

A cave devil lurches into view. Its savage mouth is open wide. Its long tongue spills out, lashing the air like a whip. Hideous, hairless gray limbs bunch with sinewy muscle as it propels itself in pursuit of its prey.

Hael takes three more running strides before she pulls herself up short, pivots, and darts into the nearest chamber. There she drops me unceremoniously on the floor before grabbing the door and slamming it shut. She hauls a nearby table screeching across the floor to bar the way.

I lie where I've been dropped, breathing hard. At least here on the floor, I can press my palms flat once more and search out whatever faint vibrations I can find. There aren't many here, but I pull what I can into my body, steady myself, find a space of clarity within the storm. Pulling myself upright, I look across at Hael as she adds to her barricade. "Hael!" I shout.

She pauses, looks over her shoulder at me.

"Those women! They need your help!"

She shakes her head. "My duty is to protect you, Princess."

I stare up at her. Even now, even with the thrum of the crystals to steady me, I feel the fear, the terror, the death outside that door. I can't hide in here and just let it happen. Swallowing back my own agonized screams, I pull to my feet, stagger across the room. I all but fall against the table Hael has pushed in front of the door and lean heavily on it for support. Then I grip its edge. "Pull it back," I demand. "We're going to help them. Now."

Hael meets my eye. "I have only one duty here," she says, but her face is agonized.

"Yes," I reply. "To serve me. And I am giving you an order, Captain."

Mine is not the voice of a prisoner. In that moment, I am her queen. It doesn't matter if it's true. It doesn't matter if my marriage was consummated, if I am Vor's wife in name or deed or only in my dreams. In that moment, I am what I must be.

"*Open this door.*"

Her lips pulled back in a snarl, Hael grabs the table and hauls it back. Pushing the door wide, she steps into the hall, draws her sword. I stagger after her and grip the doorway for support. The screams of the women have not progressed far. The cave devil was right on their heels after all.

Hael looks back at me. "Stay here."

"Save them!" I reply.

Then she's off, sprinting hard. I follow after, despite her demand, staggering along like a drunkard. My head pounds with the dissonance of terror. Death surrounds me. It slashes across my senses, sudden, ripping, horrific. I fall to my knees, pick myself up again, push on until I come to the end of the hall and turn the corner.

I arrive just in time to see Hael plunge her blade into the back of the cave devil's head. She's too late. There's already so much carnage. Blood and death and broken bodies. Three women, whose faces I cannot see, but whose emotions I'd felt so vividly in their last, dreadful moments. Hael was quick, but not quick enough.

She steps away from the monster's body and hastens to a fourth woman, who has curled herself into a trembling ball. I dare not draw any nearer. Her feelings are powerful enough to stab me through the gut. So, I hold back, and find my gaze inexorably drawn to the broken body of the cave devil.

It twitches. Stirs.

Moans.

It's still alive! Barely, but I feel the energy in it, the life force clinging with all the strength of those hideous, curved claws. There's something else there as well, something beyond the instinct for survival. A feeling I've sensed before. That roiling darkness, full of heat, full of . . . full of . . . *poison.*

Hardly knowing what I do, I draw nearer and drop to my knees beside the devil. Its head jerks slightly, as though aware of me. Pulse after pulse of feeling ripples out from it. That same darkness, that same living despair, like demonic possession. This creature's very existence is suffering.

I reach out. My hand hovers over the plated head of the beast. I know this darkness. I felt it once before, churning within Vor's soul. It didn't belong to him any more than it belongs to this poor monster. Its mind has been savagely used and broken. But maybe I can—

With a sickening crack, Hael's booted foot connects with the beast's head. Something snaps—the last lingering thread of life. The cave devil crumples in a heap of flesh and bones, and Hael stands over me, scowling. "I told you to stay where you were!"

I blink blearily up at her. "It seemed safer close to you."

She grunts. Then she bends and picks me up again. "You're mad, little princess. What were you doing touching a *woggha*? Even mostly dead, it could still bite your hand off!"

I cannot answer. I haven't the strength. "The gardens, Hael," I say softly. "Now."

She shakes her head but strides off again with purpose. I cast a last glance back over her shoulder. "Where is the woman?" I ask, struggling to get the words out. "The survivor?"

"I told her to find a safe place and block all entrances," Hael replied. "Which is what we ought to be doing right now."

I don't reply. What would be the point? I have neither the breath nor the strength to explain myself. Hael carries me through passages I vaguely recognize. The stone walls ring with the sounds of battle and the savage snarls and shrieks of the *woggha*. I grip my crystal hard, try to block out some of it. There's so much, too much! If I don't find help, it's going to kill me.

We turn a corner. Hael curses bitterly. Lifting my head from her shoulder, I see a crowd before us, blocking the way. Screams issue from the far side, and the pulse of all that terror is enough to make me cry out, "Back, Hael! Back, I beg you!"

She doesn't question me. She retreats down the passage and darts into another chamber, a small sitting room. "I'm sorry,

Princess," she says, breathing hard from her efforts. "I can't get you to the gardens. This is the best I can do. We must make our stand here."

When I don't protest, she sets me down on a chair then secures the door, checks the windows, searches for places of weakness where a devil might gain entry. Screams and the sound of pounding feet flow by on the other side of the door. I don't know if they're even now being torn apart by monsters or tearing each other apart in their need to escape. I want to order Hael to open the door again, to let at least a few of those poor souls join us here, under her protection. I cannot find the words. I can only sit where she's dropped me, gripping my crystal.

This must be the peril Vor set out to face. But the monsters are here. In the city. In the palace. Which means . . . which means . . . *Vor* . . .

Suddenly, I feel it. The *pull*. I turn sharply, draw a short breath. It was so strong, so unmistakable. Rising from the chair, I stagger across the little room to the nearest window. To my surprise, it overlooks the garden. We are situated above one of the paths, the window's ledge maybe ten feet up. From here, if I crane my head, I can see the circle of seven tall crystals on their high promontory.

They reach out to me. Call me to them. A pulse. A pull. A *need*.

The screams of the dead and dying echo in my ears, batter my gods-gift. Vor would give anything to save these people. Perhaps he has already given everything. How can I do any less?

I swallow. The idea forming in my head isn't much, scarcely more than a glimmer of a thought. But it's there. And the pull of those stones is strong, stronger even than the pain rippling through my body. I can do this. I don't know how. But I can. I will.

Hands fumbling, I find the latch, push the window open.

"Princess!"

I look back, one leg already swung over the windowsill. Hael lunges toward me, her hand outstretched. "Princess, what are you doing?"

"It's the only way, Hael," I say.

Then I pull my other leg out, grip the sill, dangle as low as I can. And drop.

# 35

## Vor

Everything fades away.

My world, my existence, is enveloped in darkness and strange silence. My only awareness is that empty space where Yok should be. Where I cannot make myself believe he is no longer.

But he's fallen.

He's gone.

A roar rips from the depths of my soul, echoes all the way up the chasm to the high cavern ceiling above. I tear a hand free of the stones and dangle one-armed from the wall. Heaving my body, I lash out, drive the spikes of my bracer into the nearest cave devil. The blow knocks it free of the wall, careening out into empty air, its legs still waggling uselessly. I don't waste a breath. Releasing my hold on the stone, I drop to a lower ledge, just catch myself. Using my body's momentum, I swing and land a solid kick into the side of another *woggha*. It, too, launches out into the void, shrieking as it falls.

It doesn't matter. None of it matters. There are too many of them. The last of the devils pour out of the cave mouth below me and surge upward, a rippling wave of death. I see my warriors on their morleth circling above. They strive hopelessly to pick them off the wall one by one.

I look from side to side. Only a few straggling, weaker devils surround me. They scrabble up the wall as fast as they can. They're so keen on their destination, they pay no attention to me. They have softer prey to hunt—all the unwary citizens of my city. All those men, women, children, whom those savage jaws will rend and rip with wanton abandon.

Black despair fills me. Maybe it would be better if I just . . . let go. Let myself fall. As Yok fell. Let the inevitable end claim me. It would be better. Swifter. Easier.

*Faraine.*

Her face springs to life in the darkness of my mind. Her name sits on my tongue, her scent fills my nostrils.

*Faraine.*

*Faraine.*

She's up there. Defenseless. Against that ravenous horde.

Suddenly, nothing else matters. I don't give a damn for alliances or kingdoms. I don't care about lies and deceptions and trickery. Whether she's a seductress or an angel, it makes no difference now. All that matters is that I cannot let go. Not while there's life left in my body. Not while there's still some small chance I might reach her, save her.

"Gods give me strength," I growl. And begin to climb once more, finding impossible handholds and footholds, inching my way up the cliff face.

A raucous bellow erupts in the air behind me. I crane my neck around to see Knar emerge in a puff of black smoke and manifest in midair. So, he hasn't forgotten me after all.

"There you are, you foul brute!" I cry. "To me, *now!*"

Knar tosses his head and sends up streams of smoke from his nostrils. But he angles his shadowy body to fly through the darkness into the space below me. I watch his coming, time my moment. Then I leap out into empty air, catch hold of the saddle, and pull myself into place. My hands grip black wisps of mane as I bend over the morleth's spiked neck. "Up now, Knar!" I cry, putting my spurs into his scaly flanks. "After them!"

In a streak of sparks, Knar speeds upward, cleaving close to the chasm wall. As we go, I shake my sword loose from its scabbard and swing the blade at several straggling *woggha*, sending them tumbling into the void. Knar soon catches up to the rest of the morleth. I surge in among my fellow riders, who shout with surprise at my sudden appearance. "Faster!" I bellow, pointing the tip of my blade. "To the top! Don't let them into the city!"

It's already too late. Though the morleth puff and pant with exertion, they cannot keep up with the swarm of devils. By the time Knar draws level with the high white wall, *woggha* already pour over and into the streets. Lur and a dozen others are battling along the ramparts, desperately trying to fend them off. The swarm is too great, too fast. For every one they manage to bring down, ten or twenty more take its place. This is far more than the numbers I glimpsed in the pit below. Every devil in the Under Realm seems to have been summoned by some unseen, malicious force sent to ravage my city, to destroy every living thing they encounter. Soon, the streets will be bathed in blood.

"*Ortolarok!*" I raise my sword above my head, swing it forward. "*Drag-or!*"

Knar surges at the sharp kick of my spurs, gallops over the city wall and into the streets. I do not look back but trust my warriors to follow. We catch up to ten devils in the first street we enter. Two of them have already brought down a screaming victim. Three more scrabble at the doors and windows of a residence. I see a woman fighting to keep a window shut as the *woggha* batters at the shutters with its terrible curved claws.

I drive Knar close, strike the beast a blow to the head. Not a death blow, but hard enough to knock it to the ground. It's up again in a flash, but I'm already angling Knar back to the two beasts crouched over their now-silent prey. They're distracted for the moment. I drive my blade deep into the soft place at the base of the first beast's skull. It drops dead, but the other takes a swipe at me, knocks the sword from my hand.

"*Juk!*" I hiss, and urge Knar higher, out of the devil's reach. Then I wrench the reins, turn my mount's head back around, and stare down into the mayhem in the street. One of my warriors rides his morleth close enough to stab a crouching devil but doesn't see another on his blind side. It leaps, pulls him from his saddle, and pins him under its bulk. Claws rip into his armor, a terrible scraping sound.

With a roar, I drive Knar in hard and kick the *woggha* in the head. My man takes the opportunity to roll free. I don't wait to see if he makes good his escape but keep Knar close to the ground. Leaning far out in the saddle, I swipe my sword off the ground.

Then we're rushing on to the next street over. More bodies. More blood. One of my warriors lies disemboweled in the middle of the street. Glassy eyes stare up to the high *lorst* lights. All around me, hell has come to Mythanar. I hear the screams of men, women. Children.

There is no plan. No strategy. I spur my morleth on, saving those I can, killing every beast that comes within reach of my blade. There are too many of them, all savage and rabid. They kill for pure blood-lust, not even pausing to feast upon their victims. It's just blood and more blood.

Every instinct tells me to take to the upper air, out of the streets. To fly as fast as Knar can carry me straight to the palace, straight to Faraine's balcony. There I would catch her up in my arms and bear her away from all of this. All the way back to the Between Gate, where I'd send her through to her own world as gods alone know I should have done long ago! How could I have been so foolish, so selfish? To hold her imprisoned here, making every damned excuse to keep her close.

Now she will die. Because I cannot reach her. Because I cannot abandon these screaming citizens to their fates, even as I know I cannot possibly save them all. Because I've failed her and failed them and failed all of Mythanar.

From the tail of my eye, I see a devil dragging a man from an upper-story window while his family screams and clings to his arms. With a cry, I drive Knar straight into the beast. We make contact. The impact jars it loose from the side of the building. It falls, but Knar staggers. I lose my seat, tumble from the saddle. Wind whistles past my ears.

Then I land flat on my back. For a moment, I cannot move. I have no breath. Every bone in my body rattles, and I wonder if they're all broken.

Instinct flares. Death is coming, coming, *now*.

I roll, lose my helmet, and narrowly avoid the swiping claws of a devil. I lash out with one arm. Bracer spikes bash the side of a *woggha*'s snarling face. Pulling myself up into a crouch, I face three devils. They circle me. Their long tongues waggle and drag on the ground, dripping streams of greenish foam.

My sword. Where is my sword?

The first devil lunges. I get my hands up just in time, catch it by the jaws. As its sharp teeth pierce through my gauntlets, I force its jaw wider, wider. It roars. I roar back. The sound bellows up from the depths of my soul as I scream into that monster's ugly face. Something cracks. The *woggha* falls at my feet, writhes. Goes still.

There's no time for triumph. A second devil hits me in the side. I fall beneath it, twisting, fighting, lashing out with my bracer spikes. One razor-sharp claw glances off my breastplate. I cannot let it pierce my armor or I'll end up gutted like the others. Somehow, miraculously, I find my feet again. Two devils close in on me, heads low. One of them growls softly. I brace myself, arms out, body low. The first one lunges. I hit it with the bracer spikes, knock it off-balance, but the second goes for me in the very next breath. I don't have time to recover.

I hit the ground hard. This time, I know I won't get back up. This time, it's got me pinned. Wrenching one arm up, I stick my bracer into the beast's open mouth, drive a spike into its tongue. It doesn't care. Its teeth crush into my armor. I feel the bones of my arm ready to break. Its claws scrabble at my chest plate, trying to crack me open like an egg. One gnarled hand slices at my head. I dodge, but a claw scrapes across my temple. Hot blood gushes.

The beast lunges harder. Foul breath blasts into my nostrils. I stare into that awful maw. It will be the last sight I see.

*Faraine.*

Her shining eyes, laughing at me from beneath that trolde-style tiara.

*Lorst* light soft and gleaming in her hair.

Her lips, curved in a warm smile, full of promise. Full of hope.

I've failed her. I'll never reach her in time.

She will die. Horribly. Wondering where I am. Wondering why I do not come to save her.

# 36

## Faraine

A sickening crunch.

Pain shoots up my ankle, a white-hot line that shocks the breath from my lungs. I fall, limbs folded under me, and land in a heap on the gravel path below the window. Curses leap to my tongue but cannot get past my grinding teeth. Sucking in a determined breath, I brace my arms, push myself upright. Somehow, I get to my feet, but when I put weight on my left foot, pain spikes again, and I crumple.

Somewhere, far off, Hael is shouting. I cannot make myself hear her. All my concentration is on rising again, hobbling forward three agonized paces into the garden. The circle of tall stones feels like a whole world away to my pain-sparked gaze. I must reach it. Somehow.

Heavy breathing. A low, guttural growl.

I spin to my right. A cave devil approaches. It creeps along with its belly close to the ground between clusters of crystals. Just as I spot it, it seems to become aware of me. Its nostrils flare, and its tongue tastes the air in little flicks. Then it crouches. Powerful muscles bunch, prepare for a single, deadly spring.

I have one moment in which to act. I can either try to flee on my damaged ankle, be knocked flat before I've taken two steps, have my spine snapped by those powerful jaws, or . . .

I drop to the ground. Plant my palm.

Even from a distance, the deep resonance of the Urzulhar stones vibrates beneath me. It calls to all other *urzul* crystals in the vicinity, great and small; draws their voices into a profound harmony. The vibration wraps around me, a small maelstrom lashing at my soul. I take hold of that power, that energy. Raising my other hand, I point at the cave devil. Just as it begins its leap, I send the resonance rippling *out*.

It catches the monster in midair. The beast drops to the ground in front of me, its mouth open, its hideous claws tensing and relaxing. It breathes out a long gurgle as its purple tongue spills over the cage of its teeth.

So we remain: me in a crouch, one hand to the ground, the other extended; the beast before me, held in stasis. Even its mind, so full of savage bloodlust, stills. But underneath that stillness . . . trapped beneath the resonance of the stones . . .

Something rages.

Something dark.

Something terrible.

Something . . . other.

*Who are you?* I whisper.

The darkness within the monster roils, thick and black as smoke. I struggle to peer into it, to discern the truth, to see—

A flash of bright red light. I cry out, fall backwards. My limbs scrabble in the dirt and gravel. When my vision clears, Hael is there. She stands over the cave devil's decapitated body, sword in hand. Her face is blood streaked, her eyes wide and pale beneath her stern brow as she lifts her gaze to me.

"It should have killed you. It had you." She shakes her head slowly, her expression mingled wonder and fear. "What did you *do*?"

There's no time to explain. I pull myself up. My limbs shake, my bad ankle throbs, and pain explodes in little lightning bursts inside my head. But I draw my shoulders back, meet and hold Hael's gaze. "Take me to the Urzulhar Circle." Her lips part. I feel her urge to protest, to demand answers. "Do as I say, Captain."

Hael clamps her jaw shut. The next moment, I'm in her strong arms again. She races through the garden, her breath hard and fast. At this close proximity her fear is almost blinding. My head whirls with nausea, and I fight to suppress the bile rising in my throat. I've got to hold on. I've got to be strong. Because if I could hold one cave devil then maybe . . . maybe . . .

There are devils all around us now. Long, low, loping bodies, darting through the crystals and rock formations. Mothcats screech as they flee, but their fear is nothing compared to the cloud of terror that rises from the city and throbs through my soul. I cannot take much more of this. I grip my pendant hard, praying all the desperate prayers I can utter through pain-clenched teeth.

Hael has just left the path and begun the final climb up the rise when she stops. A single word snarls from her lips: "*Juk!*"

I lift my head from her shoulder, peer up the rise. Three devils stalk toward us, one from directly above, two more from either side. It's like they knew we were coming. Like they knew my mad, foolish plan. Or like someone else knew and sent them on purpose to intercept us.

Hael sets me on my feet. I stagger, stumble, only just manage to keep from collapsing yet again. "Courage," she says, but more to herself than to me. Her fear is like knives, slicing at my awareness. But she draws her sword again, braces herself in front of me.

The first devil launches at us. Hael roars a wordless battle cry. Her blade flashes in the crystal light as it carves a terrible arc. It strikes the devil a ringing blow, cuts a deep gash into its gray, sagging flesh.

The second devil leaps before Hael has a chance to recover her balance. She drops her weapon, turns, catches the beast as it comes. With a powerful lunge, she hurls it over her head directly into the third beast. They crash in a tangle of limbs, but are up again a moment later, spitting foam from their sagging jaws.

"*Go!*" Hael casts me a short glance over her shoulder. "I'll hold them off as long as I can."

I don't have any choice. I race up the steep rise. Pain explodes in my ankle every time I put weight on it, but now survival instinct bursts in my veins, driving me harder, faster. I cannot move swiftly enough. All I can do is keep going as long as I have breath. When I can no longer run, I crawl upwards, pull myself along on my hands and knees, drag my bad leg behind me. Hael's vicious roars echo in my ears while the fear of the city reverberates in my head.

But the gods are with me. For the moment at least. I reach the summit, am within just a few paces of the crystal grove. I'm sobbing now. Tears stream down my face even as a gleam of hope lights my heart, breaks across my face in a smile. I surge forward, ignoring all other pains, and scrabble into the shelter of the crystals.

Teeth clamp down on my dragging foot.

I scream, shocked at this new burst of pain, and writhe around. A devil holds me fast. It bleeds from multiple wounds dealt by Hael's sword, but madness has driven it into a frenzy. It shakes its head, dragging me across the ground. My hands desperately grasp the crystals, call on their resonance to aid me. There's too much pain, too much fear, too much, too much, too—

A bolt of brilliant color streaks across my vision. The next moment, a mothcat lands on the cave devil's back. Tiny claws scrape and gouge, and the devil, startled, throws back its head and bellows.

My foot falls free. Bloody, mangled. Frantically, I twist around and crawl on my belly into the circle of stones. They pulse gently, their deep inner song a low thrum underneath the cacophony of pain and terror in my head. Sobbing, tears and mucus dripping from my face, I peel the heavy black gown from my body so that I may lie naked.

A cool wash of the crystal song bathes my soul.

Slowly, slowly, the darkness of all those feelings—Hael, the devils, the denizens of the city—flows out from me. Flows into the mighty crystals. They draw it all to their centers, and they're big enough, strong enough, to hold it.

I close my eyes, wishing I dared simply lie here and let that resonance bathe me, heal me, make me new. But I can't. I'm not here to save myself.

Pulling to my knees, I plant my palms hard in front of me. My long hair falls across my bare skin, framing my face like a veil as I close my eyes, close my ears, close off every sense but my gods-gift. Down into the resonance I plunge. Down into the deep, pulsing song of those ancient stones. Each note of that song is a thread of light—so many lights, so many individual notes, indescribably complex and beautiful.

But there are dark threads too. All those shuddering, shivering, poisoned souls. The devils. Each one unique, a life bound in torment. There are so many of them. Far more than I realized. Hundreds, thousands maybe. All those bloodthirsty fiends, savaging the city. Suffering and bringing suffering. Can I reach them? I don't know.

But I have to try.

I stretch out my awareness. Even as my body crouches there, naked, surrounded by the great blue stones, I extend my spirit, my soul. Gathering up one black thread, then another, then another, on and on and on. Each one I grasp sends a new jolt of pain through my spirit. I won't let them go. I catch them, first in ones and twos, then in handfuls, more and more, a hundred at a time, until at last I hold them all. Hold their pain, their anger. Hold their fear, their rage. Hold them with my soul, supported by the resonance of the Urzulhar.

Something stirs. Deep down, beneath the madness of the devils. Something dark. Something vast. I recognize it. I've felt this presence before. The source of the despair that so consumes these monsters, which so nearly consumed Vor.

It begins to move. To writhe and resist. The threads in my hand tense. I won't be able to hold them much longer. I must do something with them before they're ripped from my grasp. But what? Can I push this darkness from the devils' minds the way I pushed it from Vor's? That instance had nearly killed me. And he was only one man, one tormented soul. I can't possibly manage so many souls at once! I can't, I can't, I simply . . .

*Must.*

*Will.*

My jaw firms, teeth gritting hard. Sweat drips from my forehead, spatters on the stones under my bowed head.

I will save Mythanar.

I will save Hael, my brave defender.

I will save the refugee children playing among the priestesses' huts.

I will save Tril and the market vendors. The minstrels, the dancers.

I will save these people. I will save their city.

*For you, Vor.*

*For you.*

I summon all my strength, more than I knew I possessed. All the feeling in my heart, built up over so many years of hiding and protecting myself. It all had to go somewhere. I pull it forth now, let it roil to the surface, mounting pressure, like a dam ready to burst. My body shakes. The song of the crystals booms in my head, pulses through my veins.

Then I send it out—all that rolling reverberation. I pour myself in a long stream of life and soul, down to the last drop. The threads I have gathered vibrate and sing as my gods-gift flows along them and touches the minds of each and every mad beast.

My body spasms. The tall crystals above me flicker, go dim for a moment. Then they flare brighter than ever, a blaze of clear blue light, like a star fallen into this world under stone. Their light, their song, burns me from the inside out. But I don't stop. Not even when a ragged cry tears from my throat. Not even when I feel my soul being slowly ripped in half.

The whole of Mythanar cavern fills with light, brighter and brighter. The stones sing out their triumphant song, and every crystal answers back—from the largest, most complex formations to the tiniest granules of grit. Their voices fill the world, down to the fiery river below the chasm, up to the highest stalactites of the cavern ceiling. All the shadows, all the darkness of the Under Realm, are put to flight.

The last of my strength flows out from me. I have so little left. Just enough to cling to strands of life. Did I give enough? I cannot

SYLVIA MERCEDES

know. What if what I gave was only *almost* what was needed? What if, by holding on to life, I doom them all?

I can't hold on. I must give it all.

Vor's face appears in my mind, behind my tightly squeezed eyelids. I wish I'd had a chance to tell him the truth. To tell him I love him. To tell him that nothing else that had happened between us matters. Only my love. The love I chose. The love I will go on choosing. Forever.

I draw a deep breath into my lungs.

Then, with a final, shattering scream, I give the last of my strength over to the song. A burst of light explodes within my head and then . . .

. . . *oblivion*.

# 37

## Vor

**H**ot breath blasts in my face. Savage roaring tears at my ears.

I lie on my back, my arm shoved deep into the cave devil's mouth as its teeth slowly break through my armor. Ribbons of saliva fall in my eyes, burn my flesh. Muscles straining, I put everything I have into forcing that awful maw back. It's too strong, too mad. My strength falters, will soon give out.

Suddenly, all the pressure in my arm vanishes.

The beast falls away from me, staggers like it's drunk. It lifts its head, nostrils flaring. Goes still.

I roll. Blood pumping, heart throbbing. Every instinct in my body drives me to action, to escape the devil's clutches. Pushing myself up, I scramble to my feet, back away. My eyes fix on that creature which had, mere moments ago, threatened to rip my face from my skull. It stands perfectly still, its head lifted, its eyeless face fixed in the direction of the palace.

Slowly, I turn, gaze around at the rest of the torn-apart street. There are other devils within view. Many of them. Some poised above victims, both dead and still struggling with life. Every single one of the *woggha* stands in the same fixed attitude. All the savagery seems to have drained out from them. They're like sentinels on alert, focused on some distant point.

A snarl rasps from my throat. I find my sword, brandish it high, and drive it into the back of the nearest devil's skull. It drops like a stone. I go on to the next and the next, killing as many of them as I can while this strange stasis holds them at bay. Somewhere, another street over, I hear voices. One of them might be Lur, barking commands, but it feels far away. I'm alone here, alone in this world of horror and bloodshed.

Grimly, I progress from beast to beast, until I've slaughtered eight in quick succession. As I approach the ninth, however, its grey skin ripples unnaturally. Then it throws back its head and utters a prolonged, agonized howl. My blood chills. I leap back a step, terror spiking, and brace, prepared for the next attack.

But the beast swallows its voice at last, shakes its head. Then, to my utmost surprise, it turns, flees past me. Galloping on its ungainly limbs, it speeds back down the street. More devils appear moments later, and more and more. That same stream of murderous savagery which had flowed into my city now retreats. Low, slinking, moving like shadows, they flee in total silence.

Footsteps pound on pavement. I turn to see Lur, bleeding badly from a wound in her neck. She catches my gaze, relieved to find me alive. "My king!" she cries. Her voice rings strangely. "My king, what has happened? What are they doing?"

I cannot answer. I do not know. It's as though the compulsion which had driven them to swarm has suddenly fled their bodies. Not unlike . . . not unlike when . . .

I drag in a ragged breath. Terrible certainty fills my soul.

"Knar!" I bellow, and pivot on heel. A piercing whistle, and my morleth steps out of shadow before me, eyes blazing with fire. Lur calls after me, begs for answers, begs for orders. I ignore her, swing into my saddle, and spur my mount to motion. We soar over the street, over the rooftops. Below me, people are still screaming, weeping, and the *woggha* continue to flee, soundless shadows intent on escape with no interest in fighting back. But the bloodbath they leave behind is terrible indeed. It feels like the end of the world. Perhaps it is. Perhaps my world has come to an end.

*If Faraine is dead . . .*

I bow over Knar's neck, dig my spurs into his flanks with more force than necessary. The palace towers rise before my view, white and tall above the stricken city. I soar over the gate, yank on Knar's reins, and point him straight for that small stone balcony extending from an upper story window. Was it really only a few short hours ago when I last made this flight? I can almost see myself as I was then, ignorant of everything to come. Lifting her down from the saddle. Holding her in my arms. I feel again how my blood boiled with the need to kiss her, to caress her. A need I'd succumbed to as we gave in to the craving we both felt. Would those kisses be our last? Would my last words to her be those harsh and bitter barbs I'd flung at her in my anger and frustration?

I don't wait for Knar to land. I spring from his saddle, land hard on the balcony. Staggering, I push the window wide and emerge into her room. "Faraine!" My voice echoes hollowly. The chamber is empty. The door is open.

I race from the room out into the passage beyond. Her name bursts from my lips, resounds against the stone walls: "Faraine! Faraine!" All around me, voices echo back—weeping, wailing, shouting. Some still screaming. I run. Down the passage, down the stairs. Past the dead, the dying, the wounded and those trying to help them. Past the carcasses of slain *woggha*. Faces turn to me as I go. Hands reach out to me. I feel the pressure of so much need on every side.

Right now, I cannot think of anything else. Only Faraine. Only finding her. My feet carry me to the door of the infirmary. A crowd is already densely gathered here, but at the sight of me and my bloodstained face, people shuffle back, creating a path. I burst through the door, stand at the top of the stair, gaze down into the crush of people below. Ar tends to the wounded. She has several scurrying apprentices hastening to do her bidding, but they are overwhelmed.

I stagger down the steps, push through to the healing ward. The beds are all full, as is the floor. No matter where I look, I spy no glimpse of golden hair or pinkish human skin.

"Vor!" Sul's voice draws my head to one side. My brother is propped up in his bed, which he now shares with two others. They actively bleed from gashes to their chests and shoulders. Sul does what he can, applying pressure to a wound, using his own wadded-up blanket. His face is drawn, his eyes over-large in his face as he gazes across the room at me. "Are you well, brother?"

I cannot answer. I step back into the front room and grab the first apprentice who passes within reach. "The princess," I growl. "Has the human princess been brought here?"

The apprentice shakes his head. I can do nothing but let him go, let him hurry on to his work. I stand there mute, helpless. Staring around me. Staring at all that pain, which I had failed to prevent. Pain which could have been so much worse, if not for . . .

Cursing, I retrace my way up the infirmary steps, back out into the passage beyond. I run again, suddenly certain of my destination, though I cannot say why. Some instinct, perhaps. Some knowledge imparted by the gods.

The garden feels unnaturally still when at last I step into it. I see a decapitated *woggha* carcass almost at once. An encouraging sign, perhaps. I know only a few warriors strong enough to accomplish such a feat, and one of them is Hael. Perhaps she is here with Faraine. Somewhere.

I hasten down the winding paths, sprint as fast as my feet will carry me. I've shed some of my armor by now—the bracers and breastplate, the heavy boots. Anything that might slow me down. Dimness has fallen, but the living crystals gleam bright enough to guide my way. I never slacken my pace. I try to call her name, but my throat seems to close against it. All is eerily still, without the usual chatter of the mothcats or flutter of delicate *olk* wings.

A bloody form lies at the base of the Urzulhar rise, surrounded by the bodies of several devils. My heart stops. I spring forward, crouch beside her, pull her onto her back. "Hael!" She blinks up at me, her eyes unfocused. "Hael, are you still alive? Answer me, woman!"

She grimaces, her brow tightening. Then she groans. "I'm alive, my king. And not badly hurt."

She looks a mess. Her skin is slashed in numerous places, including a great gash above one eye. But she manages to pull herself up into a seated position. "Where is Faraine?" I demand. "You were to watch over her. Where is she?"

Hael shakes her head slowly. Then she twists, grimaces, and looks over her shoulder. "She—she said she needed to—"

I don't wait for her to finish. I'm already on my feet again, sprinting up the rise. The seven sacred stones are dull this dimness, their brilliant gleam darkened from the inside out. I can almost imagine I feel a vibration emanating from inside them but shove the idea back and hasten on until I step between the towering stones and stare into the sacred circle. Stare down at that small, delicate body. Naked. Lying with her golden hair spread around her.

A little mothcat sits perched on her shoulder, its long tail draped along her rib cage, over her hips. Her skin is untorn, unbruised. White as marble. She is utterly still. One could almost believe she merely slept.

"What have you done?" The words breathe from my lips, phantoms without sound. "What have you done, Faraine?"

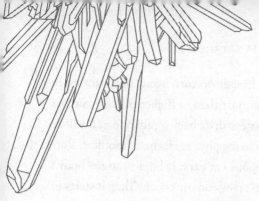

# 38

## Faraine

The pain is gone.

Well, that's a relief in any case. I feel lighter somehow. Also . . . smaller. But the smallness doesn't feel lasting. I should start to grow again soon. For the moment, however, it's nice to be merely a bit of gossamer nothing.

I turn my awareness slowly around and look down. Down through layers of reality that peel away like mist. Down into a world and realm that already feels as though it has little to do with me. Down to my broken body.

Poor thing. It was so wracked with pain. Human bodies aren't meant to bear that much pain, not all at once. It simply could not survive. A pity. That form served me well. I experienced so many joys, so many pleasures while inhabiting it. There were sorrows too, of course. There always are. But I don't know any other existence.

I suppose I shall have to find out what comes next. After one becomes unembodied.

The mists close back in. I begin to turn away, not wanting to linger on that sorry sight. But just then, a flicker of color catches my attention. I let my awareness drift back again and see a little limping creature nose its way to my physical form. A mothcat. Purple fur, orange stripes, enormous bat ears. It hops onto my body's shoulder, puts its delicate little paws on my cheek. Then it starts to purr.

I start, surprised. That purr vibrates into the bones of that body. The vibration increases and sends out a little thread of light which extends from the body until it reaches me. Though I try to pull away, the glimmering light spirals around me, loop after loop. It's neither tight nor uncomfortable, but when I try to slip away, it holds me fast. I can do nothing but hover there in that space of existence above my lifeless form.

*Let me go.* I don't have a mouth, a voice. I simply send the command back down the shimmering tether. The mothcat twitches one ear then settles down more firmly on its haunches. Its purring redoubles. The light-tether flares, strengthens.

This is foolish. I cannot remain here. My body is broken. In the end my gods-gift was simply too much for such a feeble frame. Perhaps I'll have opportunity to take the matter up with the gods themselves. Why would they bestow such tremendous power on such a weak individual? It doesn't make sense. They ought to have known better.

I tug at the life-thread, eager to be on my way. The mothcat opens its mouth. Its purr rumbles louder, the reverberation humming against the darkened *urzul* crystals.

"Faraine!"

My awareness quickens. I twist, peer through the threads of light, turn toward that sound. My spirit surges, like the pulse of a dying heart. *Vor!* Is he alive? I'd not thought it possible. I'd assumed he perished long before the cave devils ever breached his city's walls. But what if he didn't? What if he is still there, in that world of flesh and matter? What if his soul still inhabits his body?

It makes no difference. Those flesh-forms of ours are so temporary. And mine is now broken. Uninhabitable. I cannot stay here. I try to tug away. I don't want to see Vor. I don't want to feel what I know I will feel at the sight of him. But the tether won't let me go.

Suddenly, he's there, standing between two of the great stones, staring down at my empty husk. My whole being brightens at the mere sight of him. *Vor! Vor!* Alive still. Alive and beautiful. His body is a mere shadow to my gaze, but his spirit shines bright as a star, full of mysterious energies and complexity. It fairly bursts beyond the confines of his physical frame.

I watch the shadow-figure leap forward, fall to his knees beside my body. He cries out my name. I hear it like a distant echo. It catches on the delicate life-thread, ripples up to my awareness. When he touches my bare skin, some of that strange energy of his flows out from inside him and into the tether. The delicate thread strengthens, becoming a multistranded cord.

Vor lifts my body in his arms, cradles me close; presses kiss after kiss into my hair, my cheeks, my neck. Gently, softly, I float down through the misty layers of reality, until I'm close enough to whisper in his ear: *I love you, Vor. I will always love you. Wherever I go, I carry my love for you with me.*

*But now you must let me go.*

*Let me go, Vor.*

He throws back his head. For an instant, his soul shines so bright, his shadowy features become clear to my gaze, wracked with pain, with sorrow, frenzied with determination. "I won't let go, Faraine!" he cries. His voice reverberates against the *urzul* crystals, and light flickers in their darkened centers.

The mothcat lets out a protesting squeak and scampers away as Vor gets to his feet, still holding me tight. My head lolls, but he adjusts until it rests against his shoulder. Then, stepping from the confines of the circle, he hastens down the slope and into the gardens. The thread of connection stretches, strains. But the binding is stronger now that he holds me.

Up above, through many more layers of mist and unseen realities, I feel warmth and light overhead. And song. So much song. The presence of my goddess awaits. And my sisters? Ilsevel and Aurae? Do they wait for me too, ready to fold me in their welcoming embraces? I long to ascend, to find them, to enter at last into that holy eternity for which my soul longs. And yet . . .

While my soul may long to ascend . . . my heart does not want to go. Not yet.

So, I am dragged along like a child's kite through the ether. I catch only flashing glimpses of the world. Shining crystals with vibrant hearts that sing out to me like delicate songs. The hearty, glowing soul of Hael, which flares brightly as Vor carries my body into her view. These and other impressions spark at my awareness. Vor's pace never falters. He bears me swiftly back across the garden, into the palace. Past the carcasses of dead devils, the bodies of slain trolde. I feel the emptiness in those places where spirits used to be. Spirits which have since fled to their new homes as mine should have done. As I should now do.

Yet I trail after Vor into a room full of suffering souls. So many of them hang on to their bodies only by mere threads. Even as I watch, I see threads snap, break. Souls shoot away through realities, speed on to their eternities.

"Ar!" Vor's voice roars through the mists, harsh with desperation. "Ar, I need you!"

A bright, fiery soul appears as a squat, featureless form draws near to the shadowy figure housing Vor's soul. My thread has thinned. I feel myself drawing further away. I struggle to lean in, to discern the words being exchanged.

"The princess?" the fiery soul asks.

"My wife," Vor responds.

With those two simple words, the tether holding me in place strengthens. If only I had a voice with which to sing! His wife. His *wife*. At last, he claims me, names me what I am.

But it's too late. I'm already gone, or mostly gone. I am his wife . . . but only for these last few, stolen moments. Still, I will carry those words with me to heaven and treasure them for eternity.

*Vor, Vor,* I whisper, bending close to his ear once more. *Vor, it is time.*

He bows his head, hair falling across his face. Then he looks up at the healer and growls, "Do something! Help her!"

Ar ushers him further into the crowded chambers. The beds are all full, but she clears one of her worktables with a sweep of her arm. Vor lays my body down upon it but keeps hold of one hand. As though he knows that the moment he lets go, I will be gone, truly gone.

Ar looks me up and down, listens to my chest, takes my pulse. Then she lifts sad eyes to her king. "She's dead." Her voice is blunt as a grinding stone.

"No. She isn't."

The healer shakes her heavy head. "I know you don't want to believe it, Vor—"

"I won't believe it. Because it is not true."

"There's nothing to be done for her, my boy!" Ar puts up both hands and takes a step back from the table. "I don't have the means to put a living soul back into a body."

"Is her body broken?" Vor demands.

Once again, the healer bends over my flesh form. To my surprise, she seems to take the question seriously and proceeds to inspect every inch of me for signs of physical damage. She lingers a moment over my mangled ankle, but finally steps back. "I see no signs of a death blow. But her heart has given out."

"Does it still beat?"

"Not that I can detect."

"But she's not gone cold."

"It may take a little time for coldness to set in. Humans are not like troldefolk, after all—"

"Then you must not treat her like a trolde. Treat her like a human."

"I haven't the experience."

"You've cared for a human before. One whom everyone believed had died. You brought her back from the brink on the very day that I was born."

"The brink of death is not death itself, dear boy."

At those words, Vor seems to come undone. He bows over the table, over my remains. His spirit darkens, its luminous light dimming with despair. How I wish I could reach out to him, envelop him in my arms, offer him comfort. But to try would only risk hurting him more.

Oh, Vor! Vor! A small part of me had dared to hope his sheer determination would be enough to . . . But there's no use in such hopes. It's better for us both if this ends. I'm not afraid. There is no more pain for me. Only ascension and expansion and the light of eternity. My one sorrow is that I must leave him behind.

*Vor,* I whisper, crooning the words close to his ear. *It's all right. Please, my love, let me—*

Vor looks up. His eyes flash like two knives as they lock with Ar's. "If you cannot treat humans," he growls, "tell me where to find one who can."

Ar's face shutters. Her spirit dims, retreats.

"I know you know where she is," Vor continues.

"I don't know what you're talking about."

"Don't play with me." He lunges across the table, catches the shoulder of Ar's garment. "Tell where she is. Tell me where I can find her. If anyone can help me, she can."

Ar squirms in his grasp. Her soul flickers uneasily. "Fine!" she says at last. "She dwells on the Surface. I can tell you where. But are you certain, Vor? Are you certain you want to see her? After all this time?"

I don't understand. What is going on here? Of whom are they speaking? I flick my awareness from Ar's spirit back to Vor's. That determined light is back, shining brighter and hotter than ever in his soul. He leans in, drawing his face close to the healer's. "Tell me," he growls.

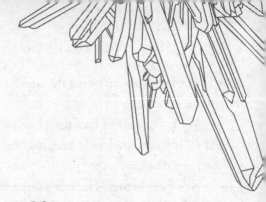

# 39

## Vor

I've wrapped her body in the black robe I found beside her among the Urzulhar Circle. It makes her look even paler as she rests against my breast. I remember when I first met her how struck I was by the pinkish tint of her skin, so different from trolde women. Now I would give anything to see that rosy flush return.

I hold her before me on Knar's broad back, much as I had the night of our first meeting. We are alone as we fly up from the city. No one can be spared to join me on this journey; everyone is needed in the wake of the attack. Those who don't chase the remaining devils from the city streets must tend the wounded and collect the dead. A bolt of shame strikes my heart. I should be down there with them. I am their king. What does it say about me that I am riding with all speed straight out of the city in the wake of its greatest disaster?

Pressing Faraine close against me, I lean over the morleth's neck and spur him on faster and faster. Were it not for her, for this frail, delicate, courageous woman, the disaster would have been far worse, the slaughter unimaginable. Cave devils would be rampaging through the stricken streets even now, tearing out throats and rending limbs. I don't understand how she did it. I don't know how she stopped them. But I know if it weren't for Faraine . . .

I look down into her still face. My chest tightens until I fear my heart will cease to beat. Gods, what a fool I was! I'd fought with everything I had to reach her, believing I was the only one who could save her. It never occurred to me that I was the one who needed saving.

Knar gains speed as he climbs into the air above the city, up and up toward the cavern ceiling. In the gloom of deep dimness, he is happy, a being of pure shadow. We make for one of the shaft openings to the Surface World. These are difficult to access, impossible by any means save morleth. And morleth do not like the air up above, so it takes a skilled rider to dare such an ascent. I've never done it before.

I don't hesitate now. Even as the massive death drop yawns below, even as my city shrinks away, I urge Knar on. This is Faraine's only chance. I would brave far greater perils for the mere hope of seeing her eyes gaze up at me one last time.

We weave in among the stalactites. There are marks left to guide the way—little white stars carved into the stone and set with small, ever-bright *lorst* crystals, which shine even when their greater, brighter brethren have dimmed. I follow these pinpoint gleamings, drive Knar with my spurs when he sniffs the air and angrily tosses his head. He knows now where we are going and doesn't like it. But he doesn't fight me.

Suddenly, I feel a blast of cool air on my face. The next moment the opening comes into view, a circle gazing out into the awful vastness of the Surface World sky. Distant stars twinkle in their celestial dance above. It's enough to make my heart quail.

"*Drag-or!*" I growl, and drive Knar on, between the massive toothlike stalactites, up to that patch of sky. The morleth gnashes his teeth. Sparks shoot from his nostrils.

The next moment, we emerge in a cloud of smoke, up from the rock and soil, streaking straight out into that terrible night. My senses whirl, sick with dread as I feel all that openness around me. After everything else I've recently endured, this is almost too much to bear.

I haul on Knar's reins, reclaiming control. He puffs and growls but obeys when I guide him back down. We skim above the tall grasses. Knar's cloven hooves shred through the delicate flowers, tossing leaves and petals, but never touching solid ground. The world around is all very wide and wild and barren—rolling fields beneath open sky, purple with twilight and alight with a million stars. I remember vividly what it was like to ride under such a sky on my way to Beldroth. I remember the sensation of Faraine's fingers lightly touching the back of my wrist, the sudden calm which came over me. I'd guessed at the time that she'd worked her godsgift on me. But I never dreamed the true potential of her power.

We leave the fields behind at last and come to a rocky place. There I search for the signs Ar described. It would be easier to fly higher and look from above, but I fear I might miss my destination entirely in this unfamiliar world. Down low, the pathway markers are easier to detect—large, gaudy red flowers on tall green stalks. Fire lilies. Their finger-length petals reach like hands to the heavens, gleaming unnaturally bright in the twilight.

I turn Knar's head. We pursue the path the lilies mark. They grow at intervals, tucked away, half-hidden among the rocks. I must take care not to miss them. I hate this pace, hate the moments I feel slipping away. Faraine grows colder in my arms, but I won't let go of hope. Not yet.

At last, I spy a stone hut with a roughly thatched roof perched on an outcropping, just as Ar had described. Warm light glows from the small windows. Orange light—sunfire rather than moonfire.

I stop Knar with a word and slip from the saddle, careful not to jostle Faraine more than necessary. Leaving the morleth behind to chomp on lilies, I stride up the rest of the narrow path and come to a halt just beyond the reach of the light. "Maylin!" I cry. "Mistress Maylin! I seek your aid."

For a long moment, no answer comes. Blood throbs in my ears. This was a mistake. I should never have come to this place. I should turn around right now, flee while I still can. Before that door opens, before . . .

I growl, shake my head hard. What cowardice is this? "Maylin!" I shout again. "I command you: come forth!"

"Command me, do you?" A flicker of shadow passes across one of the windows. The next moment, the door creaks slowly open. "Far be it from me to deny the commands of a king."

My heart leaps to my throat. In the doorway stands a small, slim, slightly stooped figure in a deep hood and heavy cloak. She rests her weight on a crooked walking stick. Her hands tremble slightly. Though her back is to her fire, the many-stranded crystal necklace she wears glints and shines, illuminating the lower half of her face, her jaw, her mouth.

She seems to study me, her eyes hidden by the shadow of her hood. At long last, her lips part. "*Grakol-dura*, King Vor," she says, her troldish strongly accented but understandable. "I wondered if you would someday find your way to my doorstep."

I widen my stance as though for battle. "I've come with one purpose and one alone. I wish neither to speak nor to barter." I lift Faraine slightly. Some of the orange light falls across her still face. "I need you to reconnect this woman's living soul to her body. I will pay whatever price you demand."

The woman's chin tilts as she redirects her hidden gaze. I feel the intensity of her scrutiny like an electric charge in the air. After a moment, she ventures forward, her cane tapping on the stones of the path. Her movements are slow, awkward, a little pained. Though she is small, she casts a long shadow before her. I shiver when it falls across me. She draws near enough that I could reach out and touch her if I dared, then moves her hood back slightly, revealing the barest glimpse of her cheek and nose. The sight twists my heart. I look away quickly. Unconcerned, she bends over Faraine, studies her closely, *hmmm*-ing softly to herself. Finally, she lets her hood drop back into place. "So. She used the Urzulhar stones, did she?"

I nod.

"Overextended herself. The resonance ripped right through her, I'm afraid."

I don't pretend to understand. "Whatever she did, she did to defend Mythanar. She saved them all. My city. My people."

The woman tilts her head back, her unseen eyes fixed on my face once more. The line of her jaw tightens. It's such a familiar sight, my throat thickens. I hastily avert my gaze, looking down at Faraine.

"I felt the recent stirrings," the old witch says at last, her voice a little softer. "There was a bad one a few days ago, yes? I felt it all the way up here on the Surface. Mythanar hasn't got much time left."

"That is not your concern." The words snap from my teeth like a bite. "You need only name your price, witch. Tell me how to save this woman."

She sighs and shakes her head slowly. Then: "There may be something I can do. But it won't be pleasant."

I frown. "Will it hurt her?"

The witch snorts. "She's already dead. How much more do you think I can do to her at this point?"

Still, I hesitate. Dead or alive, I don't want to do anything to cause Faraine distress. If she's already beyond pain, is it not kinder simply to let her go?

But no. No! I won't do it. Not until I've had a chance to tell her the truth. To speak all the things I should have said hours ago when I had the chance. Before the stirring, before the horror, before the deaths and devastation. When we were just two people lying in a tumble of limbs atop rumpled blankets. I should have spoken, even as my lips explored her body and my hands caressed her skin. I should have murmured the words as I slipped down to her secret places, as I made her moan and writhe. Or when we lay together after, when I gazed into her face, alight and shining with warmth, with passion.

All those moments, lost forever, recklessly wasted. Yet, here I am. Begging the gods for one moment more.

"Do what you must," I growl.

A low, knowing *hmmmm* sounds from beneath that dark hood. Then the witch steps back and waves a hand. "Lay her down. Gentle as you can."

I hasten to obey. The witch kneels beside Faraine and opens the front of her gown, exposing her pale bosom. From her own neck, she takes a glowing strand of crystals and drapes them across

Faraine's body. Carefully, she positions the largest crystal over her heart. This done, she looks up at me. I catch a flash of her golden eyes. "This part may be unpleasant."

I nod. "Do it."

The witch shrugs but leans over Faraine. She lets out a long breath, utters a series of words I do not know, and touches her palm to Faraine's forehead.

Faraine's eyes flare wide, blazing with white, burning light. She drags in a terrible gasp, like the exhale before a scream. Her whole body goes rigid, her back arched as though in pain.

"Faraine!" I cry.

But she cannot hear me.

# 40

## Faraine

The further he rides from Mythanar, the fainter my life-tether grows. Perhaps the *urzul* crystals sustained it, and now that I am out of their reach, it's destined to break. Or perhaps I'm simply tired of holding on to a life I've already lost. Vor is nothing but a shadow. I still feel his presence, faintly. More of a memory than a reality now. My own body I can no longer feel at all.

I study the delicate filament of life-thread wound around my awareness. It's dimming now. Which is good. I've already stayed too long. Time to let this final connection break, time to move on to the next part of my existence. It hurts to leave Vor behind, but . . . but we had our chance. And a beautiful, glorious chance it was! I'm glad of it, even if it ended in pain. Pain doesn't change the truth of the connection we had, the peace I knew in his presence. The joy, the glory. All of it was real. I wouldn't trade a moment.

I watch the shadows of the world fade. A sense of tremendous space opens above me, inexplicably great. My soul is drawn to it, upward and away. Only that last little thread keeps me from float-ing free. I should break it. I should go. And yet . . . *and yet* . . .

"Well, now. You've gotten yourself into a bit of a mess, haven't you?"

My hazy perception of existence flurries in surprise. A figure approaches through the mist, parting curtains of reality before her with the end of a crooked walking stick. She wears a heavy hood, but as she draws near, throws it back to reveal a face lined with age but still striking. Straight stern brows set above well-chiseled fea-tures, and eyes, golden as a cat's, trained on me with almost pred-atory intensity.

"Who are you?" I ask, surprised to find I have a voice.

"No one of particular importance." The woman tilts her head to one side. Her eyes narrow slightly. "The more immediate ques-tion is, who are *you*?"

There's something about the way she asks it that puts me on my guard. "Likewise," I answer slowly, "no one of particular impor-tance."

She crooks an eyebrow. "That's not what I hear. I hear you used the Urzulhar stones and saved the city of Mythanar from disaster. Pretty important if you ask me."

"I did what I could. And I . . . I'm glad it worked."

"It worked all right. But at what cost?" The woman looks me up and down. I'm not entirely certain what she's looking at, consider-ing I have no body here. But that doesn't seem to bother her. "You've gone and overextended yourself. Now look at you!" She waves a hand, indicating my vagueness.

"As long as Mythanar is safe, I am satisfied."

"Oh, are you?" At this, the woman snorts. An undignified sound coming from a face so regal. "You think driving a few *woggha* from the streets will do any good in the long run, child? What you did was like swatting the wasp on the end of the tiger's nose. Sure, you won't get stung; you'll get your head bitten off instead."

A chill ripples through my being. "What am I to do?"

"Do? What can you do? You're dead."

Once more, I look down at the little thread wound around my . . . well, not my finger. I don't have a finger anymore. But my essence. I roll the thread, watch how it sparks and glitters. "What is down there?" I ask at last, looking up and catching the strange woman's eye. "What is down in the Dark? Under the city?"

"Ah. So, they've not told you about the dragon yet."

*Dragon.*

Somehow . . . I knew. Somehow, I've always known. The signs were everywhere—the dragon motif carved into every wall, embroidered on every garment. Not just any dragon, not some fire-breathing cow-chaser such as the heroes hunt in legends. This is one of the Great Beasts. The Celestial Dancers. The Breakers of Worlds. Long lost to the mists of time and myth, yet always there, always hovering on the edges of instinctual memory.

"No," I admit. "They've told me nothing. But I know a little. I know it wants to destroy them."

"Yes. Unfortunately."

"But why?"

The woman's brows rise. "Do you think I'm privy to the motivations of dragons?" She snorts. The next instant, however, her expression grows grim. "But make no mistake, little princess—*Arraog*, the Fire at the Heart of the World, is stirring. Soon, she will wake. When that happens . . ."

I turn my awareness away from the woman. Beyond her there's a faint slip of shadow. It's Vor. At least, I think it's Vor. It's impossible to discern his features. I can scarcely detect the flicker of his soul. "When she wakes," I whisper softly, finishing the woman's train of thought, "she will destroy his world."

"Sooner or later. She will. She must." The woman shakes her head heavily. "I'd hoped to make it later. Much later. And I thought you might be the one to help me."

"Help you? How can I help you? How can anyone do anything against such a being?"

"But you're not just anyone, are you? You're gods-gifted. Bestowed with divine blessings intended for divine purpose." The woman takes a step closer. Her eyes shine like two torches, burning through realities to meet and hold my gaze. "With the right training, with the right technique, you may be just what Vor needs."

I shiver, drawing back from her. My little filament thread flickers, tenses, ready to snap. "What of the Miphates?" I ask.

"What of them?"

"Vor believes they could help."

"Maybe they could." The woman shrugs. "I don't know much about Miphates magic. I know it's big, it's dangerous, it's chaotic. It might be just what he needs. It *might*." She takes a step forward, lifts her cane, jabs the pointed end of it straight at me. "But I *know* you are what he needs. So, tell me—are you willing?"

"What?"

"Are you willing?" she repeats. Those eyes of hers seem to dance like flames before my vision. "To come back? To fight for Vor? To fight for Mythanar?"

I turn away, unable to bear her gaze. "I don't know."

"Don't say yes unless you mean it. Such magic always requires a price. It may be greater than either of you wish to pay."

"What sort of price?"

"That I cannot tell you. But when it comes, it will be harsh indeed. You may wish you had made a different choice." She tips her head, raises an eyebrow at me. "Then there's the pain to consider. Souls are not meant to reenter their physical bodies once they've left. It will not be a pleasant experience."

"I'm not afraid of pain."

"Bravely spoken, little princess. But this is worse than you've known. You might not survive the process. And if you don't, well, I cannot speak for the results on"—once more she vaguely waves a hand, indicating my incorporeal self—"all *this*."

"Do you mean . . ." I stop, uncertain I want to continue. "Do you mean I might cease to exist? I, myself? As Faraine?"

"It's a possibility. No one knows for sure what happens to souls after a failed restoration. They don't come back to tell the tale."

I draw away from her, shivering. Warm light beckons me from above, from that great space beyond this mist. I could almost swear I hear the voice of my goddess singing. Calling me home. Part of me wants to answer. Part of me wants to know the comfort and safety of that voice, the wholeness of her embrace.

Am I willing to risk all hope of heaven for Vor?

I look at his shadowy image again. Even through the layers of mist, I feel his desperation. He needs me. He needs *me*. I don't know if I believe everything this strange person says to me. But I do believe in Vor. In the two of us. In what we are and everything we could be. How could I abandon him, knowing I could have done more? How could I truly go on to heaven's light, leaving him in the Deeper Dark?

I turn again, meet the woman's strange, golden gaze. "Very well," I say. "I'll face both the pain and the price. And should I not prove strong enough, I'll accept whatever end. For him."

She gives me a narrow look. "And the dragon? Should you succeed in returning, will you face that foe?"

A shudder ripples through my essence. "I cannot say."

"Fair enough." The witch's lips tip in a mirthless half smile. "One thing at a time."

With those words, she steps back into the mist. It closes around her like curtains, obscuring her from my view. "Wait!" I call after her.

But she's already gone.

# 41

## Vor

With a sharp intake of air, the witch comes out of her trance and staggers backwards several paces. She shakes her head, recovers her balance, then immediately leaps forward and closes Faraine's eyes. The strange other-light shines through her lids for a moment longer, but when the witch snatches the crystals off her chest, that dims as well. The tension leaves her body. Soon Faraine lies lifeless and limp once more.

"What happened?" I demand, crouched protectively over her. I lift my head, glare up at the witch. "What did you do?"

She self-consciously pulls her hood back into place, obscuring what little of her face had been revealed. "I just had a chat with your pretty bride. You were right—her spirit is not far. And she's willing to attempt reconnection to her body."

The possibility that she might not be willing hadn't occurred to me until this moment. My gaze shoots down to her immobile face. More and more she does not look asleep but truly gone. Truly dead.

"Very well," I say, my voice ragged and rough. "Let's get on with it then. Do what you must."

"Not so fast." The woman presses her cane heavily into the ground, leans her full weight upon it. Whatever magic she just performed has sapped her strength. "While the girl may be willing, that doesn't mean it will actually work. And the process will be unpleasant."

A shiver creeps down my spine. "How? How is it done?"

Prying one hand from her cane, the witch points to the tall mountain across the valley, opposite her hut. "There," she says. "At the base of that mountain lies a wild pool surrounded by fire lilies. It is a sacred place, a gateway of sorts, between this world and the *quinsatra*, the realm of magic. It's located directly above the Urzulhar Circle and channels the energies of those stones. When the moon reaches the zenith of the sky and fills the waters with light, you must enter and stand in the center. Then, you and she must go under. Both of you must remain submerged until the moment you feel life restored. If you rise too soon, she will perish. Too late, and you both will. Do you understand?"

"Yes, of course." I frown, certain this cannot be all. It's too easy. If it were indeed this simple, people would be reanimating their loved ones all the time. "What of the price? I know enough of magic. There must be a price."

"There is." The witch leans on her staff again, the one visible corner of her mouth twitching. "But you'll not learn what it is until it's too late to unmake your bargain. Have a care, great king! Do not enter the water if you are not prepared to give what the magic demands."

*A life for a life.* What else can she mean? All of existence depends on balance and harmonies. Surely there can be no other answer. I gaze down at Faraine's still face again. I would gladly die for her if I could, but . . . will I abandon my city? At its most vulnerable? The weight of that choice could break me in two.

"You haven't much time." The witch's voice draws my gaze sharply back to her hooded face. "Moonrise is coming. If you must dither, dither on your way. Otherwise, the decision will be made for you. She cannot hold on much longer."

I nod and gather Faraine in my arms once more. She feels lighter than before, a mere feather which the slightest breeze might yank from my hold and drag into that horrible, endless sky. Shuddering, I turn to mount Knar.

"Wait."

I stop. Look back.

"You've not yet offered payment."

The witch's words ring in my ears. I do not answer. Cannot answer.

She steps toward me, slowly. Her body quakes, still rocked by the effort of magic she'd worked. Her necklace of crystals clatters and glints in the starlight. When she stands only a pace or two away from me, she stops.

My throat tightens. "What payment do you require of me?"

Lifting one hand from her cane, she pulls back the heavy hood, revealing an old, wrinkled face. Slowly, she turns it up to me, her golden eyes like two shining gems in the night. She smiles slowly. "A kiss. Only a kiss. Nothing more, nothing less."

Her eyelids fall delicately. She tilts her head to one side, offers up a wrinkled cheek.

I hesitate. Long ago word was brought to me of the witch's existence, of her presence so near in the World Above. I'd received the word, acknowledged it. Then done everything in my power to forget.

I'd sworn I'd never come to this place.

I'd sworn I'd never see her, never speak to her.

This? This is far worse. To embrace her. As though nothing had ever happened between us.

"Please, Vor," the witch says, her eyes still closed. "Just one little kiss. For your old mother."

My stomach knots.

Then, with a quick inhale of breath, I bend, brush my lips against her cheek.

The next moment, I'm pounding down the path, back to where Knar waits. Soon I'm in the saddle, Faraine pressed close to my breast. Without a backwards glance, I drive my spurs into the morleth's flanks. "*Jah!*" I cry.

Knar leaps to the sky and speeds across the darkness.

. . . . . . . . . . . . . . . . . . . . .

The moon is rising. We haven't much time.

The vastness of that terrible sky threatens to swallow up my sanity. I focus my gaze on our destination up ahead, determined not to forget my purpose and sink into jabbering madness. For all I know, it's already too late. For all I know, the last threads of life keeping Faraine's spirit close have already severed. But I must try. I must strive till the last of my strength gives way.

"Hold on, Faraine," I whisper against her hair. "Just a little longer now. Hold on."

The pool is readily visible under moonlight, even at a distance. The smooth clear waters gleam silver, surrounded by red fire lilies, just as Mother described. I guide Knar down, circling lower and lower until his feet prance just inches above the ground. I adjust my grip on Faraine, press her head to my shoulder as I slide from the saddle and stagger to the pool. Collapsing on my knees before it, I stare down into the dark water. There lies a perfect reflection of the terrible sky overhead.

Something resonates from below. I can't explain it. It's not unlike the crystal songs of the *gujek* minstrels. But deeper. Like the voice of the earth itself, echoing from below.

The moon glides higher and higher. It casts silvery light over the grass, the flowers. Nearby trees throw shivering shadows, like fingers rippling on the surface of the pool. I look down into Faraine's face, bathed in moonlight. She's so beautiful in my eyes. So strong, so brave. Dauntless in the face of every danger, a queen of true dignity and grace.

She is everything to me.

I would give everything for her.

Slowly, I slip into the pool. Find my footing, ease into that cold, dark water. Her hair trails over my arm and drags behind us as I carry her to the center. There the water is deep, up to my chest. I angle her carefully to keep from letting her go under too soon. The moon climbs high. It hovers almost directly over us now.

"I give it all, Faraine," I whisper, my mouth against her soft hair. "My heart. My life. Come what may, I am yours."

*A life for a life?*

*So be it.*

I throw my head back and roar to the dreadful heavens, declare before all the gods: "Whatever the price, I will pay it! Let it fall on me!"

Then, holding her tight, I tip over backwards. Black water closes over our heads.

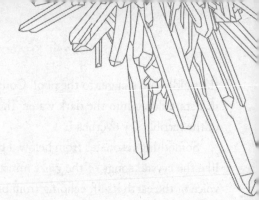

# 42

## Faraine

The crystals are singing.

I hear them. All around me. Under me. Over me.

Singing a song of the stars they once were. Singing a song of the blackness of space, the endless vastness of eternity. A song of life and love and darkness and endings and beginnings.

The song moves around me, through me. Pulls me down through layer after layer of reality until I'm submerged in black water, cold as ice. I feel the heaviness of a body all around me, like I'm encased in stone.

Still the song sings, vibrates through my bones. These are the voices of suns and moons, the voices of the higher gods. And above them and below them and through them, the great One Voice that spoke even the gods into being.

I am ecstatic. This is beyond any experience I ever hoped to know while housed in a body of flesh. It does not matter that I am cold, that I am heavy, that I am blind. Why should such things matter when such a song rings through every fiber of my being?

Then the pain begins.

Like a lance of furnace-heated iron shot straight up my spine.

I scream. There is no air, and I have no voice. It does not matter. Both my body and my spirit scream, thrash. I thought I knew what pain was. I thought I could endure it.

I was wrong.

Oh, why did I not die as I should? The worst was over. There was no need to come back, no need to feel this burning, wrenching, shattering . . .

*Faraine.*

Vor's voice. Speaking directly to my heart.

*Faraine, let me take this. Let me have your pain.*

No! No, I will not give this to him. If this is the price of my daring to defy the very laws of death, then I alone shall pay it. Not him. Never him.

*Faraine, let me take this from you. Let me give you my strength.*

With everything I have, I resist. But I'm weak. Weaker than I've ever been. The pain is too great, red-hot as it enters into me from every pore, every cell, every fragment of existence. I cannot endure it. Not on my own.

So, I fall.

Fall into the love he offers.

Fall into the strength with which he holds me.

Once again, I let him carry me, cradling me in his arms and his heart as I'm stabbed over and over again.

My body jolts. The agony of life reentering my limbs. My spirit rebels, unwilling now that the moment has come to be confined within physical matter once more. It's too late. I have no choice but to surrender my will, to go on. The light, the glory, the song—all of these fade. Now there is only darkness. Darkness, which feels as though it will never end until—

We surge up from the water, gasping for breath. The air feels heavy in my lungs, like dragging rocks down my throat to rattle around in my chest. I have lungs once more. Lungs and limbs and substance. It hurts. It hurts so much.

But I am alive.

"Faraine!"

Vor's voice. Desperate.

I want to speak to him, to ease his fear. I try to turn my head, to open my eyes. It all feels so heavy, so impossibly weighted. My tongue is like a brick in my mouth, my eyelids iron-fastened gates.

Strong arms tighten their hold around me. Then Vor's voice again, growling in my ear. "No, no, no!" The slosh of water then a blast of cold air on my skin. Every sensation is stark and terrible, a new and excruciating pain. I'm laid to rest on a stretch of bare ground, aware of every lump, every pebble, every blade of grass as it cuts into my sensitive skin.

Hands touch my face, my neck, my arms. I feel the wet heaviness of robes being drawn back. Then pressure against my skin. Vor. He presses his ear to my chest. For a moment, he holds his breath. Then: "Gods!" He gasps the word like a prayer as he draws back from me. "Her heart beats. Gods on high and below be praised!"

He's silent then for a time save for his own gasping breaths. Finally, he bends over me once more. "Faraine, do you hear me? Are you there?" His hands cup my face. "Please, Faraine, please. Open your eyes. At least grant me that."

I have to show him. But when I try to raise an eyelid, nothing happens. I'm so heavy, so terribly heavy.

I hear him draw a breath. The next moment, he fumbles with

the front of my gown again, his fingers searching. He finds the silver chain of my necklace, draws it out from under the folds of beaded cloth. Carefully, tenderly, he takes one of my limp hands, presses the stone pendant into my palm, curls my fingers around it.

Deep down inside, I feel the thrum of life at the heart of the stone.

"Live, Faraine." His face must be close to mine. I feel the warmth of his breath against my icy cheek. His voice is thick and urgent. "Live. For you are my very life. Gods damn me for not speaking sooner! But I won't lose whatever time we have now. I won't go another moment without you knowing the truth: You are my heart. My soul. *My wife.* From this day until my last, I am yours and no other's. Whether you come back to me now or not, it makes no difference. I give you everything, *everything.*" He presses his forehead against mine. A sob wracks his body. "Only live, Faraine. I beg you, *live.*"

His lips press against mine. Light at first, then deeper, fuller. I draw in a breath as warmth spreads through me, passing from his soul into mine. It's like a door has opened inside me and sunlight floods into every darkened space.

My eyelids move, flutter, open. My hand, closed around the *urzul* stone, tightens its grip. With an effort of strength beyond anything I've ever attempted, I lift my other hand and rest it against Vor's cheek.

He pulls back, gasping. Stares down into my blinking, dazed eyes.

Then the very light of heaven shines from his face as his mouth breaks into a smile.

"There you are!" he breathes.

# 43
## Vor

I sit with one leg still in the water, holding Faraine.

I am no longer my own. This plunge into the sacred pool was our *yunkathu*—our true marriage swim. Whatever perils we may face, we shall face them now together. To her will I cleave from this day forth. Her defender and her servant, her lord and her love. Whether our marriage lasts a year, a day, mere hours in this world, I shall go into eternity knowing the other half of my heart belongs to her. One flesh. One heart. One whole.

The moon passes slowly overhead. Somehow, that vast sky holds no terror for me now. Not with her here, safe, where she belongs. In my arms.

"Vor," she whispers.

"Yes, my love?"

"I'm cold."

I smile, kiss the top of her head, and press her closer. We're both soaked through, and the wind whips down the mountain and chills right through our skin, straight to our bones. "I'll take you home then. We'll find you a gown. Blankets. A bed. You must recover from your ordeal."

She nuzzles into my neck. One hand clings weakly to the front of my shirt. "It's nice here though. Just the two of us."

My lips quirk in a smile. "Which is it to be then? Shall we off for home, or remain here and freeze to death? The choice is yours. I am entirely at your disposal."

She sighs, a delightfully petulant sound. "I suppose freezing to death would be rather ungrateful to the gods. So soon after they gave me my life back, I mean. Besides, I feel I've done enough dying for one day."

I close my eyes. I cannot bear to think how close I came to losing her. How I *did* lose her. Worse still, I cannot begin to imagine the pain she endured. She still trembles with the aftershocks. But she's here.

A shadow passes over the moon. I look up, watch the cloud trailing by overhead, thick and roiling. Like the hand of doom itself. For the first time since emerging from the pool, I remember everything we've left behind, everything to which we must soon return. Now that I hold Faraine, now that she is mine, truly mine, the impending fate of my world looms large and dreadful in my mind. Still, I would not change anything. Even if all we are granted are these few, shivering moments, here in the shadow of this great mountain, surrounded by fire lilies.

After a long silence, Faraine tilts her head and looks up at me. Her solemn eyes flash with anxiety. "I didn't ask before, but . . . the city?"

I smile down at her. "You saved them, Faraine. You saved my people. You saved Mythanar. I don't know how you did it. I can't begin to comprehend that strange gift of yours. But somehow you turned the devils back, set them on their heels."

"It wasn't like that." She shakes her head then leans it against my shoulder once more, as though too exhausted to hold it upright. "The poor creatures did not want to do as they did. They were driven to it." She is silent for a moment, before finishing softly, "I merely set them free."

Of course, she did. Because she is Faraine. My valorous Faraine. Her strength is not that of a warrior; it is far stronger than mere brute force. Hers is the strength of compassion, of understanding and sympathy. A strength I've not properly understood or appreciated until now.

"Thousands of lives were spared today because of what you did." I stroke her golden hair, glory in the texture of those soft, silky strands between my fingers. "Never was there a braver Queen of Mythanar. Not in all the myths or legends throughout the ages."

She lifts her head, peers up at me from under her lashes. "Queen?" She breathes the word, little more than a whisper.

"Indeed." I tip my head, press my brow to hers. Our noses touch, our eyes lock. "You are mine, Faraine. My queen. Sovereign Lady of Mythanar and the Under Realm, from this day forth and forevermore."

She draws a quavering breath. Then, resting her hand against my cheek, she angles my mouth into her kiss. A sweet, earnest kiss, full of promise, full of longing. Full of lingering pain. Pain to which she chose to return. She was beyond all of this—all the horror, all the fear. All the hurts and shocks to which the natural body is subject. But she came back. For me.

Then and there, with her kiss burning my lips, I make a solemn vow: To be worthy of that choice. To be worthy of her love.

To be worthy of *her*. My angel. My queen.

My wife.

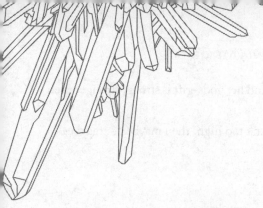

# EPILOGUE

Magic demands a price.

One life entered that pool. Two emerged.

But the balance must be found. Somewhere.

The witch observes the blissful couple, locked in passionate embrace, unaware of her scrutiny. A small part of her feels the urge to step in, all dire warnings and grim utterances. Like a proper witch from a story.

A smile creases her stern mouth. A ghost of a smile, the first she's managed in a long, long time. No, she'll let them have their moment. Those sweet kisses and caresses. Let them warm each other with lovers' glow, even as their bodies shiver in the sharp wind.

The balance will come due soon enough. For now, let them forget what they owe.

Besides, it might all come out right in the end. Years of scheming surely couldn't go to waste. After all this time, she might just manage to save them. Her son. His kingdom. This whole blighted world.

The sweet bride lives. And her gods-gift is strong, stronger even than anticipated.

If the price of her life isn't too high, then maybe . . . maybe . . .

. . . . . . . . . . . . . . . . . . . . .

Deep down, under stone.

Under lakes of fire and rivers of magma.

Down in darkness impenetrably deep, lost in a terrible dream.

The dragon stirs.

# BONUS MATERIAL

Many times throughout the writing of this book, I desperately wished I could branch off into other points of view. Particularly Hael's. With all the drama taking place between Vor and Faraine—not to mention the broader context of Mythanar and the Under Realm—I longed to explore more deeply into the lives and perspectives of those just on the outside of the main plot. But I knew if I let myself, I'd end up with an absolutely *massive* trilogy on my hands. In the end, I decided to keep the story focused, and reluctantly gave up those more indulgent side plots.

But that didn't stop me from *imagining* what was going on with all those secondary characters.

Now, with the opportunity to indulge that rabbit-trailing brain of mine, my primary challenge was picking just *one* scene to play with. So I picked the juiciest . . . I imagine this scene taking place after Chapter 10.

# Hael

"What did you do?"

Sul looks up from packing a *gunag* sack to find me standing in the door of his apartment. Light from a suspended *lorst* stone flashes in the depths of his eyes, briefly revealing an expression of surprise followed by wariness. In a heartbeat, a mask of charm slips over his features, and Sul offers me a beaming smile. "My dear Hael, always a pleasure to find myself the recipient of your growling displeasure. What am I supposed to have done now? Do tell and do make it quick—I'm setting out on a jaunt to Hoknath this lusterling and haven't time to dally. Have you come to see me off?"

I step into the room and draw the door shut behind me. My heart thunders in my throat, but I take care my expression is stone when I face him again. He quirks an eyebrow suggestively. "Why, Hael! This is a surprise. I wouldn't have expected you to—"

"Did you poison Vor?"

Sul's hands pause over his sack. Something about his eyes

tightens. "That's quite the accusation. Where has our brave captain come by her wild notions?"

I stride across the room toward him, my hands knotted into fists. "I saw him. I saw him, Sul, when he came to the princess's chambers and ordered me to leave. The look in his eye . . . It wasn't just anger. It was murder."

"Yes, well." Sul shrugs and eyes the contents of his *gunag*. "He didn't kill her though, did he? Sounds like nothing more than a lovers' spat to me."

My hand darts out, catches the front of his shirt, yanking him toward me. His eyes meet mine, glittering sharp. I hate myself for how my pulse leaps at this proximity to him. He's so beautiful, like a poisonous flower, enticing and terrifying by turns.

"I know it was you, Sul," I say, my voice low. "First the execution . . . That wasn't Vor; that wasn't the man I know. Now this? You're trying to force his hand."

Sul lets his gaze drop slowly to my straining arm then glide back to my face. "Do you have an accusation to make, my dear captain of the guard? If so, why don't you make it, slap manacles on my wrists, and drag me off to the dungeons?" His smile twists, an ugly thing on his beautiful mouth. "Or do you lack the necessary proof?"

"I don't need proof." My fingers tighten, drag him an inch closer to me. "And I have no intention of arresting you. I simply want to know. I want to hear it from your lips—did you do this?"

Sul tips his head to one side, the *lorst* light gleaming in the depths of his silver eyes. "It's been many long turns of the cycle since the three of us shared each other's secrets. Many long years since we fully trusted one another."

"Vor trusts me."

"But he doesn't. Not since you let a false bride into his wedding chamber. You're even now living out the pain of Vor's distrust—demoted, serving as a bodyguard to a *human*." He chuckles, a cold sound that nonetheless brings warmth roaring to my veins. "So much for loyalty. So much for trust."

I shake my head, jaw clenching. "It doesn't matter. It was a mistake, nothing more. Whereas you—"

"So far as you, Vor, or anyone else knows, I am the loyal brother I've always been." Sul's hand grips my wrist. With a twist, he breaks my hold on his shirt and goes back to tying the leather straps of his sack. "Now, if you don't mind, I must be on my way to Hoknath. Got to make sure all is well with the populace, sample some of the local cuisine. If you're lucky, I'll pick out a little something to bring home to you. One of their famous glowwurms, perhaps—you'll like that. Before you know it, I'll be back home to the welcoming embrace of all my dear friends in Mythanar."

I back away, stepping out of the glow of the *lorst* light. Guilt burns in my gut. After all, I stepped aside when Vor commanded me to. I backed out of that chamber and, just before the door closed, I looked into the eyes of the human princess and saw her terror. I did not know what Vor planned, but I could see the wrath in his face. His were the eyes of a madman. A killer. Fueled by uncontrollable lust and brutality.

No thanks to me, the princess survived whatever encounter followed. I'm not sure at what point the idea struck—what stray comment or look I caught from Sul that set my hackles rising. But I've learned over the cycles to trust my instincts. Every instinct is warning me of his guilt now. Though I would give anything to be wrong . . .

"If I find evidence that you poisoned our king," I say softly, "I won't hesitate."

"Oh, won't you?" Sul grins and tosses long hair off his forehead. "And what will you do? Challenge me to mortal combat? Not that I would mind perishing in your lovely arms. I can think of worse ways to go."

Deeper Dark devour me, how I hate him! Hate him for having the ability to make my skin flush and my heart throb. Hate him for making me forget my resolve to give up on these hopeless, foolish feelings which have, against all my better judgment, taken root so deep in my heart. "It was cruel," I say, my voice thick and rough. "I would understand if you had simply murdered the girl outright. But to try to force Vor's hand? To make him commit the deed? He would never be able to live with himself if he hurt that girl."

Sul shrugs. "Vor doesn't always know what's best for him. That's why he has such good friends like you and I to watch his every step."

"And who's watching your step, Sul?"

"You, apparently. It would seem I can't move a muscle without your constant scrutiny." He tips his chin, eyeing me by the *lorst* glow, a dangerous sheen in his eyes. "Believe me, Hael, I'm perfectly aware that I will never measure up to whatever standard you've set. I don't plan to waste my life trying to achieve your approval. I will do what must be done. Whatever the cost."

I take a few steps toward him. He turns to leave, but I catch hold of his arm, determined not to let this moment pass until I've wrung the confession out of him. "Sul—" I snarl.

But then he turns and kisses me. His hand wraps around the back of my neck, dragging me to him so abruptly, I stumble and fall against his chest. He drops his *gunag* sack, and his other hand wraps around my waist, both steadying and imprisoning. For a moment, I'm too stunned to react, to push him away, to pound his face into dust. My lips are hard under the pressure of his mouth, and my whole being seems to have turned to *jor*.

Then, with a flood of inferno heat, I open my mouth, allowing the intensity of his embrace to overwhelm me. His tongue slips between my teeth, tangles with mine, tasting and insistent, and I give in. I, who have carved myself into a statue of solid granite, immovable against all forces, am putty in his hands.

The hand on my hip shifts, applying pressure to which I instantly respond. He backs me up against the wall, and though my shoulders hit cold stone hard enough to knock the breath from my lungs, I feel only heat and warmth and the pressure of his mouth. He's savage, demanding, all hard edges and heat and pain. Everything I've ever longed for. What is it the priests have taught us? It is in the Dark that truth resides. Untainted, unsullied, and pure. I feel the truth of that doctrine now as Sul unearths all my secrets, delving into the darkest reaches of my heart, into those places where even I dared not venture. Those places where my desire lies, unacknowledged, unseen, but true.

He draws back suddenly, gasping for air. I pant against his lips. My vision swims as I stare up into his burning eyes. He says nothing for some moments, merely looks at me. The fingers wrapped around my neck slowly release their grip and slip around, trailing across the skin of my throat. Trailing until they reach the hard, crusty line of *dorgarag* running along my shoulder, neck, and jaw. "I thought that might shut you up," he whispers, his voice husky.

The spell is broken. I hastily grab his wrist, yank his fingers back from my marred flesh. And there we stand, my back still pressed into the wall, my fist squeezing nearly hard enough to break bone. His gaze searches my face, drops momentarily back to my lips. I wonder if he will kiss me again, wonder what I will do if he does. My breath hitches.

"*Morar-juk!*" he whispers, his lip curling in a sneer. Then he retreats a step. I let him go. Let him go and watch him turn away from me, retrieve his sack from the floor. He slings it over his shoulder and pauses, his back to me.

His chest expands as he draws a deep breath. "Miss me while I'm gone, sweet Hael," he says in that bright, charming, hateful tone of his. "And best of luck guarding that little princess of yours. I'm sure it will all be worth it in the end."

With that, he strides from the room, leaving me where I stand. And I remain frozen in place as the heat in my veins slowly cools, leaving me hard as stone.

*Photo by Chelsea Ann Photography*

**Sylvia Mercedes** makes her home in the idyllic North Carolina countryside with her handsome husband, numerous small children, and a menagerie of rescue cats and dogs. When she's not writing, she's . . . okay, let's be honest. When she's not writing, she's running around after her littles, cleaning up glitter, trying to plan healthy-ish meals, and wondering where she left her phone. In between, she reads a steady diet of fantasy novels. But mostly she's writing.

VISIT THE AUTHOR ONLINE AND LEARN ABOUT
HER TWENTY-PLUS BESTSELLING ROMANTASY NOVELS

SylviaMercedesBooks.com
AuthorSylviaMercedes

Ready to find
your next great read?

Let us help.

**Visit prh.com/nextread**

Penguin
Random
House